Moorestown Library
Moorestown, New Jersey 08057

IMPOSTRESS

Also by Lisa Jackson
in Large Print:

Mystic
The Night Before

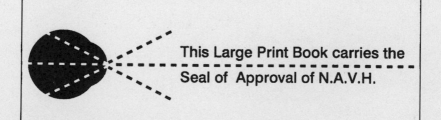

IMPOSTRESS

Lisa Jackson

WHEELER PUBLISHING

Published in 2003 by arrangement with
NAL Signet, a member of Penguin Group (USA) Inc.

Wheeler Large Print Compass.

The text of this Large Print edition is unabridged.
Other aspects of the book may vary from the original edition.

Set in 16 pt. Plantin by Al Chase.

Printed in the United States on permanent paper.

Library of Congress Cataloging-in-Publication Data

Jackson, Lisa.
    Impostress / Lisa Jackson.
      p. cm.
    ISBN 1-58724-495-0 (lg. print : hc : alk. paper)
    1. Impostors and imposture — Fiction. 2. Missing persons — Fiction. 3. Middle Ages — Fiction. 4. Sisters — Fiction. 5. Large type books. I. Title.
PS3560.A223I47 2003
  813'.54—dc21   2003053496

IMPOSTRESS

National Association for Visually Handicapped
------------------------ *serving the partially seeing*

As the Founder/CEO of NAVH, the only national health agency solely devoted to those who, although not totally blind, have an eye disease which could lead to serious visual impairment, I am pleased to recognize Thorndike Press* as one of the leading publishers in the large print field.

Founded in 1954 in San Francisco to prepare large print textbooks for partially seeing children, NAVH became the pioneer and standard setting agency in the preparation of large type.

Today, those publishers who meet our standards carry the prestigious "Seal of Approval" indicating high quality large print. We are delighted that Thorndike Press is one of the publishers whose titles meet these standards. We are also pleased to recognize the significant contribution Thorndike Press is making in this important and growing field.

Lorraine H. Marchi, L.H.D.
Founder/CEO
NAVH

* Thorndike Press encompasses the following imprints: Thorndike, Wheeler, Walker and Large Print Press.

Acknowledgments

I would like to thank everyone who helped me with this book. Special thanks to Ari Okano, who spent endless hours with my characters — I couldn't have done it without you! — and helped with the transition between editors. Thanks to Claire Zion for working tirelessly on a project she inherited, and thanks to Nancy Richie and Kathy Okano for their help in reading and rereading the manuscript.

Prologue

*The Forest Surrounding
Tower Lawenydd, North Wales
Winter 1283*

Darkness had descended when Kiera awoke on the cold, wet earth, mud and leaves clinging to her face. She had no idea how much time had passed, but the moon was high in the night sky and the forest was silent and still, not even a breeze rustling the branches. She ached all over — every bone in her body jarred, every muscle seeming bruised — and for a moment she couldn't remember how she'd ended up here in the night-darkened forest alone.

She'd been riding, she thought, and touched the coarse clothes covering her body. Yes, that was it, she'd disguised herself as a stableboy and . . . and had taken Obsidian out through the castle gates, and *oooohhh.* Her head pounded and throbbed, seeming too tight for her skull. Rubbing her forehead, she felt a knot over one eye. Obsidian! Somehow she'd lost her father's prized steed. She remembered the faint image of the black beast racing riderless through the murky undergrowth as she'd nearly been knocked unconscious. "God's teeth," Kiera muttered. "Obsidian! Come back! Obsidian!" But the horse was long gone, having disappeared into the rising mist and trees minutes, perhaps hours, ago. "Damned thing." Struggling to her feet, she winced against the pain in her shoulder, then whistled long and hard.

She couldn't return to the keep without the valuable steed, but she heard no sound of hooves approaching, no crack of twigs or rustle of wet branches as the stupid beast returned through the darkness. "Come, boy," she called, as if the temperamental horse were one of the castle hounds.

But she heard no resounding echo of hoofbeats.

She'd lost him.

Angry with herself, she took a few steps forward and felt an eerie sensation, like the breath of the very devil, against the back of her neck. As if someone were watching her. Someone close, mayhap dangerous. Which was just plain silly. She was alone and several miles from the castle. . . . For the first time she realized that she might have more troubles than just a runaway horse. She whistled again and heard a faint echo of her own high-pitched call.

The blasted animal didn't return. And she couldn't find him in the darkness. The night was closing in, becoming thick. Mist collected on her skin as it began to rise from the ground.

"Bloody hell," she swore, kicking a clump of mud from her boot.

Stuffing wayward strands of hair into her hood, she started off in the direction in which the miserable beast had fled. She'd barely taken two steps on her wobbly legs when she felt it again — the heart-stopping sensation that someone was watching her.

She hazarded a glance over her shoulder. Was there a shadow, a movement in the mist?

Her heart froze. Her throat was suddenly dry.

Through the thin curtain of fog she spied a faint image of a huge, silent man astride a pale horse. Bearing down upon her.

Fear congealed her blood. A night bird warbled.

Had the rider seen her?

Of course he had.

And he'd heard her calling for her horse. Whistling and swearing.

Stumbling back a step, Kiera sensed that he was staring at her. Though she couldn't see his face, she knew in her heart that his gaze was hard. Sinister. Elsewise why, when he so obviously saw and heard her, would he not say something? *Anything.*

Swallowing back her fear, she tried to convince herself he wouldn't bother her. Even if he was an outlaw or thief or worse, what would he want with a scrawny stable lad? "I'm . . . I'm looking for my horse," she explained gruffly, hoping to sound like a young man. "Who are you? What do you want?"

"I think you know."

Oh, God.

"You don't fool me." His voice was low, gravelly, and tinged with accusation. As if he knew her.

"I'm not trying to fool anyone," she said, her voice still disguised. *Liar! You deceived your father, the stable master, the guard at the gate . . . everyone.* She tried a different tack. "I'm afraid I was riding and got thrown off and . . ."

He clucked his tongue and the buff-colored horse moved closer.

What the devil did he want?

". . . and I'm looking for my horse. A big black stallion. Mayhap you've seen him?" She was backing up now, determined to run the second she thought she had a chance of disappearing into the fog and eluding him.

" 'Tis a silly disguise," he sneered, and her heart nearly stopped.

He *knew* she was dressed to fool people, yet she couldn't make out his features.

Her breath stilled and she didn't move. Couldn't. Surely he didn't recognize her as the daughter of Baron Llwyd. How could he? She wore ragtag doeskin breeches and a woolen tunic with a deep cowl. This miserable cur of a man wouldn't think to kidnap her and ransom her or worse, would he?

But even in the gloom she could see a flash of white teeth. "Didn't you know that I'd follow you here?"

"No . . . I . . ." Then she understood. Her hand flew up and touched the gold chain surrounding her throat. When she'd been thrown from the horse, the jeweled crucifix had slipped out of the tunic's neckline, and now, even in the palest moonlight, it glittered against the leather laces and rough fabric. Her heart thudded as the stranger slowly dismounted.

She froze.

"Where'd you get that?" he demanded, his eyes centered on the crucifix she was trying vainly to hide.

She didn't answer for a second. If she admitted the cross was a gift from her mother as she lay dying, the outlaw would realize who she was. "I stole it," she said boldly, her voice low as she forced herself to edge closer to a dark thicket. "As well as the horse. From the baron."

"So now you're a thief?"

"Yes."

He snorted. God, who was he? It seemed a deep hood covered his head, a dark beard his chin, but in the darkness, she couldn't be positive. "Surely you can do better than that." He was so close now she could smell him, feel his hideous heat, yet his face was hidden.

She had no weapon except a tiny knife in a pocket, but if he touched her she would surely use it — gladly jam it into his black heart. Carefully, barely moving, her heart beating frantically, she slid her fingers into her pocket. "Leave me alone," she warned, inching backward.

"Never."

"What?"

"You started this."

How? By falling off the damned horse? "I did nothing of the kind."

"Silly girl. You think you can fool me?"

Run! Now! While you still have a chance!

She didn't think twice. Whirling, she took off at a dead run, deeper into the woods. Dear God, why had she not sprinted out of sight before he dismounted, before he saw her, before — Her toe caught in an exposed root. She pitched forward through the leaves and brush. She put out her hands to catch herself. With a painful snap, her left wrist buckled. Pain splintered up her arm. "Ouch!"

The bastard chased her. She heard his footsteps heavy in the forest. "Where the devil do you think you're going?" he demanded, his voice so horridly close she cringed. Her wrist throbbed painfully. She saw his shadow, a dark, dangerous figure who grabbed her by

14

the shoulder and jerked her roughly to her feet. "You can't get away."

"Leave me alone."

"I don't think so."

Fear, cold as death, settled in her heart. She was alone with this . . . this outlaw. Far away from the castle. No one around to hear her scream. Strong fingers dug into her flesh.

"What do you think you're doing?" Dear God, her whole arm ached. She could barely think.

"Teaching you a lesson."

She thought he would try to rip the necklace from her throat. So be it. Slowly she reached into her pocket with her good hand. Her fingers found the tiny, wicked blade. Quickly she slipped the dagger into her palm.

"Thought you'd get away, did you?" he snarled, and to her horror his mouth crashed down on hers. He was rough, his fingers digging into her muscles, his beard scratching her face. So this was it. Not only did he mean to rob her, but rape her as well.

She'd die first.

And so would he.

He groaned and yanked her closer. She pulled the knife from her pocket. Ignored the pain. His tongue pressed hard against her clamped teeth. *Bastard!* In one quick movement, with all her strength, she jammed her tiny blade into his side.

He yelped, let go. "What the bloody — ?"

She stumbled backward and tried to run, but he caught her arm. Whirling, she slashed her wicked little blade frantically as he cursed and dodged.

"Let go of me, you miserable — oh!"

He twisted her arm back. Hot pain ripped through her shoulder.

"You little cur!" Pain forced her to her knees. Her pathetic blade fell from her blood-sticky fingers to the ground.

"Don't, please . . . just take the necklace. Stop . . ." She tried to wriggle free but he was strong, breathing hard, smelling of sweat. Blinding pain seared through her. It was all she could do to stay conscious. She was doomed. Without a weapon she was no match for him.

"The necklace?" he demanded.

"Aye, the crucifix."

"As if that would be enough!" he growled as she nearly passed out again. "You know better." She saw his teeth glint an evil white in the darkness. "Now let's hear you beg."

"Dear God, no . . ."

"You can do better than that."

A twig snapped nearby.

The thug stiffened. "What the hell was that?"

Kiera's legs were like water, her brain fuzzy, the pain so intense she heard a high pitch in her ears.

"Who goes there?" the outlaw demanded.

Twang!

What was that?

Sssst!

An arrow?

Thwack!

"Ooowwhhh!" His body jerked wildly as he screamed. His grip loosened as he fell with an earth-jarring thud to the ground.

Kiera scrambled to her feet. On wobbly legs she started running through the undergrowth, fear propelling her as wet branches slapped at her and her feet tangled in vines. She had to get away. Fast. Someone had become her savior — or had seen what was happening and wanted the cross for himself. She didn't wait to see which.

Hoofbeats thundered behind her. A horse crashed through the brush.

Her savior? Or the thug upon his horse again?

She ran desperately through the night, tree limbs clawing at her, thorns tearing at her clothes.

Could the horse behind her be Obsidian? She didn't dare hope, and crouching low, she scrambled through a thicket, her fingers scraping the bark, her shoulder and wrist throbbing in pain.

"Kiera!" Elyn's voice slashed through the night.

Her sister was here? In the forest? Nay. Her

mind was playing tricks on her.

"Kiera, for the love of St. Peter, where are you? Kiera!" Elyn's voice rang with desperation.

What if the outlaw had somehow captured her sister? What if this was a trick?

"I can't see a bloody inch in front of my eyes. Where the devil are you?"

Either way, she couldn't abandon Elyn. She dropped to her knees quickly. Fingers scrabbling the forest floor, she found a rock and palmed it. A poor weapon, but the best she could find. "Over here," she said, tripping over a stick and picking it up with her good hand. 'Twas little against the menacing beast, but she would bludgeon him with it if given half a chance.

Crouching, she waited as the hoofbeats approached.

"For God's sake, show yourself!" Elyn's words seethed with anger, and Kiera, making a sign of the cross over her chest, slunk from her hiding spot to a small clearing, where within seconds, Elyn arrived upon her sleek jennet. Small and compact upon her mare, she was leading the ghostly dun horse by the reins of its bridle. "Come on, let's go!" she ordered furiously as she spied Kiera crouching in the shadows. "There is not much time. The beast who attacked you is not yet dead. He could survive and follow us!"

That warning spurred Kiera to the pale animal. "What were you doing out here?"

"Saving you," Elyn snapped as her horse minced and danced nervously. "What were *you* doing?"

"Nothing."

"Dressed as a pauper — don't tell me, it was that stupid horse. You stole Obsidian again, didn't you?" She glanced around the night-shrouded glen. "And where is he? Where's the damned steed?"

"Lost," Kiera admitted miserably.

"Lost? How do you *lose* a prized stallion?"

"He threw me."

"Oh, wonderful. Father will flail you within an inch of your life."

"Don't remind me," Kiera sighed. She knew her punishment would be severe. Even if the steed was found unharmed.

"How did you get him out of the stable? Orson would never . . . oh, don't tell me. Joseph helped you, didn't he?" She sighed audibly. "Foolish boy," she muttered under her breath, then, with a glance at Kiera, said, "Come on. There's nothing more to do. No time to waste. Let's go!" Elyn slapped the reins of the outlaw's horse into Kiera's frigid fingers while trying to control her edgy mare.

"Did you shoot him? The outlaw, I mean?" Kiera asked, eyeing the bow and quiver slung over Elyn's back. Her sister didn't immediately answer, but 'twas folly to think anything else. They were alone in the forest. Alone with a cruel man who could be a rapist or worse. She shuddered.

"Of course I shot him," Elyn finally admitted, her words clipped with anger. "There was naught else to do. The bastard. Holy Mother . . ." She caught herself and turned to her sister. "Now, Kiera, either you ride with me or I'll leave you here."

"What about . . . ?"

"The outlaw?"

"Aye."

"I think he can damned well rot in hell."

" 'Twould be too good for him." Despite her useless arm and the fact that her skin crawled at being anywhere close to the vile outlaw, Kiera managed to climb upon his tall steed. As soon as Kiera was astride, Elyn kicked her mount. The jennet bolted, running fast as the wind, swift dark legs eating up the wet ground. Kiera followed after, clinging to the saddle's pommel and feeling the spray of mud as her own horse splashed through the puddles and bogs on this crooked path. She only prayed the horrid man who had attacked her didn't awaken and call to his horse. This stallion might heed his master's call and turn round.

Kiera shuddered at the thought. But the truth of the matter was that some animals obeyed better than that miserable beast Obsidian. She felt a pang of regret at the thought of the horse she loved so dearly. Biting her lip, she silently prayed that her father's stallion wasn't hurt and would somehow return to Lawenydd unscathed.

The path angled sharply and the forest gave way to the wide fields surrounding the castle. Elyn drew her horse to a stop, waiting for Kiera at the edge of the woods. Moonlight gave the wheat stubble a silvery sheen. Far in the distance, rising on a cliff overlooking the sea, Lawenydd stood, six square towers seeming to disappear in the inky sky.

Kiera tugged on the reins, forcing her mount to slow. The big horse responded, tossing his yellowish head and breathing hard.

Elyn was glowering at her. "Father will kill us both," she said, her features, so similar to Kiera's own, pulled into a dark scowl. Nearly sixteen, Elyn was the eldest by a year and a half. Kiera was next. Four years later Penelope had been born.

"You saved my life," Kiera said, not worried about their father's anger. Llwyd of Lawenydd was a blustery man who adored his wayward daughters and would punish them, yes, but in the end forgive them. But Elyn had truly delivered Kiera from a terrifying fate. At the thought of her attacker, Kiera trembled. Had not her sister arrived when she had, if her aim had not been true . . .

Elyn threw her a hard look. "You were foolish."

"Yes, I know, but I owe you my life."

" 'Twas fortunate that I was there."

"Aye." Kiera studied her sister's frown. "What were you doing in the forest?"

Elyn hesitated, as if searching for the answer. "Looking for you. 'Twas lucky I found you. As for Obsidian, let's hope he's smart enough to return to the castle."

"I can't thank you enough," Kiera said, glancing at her sister. "I — I want you to have this," she added in a rush as she yanked the necklace from around her neck. Pain surged through her, but she ignored it. Urging her horse forward, she dropped the crucifix into her sister's hand. "Please, take it, and know that to repay you, I'll do anything you ever ask."

"But Mother gave this to you. Before she died."

" 'Tis yours now."

"Hush. This is silly. Kiera, you don't have to —"

"Yes, yes, I do. Please, Elyn. I . . . I'm indebted to you for life," Kiera insisted, overwhelmed. "And . . . and whenever you wish the debt repaid, just give the necklace back to me and I'll remember this vow. I'll do anything for you."

"Anything?" Elyn asked, shaking her head as if Kiera was talking nonsense.

"I mean it. Whatever you ask me to do, I'll do it, Elyn. You saved my life. Of that I have no doubt. None. Now, please, take this and remember to ask me to return the favor. Please." She pressed the crucifix with its fine gold chain into her sister's gloved palm.

"Mayhap I should have my punishment from Father laid upon you," Elyn said, and for the first time Kiera saw a flash of a white — a bit of a smile — upon her sister's face.

"Yes!" Kiera lifted her chin proudly. "Ask him."

Elyn laughed a little, though the sound that rippled over the moonlit fields sounded hollow. "Nay. You'll suffer enough at his hand. I'll save calling in your debt for later, when I need a favor. Now, come on, we're already in trouble. Let's not make it any worse."

"What will happen to . . ." Kiera nodded toward the woods.

"The man who attacked you? And Obsidian?" With a sigh, Elyn blew a strand of hair from her eyes. "Any form of torture would be too good for the outlaw and we should let him rot and die, but I suppose we'll have to tell Father the truth. All of it. The horse will have to be found and the thug attended to before being imprisoned.

" 'Twould be a blessing if he were to be caught and left forgotten in a dungeon, would it not?" Elyn said, then glanced sadly up at the sky. "A blessing."

"Yes." Kiera shuddered. "I hope I never see him again."

"Me, too," Elyn said vehemently, in anger — or pain? She spurred her horse and the bay whirled, then shot forward across the silvery fields. "Me, too."

Chapter One

Castle Lawenydd
Winter 1286

"You *can't* be serious." Kiera was dumbstruck at her sister's request. "Have you gone daft?"

They were walking swiftly through the outer bailey, past the squealing pigs and bleating sheep. Wintry sunlight pierced through a thin veil of high clouds, and the smell of the sea gave a briny tinge to the odors of cook fires, burning tallow, and dung from the stables.

"You can't expect me to stand in for you . . . to pretend that I'm you and take your wedding vows!"

"Shh," Elyn whispered harshly as they slipped through the gates to the inner bailey, where displayed upon the chapel, the bans announcing Elyn's marriage to Baron Kelan of Penbrooke caught in the winter breeze. "Did you not promise to do anything I asked when I saved your life?"

"Yes, but —"

"And when I tried to talk you out of it, did you not insist?" She pulled Kiera around

the corner of the carter's hut to a path between the garden and a wagon with a broken
wheel. The spokes had splintered, and the
wagon bed was tipped as it rested on its axle.

"Aye." Kiera nodded. "But this is madness!
I cannot marry a man promised to you."

"You're not marrying him," Elyn insisted,
her full lips pulled into a knot of concentration. Her eyes, a shade of green identical to
Kiera's, pleaded. "You're just taking the vows
for me. You know as well as I do that what
is important in this marriage is not me, but
my name and position as firstborn." Elyn
sighed. "If only the estate were not entailed
upon me because we have no brother to be
the heir. It's not fair. Father has just sold me
to gain access to the river that runs through
Penbrooke to further trade."

"And you expect no one to tell the difference?"

"The chapel is poorly lit, and my veil is
heavy enough that your face will be indis-
tinct. You will whisper the vows and you will
be dressed in my wedding dress."

Kiera laughed nervously. "But the guests —"

" 'Tis a small ceremony," Elyn insisted.
"And rushed! So rushed. Because the
groom's mother ails, I am to wed so that I
may hurry back to Penbrooke to see her before she dies. God's teeth, there is no time to
do anything else!" She sighed as if all the
misery of the world lay upon her shoulders.

"If there is any bit of a blessing in this, it is that Father knows I am unhappy about the marriage. He is afraid I will embarrass him in front of his friends, so there are few who will be there."

"But those that are will see that I'm not you!"

"Nay, I've thought of that," she said, though she seemed vastly worried. "Most people, even our relatives, have trouble telling us apart. Remember we sometimes fooled Father, and now he is nearly blind with age, his eyes as white as milk these past few years. Hildy nearly raised us, so she won't give me away, Penelope will consider it a grand joke, and the priest is from Penbrooke. Father Barton or Bartholomew or something. He's never met me."

"What about the baron?" Kiera asked, not believing for a second that this plan had a chance of working. 'Twas idiocy of the highest order. "You know, the man *you're* supposed to marry."

"He's never laid eyes upon me."

"You're certain?" Kiera was disbelieving and looked to the sky where a hawk was circling. "Could he not have seen you at a tournament or at a neighboring castle during the Christmas Revels or —"

"Shhh! No! There is a rumor that Kelan was disowned by his father for a time because of his wild ways, and only recently regained favor. I've heard the guards call him the Beast of Penbrooke when they think no one is listening. He has never attended proper functions."

The carter rounded the corner, a dog limping behind him, and Elyn tugged on the sleeve of Kiera's tunic. "Come along," she said, smiling and nodding her head as the carter greeted them, then set to his task of removing the broken wagon wheel.

Elyn guided Kiera through the herb garden, where a few patches of thyme grew heartily within the clumps of rosemary and sage. The sisters sat on a bench that had once been their mother's favorite spot to work on her embroidery in the warmth of the summer sun.

"Penbrooke won't know you're not his bride," Elyn insisted as Kiera dug at a clump of weeds with the toe of her boot. "All you have to do is say the vows and beg off from the festivities, claim a headache. Everyone will believe it's a case of nerves. Then the next morning I'll return and take my place as his wife. It will not matter that it is you who has said the vows, for the marriage contract hinges on my name, which is all that is important in this mercenary union. I will be married to the man." She shuddered at the prospect, and Kiera understood why. Elyn hated the thought of being wed to a man she didn't love.

But then another thought occurred to her, a horrid thought. Kiera suddenly lost all interest in the stubborn weeds. "Wait a minute. The next morning?" She gulped. "You've not mentioned the wedding night. What am I to do when the lord comes to my chamber and expects me to . . . to . . ."

"You mean, when he expects to bed you?"

"Not me. *You*," Kiera pointed out.

Elyn rested her chin on her fists. Her green eyes narrowed on a winter bird flying past. "You don't have to sleep with him . . . well, yes, you do have to do the sleeping part, but not the other."

"And how am I to accomplish that?" Kiera hissed. "I don't believe a headache or a case of nerves will be enough of an excuse on my wedding night."

"Of course it won't. Besides, he has to think that you are — or I am — a virgin. There must be blood on the linens."

Kiera shot to her feet. "Blood on the linens? Oh, now I know you've lost your mind. How could I possibly see that the sheets were stained without . . . without — well, *you know*." Horrified, she glared at her sister. If it wasn't for the gravity of Elyn's expression, she would have thought that her older sibling was toying with her, pushing a bad joke beyond its limits. "This is a daft plan. Daft! You must have left your mind in the stable, because it's certainly missing! I think you best find it and soon."

"Just listen." Instead of anger, now Elyn seemed scared. She wrapped her fingers around her sister's wrist, touching that very spot that had broken on the night that Elyn had saved her life. A tiny bit of old pain shot up Kiera's arm. "I cannot marry the baron because I can't come to him as a virgin."

Kiera's skin prickled with dread. She pulled her hand away, didn't want to think of that fateful night and her hasty, though heartfelt, vow to do anything Elyn asked. "Why not?"

"I've already given myself." Her cheeks, beneath her freckles, reddened.

"To Brock of Oak Crest?" Kiera demanded, knowing the answer before it passed Elyn's tongue.

"Aye." Elyn was worrying her hands together, her teeth sinking into her lip. "I love him. I have from the first time I saw him at Tower Fenn. I was but thirteen years, yet smitten upon the sight of him. I have loved him ever since."

"For the love of St. Jude, Elyn." Kiera thought little of the man who had so completely and stupidly captured her sister's heart. "Is he not betrothed to another?"

"Wynnifrydd." Elyn's nose wrinkled as if she'd just smelled rotten eggs. "Of Fenn. They are to be married soon." She sighed loudly, her shoulders slumping as if from a great burden. The first drops of rain began to fall and splatter on the ground. "Brock loves me, not that scrawny wench. I know it. He no more wants to wed Wynnifrydd than I do Penbrooke."

"But you haven't given this a chance. As you said, you've never met Penbrooke. Mayhap you'll find him —"

"Attractive?" Elyn snorted, shaking her head. "Obviously you've never been in love."

"You know that Brock's a scoundrel. You've said so yourself."

"Mayhap, but the heart knows no reason." Elyn stared into the storm as if she was searching for some kind of divine intervention, some kind of insight into her plight.

"Oh, please, stop it! I've heard you spout this romantic nonsense too often, and look where it's gotten you." Kiera felt a pang of something akin to pity. Her strong sister was such a fool when it came to love, but Elyn had always been a bit of a dreamer. "I know you don't want to marry Penbrooke. Have you not said as much every day since Father announced the agreement? But what you're suggesting is mad . . . absurd; it will never, *ever* work."

"It will if you agree to it. Now, you'll not have to give yourself to him, not really." Elyn was blinking against the fat drops of rain falling from the sky. "You can give him a sleeping draft, and he'll fall asleep and I'll make sure there is a vial of blood — pig's

31

blood — that you can spill onto the sheets, so that when he awakens, he'll believe —"

"And why cannot you do this? Why can you not make sure he falls asleep, then sprinkle the sheets with blood?"

"Because I am to meet Brock one last time."

"What?" Kiera cried. This was ludicrous! Insane!

"Please, Kiera, if I can steal one more night with Brock, I will feel as if I have defied the contract that keeps me from my love. It will make assuming the duties as the Baron of Penbrooke's wife bearable, and no one but us will know."

" 'Twould only make things worse. Much worse. Nay, Elyn, this is crazy. I will do anything for you, I gave you my word, but this . . . I cannot."

"You will not have to compromise your virginity."

"So you say, but —"

"And everyone will think that he was with me. You lose nothing, Kiera. *Nothing*. And I will have one last night with my beloved."

Kiera was thinking that her virginity wasn't as precious as she'd thought, not if it could be bartered with so easily. Though, of course, Elyn was right. Kiera would never give herself to the man. Yet she could not meet her sister's request despite her promise. Kiera knew the plan could not work. She would not do it. 'Twas a fool's mission.

"This scheme is impossible," she said, gathering her cowl over her head as the rain peppered the garden. "You must go to Father and talk him out of the marriage."

"Don't you think I've tried? By the love of the Holy Mother, I've begged, screamed, cried, pleaded, and all for naught. Father will not listen to me." Her eyes darkened dangerously and her chin set in the same determination Kiera had witnessed a hundred times before. If Elyn had inherited anything from Llwyd of Lawenydd, 'twas his damned pride and stubborn streak. Rain drizzled down her neck, but she didn't bother covering her head.

"Listen —" Desperately, Elyn grabbed hold of Kiera's sleeve. "Have we not fooled our own cousins by pretending to be each other? Did we not trick our own father before?" Elyn insisted, her fire returning. "Even when his eyesight had not dimmed? We look enough alike as to be twins, as to be one, even Hildy has claimed as much!"

Kiera paused for a moment. It was true that many often swore that Elyn and Kiera were nearly identical. Indeed, they shared many of the same features. Both had brilliant auburn hair, green eyes, and chins that ended in a distinct point. Kiera and Elyn had often confused household servants and, aye, even family members about their identities. Yet while they had often played tricks, the plan was simply too implausible and dangerous. "I'm sorry, Elyn, it is not going to work. I can't do it."

Angrily, Elyn yanked on the necklace that encircled her throat. The fine chain broke, but she caught the glittering crucifix before it dropped to the ground. Rubies, emeralds, and sapphires glittered ominously in the rain. "Did you not promise me, Kiera? Did you not swear that you would return my favor by doing *any*thing I asked?"

"Yes, although —"

"So now I'm asking, begging . . ." she said, shaking her fist so hard that the bejeweled cross swung crazily from its broken links. "Are you not as good as your word?"

"Of course, but —"

"You vowed, Kiera, to me." Elyn hooked a thumb at her chest. Her eyes snapped angrily. "You insisted that you owed me this favor. 'Twas your idea, not mine."

"Yes, I know I did, nonetheless —"

"So, now, sister, 'tis time to pay."

Kiera's heart tore. She grabbed the cross and chain. "I'll do anything else, Elyn, but this . . . this I cannot. I cannot lie to Father. To Penbrooke. To God. I cannot pretend to marry the man. Elyn, please, go to Father. I'll go with you. Mayhap something can be worked out."

"Would you give yourself to Penbrooke in my stead?"

34

"He would not want me because Father has entailed the castle to you, and Penbrooke wants access to the sea to expand trade, which Lawenydd provides," Kiera said.

"So you are a liar and a coward," Elyn said, her voice cold. "You know, Kiera, I really thought better of you."

"Then you'll speak with Father."

Elyn's lips barely moved as the purple clouds roiled overhead. "Worry not, sister," she said, turning toward the keep, "I'll do what I have to."

This marriage will be little more than a sham, Baron Kelan of Penbrooke thought as he guided his horse toward the final rise and his doom. His mood was as dark as the cloudy sky, and his muscles were beginning to protest from a hard three days' ride with his pitiful handful of men, none of whom seemed to have lost their amusement that he was finally to be wed.

" 'Tis well past time," Orvis, one of Kelan's guards and a friend, had said with a chuckle as he'd raised a tankard of ale to his lips the night before they'd left Penbrooke. He'd wiped a sleeve over his ragged reddish beard. "Your days of sowin' wild oats are over."

"Aye, and now maybe some of the ladies will look my way," Tadd had chimed in, his blue eyes full of devilment as he'd fingered his dark beard. Tadd was his brother. At

35

twenty, two years younger than Kelan, Tadd was every bit as full of piss and vinegar as Kelan had once been.

"As if ye need more women," Orvis had grumbled, for he was fat and dull with the finesse of a blacksmith and the manners of the gong farmer who cleaned the latrine pits. Yet he was loyal and true, a man whom Kelan had known since his youth. "Ye need to be passin' a few my way, Sir Tadd, instead of beddin' 'em all yerself."

Tadd had lifted a skeptical brow. "And what would you do with them, Orvis?" he'd taunted.

"I know me way around a woman, don't you think I don't." Offended, Orvis had buried his bulbous nose in his mazer.

Kelan had paid the men no mind that night or any other. Their needling and jokes at his expense were to be expected, but he hadn't counted on the smug faith of Father Barton, an elderly priest who couldn't hide his pleasure that the wayward, prodigal son of Lord Alwyn was about to wed, and therefore change his heathen ways. Now that Kelan was the baron, he needed a wife. Or so thought the priest.

"Ye'll enjoy the sacrament of marriage," the old man had intoned less than an hour ago. With his thin white hair, hooked nose, and ever-pursed mouth, he had glanced at Kelan with sanctimonious piety. A bemused smile

36

had dared to soften the set of his lips. He'd clucked to his mount, a docile grayish mare, as she'd plodded along the soggy, rutted road leading to Lawenydd. "A good woman and children, 'tis all a man can ask for."

" 'Tis not what I asked for, nor," he reminded the priest, "what *you* wanted for yourself."

"We all have different callings, my son. Yours is to wed and beget children. Sons."

"So it seems."

" 'Twill be a blessing."

"How would you know? Have you ever been married?"

Father Barton had clucked his tongue. "I am married to God, my son."

"And is He a good wife?"

"There be no need for irreverence." Those old lips had pursed again in tight disapproval, and the priest's good humor had vanished as surely as if it had been swept away by the salt-laden wind.

"Nor be there a need for unwanted advice."

"Then think of your poor ailing mother." Father Barton had sketched a quick sign of the cross over his chest. " 'Twill make her happy."

There was little doubt of that. His mother, too frail to make the trip, had made it known that all she wanted from him was that he take a wife and have children, preferably a son to become the next Baron of Penbrooke. She was dying. She wanted desperately to meet Kelan's bride, had begged her son to be quick with the marriage and return. Kelan had not the heart to deny her. But despite his dead father's schemes, the priest's talk of the joys of marriage, and his mother's desperate need to know the Penbrooke bloodline would continue, Kelan felt a cold dread at the prospect of this arranged marriage to a woman he had never seen and had heard little about.

Now, with his horse a good quarter mile ahead of the others and his gloved hands clamped over the reins, he fought the urge to spur his steed and ride fast and far from his fate. His jaw was clenched so hard it ached; every muscle in his body was rigid. Soon he would meet his bride. His stomach soured at the thought. This woman with whom he was supposed to live forever.

Marriage. 'Twas a fool's sacrament.

Were he not firstborn and were his mother not on her deathbed, Kelan would never have agreed to such a hideous convention. Never.

The union was the result of two old men's wishes. His father had wanted an ally to the south, one with whom he could share borders, men, weapons, and trade, a barony with access to the sea. Even more than that, Alwyn had wanted Kelan to sire a son, an heir that would someday become baron. On his deathbed he'd elicited a promise that Kelan would marry Elyn of Lawenydd, and Kelan couldn't go back on his word.

Nonsense! That's what it was.

Because of his dead father's wishes and his mother's continued, quiet supplication, Kelan had become betrothed to a woman — no doubt a withered old maid, she was almost nineteen for God's sake and should have been married long ago — whom he'd never met. The castles were not near each other, and as he'd been banished for a time, he'd never had a glimpse of his bride. Perhaps it was for the best.

Llwyd of Lawenydd had his own reasons for suggesting the marriage. He wanted protection from the north and use of the river that cut through Penbrooke on its way to the ocean. Though the baronies did not share a border, they would make a strong alliance and could, together, force the small, weaker baronies between to do their bidding. Baron Llwyd had no sons of his own, only daughters to be used as pawns, bartered and traded as if they were wheat or cattle or horses. So an alliance had been formed, one joined by two unwilling marriage partners, to be cemented by a male heir.

Kelan's chest constricted. Well, so be it. 'Twas not as if he believed in love, he thought as his horse crested the forested hill and trees gave way to the vast fields of Lawenydd.

Dried, wintry stubble covered the ground leading toward a tall castle constructed of dark stone. Across a wide moat, the gates to the keep were thrown wide. Farmers' wagons, a peddler's cart, horsemen, and people on foot were converging at the castle while high overhead, atop square towers, the yellow-and-white standards of Lawenydd snapped in the stiff breeze blowing off the sea. He heard the sharp beat of hooves and turned in the saddle to spy his brother riding at breakneck speed only to pull up beside him.

"Ahh . . . home of your beloved," Tadd observed, eyeing the keep as if it were a prize to be won at a cockfight. " 'Tis a bit on the humble side, but 'tis no matter . . . see over there." He hitched his chin to the town and the piers jutting into the swirling gray waters. Whitecaps and swells rolled with the angry tide. Two ships were at anchor, their sails furled tight, their spars pronging upward toward the ever-darkening sky as the hulls bobbed on the turbulent waves. "What better dowry than access to the sea?"

"You tell me."

"Still not happy?"

Kelan's lips twisted. "Are you?"

"Aye. Often." Tadd slid a wicked glance in his brother's direction. "For though my fate is more lowly than yours, though I will not inherit the keep or anything of worth, I do have my freedom." His eyes were like ice as he said, "So you who reap the privilege must also suffer the consequence of being first-born. 'Tis necessary that you produce heirs, whereas I can bed any wench I choose and father as many bastards as time allows." He crooked a dark eyebrow as he stared at the castle looming in the distance. "And time, it hastens by much too quickly. Come, brother, smile. 'Tis your wedding day!"

Chapter Two

Shivering in her woolen cloak, Penelope peered through the crenels in the south tower. The wind slapped at her face and snatched at her hood as it screamed across the wide curtain wall, but she stayed unmoving in her hiding spot. Her fingers were near frozen despite her gloves. Blowing upon her hands, she spied the newcomers from her niche.

A small band of men — soldiers they appeared for the most part — entered the castle gates. There were less than ten of them, not much of a party, but they were far from what Penelope had expected. Aside from one ancient-looking man bundled in baggy, dirt-colored clothes, they were a strong, virile-looking lot. Granted they were a little on the rugged side, but then she supposed, at least to hear her sisters talk, she'd expected that these horsemen would be ruffians of the lowest order — cutthroats, pickpockets, murderers, and such. She'd heard Elyn and Kiera talking about Penbrooke and it sounded like a dark, decrepit, overgrown place where only ogres and trolls and criminals resided. And now Elyn was to marry the leader.

Except that Elyn had been missing since morning.

But that was a well-kept secret and all day long Penelope, Kiera, and Hildy, a trusted household servant who had long been the three sisters' nursemaid and confidante, had been searching for her. To no avail. Kiera had admitted the daft plan Elyn had cooked up, and was worrying that if Elyn didn't return, she would have to go through with it. It was all so romantic and thrilling. Hildy and Penelope would have to play their parts and even then things could go awry.

Swiping at her nose with the back of a gloved hand, Penelope crept from her cranny and hurried down the tower steps as fast as her feet could fly. At ground level, she burst from the tower, tripping over a calico-cat and nearly knocking flat a girl carrying two plucked geese to the kitchens.

"Hey — watch where ye're —" Upon recognizing Penelope, one of the baron's daughters, the serving girl back-stepped. "Oh, m'lady, 'tis sorry I am. I didn't see ye. 'Tis all my fault."

" 'Tis nothing. Worry not." What a twit! Penelope couldn't waste time with excuses or apologies. She raced behind her mother's bench in the garden, leaped over a puddle, and flew into the kitchen, rounding the corner as a boy threw bundles of wood onto the cook fires and another turned the spit where a pig was sizzling, grease dripping into a collection pan on the floor. A girl was grinding herbs with a mortar and pestle, another slicing apples, while the cook was stuffing sliced eels that were split from one end to the other.

But Penelope, intent on her mission, barely noticed. The cook glanced up as she raced to the back stairs. "Miss Penelope, should ye be —"

She didn't hear the rest. Her boots were already pounding up the stairs to the third floor, where breathless, she threw herself into Elyn's room.

"He's here!" she panted, flinging herself onto the bed and looking up at the white-washed ceiling while a small fire crackled in the grate and a few sparse candles flickered in the surrounding sconces. "The Lord of Penbrooke's arrived."

Kiera's stomach turned. She had two choices — to tell the truth and let both Penbrooke and her father be embarrassed, or to go along with Elyn's ludicrous scheme. Just last night, before bed, Elyn had come to her chamber and held her hand, lacing her fingers through Kiera's. "I just want you to know that I would do anything for you," she'd said. "Even if things were reversed and you were the one to marry the Beast of

44

Penbrooke, I would stand in for you, for just one night, especially since Penbrooke will not know the ceiling from the floor once he drinks the potion. After all, 'tis not that much to ask, for I am to be married to a man I detest for the rest of my life. I can only hope 'twill be short." Blinking against the tears in her eyes, Elyn had hugged Kiera fiercely.

Kiera felt as if she hadn't slept a wink. All night long she'd stared miserably at the dim shadows cast upon the ceiling by the fire and wondered if she'd been entirely too selfish. How would she feel if she'd been promised to a man she'd never met who was rumored to be a rake? She'd dozed near morning and dreamed that Elyn had come to her and whispered, "I'm sorry," as she'd left their mother's jeweled cross in her hand. Kiera had woken with a start, sweating, her heart pounding, the room empty. She'd wanted to dismiss the silly dream but found the necklace wound around her wrist. And Elyn was nowhere to be found.

And now the Lord of Penbrooke was here.

He would insist upon meeting his bride. Sweet Jesus!

Upon the bed, Penelope rolled onto her stomach.

"How many men are with him?" Kiera asked, the wheels in her mind turning, sweat collecting upon her skin. Could she go through with her sister's mad plot if only to save her father from embarrassment?

"A handful."

"And a priest?"

"I couldn't tell."

Kiera's heart was pounding wildly, her pulse racing. She rubbed her damp palms upon her skirt. It would only be for a few hours. That was all. Then her sister would be wed, her father happy, an alliance with Penbrooke in place. Soon it would be done. 'Twas nothing. Yet her throat was dry, her stomach twisting, her heart a frightened drum.

"What?" Penelope asked. "Kiera, what are you thinking?" Kiera glanced at Elyn's wedding dress. White lace and tufted velvet, draped over a screen that partitioned off part of the chamber. Could she go through with it? Don the dress and veil, utter the sacred vows . . .

"Elyn's not returned?" Penelope asked.

"Nay." Pushing her hair from her eyes, Kiera slumped onto a stool by the fire and knew she was as pale as death. Where the devil was Elyn?

"So are you going to do it? Are you really going to pretend to be her?" Penelope asked, her eyes bright with a sense of adventure. Ever since Kiera had confided in her, swearing her to secrecy this morning, Penelope, the youngest and most flighty of the three sisters, had been unable to hide her excitement.

"Did you get the vial from the apothecary?" Kiera asked.

"Aye. A concoction of herbs that he said would make even a wild man drowsy."

"And you know what to do with it?" Oh, this was insane!

"Yes!"

Penelope was to make sure that the elixir was placed in a mazer scratched with an *X* on its bottom. Kiera would know that cup was for the bridegroom. The rest of the potion was to be left in the vial and hidden in the rushes on the floor near the bed.

Kiera couldn't believe what she was contemplating, but she felt as if she had to go through with it. What other choice had Elyn left her? Anxious as a caged wolf, she paced to the window and opened the slats to stare at the inner bailey. How had Elyn left the castle so early this morning? How had she not been detected, especially on this, her wedding day? Had someone helped her? Brock? Mayhap he'd slipped inside just as the castle gates were opening and helped her escape. Oh, dear God, could she go through with the deceit? Swallowing back her indecision, she faced her sister again.

"Now, remember," Kiera said, "all you have to do is — if anyone asks — claim that I'm Elyn. I'll be wearing the dress and veil." She motioned toward the stool where the veil of thick, patterned lace rested. By the saints, this was idiocy! "No one should question you. If they ask for me —"

"You, Kiera, or you, Elyn?"

"*Me*. Kiera. If they ask for *me,* you are to tell them that I'm ghastly sick. Hildy will agree. Everyone will think that I'm in my chamber and can't come down to the nuptials."

" 'Twill be odd."

Kiera threw up her hands. Maybe she was making a horrid, horrid mistake. "It's all odd!"

Penelope looked worried for the first time. "What if Father asks about you?"

"The story is the same." Kiera rubbed her temple against a sudden headache.

"I don't like lying to Father."

"Neither do I. But . . . but we must," she said as she touched the jeweled cross at her throat. "Now, make sure that the Beast of Penbrooke drinks plenty of wine tonight at the feast. Hildy will see that there is potion in it, so that he will feel dizzy and sleepy. He'll come up to the chamber and I'll give him more wine."

"What if —"

"He'll fall asleep," Kiera cut in. "Later, when Elyn returns, I'll sneak back into my room, and she'll take her place as his bride. When he awakens he will have a pounding head but will be with his real wife. No one will know there has been a deception." The last word tasted bitter upon her tongue, yet she ignored it.

"Not even the Lord of Penbrooke?"

"Not if we're lucky."

"And if we aren't?" Penelope asked.

Kiera's eyes closed for a second. Her sister had voiced Kiera's worst fear. She sketched a quick sign of the cross over her chest. "If we aren't, then God help us."

Despite the icy air, the headstrong mare was sweating. Stomping nervously, tossing her dark head and snorting, the damned horse acted as if she sensed the lies swirling in the forest, and the guilt that Elyn felt surrounding her heart.

"Shh," Elyn commanded with a sharp jerk on the reins. "Whoa." With gloved fingers, Elyn held fast to the leather straps, keeping the jumpy horse from bolting as she cast one final look over her shoulder to the castle. Lawenydd. Her home.

But no longer.

Her throat ached and tears burned at her eyes, but she blamed it on the raw winter wind that tore through the fields, bending the dead grass. With biting cold it nipped at Elyn's cheeks as she stared at the thick stone curtain and high towers of the keep. It was nearly nightfall, but enough moonlight shone over the castle that she was left with one final impression of it before she yanked roughly on the reins and kneed her mare into the forest.

This was her choice, not to marry the man to whom she was promised, but to seek out real love, the true heart she'd met, an irrepressible spirit who had sworn to love her. *Brock. Oh, love.*

Her blood ran hot and guilty at the thought of him and what she was about to do. What she had planned was unthinkable and she felt a kernel of regret for poor Kiera. But, Elyn decided, her younger sister would survive. Kiera had promised to do anything Elyn asked, hadn't she? Then changed her mind. Elyn's lips twisted at her sister's cowardice. Pathetic, weak creature.

Certainly in the days to come Kiera would be tested. Just as Elyn had been. She'd hidden within the keep for most of the day, waiting for the perfect time to sneak away, and now she was free. Free!

Was it fair that Elyn was to have been sacrificed for her father's petty alliance, that she would have to give up her life all for duty and Lawenydd, just because she was first-born?

Nay, nay, nay!

She was still angry at how easily her father had bartered her away, with as little concern as if she'd been a lame horse, something to quickly dispose of. Well, Llwyd of Lawenydd was about to find out that his daughter was as strong as he.

Gloved fingers twisting in the reins, she guided the bay through the thickets to splash across an icy stream. She dared not ride along the road for fear she might meet someone who would recognize her and then all of her plans would be destroyed. But she had to be wary. The woods were far from safe, as she'd discovered on her own, and she'd overheard her father and the soldiers talking about the thugs and their raids upon the innocents who traveled undefended. Yet she couldn't take the chance of joining a group of travelers who might know her as Elyn of Lawenydd.

For her plan to work as she'd plotted, Kelan of Penbrooke must think that he'd married the woman to whom he'd been promised.

If Penelope, Hildy, and Kiera would only hold their tongues, play their parts, and Morwenna, Kelan's sister whom Elyn had met years ago, didn't recognize the switch . . .

Dear God, what was the chance of that?

'Twas Kiera's worry now.

Again guilt stung her, but she paid it no heed. Could not. She'd made her decision.

Aye, and Kiera will have to pay the price. Shoving aside that nagging little thought, Elyn leaned low over her horse's neck.

51

Coarse hairs from the bay's mane slapped at her cheeks. The wind whispered through the barren, skeletal branches, making them creak and moan. Elyn shivered. Her heart raced faster.

She couldn't turn back and face her father's wrath. Nor could she marry Penbrooke, whom she would never love. For Elyn refused to marry without love.

So now Penbrooke is Kiera's problem, Elyn's mind nagged. *Kiera's fate. Kiera's doom.*

Well, fine. *Better she than me!*

Yet the wind moaning through the forest seemed to mock her, to jeer at her for sneaking away like a thief in the night.

And now Kiera would have to fight the man off, night after night . . . once she understood. Then she would eventually have to give in, accept her fate. Guilt, suddenly sharp as a cutthroat's dagger, sliced through Elyn's mind once more. She closed her eyes and steadfastly brushed the blame aside. She had no time for doubt.

Besides, Kiera would make the best of the situation. She was a clever girl.

Even so, Elyn bit her lip until it bled as she thought of Lawenydd and the ceremonies about to take place. *Forgive me,* she silently prayed before forcing her thoughts to the uncertain path stretching before her.

Ahead lay Brock.

Oh, precious, precious love. Her throat tightened. He was worth every second of regret she might feel.

Far in the distance she heard the rolling peal of bells.

Wedding bells.

Chimes announcing the marriage of Elyn of Lawenydd to the Lord of Penbrooke.

"So be it," she whispered, and spurred her fidgety mare onward.

To Brock.

As the bells tolled out her miserable fate, Kiera closed her eyes, took a deep breath, and walked slowly into the chapel. So Elyn had abandoned her. Fear and anger burned through Kiera's blood, and when her sister returned later tonight, she'd be lucky if Kiera didn't strangle her.

Through the heavy veil she saw little, but she made her way to the altar, where candles burned and a man — Elyn's bridegroom — awaited. *God, help me.*

Stomach clenched, she stole a glance in his direction. Through the tightly woven lace she couldn't see his features distinctly. Yet she was able to discern that he was a tall man with wide shoulders, a straight spine, a flat abdomen, and long legs. His silhouette looked like that of a warrior. Candlelight reflected upon his head of thick, dark hair.

He was not at all as Elyn had told her. Swallowing hard, Kiera sensed that the Beast of Penbrooke's expression was hard, though she caught only a shadowy glimpse of his face.

The small room was dark; the few people were blurry, hard to recognize through the lace. *Dear God, forgive me for this deception,* she thought, her heart in her throat as she made a quick sign of the cross and knelt beside Elyn's betrothed. Upon his knees he dwarfed her, and she bowed her head, more to hide her features than for the sake of piety. Along with the smells of incense and burning tallow, she recognized the faint hint of wood smoke and leather and something else — something frighteningly male that seemed to emanate from him. Her shoulder nearly touched his arm, so close were they, and was it her imagination, or did she feel resentment, even anger, as if he was no more happy than she?

She felt him slide a glance her way.

She swallowed hard.

He was so big. So imposing. So . . . masculine.

Holy Mother, what was she to do with him? Her heart beat as fast as a hummingbird's wings; her throat was as dry as desert sand. Her stomach was knotted in a tight fist that she doubted would ever loosen.

The priest was murmuring a prayer, but she could barely hear the words over the rush of blood in her ears. This was wrong.

She'd never get away with it.

True, Penelope was to add a potion to his mazer of wine, as they had discussed earlier, but what if the herbs weren't strong enough? What if he didn't want any wine? What if all he really wanted was to claim his wife in the marriage bed?

She groaned inwardly. She should never have decided to go through with this mockery. Never. Just being this close to the man made her want to bolt. What would it be like to be alone with him in a locked room, with the promise of wedding vows hanging heavy in the air? Swallowing hard, she tried to hang on to her rapidly fleeing composure and forced her hands not to shake.

The priest was old, mumbling, but seemed joyous, as if pleased to have traveled three long days to bless this union. Would God strike her down for lying, for committing a sin in His house? Oh, she'd been a fool to ever don the wedding dress . . .

She sensed her father to one side of the chapel, and men she did not recognize on the other. Penelope was nearby, and no doubt, Hildy was somewhere in the shadows.

Kiera bit her lip. If she could somehow just get through the ceremony and the next few hours — Suddenly she realized that the small room had become silent. There was an expectant hush. The priest was waiting . . . he

55

repeated the horrid words. Would she accept this man as her husband, to love him, to cherish him, to obey him . . .

Her heart was a drum, blood pounding in her ears. Though the room was cold, sweat slid down her spine.

"I . . . I do," she whispered and wondered if she'd just damned herself forever.

Chapter Three

Every person in the small chapel let out a tiny sigh of relief. Everyone but the man kneeling next to Kiera. Kelan's back was stiff, his chin elevated in arrogant defiance. Though he, too, repeated his vows, his words were clipped and sharp. He made no effort to hide how anxious he was for the ordeal to be over.

She wanted to run out of the chapel as fast as her legs would carry her. What would happen when he lifted the veil to kiss her? Would there be someone in the room who would recognize her, who would gasp and point and accuse her of being the impostress she was?

And suddenly the rite was over. The priest offered up a prayer and announced that they were married — the Lord and Lady of Penbrooke. *God, help me,* she thought as her new husband leaned over to lift her veil and kiss her.

This is where it will surely all fall apart.

Slowly he pulled back the heavy lace, and her eyes met his in the darkened chapel. A stormy, angry gaze pierced deep into hers and seemed to see every one of her lies. 'Twas as if in that instant, he looked straight to her soul.

She drew in a quick breath. Her heart knocked wildly. Her knees nearly buckled.

He wasn't the ogre Elyn said he was.

Far from it.

His features were harsh, yes, rugged, but rough-hewn in a dangerous way that only heightened his masculinity. His silvery eyes glared from beneath thick, dark brows and rested upon cheekbones that seemed as if they'd been chiseled by God Himself. Square, beard-darkened jaw, narrow, strong nose, and blade-thin lips set in a furious hard line.

Her heart hammered noisily and she braced herself for a quick brush of those sensual lips over hers, for a fleeting touch of skin to skin, but she should have recognized the determination in the set of his jaw. His arms surrounded her and he pulled her tight, then lowered his head and waited just a heartbeat, long enough that she saw the raw power etched in his features.

In an instant, his mouth slanted over hers. Warm. Hard. Demanding. She nearly gasped and something deep inside of her started to tingle. The kiss deepened. Her head spun and the small room seemed to tip a bit and sway. *This is all wrong. It shouldn't feel like this! Not like this!*

Despite all the thoughts racing through her

head, her impulse was to kiss him back.

He jerked his head away from hers. Hot gray eyes assessed her for a split second, and she thought she recognized not only surprise, but arrogance, as if he was used to women swooning at the mere brush of his lips upon their skin.

Thankfully he let the veil drop. She was certain her face had turned a wild crimson color, and even with his weak vision her father might recognize her as she turned to face the chapel door.

God be with me, she thought, catching a glimpse of Penelope standing next to their father. The Lord of Lawenydd was beaming, but his youngest daughter was awestruck, her round-eyed gaze never leaving the face of her new brother-in-law.

Kelan's arms dropped, and somehow Kiera's unstable legs held her. He didn't so much as hold her hand or offer her a steadying arm as side by side they walked quickly out of the chapel and into the corridor. As wobbly as her legs were, Kiera wouldn't have to feign sickness, for she didn't feel well, not at all. Her cheeks burned, her blood pounded hot through her veins, and she was filled with the horrifying notion that his kiss at the altar had not been so much a bonding, nor even an acceptance, but rather a dare and a furious one at that. As if the Lord of Penbrooke was as angry about this marriage as she was. More than that, it was as if he was silently warning her he intended to take out his fury on his wife.

Which is you, Kiera. At least as far as he knows. You're the one who said the vows. You're the one who nearly tripped over your sister's name as you promised to love, honor, obey, and be faithful, along with all those other promises at God's altar. Though Elyn is his legal wife, he thinks that you are she, and as such you will surely suffer his wrath.

Oh, this was a mistake. An unforgivable mistake. She should never have let her guilt get the better of her, never have tried to help Elyn in her lie. She should make things right. This instant. Before things got worse. But from the corner of her eye she caught a glimpse of her father's face. Radiant and proud, he was shaking hands with well-wishers.

She couldn't disappoint him. Not now. She withered inside, felt far worse than she imagined she would. She wasn't cut out for deception and yet she was thick in it, so thick she saw no way out. The truth seemed to slip further and further away from her.

The deed was done. The lie complete. Kiera's misery was much greater than she had even feared it would be.

Servants held the doors open, and just outside the chapel Hildy waited, her thin lips pursed, her hands twisting in the folds of her skirt.

"Congratulations, m'lady."

"Oh, Hildy," Kiera whispered so that no one would recognize her voice. "I feel . . . faint." Though the speech was rehearsed, the words were so true.

"But the feast —" Hildy protested, on cue.

"I . . . can't . . ." Through Elyn's wedding veil, Kiera cast a glance up at her new husband. "If you could please excuse me, m'lord."

"Yes, mayhap you should lie down in your chamber," Hildy suggested.

"This is our wedding feast," he said.

"Yes, yes, I know." Kiera laid a hand upon Penbrooke's sleeve and she felt the muscles in his forearm tense. "I — I'll join the festivities later."

"Will not your father be disappointed?" he said, obviously offended.

"Nay," she whispered. "He will understand." *And he's got what he wanted.* "I — I'll join you soon."

He hesitated.

Oh, no, he had to agree!

"This is an embarrassment," he said through lips that barely moved. "The guests —"

"I know. 'Tis a pity. If I could just lie down but a few minutes." She couldn't lift her veil at the lord's table in the great hall during the feast. Even her weak-eyed father would recognize her and realize that he'd

61

been duped. She shuddered as if gripped by a sudden, intense pain.

"M'lord, she may have caught a sickness from her sister. Even now Kiera is abed. 'Tis why she didn't attend the ceremony. Mayhap the illness has spread," Hildy said. "We would not want to expose the guests or family to whatever vile sickness this is."

The man was silent at Hildy's remark, but clearly still seething.

Kiera didn't wait for his permission, but hurried toward the stairs.

Footsteps shuffled behind her, growing louder. She heard Father call after her, "Elyn!" She didn't turn around. Couldn't risk it. She sprinted up the stone risers as if her feet had wings. Upstairs, she flew into Elyn's chamber and cursed herself and her sister for this awful, stupid plan.

Yanking the door closed behind her, she gasped, catching her breath as she leaned against the thick oak panels and stared at the chamber — the bridal chamber. Inwardly she groaned. The bed was freshly made, the rushes strewn over the floor were new and fragrant. Dozens of candles had been set upon the window ledge and small tables, while a fire crackled and hissed in the grate. Upon the bed lay a sheer new chemise, pure white with tiny embroidered roses at the neck.

Kiera's stomach turned. How could she

wear the diaphanous piece of nothing and lie in this bed waiting for the man who thought he was her husband?

Panic assailed her. She should run. Hide. Let him think what he wanted. She could appear mad, that was it, crazy as the old hermit locked in his cell in the west tower . . . no . . . *Calm down. Breathe deeply. Think, Kiera! You got yourself into this mess and it's up to you and you alone to get yourself out!*

For a second, she thought of that breath-stopping kiss at the altar, the press of Kelan's warm lips to hers. Her blood raced, for she'd never expected her reaction. Rather than feeling revulsion, she'd been intrigued. Kiera even wondered what it would be like to kiss him a bit longer. She touched her lips with the tips of her fingers, then shook her head at her own folly. What was she thinking? She could feel nothing good for this man. Nothing!

Before her wayward thoughts got the better of her, she crossed the room to the bed. The marriage bed. Elyn's bed. The bed where she would spend the night with . . . no, she wouldn't consider the night.

On the table next to the bed a jug of wine and two mazers were waiting. As planned. She lifted up one cup. There on the bottom of the stem an *X* had been scratched into the silver. Lowering herself to her knees, she felt in the rushes near the table and found two small vials. The potion. And the blood. Would it work? She remembered the determination and spark of intelligence in Kelan's gray eyes as he'd kissed her. In that quick glimpse she'd recognized that he wasn't a man easily fooled, nor would he be forgiving if he ever discovered he'd been duped.

But she had no other option.

Carefully she slipped the vials into a safe place in the rushes, near the head of the bed where they wouldn't get crushed by a misplaced boot.

Faintly, she heard the strains of music. Downstairs the feast had begun. It was only a matter of time before she had to face Kelan again. No doubt he'd be more than angry. Beyond furious. At her. For embarrassing him within minutes of being wed.

She shuddered. He would never let Elyn forget how she'd shamed him on their wedding day. Nor would he let her feign sleep tonight to avoid his wrath. No doubt he would wake her and demand his rights as a husband.

Kiera would have to stay awake to make sure he drank the sleeping potion and somehow keep him at bay until he fell asleep. Once he was no longer conscious, she could sprinkle the blood on the linens. If she dared.

Sending up a silent prayer, she walked to the window and stared into the cold winter night. Spangled by moon glow, the curtain wall shimmered silver. Beyond the thick battlements, somewhere in the surrounding forest Elyn waited for the man she loved.

A hollow feeling crept through Kiera's heart and she felt a second's envy for her sister. Elyn had found true love, or thought she had. Would Kiera ever know that particular and divine bliss? Would she ever fall in love? Would she ever care about someone above all others?

Frowning, she experienced another, darker thought. If Elyn and Brock had such a deep bond, how would they ever break it? Why would her sister give up that which she most desired? Elyn had risked much to be with Brock of Oak Crest. As had he to be with her. So what was it that would force her back to Lawenydd? Kiera watched a cloud pass over the moon.

Who was to say that Elyn would return?

She promised.

Kiera fingered the cross at her throat.

So what? Has she not lied before? Did she not promise your father that she would marry Kelan? Did she not break that vow? So why would she return for you?

The thought curdled in Kiera's stomach, and though the doubts assailed her, she wouldn't believe them.

Surely Elyn wouldn't leave her to live the rest of her life caught in a lie, pretending to be wife to a man who was not her legal husband, forever an impostress.

Or would she?

Icy fingers of the wind snatched at Elyn's hood and slapped at her cheeks. Her lungs burned and exhaustion threatened to overtake her, just as it did the horse. Lather dampened the mare's coat, and her once long strides had slowed. "Come on, come on," Elyn whispered, urging the lagging beast up a final hill.

She was edgy, her stomach in knots.

What if Brock wasn't waiting for her?

What if he'd changed his mind?

What if . . . what if he was toying with her?

He wouldn't! And yet, had there not been a time when he'd been untrue?

She gritted her teeth against the cold air and the grim thoughts slipping like ghosts through her mind, haunting her.

'Tis only the night getting to you. Have faith.

But the nagging doubts persisted as her teeth chattered and Royal, the game little mare, labored up the rise. This temperamental jennet was not her usual mount. Elyn had been careful to steal a horse she'd never ridden before, a mare Kiera favored, one that wouldn't be easily missed and associated with Elyn. Leaving the castle had been tricky, but dressed as a peasant boy, as she had often enough been in the past when she'd left to tryst with Brock, she'd eased past the guard. Busy with the miller whose cart was mired in the mud just inside the castle gates, he hadn't more than glanced her way.

She'd found it easy enough to sneak the horse under the open portcullis, as there was more activity in the keep than usual, more workers, merchants, and visitors because of the wedding. But the horse would certainly soon be missed. Though the old stable master, Orson, was somewhat of a dullard these days, his son, Joseph, would discover the herd was short and would be blamed for losing one of the animals.

Elyn thought of Joseph and felt a jab of guilt, for she knew the stableboy fancied her. More than fancied, she imagined, and she'd callously used him for her purposes. 'Twas silly for him to have romantic thoughts. And yet the way he looked at her or blushed when she caught him was flattering, even heartwarming. As well as ridiculous. No doubt Joseph would get into trouble this night. Just as his father, Orson, had been blamed the night Kiera had stolen away on Obsidian, the horse that had never been found.

Easing the mare past the ruins of a burned-out hut, Elyn refused to dwell on what might happen to those she'd left behind. Beyond this final hill was a small town.

Brock had sworn he would meet her at a place called the Gamekeeper's Inn.

Unless he'd changed his mind.

Setting her jaw against the doubts that plagued her, she kicked the mare harder than she'd anticipated. The horse shot forward just as an owl swooped out of the shadows. With a frightened whinny, the little jennet shied, breaking stride and rearing.

"It's all right," Elyn said, clinging tight to the reins. "Shh . . ."

The mare's front legs landed on the ground with a jarring thud that rattled Elyn's spine.

The fight between rider and mount wasn't over. Bit firmly clamped in her teeth, the horse charged forward, hooves flying. "Damn it all! Stop. Whoa!" Elyn struggled with the frightened animal, pulling hard on the reins, using her weight to force the mare to slow. But the bay was spooked. Her eyes rolled, showing the white rims, and she fought the bit. "Easy girl. That's it. 'Twas nothing," Elyn assured the beast, slowing her into an easy lope.

An owl was the least of Elyn's worries . . . right now she had to think of her future. And Brock.

What if he's not there? Doubts clawed at her as images black as the dark night swept through her mind. *Where will you go? What will you do? Return to Lawenydd?*

But you can't. Bile rose in the back of her throat.

You can never go back again. Never!

Her stomach was knotted and sour, sweat collecting on her body though she shivered. Brock wouldn't abandon her. Not now. He couldn't.

She tucked her head low and pushed those frightening thoughts into a dark corner of her soul as the horse galloped along the winding road. Hurrying past a few solitary huts and farms, Elyn felt the harsh slap of the wind as it tore her hood from her head and her dark hair unfurled behind her. Faster and faster the little horse raced. Faster and faster her own heart beat.

Brock was her first love. She believed he would be her only love, even though he'd betrayed her once before. 'Twas but three years past. . . . Though it seemed a lifetime, she'd felt that sharp, painful prick of deceit, felt its scar even now. Though it was long past, could he not deceive her again? What would she do then?

'Twas simple enough.

She'd kill him.

Chapter Four

Where the devil was his bride?

From his seat at the lord's table, Kelan viewed the great hall. Musicians were playing from an alcove set high into the far wall. Servants carried trays laden with food and drink from the kitchen to the head table. Magnificent sugar sculptures decorated the tables. The mood was merry, the company jovial, but Kelan's temper darkened by the second.

The seat next to him remained empty, as if his new wife was deliberately trying to embarrass him, making her distaste of him known. He suffered through the nothing-talk of his new father-in-law and the stares of the twit of a sister. She was a mite of a thing who, every time he glanced her way, would quickly look aside, blush, and bite her lower lip. As if she was guilty of some dire deed.

Which was foolish thinking.

Courses came and went. Roasted stag and peacock, jellied eggs and crisp, sweet tarts. Stuffed eel and pike with ginger. Baked apples and wine. Mazer after mazer of wine. His cup was never left to empty.

70

Settled low on his back he watched without any interest as jugglers and dancers and an insipid jester with bald jokes passed by the table. They were meant to entertain the honored guests, the Lord and Lady of Penbrooke, which only made it more obvious that the seat next to him remained vacant. As each platter was served, he expected his bride to appear and caught the glimpses, raised eyebrows, and not-so-quiet jokes at his expense.

"Hasn't been married but a few hours and already 'tis obvious who will run the keep," one fat merchant muttered under his breath.

A snort. "Would you expect anything else from Lady Elyn? A feisty one she is. With a mind of her own."

"Would ye not like to be a mouse in the rushes tonight when the lord takes her to his bed?"

Hearty chuckles at that. Kelan's back teeth ground together painfully.

"Mayhap *she'll* do the taking."

The two men laughed loudly over the plaintive strains of the lyre. Christ Jesus, did the woman mean to string him up by his balls for all to see and jeer at? This flagrant disobedience was more than embarrassing; it was a mockery of the vows they'd spoken only hours earlier and meant to make a needle-sharp and very public point. She would pay for this insubordination, oh, she would pay and pay dearly for every titter, raised eyebrow, and knowing smile cast at his expense.

'Twas no wonder Kelan felt as if he'd been played for a fool. Everyone in the great hall sensed it as well. His wife had better appear and soon, or he'd be the laughingstock of not only this keep, but his own as well, for gossip traveled faster than the swiftest steed, racing through the villages, along the dark roads, and through the neighboring keeps.

Irritated, his temper darker with each passing minute, he swilled mazer after mazer of wine, ignoring the stares of the curious, trying to concentrate on the worthless talk. But all the while in his mind he was conjuring ways of making his wife atone for his shame.

Tonight, when they were alone, he'd find a way to make his wayward bride understand that he would never abide disobedience from her. At the very least, she should have made a brief appearance and sat with him.

" 'Tis sorry I am about Elyn," the old man said as if he'd finally realized his daughter was missing. Sighing, he set aside his cup. "A headstrong one, she is . . . well, they all are. Mayhap you will be blessed with sons." His smile twisted sadly and his eyes, milky white with age, looked over Kelan's shoulder to a spot only he could see. "Not that the girls aren't a godsend, mind you. A godsend, but

. . . they lost their mother when they were young and, I suppose, I should have remarried . . . they needed a woman's touch . . ." His frail voice faded as if he'd said too much or his mind had wandered to new, unclear territory. "Yes, sons. That's what you need." Slapping the table as if he'd said something profound, he motioned the serving girl for more wine. "Zelda . . . our guest of honor's cup is nearly empty."

As the serving maid scurried off in search of a fresh jug of wine, Kelan glanced again toward the arched entrance of the great hall, where the bottom steps of the staircase were visible. Much as he willed her to, his wayward wife, of course, did not appear. Rage burned through his blood and he could feel the wine he'd been drinking was going to his head. He could usually drink as much as the next man, but tonight, mayhap due to his irritation, he felt a little light-headed and fuzzy, as if his mind was one step away from his body.

He glanced to the far end of the table where Baron Llwyd's youngest daughter, Penelope, sat. But she'd moved and was talking to the serving girl . . . with the wine. When she caught him staring at her, Penelope quickly ducked her head and scurried from the great hall. Kelan felt the hairs on the back of his neck rise in warning, but he didn't know why.

Tadd, seated on the other side of the bride's empty chair, leaned closer. He was picking his teeth with a small rabbit bone and motioned to the vacant space with the cleanly picked rib. "Already scared her off, have you, brother?" he asked.

"I told you she's not feeling well."

"A bloody excuse."

On the other side of Tadd, Orvis, eavesdropping, grinned widely. "A case of the marriage bed jitters. It happens."

"Not to me it won't," Tadd said as his gaze traveled quickly from one serving maid to the next.

"Cuz no one would marry ye, that's why." Orvis guffawed at his own joke.

"Nay, 'tis because I keep my women satisfied." To prove his point, he winked at the serving girl named Zelda. She was a pretty lass with pillowy breasts and sly, dark eyes. Lifting an interested eyebrow in Tadd's direction, she stuck out her lower lip almost petulantly, then twirled away, her skirts swishing loudly as she scuttled behind a curtain.

Orvis snorted and stuck his nose in his mazer. "Not all women, it seems."

"She'll be back." Tadd's confidence didn't falter a bit. "But what about your wife, Kelan?" Tadd couldn't hide his amusement at his brother's discomfiture. "Is it not time to bed the lady?"

"Soon."

"If I were you, I'd already be up the stairs. I caught only a slight glimpse of her face, but she's a comely one, your new bride."

Kelan glowered angrily and tried to pay attention to a singer who had joined the piper in the musician's alcove.

"Ah, to have a glimpse of that chamber tonight." Tadd's eyes glinted.

Better you than me, Kelan thought with disgust. He had no need of the stubborn, disrespectful woman. He wouldn't admit, not even to himself, that the kiss at the altar had caught him off guard, and the shadows in her green eyes when he'd lifted her veil had disturbed him. He'd expected cool disdain in her lips, but he'd experienced something more, something vexing. Something he didn't want to consider. "Have you not anything better to do?" he asked his brother.

The saucy serving maid returned with another jug of wine, and though she tried to hide it, she slid a cunning glance in Tadd's direction. Orvis caught the look and muttered, "Bah" before plowing his nose into his cup again.

"Aye, Kelan," Tadd said, smiling wickedly, "as luck would have it, it seems I might have something better. Something much, much better."

Nothing good will come of this.
Hildy threw the stones, and her handful of

colored pebbles tumbled noisily across the scarred wooden table to land in a beam of moonlight cast through the open window.

'Tis the devil's work.

Her old heart knocked painfully and she rubbed one spotted hand over the other. From the keep came the sounds of rowdy laughter, faint music, and the pulse of deceit. How had she let this happen? She glanced at the stones again and swallowed hard. She'd failed.

The promise she'd vowed to Lady Twyla as she'd lain upon her deathbed had been broken. Had been destined to break.

"Take care of my girls, Hildy," the lady had begged in the barest of whispers as a rattling cough had overtaken her thin, bony form. "Promise me that you'll see them all happily wed, that they will have children of their own."

"I will, m'lady," Hildy had sworn in the flickering half-light of a few sparse candles.

There had been a faraway look in the lady's green eyes. Her white skin had been thin, nearly translucent, as it stretched tautly over high cheekbones and a strong, pointed chin. Her chemise had been wet with sweat, her hair in damp ringlets despite the cool cloth Hildy had pressed to her forehead. The lady had fingered the cross she'd forever worn around her neck. "I have not had a happy marriage, as you know. 'Twas a union that my father conceived, but . . ." Sadness had touched the corner of her pale lips. " 'Twas good enough. Mayhap there is no thing as true happiness. Mayhap it is impractical, a romantic notion." She'd blinked and swallowed over the pain. "Just see that the girls are married to men who will be kind to them, who will treat them well . . ."

"I have no say in who they will wed," Hildy had protested.

In a moment of clarity, Lady Twyla's eyes had sharpened, focused as hard as a hawk's upon her maid. "You have the baron's ear. He trusts you."

Hildy's heart had nearly stopped. Her mouth had gaped.

"Aye. I have known for a long time," Twyla whispered, and one gaunt hand wrapped surprisingly strong fingers over Hildy's wrist. "I blame you not. I know of my husband's . . . needs. I know also of his beliefs in your silly omens and predictions. He is not always a Christian man. He thinks you are gifted, that you have the sight, that you . . . that you are a damned charm. A good luck piece." Her lips had twisted painfully at the thought. "Mayhap he thought that some of that luck might rub off on him."

"Nay, m'lady, nay, I —"

" 'Tis true!" She'd snapped at Hildy, nearly ten years her elder. Sighing, she'd shaken her head and brushed a wayward strand of hair out of her eyes. "Since he trusts you, you must advise him about my daughters. Promise me that you will do everything you can to see that they are wed to good men with true hearts."

"I will, m'lady, but —"

The talonlike fingers tightened with the same desperation mirrored in the lady's eyes. "Promise me," she'd insisted and, with her free hand, had found the cross half buried in the slit of her chemise. She'd held it out, then wrapped Hildy's unwilling fingers around the bejeweled piece. "Promise me. With God looking on. Now." When Hildy had hesitated, Lady Twyla had insisted. "Now!"

"I — I promise," Hildy had choked out as the lady had collapsed onto her pillows. Satisfied and drained.

But Hildy had lied. She'd known it then. And with chilling certainty, she knew it now.

Hildy had lost her influence over Llwyd of Lawenydd with his wife's death. Mayhap it was guilt over his wife's passing, or perhaps he had simply tired of her. The only relationship Hildy had maintained with the baron was through his children.

No matter the cause for her loss of Llwyd's favor, the result was the same. She had known her attempts to direct Lady Elyn's fate would be ignored by Llwyd. She had foreseen danger in the union with Kelan,

Baron of Penbrooke. But nothing prepared her for the future she now saw for the baron's daughters.

As she stared once again at the damning stones, she knew that because of this sham of a marriage, tragedy and death were about to descend on Lawenydd.

'Twas time to teach his wife a lesson, Kelan thought angrily. He'd tried to hold his rage in check, attempted not to let his irritation and his embarrassment show, but as each second passed, his anger had mounted. He'd suffered through enough of the festivities and the curious glances, lifted eyebrows, smug smiles, and twitching lips. He'd been married less than four hours and already the wench had the upper hand. Fortunately Tadd, sniffing at the skirts of the comely and willing serving maid, had disappeared. Orvis had consumed enough ale that he was certain to fall asleep at the table, his thick fingers curled over the stem of his mazer.

Kelan, more than a little drunk, scooted his chair back, excused himself, and, feeling the effects of too much wine, made his way out of the smoky great hall to the staircase. His legs were unsteady, which surprised him, for he was a man who could usually drink without too much effect.

Lord Llwyd's wine was potent.

More carefully than was his custom, he

strode up the curved stone staircase to the third floor, which, he'd learned from his conversation with his new father-in-law, housed the private chambers of the lord and his children. A single hallway divided the center of that top floor. One half was the baron's private quarters, and the three chambers opposite were occupied by his daughters. The first room belonged to that silly waif of a girl who'd stared at him in fascination as he'd endured the feast. The second was inhabited by Kiera, the sister who was so ill she couldn't come down to the wedding nor the feast. Which, of course, the bride hadn't attended either. She'd hidden herself away and had pointedly avoided her new husband, making him appear a bloody fool. Again a deep rage curdled through his blood. Either these daughters of Llwyd were a sickly lot or a prideful, stubborn one.

Kelan suspected the latter.

Gritting his teeth, he made his way to the third door, considered knocking, then thought better of it. Damn it, the woman was his wife. A wife he hadn't wanted.

He tried the latch, expecting that she might have dared to lock him out, but the door cracked open. Dim light from the sconces in the doorway sliced into the dark room that seemed to swim before his eyes. He leaned one shoulder on the doorjamb to brace himself as he caught sight of her. She was sitting up in the bed, the blankets drawn tight into one fist that she held over her breasts. Her eyes were round and wide, and she looked as frightened as a sacrificial lamb.

"Wife," he slurred, his tongue impossibly thick.

"H-husband."

" 'Tis comforting to know that you are, indeed, alive," he chided. Stepping inside, he closed the door softly behind him. It latched with a quiet click, and she nearly jumped out of her skin. Her green eyes, luminous in the shadowy room, stared at him, and he read confused messages there. She was scared, yes, but there was something more in her gaze — guilt? But why? For not joining him at the feast? For not loving him? For . . .

The thought crossed his mind that she might not be a virgin, that her fear was because she'd already lain with a man and was about to be found out.

The fire had died to glowing embers; the candles burned low, tallow dripping onto the table. "You didn't come down to dinner," he said, his words louder and more accusing than he'd meant them to be.

"Nay," she said, swallowing hard.

She was a pretty thing, he saw in the half-light. Tangled reddish brown hair that caught gold in the firelight framed her small, oval face complete with finely arched eyebrows, high cheekbones, and a small mouth. He'd caught but a glimpse of her when he'd lifted her veil to kiss her at the altar, but even then he'd noticed the regal tilt of her chin, the spark of intelligence in her green eyes, the dusting of freckles over the bridge of her nose.

"You were ill?" Dear God, why was it so hard to speak? His tongue felt thick; his thoughts were sluggish.

"Yes."

"And now?" He was walking unsteadily to the bed, trying to contain his temper, wondering what he would do with this strange creature who was now married to him.

"I, um, I still feel . . ." She searched for the correct word and tiny lines of vexation appeared between her eyebrows. He'd expected a spinster — since she was by every right long past marriageable age at nearly nineteen — but this woman was far from that. Her breasts were full as they pressed against the fabric of her chemise, her limbs long and supple. " 'Tis of no matter."

"It is to me. You made me look a fool."

"What?" She glanced upward quickly and something flashed in her eyes.

"I sat alone. Waiting for you."

"I'm sorry, I thought you knew —"

"What I know is that my bride humiliated me."

She gasped. "Nay, I — I am feeling poorly. I — I —"

"Are lying," he said succinctly, all the rage he'd experienced for four long hours returning, momentarily seeming to clear his head. He leaned over the bed. "I waited for you," he repeated.

His nose was nearly touching hers and Kiera swallowed hard. He was too close. Even though he was obviously drunk and the room was nearly dark, he was staring at her with such intensity that she was certain he was memorizing each and every one of her features. Her heart was beating so fast she could barely breathe, and she remembered their one, fleeting kiss, the repressed fire in the meeting of their lips.

"Have you nothing to say for yourself?" he demanded, so close his breath, warm and smelling of wine, whispered across her cheeks.

"I think I just apologized."

"Too little and much, much too late."

Kiera wished he would disappear. Why had she felt she could go through with Elyn's plan? It would have been better for the Lord of Penbrooke to realize that the marriage would never work, for her father to be shamed but at least face the truth. As it was, Kiera was trapped until her rebellious sister returned.

And when will that be?

She swallowed hard. She hadn't lied when she'd told him that she was ill. Though the room was cool, sweat collected on her skin. Her fingers were curved in the blankets, and half lying here, in Elyn's bed, wearing Elyn's chemise, talking to Elyn's *husband*, she thought she might lose consciousness.

Silent, glowering down at her, he seemed even taller than he had at the wedding. A muscle worked at the edge of his jaw, and his big hands were coiled into hard, furious fists.

She had trouble finding her voice but finally whispered, "I should have sent word —"

"You should have joined me."

"But I could not."

"Or would not?" he challenged, his eyes narrowing suspiciously.

Rage pulsed from him. A sheen of sweat glistened on his skin, but as he rounded the bed she noticed that he seemed to walk unevenly. His strong, impossibly long legs wobbled slightly. Good.

"I — I am sorry if I offended you," she said, lowering her eyes. She could not risk infuriating him, not if the plan was to work. And though she wanted to snap back a hot retort, it would not serve her purpose. "I will not do it again. Now . . . mayhap you would like a cup?"

She smiled and reached for the jug of wine. She'd already added more potion into the marked mazer, just a little from the vial to make certain it worked.

Quick as a snake striking, strong fingers

grasped her wrist so tightly she gasped. "Understand one thing, wife," he said through clenched teeth. "I will not tolerate being humiliated. Not ever."

She gulped, tried not to notice the pressure of his fingers against her skin. "I know."

"Do you?"

"Yes!"

"If you ever, *ever* embarrass me again as you did tonight, you will regret it."

"You are threatening me?" she asked, her temper sparking. *Be careful, Kiera, don't bait him. Let it be.*

" 'Tis not a threat, wife, but the truth. I will not tolerate disobedience."

"Then I will try hard to be the ever obedient, loving, meek little wife," she mocked, unable to hold her tongue. "Anyone who meets me will know that I am only there to serve in your shadow, *m'lord*."

"You test me," he ground out.

"As you test me."

He hesitated, then let his hand fall. " 'Tis not a secret that I didn't want this marriage. No more than you did. But here it is. We are wed." He threw up a hand and stepped away from the bed, allowing Kiera to breathe a little. "We now have to make the best of it."

"Aye," she said, trying to hold her sharp tongue. "That we must."

He glanced at the table and she thought for a heart-stopping minute that he might want to pour the wine for himself. "Here, let me get you a cup," she offered quickly and let the blankets fall, aware that her breasts and their hard nipples would be visible through the thin silk. She grabbed the jug and splashed wine into the cups, spilling a bit and silently praying that the sleeping potion wasn't lost.

"I think I've drunk enough."

"Nay! We . . . we should share some wine."

"That we should have. *Hours ago.* Downstairs." His eyes slitted distrustfully. "You don't seem ill."

"I'm — I'm trying to please you," she said and managed a smile she didn't feel. Her hands were shaking as she handed him his mazer, yes, the one with the *X* scratched onto the bottom, though she could barely make out the marking.

He snorted in disbelief. Then, his gaze locking hard on hers, he touched the rim of his cup to her mazer. "Well, wife," he drawled, his lips twisting at the irony of it all, "here's to loving husbands, obedient wives, and, oh, yes, to wedded bliss."

Chapter five

The toast echoed through the chamber as Kelan touched the rim of his mazer to hers.

Kiera swallowed hard, felt herself turn ashen at the thought of her lies. So many lies. To her father, to the priest, to God, and to this man who mistakenly thought she was his wife. "To bliss," she forced out and saw those steely eyes staring at her, taking in the features of her face as if searing them into his brain.

Scooting back quickly, away from the shifting light of the candles, she turned her face from him, hoping her hair created a curtain that would disguise her features. What had she been thinking? The room was dark, yes, but there was still enough light that if he caught a decent view of her he might realize upon awaking with Elyn that he'd been duped. She could only hope that he was already too drugged to remember.

She took a swallow of her wine, then another as he drained his cup and lifted a dark brow, silently daring her to do the same. From her corner of the bed, she took the challenge and emptied her mazer, feeling the cool wine slide down her throat. "Another?" he asked.

Before she could reply, he reached down and poured from the jug into the two mazers. Oh, by the gods, now how was she supposed to add the draft of sleeping potion to his drink?

He glanced over his shoulder, one dark eyebrow raised, his hand poised over the jug.

"What . . . oh." She felt herself coloring under his gaze. "Please, m'lord." 'Twas difficult to spit out the word, for she didn't like even the idea that he was her master.

"You may call me Kelan, or husband."

Never, she thought. She accepted the cup and, after he touched the rim of his mazer to hers again, drank, watching as he did the same. How long was it before the elixir would take effect?

"Thank you . . . Kelan." Her heart hammered and she could barely breathe. This was all wrong. So very wrong.

Resting a hip upon the bed, he eyed her over the rim of his mazer. "And what shall I call you, I wonder?" he asked, sipping. "What would you like?"

"Me?"

"To be called."

"Oh." *Think, Kiera, keep him talking.* "Elyn," she said, her tongue tripping over the name. Dear Lord, he was so close. Too close. Her bare foot was near his hip but she didn't dare shift away like a frightened rabbit. He was supposed to be her husband.

"Not wife?"

"No!"

He waited in the dim, glimmering candle-light.

"I mean . . ." She fought the urge to make the sign of the cross as he stared at her with the sharp-eyed intensity of a hawk. "I mean, Elyn is fine. Yes. Call me Elyn." She forced a tiny smile. "This is all so new."

Again the twitch of his eyebrow.

Inside she felt undone. Shaken. She licked her lips nervously, then saw that his gaze was drawn to the movement. What now? He seemed a little drunk, but just a little. Not near enough. And beneath his mask of civility she sensed a smoldering fury, anger that he was trying to keep from sparking. " 'Tis new for me as well," he finally said and shoved his dark hair off his forehead. As if fighting a headache, he closed his eyes.

Finally.

Now if he'd just fall asleep so that Elyn could return and they could exchange places again. Kiera felt a little bit of relief and yawned slowly, her bones beginning to melt a bit. In her nervousness, she'd drunk too much wine after not eating all day. Her head had begun to spin a little and the golden shadows crowding the room seemed warmer and more enticing. If it weren't for this beast sitting on the edge of her bed, she might even find the evening pleasant.

"You must never embarrass me again," he said suddenly, his voice brooking no argument. She saw it then, in his coiled muscles, in the tense corners of his mouth, the tight, white fury he could no longer contain.

"I meant not to —"

"Liar!" His whisper was harsh as sand. His eyes flew open and he lunged suddenly, leaning over her, grabbing her wrists. "Something is amiss here," he accused, his nose nearly brushing hers. In the half-light his eyes were nearly black, so large were his pupils.

The fingers surrounding her wrists were manacles. The arm she'd injured long ago on the night that she'd lost Obsidian ached, reminding her of the night another man had hurt her, a dark, faceless attacker who had never been captured. She swallowed back fear though inside she shuddered at the memory.

"What is it, wife? Do you find me distasteful?"

"Nay," she said, her lungs constricting. That she remembered the attack now was unsettling.

"Unattractive?"

She swallowed. "Nay," she whispered and reached for the coverlet again, but his unforgiving fingers forbade any movement. The fire spat noisily and from the hallway she heard the sounds of footsteps as the guard changed.

"Then what, Elyn? You're acting like a frightened foal."

She met his gaze. "I have never been with a man before," she said, stalling for time.

"I expected you to be a virgin," he said, but she saw the unspoken questions and she knew that in the back of Kelan's mind, he wondered if his wife's skittish behavior stemmed from fear that her new husband would discover she was impure.

Boldly she lifted her chin. "But I know you are not so innocent, husband. You have had others. Mayhap dozens of others."

"Which should please you. Do not try to make us equal, Elyn. You are a woman, and I am man. 'Tis different we are."

"So I should not judge you, but you have the right to judge me?"

He didn't answer, didn't have to. He just stared at her and her brassy impudence with night-darkened eyes, eyes she was certain could see into her soul and carefully ferret out all of her lies. His gaze roved over her face and body, silently claiming her. Oh, Lord. Her breath got caught between her throat and lungs, and when he closed the distance between them, his lips hovering over hers, she heard her own heart knocking. Wildly. Loudly. Wantonly. She wanted him to kiss her, wanted to feel his lips against hers again. Oh, this was madness! With the tiniest of smirks, as if he guessed what she was thinking from the fluttering of the pulse at her throat, he lowered his head. Hot breath seared her skin. She fought the urge to writhe.

The kiss was a light brush of skin to skin, hard lips grazing hers ever so slightly, ever so seductively.

Oh, by all that was holy, no!

As he lifted his head to stare at her, his features seemed less severe, softer, the dim room a little fuzzy. He glanced down at her breasts, to her traitorous nipples pointing hard against the thin silk of her chemise. His grip loosened, letting her go.

"May-mayhap another cup," she suggested, barely recognizing her own husky voice as she reached for the jug.

A big hand covered hers. "I'll get it, wife."

She cringed at the endearment, then realized the word had been spoken without any hint of kindness or affection, as if he was trying it out, trying to impress it upon his memory.

"I realize you are no more happy about this marriage than I am," he said as he handed her the mazer. When was the last time she'd added the potion . . . would it linger in the cup? Why the devil wasn't he falling asleep?

He was staring at her. Again. She blinked

against suddenly heavy lids. Oh, no . . . he couldn't memorize the lines of her face.

"Well?" he demanded.

"Well, what?" Had he asked her something? Her brain seemed to be swimming.

"The marriage. You opposed it."

"Oh! Yes." *Remember, you're Elyn.*

"Why?"

"I . . . I didn't want to be . . ." *To be what?* ". . . wed."

"But you're of age. Past."

She remembered Elyn's fantasies. "But . . . I think . . . 'twould be nice to be . . ." She felt her face flood with color. How could she admit her sister's dreams, dreams she didn't trust? He was waiting. She forced out the words. "To fall in love with my husband."

"You're a romantic?" he said with the hint of a sneer.

She nodded sluggishly, some of her wine sloshing out of her mazer. Quickly she sipped from the full cup, then noticed the stains on the white of her chemise, purple blotches over her breasts and abdomen.

"Oh . . . dear . . ."

Catching her staring at the spots, he smiled . . . a wicked, devilish smile. He pried the cup from her fingers, then set each of their mazers on the table. Shimmering light reflected in his eyes for a second and she knew in an instant that the moment of truth had come, that she could not avoid his touch.

Slowly, he lowered his head and his lips pressed against the thin cloth over the dark splotches.

Hot and moist, his breath seared through the chemise to burn against her skin. She writhed. Moaned. Experienced a new and frightening want. Slowly his tongue traced the outline of a stain, and she felt a tingle deep inside, a yearning so deep it was terrifying and, oh, so seductive. She felt a need to wiggle against him, to feel his flesh against hers. He turned his attention to another stain, one that started below her neckline and spread dark over one breast.

His tongue found the discoloration. Flicked against it.

Her nipples tightened to hard pebbles, eager for more of his touch. Oh, God, this was not supposed to happen.

Want rippled through her.

She tried to move and couldn't.

As she watched him, she wondered what it would be like for him to kiss her bare skin, to strip off her clothes and touch her in the most private of places. Oh, she was a wanton. This was her sister's husband. The man Elyn was to live with for the rest of her life. Yet Kiera couldn't push him away. The sensations running through her body were new and treacherously delicious. Erotic pulses snapped through her blood, pounded in her heart. The thin, frail fabric of her chemise was little barrier, yet she wanted to cast it off.

No. Don't do this, Kiera. You can't.

His tongue found the stain and pressed hot and rough through the slick fabric.

She let out a soft moan. This shameful act couldn't be happening. Couldn't. She would stop it right now. "I — I don't think . . . oh!"

His mouth found her nipple and through the lace and silk he kissed, wetting the fabric so that it clung to her as tightly as a second skin. "Then don't think," he whispered against her, his breath fanning already hot fires deep within her belly.

Slowly he slid a hand upward to touch her other breast, gently kneading, strong, callused fingers massaging her skin and toying with her nipple. Dear God, she ached inside, began to move, found her own fingers running eagerly, desperately through his hair. Sinful as it was, she wanted him. All of him. Upon her, around her, beneath her, inside her. Touching, melding, kissing. Erotic images filled her mind, images she'd never witnessed, never experienced, but now seared through her brain in exciting and sensuous detail.

All thoughts of denial fled. His teeth scraped against her nipple and she arched her back.

"That's it, little wife," he growled, sliding

upward to kiss her full on the lips, his mouth open, her own an invitation. His tongue slid between her teeth, the tip skimming the roof of her mouth, then mating with her own. The world spun, the chamber seemed to melt away, and all Kiera could do was return his feverish kisses.

She couldn't think, didn't try as he pulled her chemise upward, exposing her legs. She knew she should stop him, but as his fingers caressed her calves and thighs, and delicious shivers slid down her spine, she didn't. She had vague thoughts about the elixir and why it wasn't working, and why she was so weak when it came to refusal of this man, but her musings disappeared as he touched her, probed her, sending spasms through her.

"You're so tight," he whispered, his voice thick with pleasure as he began to stroke. She was moving with him, accepting him, opening to him, kissing him and wanting more . . . Somewhere deep in the back of her mind she knew she was making a vast mistake, an irreversible error that could never be forgiven, that she should try to stop this now, but the pleasure of the moment, her dizzy head, and the incredible ministrations of this man held her tongue. She spread her legs further and he growled as he kissed her through the bunched fabric that had collected over her abdomen.

"Beautiful . . . beautiful wife," he said.

"I'm not —" she said, trying to explain that she wasn't Elyn.

"As beautiful as any woman." While still touching her with one hand, he slowly untied the laces of his breeches, and his manhood, straining against the fabric, slipped out. She swallowed hard upon seeing the length of him, the thickness. No . . . this could not happen. She gasped and tried to draw away, but he swore, "I'll be gentle. Tell me if anything displeases you."

"I can't," she whispered as he kissed her again, then stretched atop her, his weight pressing into hers, his hand slowly sliding from her, his shaft hard against her skin. She felt bereft, wanting more of him, and then he kissed her again. Hard. His hands tangled in her hair, his muscles straining.

"I'll be careful."

No! She couldn't do this. He was Elyn's husband and yet . . . she wanted him. "Wait," she begged.

He paused, took the time to stare into her eyes and brush a wayward strand of hair from her skin. "For?"

She couldn't think of a single excuse other than the truth. Why wasn't that damned potion working? He nuzzled her neck, tingles raced over her skin, and the heat within her was a palpable ache. "I don't feel that we are wed," she said breathlessly, her head spinning.

"Were you not there?"

"But I knew not the priest . . ." Her words were thick. "Mayhap we should wait until Lawenydd's priest returns and . . . and have another ceremony and . . ." He stared down at her as if she were a half-wit and then a small smile curved his lips.

"I don't think another wedding would change things." He kissed her then, harder still, his lips molding over hers and his tongue touching and seeking hers. Kiera's arms wrapped around him of their own accord, her fingers tracing the grooves of his shoulder muscles, her mind swimming. His mouth and hands were everywhere, caressing her buttocks, kissing her nipples, rubbing the curve of her spine and holding her close. His tongue was moist and anxious as it trailed across her skin, his fingers kneading, stoking the fire that was already burning white-hot within. She writhed and ached. A deep, dusky want that no amount of rational thought could deny pulsed through her blood. His lips found the most intimate part of her, his fingers and tongue probing, gently teasing. All her doubts were lost in the darkening room and she bucked as the first spasm hit her. A primal cry tore from her throat, the ceiling spun, and she had barely time to catch her breath before he was atop her again, his mouth covering hers, his knees parting hers, his body melded against her damp, flushed skin. The chemise bunched as he pushed forward, the tip of his shaft grazing the sensitive skin surrounding her womanhood. She gasped; he pressed forward. Oh, God, she wanted this.

Her fingers curled in the bedding.

He moved, prodding deeper.

"Oh!"

There was a rending, a burning pain, and she tried to wriggle away, but he kept moving, straining above her, holding her close and kissing her.

"The pain does not last long," he whispered against her neck. His breath came in short, shallow bursts, and the pain gave way to a warm, needy pleasure. She caught his rhythm and began to move with him, faster and faster, as wild as a swollen river, as hot as the sun. "Kelan," she cried out as her body arched and all the dying flames in the room seemed to burst behind her eyes . . .

A growl escaped his lips as he threw back his head and shuddered with his release.

His breath covered her face and he collapsed atop her, his weight flattening her breasts.

"Elyn . . . sweet, sweet Elyn."

She froze. *Elyn . . . oh, God . . .* All her warm thoughts turned to ice. What had she done? Oh, no . . . this wasn't supposed to happen. As if aware of her distress, he kissed her lips and rolled onto his side, then cuddled up behind her. Her buttocks pressed into his groin and he rubbed against them, his manhood probing even deeper. Her mind was still fuzzy, yet guilt grabbed hold of her soul. Deep inside she felt him and he seemed to thicken yet again. No . . . she couldn't . . . but he pushed her hair aside and kissed the back of her neck, his fingers splayed upon her abdomen, pulling her tight. Oh . . . no . . . but her rump pushed into him and he moved, stretching her further, rubbing against a spot that caused delicious pain to wash over her.

Moaning like a wanton, she knew that she was lost. As long as she was in bed with him, she couldn't deny herself the sinful pleasures he offered.

"I will bed you like this for the rest of my life," he vowed, his breath fanning her fevered skin as he touched her in a spot that sent delicious thrills through her.

"Nay —"

"Shh . . . I know. Neither one of us wanted to marry, but —" He moved just so and she gasped. "Is this so bad?"

"Heaven," she sighed, and twisted to kiss him on the lips.

Chapter Six

Dear God, what have I done?

Kiera's head thundered in pain as she opened a bleary eye. One strong male arm was wrapped around her midsection, and a muscular leg trapped one of her own.

Cautiously she opened the other eye and, wincing, found herself staring into Kelan of Penbrooke's rugged face. Her sister's husband. Although Kiera had said the vows and consummated this lie of a marriage, she was not legally Kelan's wife, nor would she ever be. Elyn's name in Welsh law took precedence over Kiera's acts, though Kelan would certainly have grounds for an annulment, should he want it . . . oh, by the fates, she'd made an irreversible, sinful mistake . . . many mistakes. And now . . . and now she'd suffered the loss of her virginity, her own purity. What man would ever want her now?

And what other man would you want? Can you even think of another when still you are sore from the pleasures this man, your sister's husband, brought you?

She hazarded a glance at Kelan and noticed the small details. His face was relaxed,

101

his mouth slightly ajar, and the warmth of his breath teased her skin. Dark hair fell over his forehead and he seemed almost boyish in slumber. But all he had to do was open one eye and he would be the lord of the manor again, the hard warrior. Half lying over her, his chest pinned her arm, while his own arm was flung across her chest, his hand cupping her bare breast.

She felt a flush steal up the back of her neck. What was she to do? When Elyn returned . . . oh, God, mayhap she was already within the castle walls . . . waiting to take her rightful place!

Elyn should have been here in this bed. *Her* bed. She should have been the one whose chemise was drawn over her head, whose breasts were kissed and laved, whose legs were parted . . .

Images of the night before flashed behind Kiera's eyes, and the ache pulsing through her head was intensified by her guilt. Once more the sharp soreness between her legs reminded her of how foolish she'd been. Throughout the night, she'd given herself to Kelan of Penbrooke over and over again. As if he were truly her husband. She'd known it was wrong, but hadn't been able to resist this man, this husband of her sister.

Oh, Lord, what would happen when Elyn sneaked back into the castle? She could never know, *never* learn that Kiera had made love with her husband. Shame burned through Kiera as she tried to inch away from Kelan. What would she do now that she had known this man's touch? What was to be become of her now that she no longer had her virginity to bring to her own real marriage?

And where the devil was Elyn?

Had she returned from her tryst with Brock, and was she already waiting in some alcove, ready to trade places?

Or was she still missing?

Hardly daring to breathe for fear she would wake Kelan, Kiera slowly extracted her arm from beneath him and, wincing against the pain running through her body, slid her legs to the side of the bed. She noticed the stain on the rumpled sheets and thought of the vial of pig's blood that had been wasted. *Think not of it. Find Elyn. Now. Explain that . . . that what? That even though you finally agreed to her plan, you didn't hold up your end of the bargain? That the potion took too long to work? That you couldn't refuse Kelan of Penbrooke? That you were so overcome by drink that you found the man irresistible? What kind of pathetic excuses are those?*

Kiera shoved aside the nagging recriminations pounding through her tender brain. There was no turning over the hourglass, or changing the sundial. 'Twas done. She'd pretended to be her sister as planned, but then things had gone awry. Last night she'd made love to her "husband," and could even now be carrying his child. Her mouth turned to sand at the thought. *What then? What then?*

No! She couldn't think of that. Noiselessly she placed her legs over the side of the bed though her mind was still unclear. *Hurry, Kiera. You don't have much time. He will eventually awaken. You must locate Elyn.*

Standing woozily, she took a deep breath, and was determined to set things right. Well, as right as they could be. She snatched her soiled chemise off the floor and threw the flimsy garment over her head. From the corner of her eye she caught a glimpse of Elyn's wedding dress. Shuddering, she told herself she would *never* wear that horrid gown again. Never. There had to be something else. Her feet bare, Kiera hurried to the small alcove where Elyn kept her clothes. All the tunics and gowns were in the vibrant colors her sister loved. Red Lincoln velvet, yellow damask, a deep blue silk . . . suddenly, she imagined Elyn as if her sister were close by, and she felt deep, unbearable shame at what she'd done. A lump filled Kiera's throat, yet she felt anger as well. For Elyn had left her to her fate.

Curse you, Elyn, where are you?

Have you not returned? Mayhap because you didn't believe I would take your place. Mayhap you didn't expect me to go through with your plan.

But why then did Elyn visit her in the early morning? More important, Kiera thought angrily, why put her in this impossible situation to begin with? Everything that could go wrong *had* gone wrong, and horribly so.

Without any answers, Kiera angrily pulled on the first tunic she reached. Then, refusing to gaze at the man sleeping so damned peacefully in Elyn's bed, she edged silently to the side of the bed where she'd left the vials. She needed to retrieve them and hide them on the off chance that he might waken before she returned.

She noticed one of the vials pushed near the wall by the bed. Silently she bent down to pick it up just as Kelan snored loudly and rolled, throwing an arm in her direction, his fingers narrowly missing her shoulder. She froze. Didn't move a muscle. He muttered something and his eyes moved beneath his eyelids.

She tried again, stretching her arm just as he sighed and, to her horror, opened an eye.

Her heart stopped.

Slowly she drew back her hand and saw his eyelid lower, as if he hadn't caught a glimpse of her.

She couldn't risk him seeing her with the vials. She could explain being out of the bed, that she needed to go to the latrine and relieve herself, or that she needed to send for her maid. But she would have no excuse to be carrying pig's blood and an empty little jar that had been used for sleeping potion.

Carefully, not making a sound, she kicked the rushes a bit, hiding the vessels. Then, holding her breath, she quickly made her way to the door.

Kelan didn't stir.

She paused with her ear to the thick oak and strained to listen. It wouldn't do to have someone in the castle see her sneaking out of Elyn's bedchamber. Through the panels she heard not a sound, yet her palms were wet with sweat as she unlatched the door. It creaked open and she cringed inwardly.

The hallway was empty and nearly dark.

She glanced over her shoulder one last time.

Kelan didn't move.

Good.

Slipping noiselessly into the corridor she closed the door with a soft thud. Torchlights burned low in the hallway, giving off smoke and some light. And the early morning sounds of the castle stirring, muffled conversation, footsteps, and even quiet bursts of laughter filtered through the darkened corridors to her ears.

Heart constricted, sweat collecting down her back, she hurried into her own chamber and prayed that Kelan wouldn't wake up. Not for hours. If she was to find Elyn, she would need time. That was, if Elyn had decided to return.

Don't think like that. Of course she wants to return. She wouldn't leave you in this predicament forever. Nay!

But that little nagging worry didn't leave Kiera's mind as she hastily washed herself with the water in a basin. She wiped her face and arms and even quickly cleansed the sore spot between her legs with the cool water. Afterward, she finger combed her hair and changed into her favorite gold-colored tunic and deerskin boots. After swinging her heavy mantle over her shoulders, she pocketed her dagger, a weapon she never failed to carry since her encounter with the thug in the forest, which still haunted her.

Her stomach was in her throat as she entered the hallway again. What if someone had realized she was not Elyn during the ceremony? What if Elyn had been caught stealing back into the castle and now their father knew of their deception? What if, God forbid, Elyn had been hurt and couldn't return?

Kiera hurried down the back staircase and braced herself as the sound of footsteps pounded up the stone steps.

"Oh!" Penelope cried, nearly running her sister over. "*There* you are." She seemed relieved. "Where's Elyn?"

"I don't know."

"What? But I thought the plan was —"

"She didn't return last night," Kiera whispered as Penelope followed her down the staircase to the second floor. "I was hoping that you or Hildy may have heard from her."

"No. I've heard nothing."

"Damn."

"Then . . . then . . ." Penelope's eyes rounded in comprehension. "But I thought she was to come back and —"

"So did I!" Kiera pulled her sister into an alcove and pressed a finger to her own lips. "But then it wasn't as if we had an agreement. She could have thought I wasn't going to take her place, for I never said I would. Oh, damn." Frustration burned through her. "Listen, Penelope, not a word of this to anyone!"

Penelope nodded, her head bobbing in hasty agreement. "No one."

"Just Hildy. We'll need someone to help us. Now, I have not much time. I must find Elyn before her husband awakens."

"Her husband," Penelope repeated thoughtfully as she stared at Kiera. "What happened last night? You know, after Lord Kelan went upstairs to Elyn's chamber?" Penelope blinked and swallowed at the horror of it.

"Nothing," Kiera whispered harshly, though she felt her cheeks flame. "I mean he was drunk and I gave him the potion and . . . he's still sleeping. Now, I'm going to go see

Father, show the servants that I'm feeling better. But I'll say that I ran into Elyn in the hallway when she was going to the latrine and . . . oh, bother, what will I say . . . oh! That she is still feeling ill . . . nay, that she is tired, that's it, and she wants — no, she and her new *husband* want their food brought to them and left outside the door. Then you must see that no one goes into the room."

"But why would they not come down-stairs?"

"Because they're so . . . so involved."

"What? Oh . . ." Penelope rolled her eyes. "I couldn't — oh!"

Kiera grabbed the front of her sister's tunic. "You can and you must, do you hear me? If anyone finds out what I've, I mean, what Elyn and I have done, 'twill be hideous. Unthinkable! Father will probably collapse and die, just after he's flailed Elyn and me — and, yes you — for lying, until we are near dead; the Lord of Penbrooke will be embarrassed at being played for a fool and will . . . will probably flog me yet again, as well as Elyn and anyone else involved in the plot."

"Y-you mean me?" Penelope whispered, properly terrified as she finally grasped the solemnity of the situation.

"Of course, you, too," Kiera said to make her point. She remembered all too well the steely edge to Kelan's words last night, the furious glint in his eye when he'd warned her not to play him for a fool. "And Hildy! Do you want her death on your hands? Listen to me, we are all in this together." Kiera was desperate. "Please, Penelope, help me."

"I — I guess I have no choice," she said, looking over her shoulder as if suddenly aware they might be overheard.

"That's right. This is your only choice. So you must make sure that no one goes into Elyn's chamber."

"What if *he* comes out?"

"That should be all right. As long as he doesn't see me. He'll sleep a long time, though, I think."

Penelope's eyes narrowed. "Why?"

"Because he is tired!" Kiera snapped, then realized she, too, was near dead on her feet. She'd slept so little . . . "He rode for hours before he got here, then there was the wedding and the feast and . . . and all the wine and the elixir. He drank a lot. He'll not raise his head for hours."

Penelope's eyebrows raised suspiciously, as if she didn't believe Kiera's excuses. "And so you actually slept with him?" Was there a trace of awe in her voice?

"I slept very little," Kiera admitted, for that much was the truth, but she embellished it enough to satisfy her sister's rampant curiosity. " 'Twas difficult with him there snoring."

"In the bed with you?"

"Yes," Kiera hissed, for her sister would believe nothing less. "I was jumpy and nervous all night. Never closed my eyes. Now, see that meals are brought up and left outside the door! You can suggest that Elyn and her husband want to dine . . . in privacy." Her head was really pounding now. How long could she keep up this pretense? Elyn had to return. She *had* to. And soon. "Check Elyn's favorite hiding places, the bell tower, and the weaving room and . . . the wine cellar. I'll search the hayloft and . . ." A heavy tread clambered up the stairs, and the fat laundress carrying a huge basket of bed linens waddled, breathing hard, along the hallway.

"M'ladies," she said with a nod of her head. "Good mornin' to ye both."

"And you, too," Kiera said. Penelope looked as if she was about to faint dead away.

"She saw us," Penelope hissed as the laundress disappeared around the corner.

"She sees us every day."

"But not . . . you know, plotting and scheming and lying here in the dark."

Kiera wanted to slap Penelope silly. The girl was such a twit! But a good-hearted one. "Come on." Kiera tugged her younger sister from the shadows. "Think nothing of it. Now, if you find Elyn, for God's sake send her to her bedchamber!"

"Won't the Lord of Penbrooke know that

111

she's different? I mean, a different person? Not you?"

For an odd reason Kiera didn't want to acknowledge, her heart twisted, adding to the ache already pounding dully through her brain. "It was dark last night. He was in his cups. As I said, he . . . he fell asleep."

"But —"

"Just do your part, Penelope, please!" Kiera snapped. "Try to find Elyn, for surely, if she's returned from meeting Brock, she's hiding somewhere so that no one will see her, as she's supposed to be in the bedchamber with her new husband!"

"I shall, but what if something goes wrong?"

"Such as?"

"Such as we don't find her."

Kiera's heart dropped, for Penelope was voicing her own worst fears. "Then I'll go out and look for her. Meet me at the stable and let me know . . . either shake your head if you haven't found her or nod if you have." She grabbed her sister's slim shoulder. "And whatever else you do, don't let anyone into Elyn's bedchamber. Make sure that Father, the serving girls, and the nosy steward realize that the newly wedded couple want their privacy."

"If that's possible."

"It has to be! Now go. We have to find her before her husband wakes." Again Kiera's silly heart wrenched, but she paid it no mind. She could not, would not, so much as think she might care for the man with whom she'd spent the night. Oh, Lord, this was such an impossible mess.

She passed by the solar and paused, thinking she should take the time to explain her absence at Elyn's wedding. But Kemper, the steward, was just closing the door to the chamber.

"The lord doesn't wish to be disturbed this morning," Kemper insisted when she asked for access. A tall, narrow-shouldered man with clever eyes and tight, disapproving lips, he was forever looking down his hooked nose.

"I would like a word with him."

"Can it wait?" If possible, his mouth pulled into a tighter line. Better not to raise his suspicions.

"Aye. I'll be back later after . . . after I go for a ride, but please, if you speak to him, tell him I would like to see him as soon as I can."

"I'll pass it along." He offered what was a thin pretense of a smile.

"Thank you," she said, and found she felt grateful after all that she didn't have to face her father. Even though his eyesight was dim, Llwyd could sense things and would probably feel her discomfort. From the time she'd been a child, her father was able to ferret out the truth and seemed uncannily able to smell a lie even before it was spoken. And right now she had little time to waste. Who knew when Kelan would awaken?

And then what? What will you do when you have to face him in the morning light?

"Oh, fie and fiddle." She wouldn't think of it now. Surely she would find Elyn, wherever she was. And when she did, she'd shake the living devil from her.

Chapter Seven

"But I don't understand." Elyn studied the lines of Brock's face. He seemed older somehow and embittered, the creases around his mouth severe. His lips were thin, and his gaze was lost somewhere as he stared up at the ceiling of the inn where they'd spent the night.

"I cannot run off just yet," he said, his voice, as ever, smooth as velvet.

Disappointed, she cuddled up to him in the tiny bed, feeling his warmth upon the cold sheets, listening to the pounding of his heart. He was tense, every muscle taut. He didn't so much as notice as she pushed her fingers through the curls of blond hair covering his chest and rested her head upon his shoulder.

"But I did. I ran off."

His smile was wicked. "You didn't run to me," he reminded her. "You ran away from *him*."

"Did I not come to you?" she demanded. Why was he being so distant?

"That you did." He placed a kiss upon her crown and she remembered why she loved him so. His kiss robbed her of her breath; his touch was pure sorcery. "We must be patient," he said and squeezed her shoulder.

"For what? I left my family. My keep. My sister who is now married to the Lord of Penbrooke. And I gave up everything, lied to everyone in my family, all for you." Levering onto an elbow she glared down at the man she loved with all her heart. Petulantly, she reminded him, "I did everything we planned. I held up my part of the bargain and avoided the marriage my father arranged. All I expect in return is for you to take me away. As you promised."

"What of Kiera?"

Elyn swallowed hard and her glance slid away. Guilt, ever at her side, raked rough talons down her heart. But then Kiera had lied, too, hadn't she? After offering to do anything in return for Elyn's having saved her life, she'd balked when asked to stand in for her. "What of Kiera?" Elyn whispered now, refusing to feel guilty. Kiera got what she deserved.

Brock laughed suddenly and pinned her onto the mattress with his weight. "How am I to trust you, Elyn, if you would gladly give up your sister's freedom for a turn at your own?"

"I love you," she said simply.

"Do you?"

"Aye. And you?"

"What do you think?" He growled as he caught her lower lip between his teeth. One hand covered her breast, his fingers toying with her nipple.

"I — I think you are trying not to answer me."

"You can trust me, Elyn . . ." He leaned down and licked her nipple, though he looked up at her as his tongue teased the very tip. "Everything will be as I planned."

"As we planned," she corrected, but she was already writhing under him, wanting more of him, needing to hear the words of love, to feel his weight upon her.

His teeth scraped a bit. Delicious pain seared through her.

"Aye," he said, his breath warm against her wet, sore skin. His fingers lowered to her buttocks and he pressed her firmly against him. "Just as *we* planned."

It was still early when Kiera swept down the stairs and along a narrow corridor that led past the kitchens. The scents of sizzling meat, baking bread, and cinnamon followed after her, and she realized, despite her aching head, she was hungry. Her stomach rumbled, but she had no time to waste.

Outside a fine mist had shrouded the keep and clouds hung low, letting in few rays from the winter sun that climbed ever higher in the sky, telling her that she had but a few hours before the midday meal would arrive at Elyn's door. Kiera flipped the hood of her cloak over her hair and hurried around tall stacks of firewood. Two huntsmen were hauling a stag and several rabbits strung upon poles toward the tanner's hut. Through an open doorway Kiera caught a glimpse of the strong-armed alewives stirring huge, bitter-smelling vats of beer.

Hammers banged as the carpenters repaired the roof of the candlemaker's hut, and the sweeps of the windmill swished through air so cold Kiera's breath fogged. Hastily she skirted puddles that had formed in the cart ruts while ducks and geese squawked and flapped noisily out of her way.

Avoiding conversation, she walked through the fog-shrouded bailey as if she were going for a morning's breath of fresh air, but her gaze was forever moving, hoping for a glimpse of her sister.

So that Elyn can take her rightful place at Kelan's side, even though you yourself have allowed him to bed you. Biting her lip, she told herself that it was of no matter, that she had no claim on Kelan, that, in fact, she didn't want him.

Or did she?

The thought of his lovemaking . . .

Oh, stop it! You're as bad as Elyn, a hopeless, sorry romantic. What's wrong with you? You don't even know the man. What should worry

118

you more is that because of your rashness and lust you are no longer a virgin, no longer suited to marry anyone.

Quickly she took a path past the potter's hut, her gaze anxiously scouring its dark interior. She saw nothing but the potter at his wheel, his black cat curled at his feet. She stopped at the apothecary's hut and the baker's niche, managed to make small talk, then hurried through the garden and into the storage rooms, even climbed into the towers to open the hermit's cells and peer inside. But there was no sign of her sister.

Curse and rot Elyn! God's teeth, where was she?

With Brock, you ninny! She's not coming back. Why would she?

Kiera was halfway down the stairs of the west tower and stopped dead in her tracks. The ugly thought took root. Was it possible? Nay, nay, nay! She couldn't believe that Elyn would deceive her so.

But didn't she trick Father and Kelan and everyone else in the keep? Why do you think she wouldn't do the same to you?

'Twas impossible. They had a pact . . . a bargain . . . a . . . promise. She would find Elyn. If it killed her.

More determined than ever, Kiera checked the dungeons and the armory and any other spot she thought her sister might hide. To no avail. Elyn was still missing. And Kiera was swiftly running out of time. The Lord of Penbrooke wouldn't sleep all day.

Her only hope was that Penelope was luckier than she and that by some twist of fortune their youngest sister had found Elyn.

She left the tower and ducked around a hayrick, avoiding the kennel master, who was walking four dogs, all of whom wagged their tails and strained their leashes at the boy who was carting ashes from the keep in a large wheelbarrow. Kiera veered away from the center of the bailey, taking a crooked path that wound through the orchard to the stable.

She stole quietly inside, where she was greeted with the musty scents of dry hay, dung, and dust. Pale morning light oozed through the slats in the windows, and she spied Orson, the near crippled stable master, seated upon his favorite stool. He didn't look up from his work as his gnarled fingers feverishly polished the bit of a bridle.

"Orson?"

"Oh! M'lady. I didn't hear ye come in." He got to his feet as Kiera entered the dark interior. A lantern sat on a ledge above a water trough, its flame low. The inside of the stable remained shadowy and warm, with horses shifting and snorting from their stalls. The stable was one of Kiera's favorite places within the walls of Lawenydd.

"Easy, now," Orson said to the animals.

"We've a lady among us." He chuckled. "Goin' ridin' today, m'lady?" he asked. He should have been relieved of his duties years before, but he was a favorite of her father. Since his son, Joseph, had inherited Orson's way with the horses, the old man had retained his position. Even after Obsidian had turned up missing, Kiera thought with a familiar pang of guilt.

"Aye, Orson." She managed a smile and hoped she didn't seem nervous. "I thought a ride might be good this morning. On Garnet."

"Ye're feelin' up to it, are ye? It's cold this morn and I heard ye were so ill yesterday that ye missed yer own sister's weddin'."

"I was feeling poorly, but I'm much better today," Kiera said and ignored the questions in the stable master's gaze. Beneath the wrinkled folds of skin, his brown eyes gleamed as if he were privy to some private joke, and she imagined that everyone in the castle knew of her deception.

Orson yelled over his shoulder, "Joseph . . . the lady needs her jennet."

"Right," a deep voice called and then Orson's son appeared from around the corner. As tall and strapping as Orson was shriveled and stooped, Joseph inclined his head and offered a smile of white teeth. His yellow hair was as coarse and straight as the straw he fed the animals, and his features were spread wide upon a friendly face. Kiera had grown up with him, and as children, she and Elyn and Joseph had been friends. Until their mother had changed all that. He, after all, was a stableboy. Lady Twyla hadn't wanted her daughters to consider him anything but a servant. "I'll bring Garnet round," he said with a quick nod.

"Thank you." She smiled at him, but he'd already disappeared through a doorway.

Orson hung the bridle on a peg and squinted hard. "Ye're not plannin' on ridin' alone, are ye?"

"I won't be gone long."

His frown became a scowl. "I could send Joseph or one of the other stableboys with ye. Or one of the guards. The forest, it isn't safe. There's robbers and henchmen and outlaws in the woods, but then you should know that better than anyone."

"I'll be fine," she insisted. "Worry not."

"Does yer father know about this?" he asked, then quickly cleared his throat, as if he realized it wasn't his place to question her. "Well, ye be careful," he added, "and that's all I have to say to ye, except ye have a nice ride."

"I will, Orson, thank you." She turned quickly and hurried outside to find that Joseph was already waiting for her, holding tight to the reins of Garnet as her favorite tall red-coated mare fidgeted and stomped, then tossed her head.

"She's ready to run," Joseph observed with a grin.

"She's always ready to run."

"Like her mistress."

Kiera grinned despite her fears. "Aye, Joseph, like her mistress." If only he knew that she would like nothing better than to run as far as this game mare would take her. She cast a glance over her shoulder to the third floor of the great hall and the window of Elyn's room, where she imagined, for a fleeting second, she spied the Lord of Penbrooke glaring down at her. But she blinked and he was gone, as if he were a ghost, or more likely nothing more than the play of pale sunlight through the fog. Kelan was asleep and would probably not waken for hours. At least she hoped so.

"Have a good ride."

"I will." Kiera swung onto the mare's back, and the pain between her legs caused her to wince as she took up the reins. She had to work fast and find Elyn . . . wherever the bloody hell her sister was hiding.

Mayhap she's hurt. Even dead. Thrown from her horse. Kiera's heart turned to ice. Her fingers twined in the reins. Nay. The worst that could have happened was that Elyn had changed her mind and wasn't returning. Kiera had kept that wayward thought at the back of her mind, but it was there just the same even though she prayed her sister wouldn't have betrayed her.

But why would she not?

Had she not risked life and limb and banishment to be with her beloved? Perhaps she'd left Kiera to deal with Penbrooke forever. Kiera urged her mare toward the main gates. She had to find Elyn.

Or else she would be forced to play the part of Kelan's bride again tonight.

And would that be so bad? The damage is already done. Why not spend another night learning the ways of lovemaking?

And what then? Would she not be further enmeshed in her own web of lies? She guided Garnet through the bailey and under the portcullis. One way or another, she had to locate her sister and insist she return to take her place as Kelan of Penbrooke's bride.

His head felt as if it weighed as much as a destrier.

With a groan, Kelan shifted on the bed. The room was dark and cold, the fire having smoldered to ash during the night, the window shuttered. And the bed was empty. His wife had already risen.

His wife.

What a strange thought. But no longer disgusting. The woman had surprised him. Time and time again. In the short span of their marriage he'd felt rage, humility, and then, unexpectedly awe.

Despite the hammering in his brain, he grinned at the memory of their lovemaking. While he had questioned her purity due to her unusual behavior throughout the day and later in their bridal chamber, at heart he'd expected his new wife to be a virgin, and he'd pleasurably discovered she was one. She was also a headstrong woman, one who had willingly embarrassed him. But he'd never thought he would find himself in bed with a sensual creature who, though frightened at first, had become as eager in the pleasures of the flesh as he. Perhaps this marriage would not be the torture he'd anticipated. He was too sane to believe in wedded bliss and happily ever after, but he did allow himself the notion that this union might not be as unpleasant as he'd convinced himself it would be.

Never forget how she embarrassed you. Do not let that hardheaded woman ever again get the upper hand.

He reached for his breeches, his fingers scraping through the rushes and brushing up against something solid and cold in the fragrant straw. "What the devil?" He picked up the small container, a vial, and opened it. The metallic scent of blood filtered to his nostrils and he dipped a finger into the cold purple liquid. Aye, it was blood . . . but why here in this chamber? It belonged to his wife or someone who had been in the room, perhaps a servant. Someone who believed in the dark arts? Mystified, he scoured the floor and found another small container, this one empty and carrying no scent. Odd . . . very odd.

He rubbed the back of his neck and wondered at the kind of woman he'd married.

Blood? Why blood?

And what had been in the other vial?

He'd heard of women who had used the blood of a chicken, or goat or some other animal, to sprinkle upon the bedsheets of a man they were duping, when they were trying to prove a virginity that had no longer existed. But his wife, she had not used the blood — the vial was still full and the sheets were stained. And she had been tight, so tight. As blurry as his memory was, he clearly remembered that she was pure. No doubt a virgin.

Then why the vials?

Straightening, he studied the bed, trying to remember the night before. 'Twas all so fuzzy and dark. He opened the shutters to let in the gray morning light. From his vantage point he looked over the bailey. Children were playing with an old hoop, women were gathering eggs and hanging laundry in the shadow of an overhang, a smith was pounding horseshoes at his forge, and a woman was climbing upon a reddish mare.

For a second he wondered if the woman was his wife. She wore a brown cloak with a cowl covering her head. She glanced in his direction, then looked quickly away.

A stone settled in his stomach.

Surely the woman was not Elyn. For there was no reason for his bride to leave.

Astride the horse, she leaned forward. The animal took off, breaking into a gallop and streaking through the gates to the outer bailey and out of Kelan's range of vision. 'Twas not Elyn. She would not defy him so. Not after last night. And yet, she was not a predictable woman. He'd learned that much in less than a day. He fingered the vials in his pocket and thought about the mysterious female upon the red mare. Why would she leave? Where would she go?

Those thoughts taunted him as he found a scrub basin and splashed cold water over his face, wincing at the ache slicing through his brain.

The woman he saw was not Elyn. His wife was here. In this castle. And either she'd return to their bedchamber soon or he'd go searching for her.

Just as soon as the throbbing in his head subsided. He found his empty mazer, filled it from the basin, and poured the water down his throat. He'd give her a little time . . . but just a little, he thought as he stumbled to the fire.

He managed to toss a few pieces of oak onto the embers still glowing in the grate, but that one task was all he could manage. He, who awoke each morn ready for the day, eager for his day's work. He was now lethargic and dull . . . too much wine . . .

As he straightened, he heard the vials clink and he wondered, just fleetingly, if some sleeping potion had been added to his wine. But why . . . nay, he was just tired, that was all.

He needed sleep.

Before another thought could cut through his brain, he stumbled back to the bed. This was not like him . . . but he was too tired to try and piece it all together. When his bride returned . . . then he'd question her. Then he'd demand answers . . . he'd insist upon knowing the truth . . . but now, drowsiness was overtaking him and he gave into it, letting the darkness come, no longer fighting, and falling asleep with the worrisome thought that his new beautiful wife wasn't all she appeared to be.

Chapter Eight

Elyn was nowhere to be found. *Nowhere.* Above the clouds, the weak winter sun had risen high overhead, and Kiera knew she had to return to the keep.

She had hastily searched every hiding spot she and Elyn had discovered while growing up. Kiera had ridden for hours. First to the cave in the cliffs above the sea, then the ledge behind a waterfall. She'd galloped across the meadow where they'd caught butterflies, and ended up at the gnarled oak tree they'd climbed to watch the ships sailing into the harbor.

When all else failed, she searched the old, abandoned mill where they'd swum naked in the millpond by day, and at night, away from the eyes of their father or Kemper or the castle priest, they'd huddled around a fire and learned of the old ways from Hildy. It was here where Kiera had seen her first spell cast, here where she'd learned to draw runes in the sand, here where she'd listened as Hildy had explained about the magic of the forest and the power of earth, fire, and water.

However, now there was no trace of her sister.

It was as if Elyn had disappeared into the thick mists that rose through the dripping ferns and skeletal trees.

Or somewhere with Brock.

"Where the devil are you?" Kiera asked in frustration as she combed the woods. She couldn't spend all day searching for her, not if she had to keep up the lie that she was her sister. As the hours had passed, Kiera had become more certain that she was trapped, at least for another day, in her ruse.

After scouring every copse of trees and stretch of fields she could think of, she gave up her fruitless search and reined Garnet toward the keep. She could waste no more time.

Even now, Kelan could be stirring. Worse yet, he might already be awake and wandering about the castle searching for her. What if he caught her returning from her ride and what if someone in the castle was there — the stable master, or the carter, or even the gong farmer? If he acted as if they were wed and she was his bride, the peasants would point out that she wasn't Elyn . . . oh, no, she couldn't let that happen.

"Hurry," she whispered, riding through a final thicket of oak, thinking of the day ahead and the pitfalls she would have to avoid. She leaned forward in the saddle as the scent of the sea filled her nostrils and a few rays of sunlight pierced the clouds. How long could she keep up this deception? How would she keep her "husband" in Elyn's chamber? She couldn't very well lock him in. She thought of the sleepless night she'd spent and how she'd behaved, how easily he'd sparked the womanly fires deep within her, how even now she would like to feel those breath-stopping sensations just once more.

"Don't think of it," she growled to herself as she dug her knees into the mare. Strong muscles responded. Red legs flashed as Garnet sped across the damp fields of yellowed grass, racing over the uneven ground in long, quick strides. Kiera felt the rush of the wind, her fingers twining in the reins, her face slapped by the mare's coarse mane. Through the rising mists, she saw the castle emerge, its towers spiring high enough to disappear into the low-hanging clouds.

There was a chance that Penelope had found Elyn hiding within the castle walls. Mayhap even now she was with her husband . . . Kiera's stomach twisted at the thought. Could her sister take her place in Kelan's bed? Was it possible for Elyn to have spent one last night of lovemaking with Brock, then slip into her discarded identity once again and take Kelan, her husband, as her lover? The thought was like a drip of ice in Kiera's heart, though she didn't want to think about why it mattered to her.

Tugging on the reins, she guided Garnet onto the rutted, muddy road leading to the main gates. Dirt flew from the horse's hooves, and the wind, tugging off her hood, whistled past Kiera's head. Her heart was pounding, but not so much from her wild ride as from the thought of facing Kelan. If Elyn had returned, Kiera would have to avoid Kelan entirely. But if her wayward sister was not within the keep, Kiera would need to take her place in his bed. If for no other reason than to keep him in their room.

Her pulse jumped at the thought, for she would like nothing better than another night learning the secrets and pleasures of love-making and yet . . . it would be best for all if she never was with Kelan again, if she never felt his touch upon her skin. The sooner she ignored her silly fantasies, the better for everyone.

She raced around a miller's wagon filled with flour sacks. Oxen were straining at their yoke, and the miller was growling orders at his team. Slowing as she reached the draw-bridge, she guided the mare past a woman shepherding four children through the main gate and had to slow nearly to a stop when a peddler's mule balked and brayed in protest at pulling his overladen cart past the guard. Silver trinkets in the cart jangled noisily and the florid-faced peddler snapped his whip angrily over the obstinate beast's ears.

"Move, ye bloody slug!" the peddler shouted as Kiera guided her mare through the narrow opening between the cart and the sidewall of the gate. The horse perked up her ears and loped easily to the stable, where Orson, seated upon a worn stump, was watching with a critical eye as a stableboy held fast to a tether restraining a young, headstrong colt.

"Don't fight him," Orson barked as the black colt bucked and tossed his head as he ran in tight circles. "Hey, there, lad, let him know ye're the master, but with a gentle touch. Ah . . . that's it." The colt straightened his gait, galloping easily around the red-haired boy.

Kiera reined Garnet to a stop, which ruined all the lad's hard work. His colt shied, nearly stripping the leather straps from the boy's hands and jerking him off his feet. Scrambling in the dirt, he managed to hold on to the sweating, wild-eyed black, but the lesson was over for the day.

"Don't lose him, now," Orson warned, shaking his head. He lifted his cap, scratched his pate, then settled the woolen hat squarely upon his head again. "Bloody beast."

Kiera slid to the ground and Orson glanced in her direction. His old eyes crinkled at the corners as he took the reins from her outstretched hand.

"A good ride?" he asked.

"Perfect." Kiera patted the mare's sweating shoulder and tried to appear calm while from the corner of her eyes, she was searching the grounds. Had Elyn returned? Or not? She glanced to the window of Elyn's room, but there was no figure of a man in the recess. "Garnet runs like the wind."

Orson took the reins from her just as she saw Penelope hurrying along a path leading to the stable. Upon spying Kiera, she shook her head so violently it seemed as if she were trying to dislodge water from her ear.

So Elyn hadn't come back. Kiera's heart sank. Something was wrong. Terribly wrong. Elyn would have returned unless some horrid fate had befallen her. She'd promised to return. She couldn't have decided to desert Kiera. Not truly.

Some ghastly misfortune must have happened.

Or this time she's deceived you.

"I — I found her not," Penelope whispered, her cheeks ruddy from the cold. The fog was lifting, thin clouds blocking the sun.

Kiera glanced over her shoulder and saw the stable master following her with his eyes. "Shh." She grabbed her younger sister by the elbow and propelled her around an empty wagon. "Say nothing. Where's Hildy?"

"I know not."

"Find her and send her to my room. Oh,

and bring one of Elyn's dresses from the laundress."

"Which one?"

"It matters not!"

"But to which room: yours or Elyn's?"

"*Mine*. Now, hurry along." Releasing Penelope's arm, Kiera cut past the well and hurried into the kitchen, where the cook, a fat woman with fleshy arms that jiggled as she worked, was glaring at two boys. One thick finger was pointed at the older boy's nose. "And if I ever catch you stealing apples again, I'll wring your neck like that." She snapped her fingers and the boys jumped, the younger one nearly stumbling back into the fire, where a boar was roasting upon a spit tended by yet another lad. A young girl with frizzy hair was sneaking a peek at the boys and madly chopping onions at a scarred table in the corner. Two other girls, struggling to hide their grins, worked at a table near the door.

The smell of roasting meat and spices caused Kiera's stomach to growl from hunger.

"You've seen me do it now, haven't ye?" the cook demanded of the boys. "When I want a particularly fat hen for the lord's supper?"

The younger boy gulped and nodded, his face bright red, while the older lad flattened his lips and glared through strands of unruly brown hair at the cook. "You don't wring their necks. You cut off their 'eads with an ax," he argued while grease spattered, sizzling as it landed on the hot coals.

"Well, maybe that's what I ought to do to ye, John Miller. I'll tell your father, I will, and he'll make you wish I'd put a quick end to ye with my ax. Now, git outta here! Go before I change me mind. I be sick at the sight of ye." The boys took off through the back door.

"Bloody thugs." She turned quickly for a heavy woman. "Oh, m'lady. I didn't see ye."

Kiera managed a smile she didn't feel as one of the serving girls pounded sugar at a nearby table. Just in case Penelope had forgotten Kiera's earlier orders, Kiera decided to address the cook herself. "I spoke with my sister, Lady Elyn, this morning, and she would like me to bring a tray of food to her and her husband."

"You? Oh, no, m'lady." The cook was aghast. Fat fingers splayed over her huge breasts. "Lady Penelope already asked that trays be brought up and left at the door to the bedchamber. I'll send up a tray with one of the girls right away if that's what Lady Elyn wants. But won't the lord and lady be dinin' with your father?"

Kiera glanced at the floor, blushed, then met the cook's curious gaze. "Elyn, she says they, um, want their privacy."

"Oh, they do, do they?" The heavy woman chuckled as she walked to a wide table near the door where one girl was mashing spices with mortar and pestle and another was rolling dough. "Well, I remember when I was first married. Couldn't get enough of me husband, I couldn't. That all changed, let me tell you, after the fourth child. I wanted no more of 'im, I did. And now, he's gone." She sighed, then turned her attention to the girl rolling the dough. "Hey, mind what ye're doin'," she growled. "Use a light touch, will ye? Here, let me show you how to do it proper like." She edged the bony, disgruntled girl to the side. "Tend to the fire, would ye, Mary?" she ordered without looking up.

"Well, my sister's been married less than a day," Kiera persisted.

"Aye, and she'll be plenty tired unless I miss my guess. Did you see her new husband? A handsome devil he is and strapping." The cook's bushy eyebrows twitched as she kneaded the dough while the scrawny girl she'd replaced sulked as she threw chunks of wood into the fire. " 'Tis no wonder the lady doesn't want to come downstairs for a while. Neither would I if I could spend some time in the Baron of Penbrooke's bed."

The girl at the fire snorted, the one grinding spices swallowed a smile at the unlikely image, and Kiera felt her face flame more brightly than the coals beneath the spit.

The cook continued to chatter as she worked the dough. "I'm just glad she gave the man a chance after failing to attend the celebration of their union last night, the wedding feast I prepared."

Kiera blushed as the cook looked her over. She realized that she had injured more than her new husband's pride by not showing up last night.

"I'll send Gladdys up in a while," the large woman promised. "Is there anything else I can do for ye?"

"Just see that Lady Elyn and her new husband are not disturbed. Gladdys can knock, then leave the tray at the door," Kiera emphasized.

"I'll see to it."

"Thank you."

As Kiera hurried toward the back stairs, she caught a glimpse of the cook mopping her brow with the back of her hand.

"Where in the name of the Holy Mother is Zelda?" Cook growled, sweat gleaming on her skin. "I swear keeping my eye on all of you girls will send me to an early grave."

Kiera stole up the stairs on silent footsteps. There was a chance Elyn was waiting for her, in her room. Though she had to admit, she had little faith she would find her sister patiently awaiting her return. At the third floor, she was about to slip into her own chamber when the door to Elyn's room creaked open.

There, with one shoulder braced upon the doorframe, was Kelan.

Kiera nearly jumped out of her skin.

Without a shirt, his black hair rumpled, his breeches unlaced, he stared at her. "You were out riding?" he asked, bewildered. Rubbing the back of his neck, his arm bent over his head and stretching the hard muscles of his flat abdomen, he blinked as if trying to focus.

Kiera swallowed hard. In her mind's eye, she saw him as he had been the night before, naked and stretched upon her, his skin burnished from the light of a dying fire.

"Oh . . . er, yes," she said. "I didn't want to wake you." She hurried toward him and, afraid someone would see them and recognize her, stood on tiptoe to plant a quick kiss on his lips. His gray eyes cleared a bit.

Smiling despite her anxiety, she laced her fingers through his and drew him back into the dark chamber. As if it was second nature, she replaced the latch. "I . . . always ride in the morning." Playfully, she pulled him to the bed.

"You should have awakened me," he said, yawning. "I would have joined you."

"You were tired."

"That I was," he admitted, his dark eyebrows knitting thoughtfully. "Were you not?"

"A little. And I hated to rouse you. You snore, you know." She threw a flirty smile at him and was astounded at her own sassy tongue. She was teasing him, and she knew by the gleam in his silvery eyes that she'd goaded him into thoughts far from her early morning ride.

"Do I?"

"Oh, yes! 'Tis an awful sound . . . like an old boar grunting hungrily in the trough."

One side of Kelan's mouth lifted. "And you know of old boars, do you?"

"Mmm. I have always been interested in the animals of the keep."

"And what else?" he asked as he wound his arms around her and stared deep into her eyes. Her blood turned hot and she worried again if Elyn was nearby, even hiding in the next chamber, waiting to take her rightful place.

"Many things. Mayhap I should change from these riding clothes?"

He toyed with the laces at her throat. "I'll help."

Oh, the seduction in his eyes. *Keep a clear head, Kiera. Think! Do not be distracted. You slept with him once, do not make that mistake again. Just keep him here without tumbling into bed with him!* "Nay, I, um, didn't want to disturb you, so I changed in Kiera's room next door. If you will but wait for me, I will return —"

"Oh, no, you don't," he said, his arms tightening over her waist. "You lured me back here, wife, and now you must pay the price." Holding her close with one arm, he lifted his hand to the opening of her tunic and ever so slowly unlaced the slit at her neck. Her throat turned to dust as she watched his fingers graze her skin, and deep inside, in that dark, moist, oh-so-feminine part of her, she began to ache with a now-familiar want.

God help me.

Her breasts were half exposed and he bent his head to run his tongue along her already warm flesh.

She quivered.

"So you do want me, you little wench."

"Nay . . ."

"Oh, I think so," he said, breathing hard. Kissing her, he reached lower, bunching her skirts as his fingers slipped upward, along her thigh, light touches teasing and tormenting. She began to wriggle and writhe, for the memories of the night before crashed through her brain, and Lord help her, she did want him, nay, yearned for the feel of him, all over again.

He backed her against the wall and she, gasping, felt the gentle prod of one finger and the bittersweet pain that lingered from the night before. She sagged a little, opening to him as he penetrated her with one, no . . . two . . . stretching . . . She was breathing in gasps, her blood pounding in her ears as he manipulated her, touching, stroking. She moaned, her fingers in his hair, and suddenly he released her, pushed down his breeches, and, lifting her, placed her firmly upon his rock-hard shaft.

"Oh!" Her eyes flew open as he began to move. "Oohh . . ." Her fingers dug into his bare shoulders, and her legs wrapped around him. The soreness eased with each of his strokes. Slowly at first, then more quickly, he moved within her. She gasped. Couldn't think. Could not catch a breath. His face buried in her breasts, his arms providing support, he took her, laid claim to what he thought was rightfully his, making love to his wife.

And Kiera couldn't, wouldn't, stop him.

The room tilted and swayed. Heat burned through her and she thought of nothing but that one vital, aching spot where they joined. She was gasping, holding on to him for dear life, riding a rising tide of desire — "Elyn," he whispered, and she froze. "Oh, Elyn . . . wife . . ." He stiffened, throwing back his head and letting out a raspy cry as the sweat upon her skin dried in the cold chamber. What was she doing? What was she thinking? In essence she was committing adultery with her sister's husband, sinning wildly, passionately, eagerly, and refusing to think of the future. For now, for a few blissful minutes, she was caught in the moment, the glorious, seductive moment.

Kelan, holding fast to her, tumbled onto the bed, where they tangled in the bedclothes. He kissed her again, his mouth claiming hers, and she tried not to respond, but they were still joined. Still one. As his tongue teased and played with hers, she felt his member swell within her again, realized that her fingers were tracing the sinewy muscles of his shoulders and back, touching old scars and smooth flesh. Despite the denials raging through her head, she gave in to the pure animal pleasure of him and closed her mind to all the nagging doubts that continued to plague her.

Perspiration oiled their bodies as he rolled her onto her back. Levered upon his elbows, he locked his gaze with hers. He penetrated more deeply, thrusting hard, creating a swirl of pleasure that consumed her and chased away any concerns that making love with him was wrong. For the moment, perhaps this last moment, they were one.

He withdrew slowly and she cried out.

With a smile he slid in again, deeper still.

Her fingers dug into his shoulders. "Kelan . . ."

"Aye, little one, I want it too," he said and moved a bit.

She wriggled.

He came to her. Harder this time.

"Yes!"

Again.

Hotter. Wilder.

"Oh . . . love . . ." she cried out as a spasm jolted through her body and for an instant brilliant light flashed behind her eyes.

Every muscle in his body flexed, strident one second, relaxed the next as he settled upon her, his weight pinning her to the jumble of bedclothes.

Her breath was ragged, her heart hammering, the soft, sweet glow of being with him ever so slowly evaporating as she realized that she was here, alone, half naked with her sister's husband.

What have I done? Why can't I stop this? Oh . . . God help me, Kiera silently prayed as she held him against her and wished this moment would never end.

Chapter Nine

What had happened to her in the span of a day? Kiera glanced at the sun shining brightly outside, dispelling all remnants of the early morning mist she had ridden through earlier.

As she lay on the bed next to Kelan, feeling his hot breath, Kiera told herself that she didn't love him. Nay, even that thought was preposterous. And yet she'd cried out . . . oh, she couldn't think of it. He was a stranger. A handsome, well-muscled man who knew of the art of lovemaking. But he was her sister's husband and they were lying in her sister's bed. All was lost, for after this second bout of lovemaking Kiera knew deep down that her sister's ruse was bound to fail. There was no way that Kelan would mistake Elyn for Kiera once her sister returned . . . or was there?

With one hand she reached for her clothes.

There was a tap on the door.

"Who is it?" Kelan yelled.

"Gladdys, m'lord," came the muffled reply. "I brought ye something to eat as Lady Kiera asked."

"Leave it," Kiera said quickly, for she couldn't take a chance that Gladdys, who had been working in the kitchen earlier, would hazard a peek inside and see either her or the gold tunic pooled upon the floor. She silently prayed that Gladdys had not recognized her voice.

"Aye, m'lady," the maid said and Kiera felt a spot of relief as she heard the girl's footsteps recede. Quickly, she rolled away from Kelan and scooped up her tunic. Throwing it over her head, she climbed to her feet.

"Stay," she said when Kelan seemed about to get up. "I'll get it." She turned her back to him and hastily made the sign of the cross over her bosom.

Her bare feet swept over the rushes to the door, where she hesitated but an instant, then silently threw the latch. Offering up a prayer, she poked her head into the hallway and gratefully saw no one lurking in the corridor.

Thank the fates!

Swiftly, Kiera snatched the tray from the floor, shut the door behind her, and slipped the latch into place. Once more she'd been lucky, but how long would it be before her luck ran out?

Forcing herself to appear calm, she carried the tray to the bed, where Kelan, eyeing her as if she were the most interesting woman on earth, lay waiting. He hadn't bothered with his clothes and Kiera tried her damnedest not to stare at his long legs or the mat of swirling dark hair stretched over his chest, or his manhood, now slackened a bit, resting at the juncture of his legs. Nay, she would not even glance his way as she set the tray upon the bed next to him.

Instead, she turned her attention to the platter and the delicious odors emanating from it. The smells of salt pork and fish pies assailed her nostrils, and her stomach growled hungrily as she eyed the fruit tarts, slabs of cheese, vessel of thick honey, and slices of warm bread. How long had it been since she'd eaten? Could she risk but a few bites, then go look for Elyn again?

"Would you not like wine or mead?" she asked, spying the empty jug on the small table near the bed. "I can ask it to be brought up." She started to leave, but his hand reached out and encircled her wrist.

" 'Tis not important."

"But —"

"Can it not wait a few minutes?" he asked, and she dropped onto the edge of the bed. She couldn't risk making him suspicious, and her mouth was fairly watering with hunger.

"Of course."

Letting go of her arm, he sliced the bread and topped it with a chunk of cheese, then offered it to her. She reached for it, but he shook his head. "Uh-uh-uh. Bite." Holding the food to her lips, he waited as she accepted the morsel and savored the burst of flavor. As she was swallowing the cheese and bread, he tore off some of the pie and held that to her lips.

"I can feed myself."

"Can you?" He smiled and brushed her mouth with the morsel.

"Aye." But she took the tiny piece he offered and felt his finger slide between her teeth. Her tongue surrounded it before he pulled it away.

"Is this not more fun?" he mocked, sucking his own finger clean before turning his attention and knife to the pork.

"Different," she said and watched as one of his dark eyebrows raised. "But it would be more complete with the wine. Give me but a minute . . ." Before he could snag her wrist again, she was off the bed and across the room. She opened the door slowly and found no one in the hallway, so she quickly edged to her own room, where the door had been left ajar. Noiselessly she slipped inside and slid the latch into place.

"What took you so long?" Penelope whined. Kiera jumped with surprise to find her sister there but then quickly placed her finger to her lips as she hitched her head in the direction of Elyn's room. The two chambers were separated by only one wall.

"Keep your voice down," she whispered,

spying Elyn's blue silk gown hanging upon a screen. Oh, where the devil was her sister?

The last time Elyn had worn the pale dress was during the Revels a few months before. Kiera remembered that night.

Elyn had been happy then, carefree, her eyes bright with a secret as she'd danced with one knight after another. "Tonight I meet Brock," she'd whispered to Kiera as they'd met in the hallway when the music had stopped.

"Brock? But I thought Father forbade it. Are you not to marry the Lord of Penbrooke?"

Elyn's smile had faded as she dabbed at her brow with a small cloth. She was sweating, as she'd danced without a break for nearly an hour. "Mayhap. But I'm not married yet, am I?"

"You cannot go against Father's wishes."

"Nay?" Elyn had arched an impetuous, naughty eyebrow. Her smile had been pure defiance.

"Oh, no! Don't do it. You'll get caught." Kiera was frantic with worry, and the deed had not yet been done.

" 'Tis a risk I'll willingly take."

"And if you're found out, Father will have you flogged and banished, or locked in the east tower." Kiera had pulled her sister away from the crowd and behind a thick velvet curtain. Inside the darkened alcove there was less chance of being overheard.

"He'll never know." Elyn had placed a hand upon Kiera's shoulder. "Someday, you, too, will fall in love and then you'll understand. Nothing is more important."

"Not your freedom? Not your life?"

"No," Elyn had said and laughed gaily as she'd thrown back the curtain and hurried up the stairs, her dress, this very silk gown Kiera held in her hands, shimmering beneath the rushlights.

Now, Kiera's shoulders slumped as she began to peel off her wrinkled tunic. Her sister had been foolhardy when it came to love, a woman blind to her beloved's faults and her own folly. Until last night, Kiera had never understood this rash side of Elyn. Even yesterday she would have thought her own rashness when it came to love impossible. Today, after sleeping with Kelan, she wasn't so certain.

There was a quick, light rap on the door. She froze.

Kelan?

Penelope shot to the door.

"No, wait!" she whispered to Penelope, then more loudly called, "Who is it?"

" 'Tis I, Hildy," the nursemaid responded, and Kiera nodded at Penelope, who unlatched the door to let the old woman inside. Hildy's eyes were dark with worry, her hands rubbing together nervously.

"Have you not found Elyn?" Kiera asked, though she knew the answer before the old woman could respond.

"Nay, she has not returned." Hildy shook her head and rubbed her arms as if suddenly chilled. "I've inquired in the town, listened to the gossip, hoping to hear something. Anything. But no one suspects there's something wrong."

"That's good," Kiera said.

"Mayhap, but I found out nothing. No one has seen Elyn, or if they have, they talk naught of it." Frowning, she walked to the window and stared through the slats of the shutters, as if by simply willing Elyn to appear, she could conjure up the missing daughter of Baron Llwyd. "I fear something dire has happened."

"Something dire?" Penelope asked, her eyes rounding.

"Trouble . . . ill will . . . I know not. I've cast the stones."

Penelope gasped. "And what? What did you see?"

"Trouble. Coming to Lawenydd."

"What kind of trouble?" Kiera asked, goose bumps rising on her flesh. Hildy was known to see into the future, to have glimpses of how each person would meet his fate.

" 'Tis still unclear." Hildy's old hands opened and closed, as if she was grasping for something she couldn't hold on to. " 'Twas foolishness for Elyn to run off," Hildy murmured.

"Aye," Kiera agreed. "But she did and now we have to make things right by finding her."

"If she can be found." Hildy's eyes were dark.

"Did the stones say otherwise?" Kiera asked.

"As I said, 'twas unclear."

"What will we do?" Penelope asked, her face without color.

"Find her." Kiera wriggled into Elyn's gown. Though it would not matter to Kelan, since he had never seen Elyn, the servants would be more likely to mistake Kiera for her sister if she was glimpsed in Elyn's clothing.

"What if she intends not to return?" Hildy asked.

Kiera's heart turned to ice. 'Twas what she most feared. "Then we'll have to search her out. I'll need your help," she said to Hildy as she adjusted the dress around her waist and shoulders.

"How?"

"More wine and more of the potion." She straightened a sleeve and tossed back her hair. "Stronger this time."

"Stronger?" Hildy repeated softly. "Are you sure?"

"Yes! I think I could tell if someone is asleep."

"Penbrooke was awake?" Penelope asked, her eyes rounding even further. She blinked hard, as if she was astounded. "Then how . . . how did you . . . you know, keep him away from . . . well . . ."

"From bedding me?" Kiera asked in a harsh whisper. " 'Twas not easy, but worry not of that, for now we must find Elyn and switch places. There is a likelihood that he will recognize the change, but we will face that problem if it arises. Hopefully the drugs will make his memory hazy, so it is important that he is given the elixir and wine. More wine."

Hildy wrapped her thin arms around her middle as if to ward off a chill. "Too much of the medicine could harm him."

Every muscle in Kiera's body tensed. No matter what, she would not want Kelan harmed. "Hurt him? How?"

"A sleep from which he doesn't awaken. Or even . . . even death."

"Dear Lord." Penelope flounced onto the bed. "You mean we could kill him?"

"He won't die," Kiera said as she thought of his muscled body. "He's healthier than the best stallion in the stable."

"But — if he goes into the deep sleep?" Hildy asked.

"Then it will give us more time to find Elyn." Kiera felt a niggle of guilt. What if she damaged Kelan? Nay, she could not do it.

She bit at her thumbnail, then dropped her hand to her side. She couldn't bear the thought of harming him. They would have to be careful. Very careful.

"Could we not just tell Father the truth?" Penelope asked.

"*Now?* Don't you think we should have done that sooner?" Kiera remembered her vow to her sister, her promise to do anything Elyn asked in repayment for saving her life. Then, she'd objected to Elyn's request. And now . . . oh, Lord, perhaps deep down she wanted to pretend to be her sister for just a little longer. "We're stuck with it now, aren't we? Until we locate our sister. Then mayhap we'll go to Father and my . . . Elyn's husband . . . and tell the truth." Bending her head forward, Kiera reached behind her, quickly plaited her hair, and tied the end with a ribbon that matched the fine strings that laced the neckline of her dress. "Just make sure no one spies me with the lord. And see that more wine is brought to the room."

"With the potion?" Penelope said.

"Of course!" Was the girl a half-wit? "And please, see that you mark the cup clearly this time. There can be no mistake." Kiera straightened and tossed the plait over her shoulder as she faced Hildy, the old nurse-maid and sorceress. "You can send the extra vial of potion by wrapping it in a cloth and hiding it in a basket of . . . bread or cheese or clothes to wash . . . or whatever." She crossed to the door. "But please, hurry!"

Penelope fidgeted with the neckline of her dress. "What will you do?"

Kiera paused, her hand resting upon the latch. "Get Elyn's husband drunk again and hope that he falls into a deep sleep that lasts for hours." She felt a jab of guilt for this deception, but ignored it. She couldn't let recriminations stop her, not now. "After he falls asleep, I will retrieve the old vials, escape the room, and try again to find our sister."

"How?" Penelope asked, clearly doubting this was possible.

"I know not, but we have to do something. And soon," Kiera admitted as she opened the door. "Elsewise this deception has all been for naught."

Chapter Ten

His new wife was a puzzlement.

Kelan rolled off the bed. He'd been dozing on and off most of the day, which, it seemed as he glanced to the window, was now waning to dusk. He winced at the pain blistering through his brain. 'Twas as if a dozen steel-shod horses were galloping through his head. Any light burned his eyes, and his bladder was stretched to its limit.

Yet he couldn't help but consider his bride. An enigma she was, a pleasant surprise.

Kelan had met more than his share of women in his days and they were all different, all unique. But this one, this female to whom he was married, intrigued him as had no other. He'd known her but a day . . . no, that wasn't true; he didn't know her at all. Most women, given enough time, revealed themselves, but he had a feeling about his wife that suggested he would constantly be surprised by her.

He set the tray with its few remains of their shared meal upon the floor and made his way out of the darkened room. His legs were still unsteady, his muscles tight, and the pain in his groin reminded him of the pleasures of the night before. Aye, she was a wild, beguiling woman, Elyn of Lawenydd.

He stepped into the hallway, where the rushlights burned low, then made his way to the latrine to relieve himself. The corridor was dark and deserted, the tiny garderobe icy cold from the open slats on the windows. His member was sore, but the pain was pleasant as it hinted at pleasures yet to come. This marriage might not be as bad as he'd expected. He laced up his breeches and walked down the short flight of stairs to the third floor.

As he entered the corridor he heard voices. They emanated from the room next to his wife's, the chamber that belonged to Elyn's middle sister, Kiera. He wondered about that one. He'd learned that Kiera was close in age to his bride, and yet she had not been at the wedding. He'd been told that she'd been too ill to attend, and yet now she was in her room with others. One voice sounded as if it belonged to an older woman. Another, he swore, was his wife's.

Woman talk, he thought with a snort and reentered Elyn's chamber. The smell of sweat and sex was thick over the fragrances of the rushes, but the room was as cold as a tomb. Empty.

Plowing stiff fingers through his hair, he wished his bloody headache would fade. He couldn't help but wonder about the wine he'd consumed and whatever else might have been in it, for the vials were testament that something was amiss. Seriously so. He fingered the small vessels again, smelling them and deciding that once Elyn returned he would confront her with them.

In the meantime, there was much to do. He needed to get dressed, find his small company of men, and make plans for leaving Lawenydd. 'Twas time to return to Penbrooke. His frail mother would be impatiently awaiting his return. Imagining Lenore's pleasure at seeing him happily wed, Kelan grinned and reached for his tunic. He would find Tadd, Orvis, and the priest, tell them that they would leave at dawn.

But first things first. He made his way to the grate and found a stack of split, mossy oak, which he arranged in the fireplace, then blew on a few remaining coals. The embers glowed red and slowly a flame emerged, crackling as it began to devour the dry, moss-laden oak.

Kelan rocked back on his heels. He'd thought Elyn's odd behavior during the wedding had been due to shyness, and then her refusal to come to the feast, evidence of a defiant streak. He'd come to this room intending to make her bend to his wishes . . . and he'd ended up making love to her and caring more for her own needs than his. She was bold one minute, flirtatious the next, then incredibly demure the following. He'd suspected she had feigned her illness, that she had been avoiding him, and even that she was impure. Yet when he came to her, she was living, breathing passion. A virgin, yes, but one who was a willing, nay, eager lover. Just thinking of the night before brought his manhood to attention. So why had she slipped out of bed and gone riding? Then returned and insisted upon bringing him a meal rather than allow the servants to carry in the food? And what of the damned vials he'd discovered in the rushes?

'Twas troubling. And his head, oh, how it thundered. From too much wine? Too little sleep? It was unlike him.

The latch of the door clicked. Turning, he caught a fresh glimpse of his wife entering the chamber. She'd tied her hair back and changed into a dress that shimmered and rustled as she moved.

"I've asked for more wine to be sent up," she said, and even in the darkening room, where the light was fleeing with the setting sun, she was beautiful to him, her features muted by the shadows.

"Should we not join your father?"

"Later," she insisted and sent him a glance from the corner of her eye, a glance that was innocence and seduction.

"I was about to meet with my men and

discuss leaving. We should set out for Penbrooke early tomorrow, as soon as dawn breaks."

Was it his imagination or did she stiffen just a bit? "So soon? Can we not wait another day or two?"

"I think not." Again the reticence. She walked to the bed and he noticed that her small hands were clenched into tight fists.

"Don't you want to see Penbrooke? 'Tis your new home."

"In time." Again he noticed that hardening of her spine. She picked nervously at the folds of her skirt. " 'Tis just so soon."

"You can visit here often, if you like. 'Tis but three days' ride."

"I know, but . . ." She bit her lower lip, then seemed to find some inner strength.

He felt himself cracking. Giving in. His mother would surely survive a few more days. When he had left four days ago, she had been frail but in good spirits at his upcoming nuptials. "If it would please you, we can stay another day, mayhap two, but then we must be off."

"Yes, oh, yes," she said hurriedly. "Two days. 'Tis all I need; then I'll gladly ride with you to our new home." She offered him a smile, though there were doubts shadowing her eyes, and something else. Fear?

"So be it." Straightening, he dusted off his hands. 'Twas time to ask her of the vials. "I found something," he said, reaching into his pocket just as someone tapped on the door.

She visibly started.

"I'll get it," he said. Already half across the room, he noticed that she walked to the window and stared out, turning her back at the visitor as he yanked the door open. An older woman servant stood in the corridor, one he'd seen at the nuptials. Her face was lined and grim, her eyes dark as stones. She balanced a tray upon which was a large jug and two half-filled mazers as well as a smaller platter of tarts.

"M'lord," she said, bowing her head of black hair streaked with gray. "Congratulations on your marriage." Her old voice cracked a bit, but he recognized it as the same one he'd heard earlier talking in Kiera's chamber.

"Thank you."

Some of the starch left Elyn's spine as she turned to greet the woman. "This is Hildy. She was my mother's maid, our nursemaid, and now attends me."

"Aye, 'tis true, I'm afraid. I've known the lady since she was a babe. How are you this day . . . Lady Elyn?" she asked, setting her tray upon the small table and brushing some crumbs to the floor as she glanced at the bed.

For a mere second, there was a flicker of disapproval in her eyes, her lips pursing a bit as she caught a glimpse of the rumpled bedsheets.

"May . . . may your union produce many strong sons and daughters," she said as she handed him a cup. "And for you, m'lady." Cradling the other mazer, she approached his wife. "Is there anything else I can do for you?"

"Not right now." Elyn took the cup from the older woman's outstretched hand. "Thank you, Hildy," she said as the maid picked up the tray with the remains of their earlier meal, then disappeared through the doorway.

And then they were alone again.

Elyn flashed him a smile. "To us," she said, her back to the fire, her face in shadow, as she lifted her cup.

"The Lord and Lady of Penbrooke." He touched the rim of his cup to hers and they both took a drink. "May we reign forever."

"Forever's a long time."

"Mmm. And maybe just enough for me to get my fill of you."

She smiled and his heart caught. Even in the dusky light, he saw her beauty. She buried her nose in her mazer and he drank as well, letting the sweet liquid slide down his throat. He thought fleetingly of the vials he'd found, but finished his cup and couldn't believe that she would be a part of any deception. Not when she was smiling at him so, her chin elevated a fraction, her lips twitching in amusement, her eyes shining with the secret they shared.

Before she finished her mazer, he took the cup from her fingers and set it with his on the floor. Before she could utter a word, he straightened and looked down at her upturned face. By the gods she was a beauty.

"There is much we need to discuss," he said.

"Much."

"But it can wait until morn."

"Can it?" Her smile was positively wicked.

"Oh, yes, lady." His arms surrounded her and she didn't resist, but fell readily into his embrace. He lowered his head, gently brushing his lips over hers. She let out a soft little sigh and turned her face up to his.

'Twas his undoing.

While thoughts of deception and vials and strange conversations skittered from his mind, he fastened his mouth to hers. Her lips were full and soft and tasted of wine. She gasped and he took advantage, sliding his tongue between her parted lips, bowing her back as he pulled her tight against him.

"Kelan, love," she whispered, blinking and pulling back inexplicably. "I — I cannot." Her voice caught and she looked away.

"Why?"

He noticed her swallow hard and though she tried to pull away, he held her fast.

"There is much to do."

"We have time."

Slowly he untied the ribbon holding her hair back, then leaned her over the bed. Her protests were weak and she didn't say another word as he loosened the laces of her dress. It fell over one shoulder and he worked with the ribbons of her chemise, opening the cloth, exposing her skin to him.

She sucked in her breath as he pressed his lips to the top of her breast and as he slid the dress lower, he discovered her nipple, a hard, ready button that he licked until she groaned and her arms surrounded him. He suckled, pulling hard. Her knees buckled, and they fell onto the bed. His erection was thick. Throbbing. His blood pounded with the want of her, and yet he took his time. Deliberately peeling her silky dress over her head, he kissed her, massaged her, made sure that she was ready. Her skin flushed in the firelight, her legs parted, and he quickly loosened the laces of his breeches and pushed inside her sweet, moist warmth. Dear God, he wanted to claim this woman, to make her his own, to . . . for a second his concentration shattered. He felt woozy again . . . like before.

Suddenly she surrounded him, her legs hooking over his waist, and he pulled her up, propping that delicious rump on bedclothes so that he could delve deeper, harder, thrusting in and out, the world fading into the shadows. Nothing seemed to matter, just that white heat between them. He heard her cry out, felt his own release, and then, in an instant, tumbled forward, losing consciousness.

Joseph counted again.
Thirty-nine horses.
Not forty.
Standing on a knoll overlooking the pasture, Joseph's gaze swept the herd as he mentally clicked off each familiar animal. Lawenydd's stable boasted jennets and palfreys for everyday use; sumpter horses for heavy work; roundseys, which were usually ridden by the peasants; and, of course, the pride of the castle, the destriers. Joseph knew them all.

His jaw hardened and his eyes narrowed. He must've made a mistake. Bay, sorrel, dun, gray, black and dull brown, the horses ambled in the weak light as the sun sank lower in the sky. Snorting, they picked at the winter grass. A few newborns scampered at their dams' sides, frolicking on their spindly legs, or nudging at the mares' flanks with their noses, ready to nurse. The stallions were kept separately, tethered away from the herd. But as Joseph's gaze shifted to the field on the other side of the creek, he knew he would come up with the same damning number. One horse short.

Nonetheless, he checked again, taking into account that three horses were being used on

165

a hunt, five by soldiers patrolling the forest, two were at the farrier's hut being reshod, four of the mares were housed in stalls while awaiting the imminent arrival of their foals, and one old stallion had pulled up lame and was hopefully recovering in yet another box. Thirty-nine.

That left the missing mare. The small, feisty jennet who always fought the bridle and, if given the opportunity, would take the bit between her teeth and ignore her rider's commands. Temperamental and fiery, the sleek bay was a small, compact animal that few of the soldiers favored. However, Lady Kiera was known to ride the bay when Garnet, her favorite, wasn't available.

Lady Kiera. The sweetest woman in all of Lawenydd, mayhap all of Wales. Not like her sister Elyn, whom Joseph unfortunately had fallen for long ago. It was foolish to even think of her. Yet think of her he did. All too often.

Some people in the keep insisted that the eldest two of Baron Llwyd's daughters looked so much alike as to have been twins, but Joseph thought that was nonsense. Physically, aye, they resembled each other much in face and stature and, yes, even in mannerisms. But that's where the similarities ended.

Whereas Elyn was competitive, sharp-tongued, and a general pain in the arse, Kiera was much warmer. She, too, had a temper, but it was cooled by a sense of humor, and no matter what, she always had a kind word for him. Though Elyn had intrigued and attracted him as a younger man, 'twas a foolish notion on his part. Wrong.

The trouble had started when he'd turned eleven and had begun having dreams of Elyn, of taming her. Dark and sexual, the dreams had oftentimes caused him to wake up hard as granite, lying in the straw over the stalls of the stable. Alone in the hayloft, with moonlight streaming through the small window, he'd conjured up her beautiful haughty face time and time again.

Her eyes were wide and green, like the mists at dawn, her cheekbones sculpted, high and regal, her lips the color of roses in full bloom. And he'd seen her naked once, when she didn't know he was about, years ago when she and Kiera had taken off their clothes and swum in the millpond. He'd never mentioned it to a soul.

But in those long, long midnight hours alone in the hayloft, he'd remembered her white skin, dark hair, and the glimpse of a rosy nippled breast. Though he could be damned to hell for his thoughts, he'd allowed himself to imagine what it would be like to bed her, to slide between cool sheets and feel her hot body next to his.

Oh, 'twas a sin and he knew it, but his own mind was sometimes his worst enemy.

167

What would it feel like to bed the lady? To his shame, while in the midst of his erotic musings, he'd even gone so far as to touch himself as he fantasized about her.

Afterward he'd always felt dirty and foolish, and his conscience and faith had forced him into the chapel, where turning ten shades of scarlet, he had confessed his sins to the castle priest.

Never once had Joseph mentioned Elyn's name in his confessions. He would never defile her name so, nor embarrass himself further. Not even to God.

He tried to be pious, to do God's will, though sometimes it was difficult. And he attempted to be truthful and confess his sins. He'd even owned up to the fact that it was he who had allowed Kiera to ride off on Obsidian that evening three years earlier, he who had disobeyed all reason and saddled the horse for her, promising not to tell a soul that she was borrowing her father's prized stallion. His mistake had cost the baron a priceless steed and nearly cost Kiera her life. The flogging he'd received was small punishment for his stupidity. That his own father, Orson, had not lost his job as stable master was a miracle, one Orson never let Joseph forget.

Even so, even with his attempts at piety, he'd held his tongue when it came to his feelings for Lady Elyn. And his passion for her had cooled. Now, 'twas her younger sister, the kinder of the two women, who caused his blood to heat, his stupid member to rise as sturdy as an oak tree at the most awkward of times. Christ Jesus, he was a fool.

He couldn't think of either lady now. Not with the horse missing. Squinting hard, hoping he was somehow mistaken, Joseph again studied the field only to find no sign of the temperamental mare. She was gone. Vanished. Or . . . his gut tightened at the turn of his thoughts.

"Hey! Joseph! What's the matter with ye?" his father demanded. Carrying a whip rolled tightly between his fingers, Orson limped up the crooked path traversing this hillock. "We've got work to do, if ya haven't noticed. The red mare's in labor and havin' a time of it. Don't ye think ye should tend to her?"

"Aye." Joseph nodded. "I'm on my way." He hesitated, then decided his father needed to hear the bad news. "I think a horse is missing," he admitted. "Royal, the little bay with the crooked star."

"Royal's missing? What d'ye mean?" Orson asked, but his gaze was already skating over the herd while he mentally checked off those that were elsewhere. "She was here this mornin', wasn't she?"

"I don't know." Joseph rubbed the back of

his neck and thought hard. "I don't think so."

"Yesterday?"

"I'm not sure."

"Ye're talkin' 'bout the ornery little jennet who kicked the carter last fall and near broke his leg?" Orson asked, disbelieving.

"Aye, Royal, as I said," Joseph snapped angrily. "She's gone. Not a trace of her." Joseph turned to look at the herd once more as if in so doing he'd spot the mare in the shadow of a taller horse.

"Are ye sure or not whether someone took her out for a ride?"

"Who?"

His father lifted a hand toward the sky. "I don't know. Anyone. The Lady Kiera, she rides her, don't she?"

"Sometimes, but not today. This morn she came to the stables and requested Garnet, as you know. But she returned her a few hours later — see there, near the tree." Joseph pointed a long finger toward the jennet in question. As if she knew she was the center of attention, Garnet lifted her head for a minute, then went back to sedately plucking grass and swishing her long tail.

"Curse it all," Orson muttered under his breath. "How could you let this happen?"

Joseph didn't answer as his father, a tic starting beneath his eye, studied the herd. His old eyes narrowed thoughtfully. "Is she not being shod at the farrier or used by a huntsman or —"

"Or what?" Joseph demanded. "I've thought about everywhere she could be and she's not there. She's missin', I'm tellin' ya."

"But who would take that one? If someone was to steal a horse, I mean."

"I didn't say she was stolen," Joseph replied, but the thought had crossed his mind.

"Well, she's gone and unless she ran off by herself, then someone took her. So where's the sense in that?" Orson motioned toward the destriers in the next field. "Now, if Rex was missin', that I'd understand. Or Falcon, there, a great one he is. But that mare." He snorted as if the thought was absurd. "Royal. Humph!" Lifting his cap, he ran stiff fingers over his near bald pate.

His voice was lower when he said, "Let's find her before the steward or his lordship himself hears of this." Orson glanced at the setting sun, and Joseph could read the older man's thoughts. Soon there would be no light by which to look for the missing horse. Damn it, the day after the union of Penbrooke and Lawenydd should not be marred by a missing horse. Settling his cap onto his head again, Joseph's father worried the handle of his whip. His tic was still trembling frantically. "Don't tell anyone. Not yet. The damned horse might turn up and then we've riled everyone up for no reason."

His old eyes met his son's and Joseph read the unspoken message in his father's gaze, the fear that he could very well lose his job this time. Or worse. Banishment was possible. They both knew it. "Now," Orson said through clenched teeth, "I'll tend to the mare in labor. You, son, find the damned jennet."

Chapter Eleven

As she stood on the parapet and stared out to sea, a chill wind cut through Hildy's soul. The sky was now dark, and another day had passed without any sign of Elyn's return. But then, what made Kiera so certain that her sister would reappear? Duty? Love? Responsibility?

Bah.

Elyn was only interested in herself.

Hildy suspected the selfish woman would never show her face in Lawenydd or Penbrooke again.

A storm was brewing on the horizon. Sunlight had fast faded, hidden by roiling purplish clouds. The ships anchored in the twilight waters seemed ghostlike with their tall, skeletal spars stretching to the dark sky.

'Twas her own fault, Hildy decided, fingering the beads surrounding her neck. She should have stopped this madness. Before it got out of hand. She'd known of the trouble even before it began, for she'd seen the glint of uncompromising rebellion in Lady Elyn's eyes.

Had Hildy not expected it? Elyn had always been a willful, spoiled child. Mayhap if the lord and lady had been fortunate enough to conceive a son . . . but they had not.

When she was younger, Elyn had been sent to Castle Fenn to learn the ways of running a household, to learn how to be a proper lady. But of course, that was not to be, for while she was at Fenn, Elyn had met Brock of Oak Crest.

As fate and the stones had predicted she would.

A few years older than Elyn, Brock was already a squire at the time, a roguish, wayward boy. While learning the skills and duties of a knight, he had somehow burrowed his way into Elyn's naive heart.

And now she'd been gone for nearly two days. Gone to be with him. Nay, she would not return. Would not be separated from him. Would not endure her father's and husband's wrath.

So what to do now? Hildy closed her eyes and sent up a prayer to the Holy Mother.

Could she confess to the baron?

Insist that Kiera do the same?

Now, after the false marriage?

Hildy imagined Lord Llwyd's embarrassment, his shame. He would be furious. And yet, his anger would be naught in comparison to Kelan of Penbrooke's rage. He would look a fool, duped by Kiera, Elyn, and, he would surmise, everyone in Lawenydd. He would never live down the shame of it. Nor would it go unpunished.

The gossip would spread like fire through the baronies, and the Lord of Penbrooke would become a laughingstock, considered a buffoon or worse, a prideful man duped by a mere woman.

What would he do to Kiera?

To Elyn if he found her?

To all of Lawenydd to reclaim his pride?

Tears filled Hildy's eyes and she made the sign of the cross over her bony chest. Lips moving silently, she sent up a prayer to a God who had rarely given her His ear. "Have mercy on us," she whispered. "Have mercy on us all."

If only she could find Elyn. But alas, it was already too late. With a premonition of doom weighing heavily upon her, Hildy hurried down the steep steps of the north tower. The rushlights were flickering dim, cobwebs clinging to the smooth stone walls. She heard the scrape of tiny claws over the sound of her own footsteps. The sound of mice and rats scurrying out of her path, though she barely noticed. Her mind was on Brock of Oak Crest, a son of Satan if ever there was one. Handsome, cruel, and self-serving, he promised to be a tyrant.

Yet Lady Elyn was certain she loved him. *Have you not known the pain of a love that could never be? Would you not, if given the chance to live your life over, chase that dream more feverishly rather than die a shrunken, barren old woman?*

She shouldered open the door and bent her head against the wind as she made her way along the path to her hut. Aye, she'd been foolish over a man, but he was twice the man, nay, thrice the man that Brock of Oak Crest would ever be.

Elyn had met and fallen for Brock when she'd been sent to Castle Fenn, shortly after her mother's death when she was thirteen. It had been a dark time for all, and realizing that Elyn would be the first to marry, Llwyd had sent his eldest daughter to complete her training as a lady at Fenn. As a youth Brock had been cocky and brash, irreverent and a rebel, a boy after Elyn's own wayward heart. Elyn had fancied herself in love with him, it seemed, from the moment she'd set eyes upon him. They had been together at Fenn but had been separated when Brock had returned to Oak Crest and she to Lawenydd. Then, as cursed luck would have it, Brock, who had become a knight, had been loaned to Lawenydd before assuming his duties as firstborn at Oak Crest.

'Twas a dream come true for Elyn, and though Hildy disapproved, she could say nothing.

The passion between Brock and Elyn, always smoldering, had once again sparked when Brock had come to Lawenydd more than three years ago. Hildy had seen it then but had held her tongue, for Elyn was not allowed a choice in the matter of her marriage. Lord Llwyd had thought the alliance with Oak Crest was not important enough for his firstborn and heir to Lawenydd. Oak Crest was a poor keep, the old baron a drunkard, Brock unlikely to make the castle flourish and prosper. Nay, Llwyd had been set to make a pact with Penbrooke, and had succeeded.

Hildy had watched the events of Elyn's life unfold and she'd seen far more than Lady Elyn would have liked. For there was something besides hot passion simmering between the two lovers, something darker, a secret Elyn dared not confide.

Hildy had yet to understand what it was. She passed the candlemaker toting sacks of candles into the great hall to brighten the darkness of the evening as she rounded the corner to her hut.

"Good evenin' to ye, Hildy," he said with a nod of his head.

"And to you, Thomas. Give Belinda my best. The babe, it's due next month."

"That it is," he said, offering a wide grin missing several teeth. "Our fifth. Belinda, she'd like ye to come over and" — he glanced over his shoulder as if he expected someone to overhear the conversation —

"and, you know, bless the birth."

"That I will," she promised.

"I wouldn't want the priest to know about it."

"Worry not, Thomas."

With a nod, he hitched his load to his shoulder and strode quickly away. Hildy stepped into her small quarters. The hut smelled of dried herbs and spices. Carefully she lit a candle from the embers of the slow-burning fire.

Her nimble cat hopped atop the table. "A bold one ye be, Sir James," she chided, stroking his sleek black coat. "And have ye caught me a mouse today? Or a rat? Or a snake? No?" Smiling, she scratched the skinny animal's chin as the door burst open, causing the fire to glow bright.

Baron Llwyd loomed in the doorway, his expression dark as midnight, his walking stick in one hand. Sir James hissed and scrambled up a post to the rafters as Llwyd's favorite hunting dog, the one forever at his heels, sniffed his way inside. "Something is amiss here at the castle. I think you may know what," he said, his cloudy eyes trained on her.

"M'lord, I know not of what you speak," she said, lying as easily as she had all her life.

" 'Tis Elyn. And Kiera. They both are acting strangely." He threw up his free hand in disgust and made his way into the hut. The dog was sniffing around the table, and Sir James growled, his hair standing on end as he hid upon the rough beam.

"Why have I not seen my daughter and her groom?" Llwyd demanded as the dog whined. "You, hush!" he tapped at the dog with his cane.

Though the years had stooped Llwyd of Lawenydd's once broad shoulders, and taken most of the sight from his eyes, he was a handsome man and, in Hildy's estimation, still more noble than any other. The skin surrounding his jaw was looser, his girth wider than it had been in his prime, but he still was commanding. Every time Hildy saw him, her old heart skipped a guilty beat.

"It's been nearly a day since the wedding." He leaned one hip against the smooth planks of her table. "Though I am pleased that Elyn has accepted her marriage, 'tis odd that they have not come down from her chamber for any of the meals. Nor has Penbrooke spoken alone with me. There is much I would like to discuss with him, agreements to be made."

"Mayhap you should be thankful that your daughter is so taken with her new husband."

"Humph. 'Tis odd. She was against the union, I know. She even claimed that the arranged marriage was archaic. Can you imagine? What did she call it? 'Hideously old-fashioned' or some such rot."

Hildy opened her mouth to protest, but the baron lifted a hand in her direction, effectively cutting her off. "There are other strange things as well. Elyn has never been one to stay in the castle. She and Kiera . . ." He shook his head, some of his white hairs glinting in the light from the fire. "Both of my older girls are much like me . . . too much, perhaps. I encouraged it, of course, and Twyla never forgave me for it." Sighing, he made the sign of the cross over his chest. "Well, she never forgave me any of my sins."

Watching as the dog circled and nestled upon her hearth, Hildy ignored the shame that touched her tired old soul.

"And what of Penbrooke? Does he not want to settle some things between us? We are now family, aye, but I would like a formal agreement that we are allies . . . oh, bother . . ."

For the first time since entering her hut, he stopped ranting long enough to look at Hildy. She wondered what his murky eyes saw. The young woman he'd first taken to his bed nearly forty years earlier, or a haggard old crone who had never loved another man? Distractedly, she pushed a strand of coarse hair from her face.

He reached forward and touched her arm. "You're still a beauty, you know," he whispered as if he'd read her thoughts.

But that was always the way it had been

between them. Oftentimes, after a few stolen hours of lovemaking, they had lain in silence upon the cold bedsheets, touching only fingers, and it had been as if they were still one. Oh, how she'd lived for those days.

"And you're half blind."

"Not enough that I don't see into your heart, Hildy-lass."

She swallowed hard. Fought hot tears. "What is it you want?"

His fingers rubbed her shoulder. "Throw the stones for me. Tell me of the future of Lawenydd. I have the feeling something is very, very wrong within the keep."

She moved away from the seduction of his touch. What they had shared was long over. Years of passion and love had ended with the baron's guilt. Guilt due to his wife's death and the acts of adultery he had committed with Hildy. But she still loved this man. "You asked me once never to toss the stones," she reminded him. "No matter how you begged, pleaded, or beguiled me, I was never to do what you just asked."

He frowned. "That was long ago. I . . ."

"I understand. But you were serious about it then."

"My wife had died," he said, and looked at her as if his blue eyes were clear again. "Just as you'd predicted. I hadn't listened, but now . . . now I need to know."

"You are certain?"

"Aye." He pulled her into his arms and rested his forehead against hers. "I've been a fool most of my life. I've hurt those who were closest to me. I know I misused you as well as my wife, but it was because I was torn between the two of you. I make no excuses, Hildy; you know that. I was wrong and have had the misfortune to live long enough to regret each and every day. I thought your magic was nonsense, or dangerous, but I must have the truth. Because of my children. Please."

She sighed, hearing his steady heartbeat over the quiet hiss of the fire and the dog's soft snores. How could she deny him? Had she ever? Nay. "As you wish, m'lord." She turned to reach into her cupboard, but he spun her around to face him and placed a warm kiss upon her lips, the first one in years.

"Thank you," he whispered.

Blushing, she pulled out of his embrace and dashed away the spiteful tear that had fallen from her eye. What was wrong with her? She was no longer a naive girl whose heart was young and free. To mask the emotions that strangled her, she scrounged quickly in her cupboard. There, within a small, chipped dish, she found her threadbare pouch. Oh, this was a mistake. She knew it.

The stones clinked as she opened the sack and rolled them into her open hand. They were different sizes, their colors distinct but far from brilliant, the edges worn soft from being rubbed together.

She felt the baron tense.

As she whispered a soft prayer to the Mother Goddess, Hildy closed her eyes and tossed the polished pebbles onto the table. Rattling ominously, they tumbled across the scarred boards, bounding and rolling to stop suddenly, the fates visible in the way they settled.

Hildy's soul turned as dark as night. 'Twas as if a demon had cursed them all. For the briefest second she closed her eyes.

"What? What is it?" Llwyd demanded, pointing at the stones. "What do you see? Tell me!"

"You were right. There is trouble," she admitted, forcing the words out and feeling as cold as if she'd been cast into the winter sea.

"What kind?"

"I know not," she lied, avoiding the baron's gaze. Worrying the beads at her throat, she glanced back at the damning position of each pebble. "But it will be dire."

"I knew it." He leaned heavily against the table. "I've been a fool, Hildy. This marriage that I wanted so badly is cursed." Scratching the whiskers on his chin, he asked warily, "What is it you see there, in the stones?"

She hesitated. How could she tell this man whom she loved with all of her heart that because of his greed, because of his misguided goals, one of his daughters would die? She could not. Gathering up the cursed rocks, she offered him a sad smile. "I see a man who loves his children, a man who cares about his keep, a good man who has made mistakes throughout his life and will probably make more." He was staring at her through those milky eyes, silently willing the truth from her lips. She cleared her throat and said, "I see also that we must accept what the fates have cast in our direction."

"Mayhap I can change things. Annul the marriage. Send Penbrooke back to his keep." Llwyd hobbled to the fire and glared into the hungry flames. Deep lines creased his face. Worriedly he rubbed the worn knob of his cane. "I'm afraid, Hildy," he admitted as he stared at the fire. "In my life, there has been little I feared; you know that. But right now I'm certain I've damned my own soul to hell."

Chapter Twelve

Kiera smiled. She had successfully kept Kelan from leaving Elyn's room almost all day. Now it was nighttime, and she could breathe a small sigh of victory. She watched as he stoked the fire, his bare back scarred, his thighs thick as he bent on one knee. He was wearing only breeches and they strained across his buttocks. She, herself, was half dressed, wearing only her chemise. She had spent the large part of the early evening hours making love to Kelan. Guilt lay on the edge of Kiera's conscience, but her body felt too magnificent to worry for the moment. She was definitely sore, but she had never felt so content in her entire life.

With your sister's husband, you ninny. What are you thinking?

'Twas time to forget her fantasies. She had to keep Kelan in the bed another day or two and soon he would want to get up, to meet her family again, to bargain with her father. Her only hope of continuing this hateful, wonderful deception was to use the potion.

She tossed a naughty smile his way and, lying back against the pillows, motioned to the small table near the bed. "Perhaps some wine, husband?"

"You would have me drink more?" His voice was gruffer than it had been. He seemed restless.

"Why not?"

"Why?" he asked, casting a look over his shoulder, a cold stare that caused a sliver of concern to burrow into her heart.

"To . . . celebrate our marriage."

"Ah." He nodded slowly as he stood and dusted his hands. The fire was burning bright, crackling and sparking against the cold of the coming night. "Our marriage," he repeated, and his voice had an ominous edge. "Mayhap we should discuss it." The warning hairs on the back of her neck rose, and as she looked him in his eyes, she saw that some of the rage he'd heretofore tamped down now burned bright.

"If you wish." She lifted a shoulder as if it were of no matter when inside her heart was beating like a drum.

"You've been deceiving me, little one, and not just today." He approached the bed.

"Kelan, no —"

"Do not lie. From the moment I set eyes on you," he said through lips that barely moved, "I have sensed it. Seen things, but ignored them with your seduction in this chamber. I can no longer. Something is wrong here. Very wrong. For a reason I have yet to understand you've been lying through those beautiful teeth of yours. Deceiving me. Playing me for a fool."

"I would not."

"Of course you would."

"But — have we not . . ." She motioned to the bed and his gaze skated across the crumpled bedclothes.

"Marriage is not just lovemaking." He was so determined, his jaw set so tight. What could she tell him? What could she say?

"I suggest you tell me the truth. Right now." Looming over her, he appeared dangerous, and yet she refused to cower.

"I have been."

A muscle worked in his jaw. "By the gods, you confound me."

"As you confound me."

"Nay. 'Tis different. Either you tell me what you've been doing, wife, why you have been determined to keep me penned up here in your chamber, or make no mistake, I promise you, you'll pay for your lies and pay dearly."

"You threaten me?" She climbed out of the bed and, standing near the wall, forced herself to glare up at him. "Why?"

His eyes narrowed as if in squinting he could see past her lies. "I saw you through the window this morn, mounting to ride, and you looked about as if you were searching for something, or someone."

She was doomed. She had no choice but to tell him the truth. Oh, God. Desperation tore at her soul. "You were spying on me this morning?" she managed, remembering Kelan's shadowy form in Elyn's window. She inched her chin up a notch, hoping to appear outraged though her buttocks were pressed against the wall.

"Only because I couldn't chase you down. I was much too tired from our lovemaking to run after you." A dark, suspicious eyebrow arched and she wanted to die, to drop right through the stone floor and disappear. "Is that not odd? That while I could barely raise my head or drag myself out of bed to go to the latrine to relieve myself, you are racing through the keep so fast that I swear the castle dogs would not be able to keep up with you. And I am not one to be bedridden from drink." He paused.

Her heart was drumming wildly. Loudly. Thundering with fear. *Tell him the truth. Now! Let him hear it from your lips!* "You seem angry, husband," she said, her insides shaking.

"See how perceptive you are?" he mocked, not touching her but standing so close she could feel his heat, his rage.

Tell him!

"There . . . there is much we have to discuss, 'tis true." God's teeth, could she admit the depths of her deception? Here? Now?

What would he do? To her? To Elyn? To their father who was an innocent in this scheme? "But . . . perhaps we should sit down." Kiera indicated the bed.

"So you can seduce me?"

"What?" Her head snapped up.

"Is that not part of your deception? To make me weak from lovemaking, or is there more? Do you ply me with food and drink that causes me to lose my strength?"

This was worse than she thought. "I — I don't understand."

"Do you not?" His lips twisted cynically and he shook his head as if disappointed that she would continue to try and deceive him.

"Are you suggesting that I do something to you? Poison you or — or what? Make love to you until you cannot stay awake?" She feigned innocence though her insides curdled with the deception. How long would she have to lie? Forever?

What if Elyn never returned? Dear God, and what if she did? What if she showed up here, now, to take her place, and for the rest of her life Kiera would have to pretend that she'd never known the feel of Kelan's lips upon hers, the touch of his hand upon her thigh, the smell of his skin as she lay with him. The niggling thought that had plagued her since last night emerged yet again. What if she'd become pregnant? What if even now she was carrying his child? *Confess to him!*

"I don't know what to think of you, wife," he admitted, so close that his breath was warm against her face. His eyes delved deep into hers, searching for the truth and touching her rueful soul. "You're not what I expected."

"Nor, Kelan, are you," she said with heartfelt honesty. Never would she have guessed he would be a man who could intrigue, entrance, and frighten her so. She was breathing hard and his gaze strayed down her neck, to the telltale pulse beating at her throat. He hesitated and she was certain he noticed the rapid rise and fall of her chest. If possible, he stepped closer, his body a hair's breadth from hers.

"And I found vials near the bed this morning. One empty. One filled with blood."

She nearly dropped through the floor. Felt her face turn ashen. "Vials?" she repeated, her voice close to cracking. 'Twas too late. He *knew*. For the love of the Holy Mother, he *knew*. "And you did not tell me?"

"I'm telling you now."

"But why would you not speak of it sooner?" she demanded. "If you thought something was amiss —"

He grabbed her roughly by the shoulders as if he intended to give her a quick shake. Instead he said, "Do not try to turn this around! I found the damned vials and I wondered, what were they for? Who put them there?"

"Perhaps a servant dropped them."

He snorted. "The room was clean, the rushes fresh, the firewood stacked, water in the basin clear. The linens clean. Nay, wife, this very room, the chamber in which we were to consummate our vows, had been carefully prepared."

"But a servant could have mistakenly dropped the vials and —"

"Hush! Lie no more! Don't forget that I saw you deter the servants from entering the room," he growled, eyes blazing, nostrils flaring. His hands tightened over her shoulders. "The blood, I understand not, though I have heard of this ploy if a bride comes to her marriage bed no longer a virgin." Kiera forced her legs to support her, hoped her face did not betray her. "But you, little one, I have no doubts of your virtue, and the vial of blood is still full. Untouched. Now, the other vessel, it poses another question. What did it hold?" He paused, as if lost in thought, or waiting for her response.

"I — I know not," she stammered.

" 'Tis a puzzlement, but considering my lethargy, I can only guess it contained some potion intended to make me sleep the sleep of the dead."

"What are you suggesting?" she asked. "That I tricked you? That I tried to harm you? That somehow I was plotting against you? But why?" Oh, she was tangling herself

191

more with each question. *Tell him now that you're not Elyn; try and explain that she left. It's not your fault. You never agreed to this foolish plan; she left and you had to save your family's honor. . . .* But she had lied and what honor was there in deceit?

"That's what I'm asking you. If you wanted me dead —"

She gasped. "No!"

" 'Twould have been easily done when I slept, yet here I am. Alive. Though something is not right, nay, 'tis very, very wrong, and I want to know what it is." With deliberation he reached into his pocket and withdrew the damning vials. Kiera stared at them and realized she'd met her doom. Her luck had finally run out. She had to confide in him. Now. There was no escape. Elyn's fate had been sealed. As had hers.

From outside the chamber Kiera heard footsteps rushing up the stairs. Oh, God. Someone was coming. Running. Toward this very room. Before she had a chance to unburden herself. She had to tell him. Now, before — "Kelan, I —"

'Twas too late. Someone was pounding on the door, demanding to be let in, and before Kiera could protest, Kelan walked over and flung it wide open as Kiera spun, putting her back to the entry, hiding her face.

"There you are!" an unfamiliar male voice boomed.

Who? Was he talking to her? Or the Lord of Penbrooke?

She dared not peek over her shoulder until she was certain it was someone she didn't know. "Have you not heard?" the man demanded.

"What?" Kelan asked.

"Reginald arrived a few minutes ago with news from Penbrooke." His voice lowered, became more sober. "It's our mother."

Our mother? Kelan's brother? She glanced around just in time to see Kelan's face drain of color. "What of her?"

Cautiously, Kiera looked over her shoulder. The man was tall and dark, his brow creased, and his lips were compressed into a sharp line beneath a dark beard. Blue eyes were troubled; his expression was bleak. "She's fallen," he said tightly. "According to Reginald, the physician thinks she has but a few days to live, and that was nearly three days ago."

"Then we leave now," Kelan said.

" 'Tis dark out."

"We'll ride by torchlight." His gaze swung to Kiera as he pocketed the vials. "Get ready."

"I can't leave tonight. We had an agreement," she protested. But she'd always known Kelan had to return to his ailing mother. Wasn't that why they had hastened into this marriage and why Elyn had to boil up this insane lie in which Kiera was now stuck? No, this was all wrong. She needed time to confide in him. Alone. And she couldn't leave Elyn and Penelope and her father without explaining. Yet she couldn't deny him a last chance to see his mother.

"Aye, *wife,* you can. And you will!" Turning again to his brother, he said, "We leave within the hour. I'll say my good-byes to our host, and you, Tadd, see that the stablemen have our horses ready."

Panic grabbed Kiera by the throat. "But I've not packed; I've not told my family good-bye; I've not —"

"And my mother is dying!" he snapped, grabbing her roughly by the arm again. "We depart within the hour, wife. Perhaps you should start saying your good-byes now."

"But you can't leave," Penelope wailed, pacing from one wall of Elyn's room to the other. She was wringing her hands, her face a mask of worry.

Kiera stuffed a few meager pieces of Elyn's clothing into a bag. She had little time. The rest of Elyn's belongings would be sent on a wagon within the week. And by that time she would certainly have had to confide the truth . . . unless Elyn miraculously appeared. Then they would have to explain, or think of some new plan; simply switching places would never work. Not now. Too much time had passed. Kelan knew her and would sense the difference.

"What will happen when Elyn returns?" Penelope asked.

"I know not!" Kiera flung a tunic into her leather pouch as her younger sister anxiously rubbed her elbows. "Kelan found the vials from the wedding night, before I could remove them from the room. He showed them to me before the news of his mother arrived and accused me of drugging him."

"Father, protect us," Penelope whispered. She flung herself onto the bed and seemed about to burst into tears.

Kiera cleared her throat. Could she really leave? Had she any other choice? "Listen, if Elyn should return, she will have to catch up to us and we'll switch."

"Will your, er, her husband not know?"

"I hope not, but, aye, I think he would. He's . . . he's not stupid and this has gone on much too long. As I said, he's already suspicious because of the vials and his inability to stay awake. Oh, I was foolish. This entire plan was a mistake from the beginning. I'll leave Elyn to explain it to him or to . . . or to come up with some other mad story." She was almost certain there was no way for Elyn to take her place undetected. She and Kelan had spent so many hours together, and though it had been dark in the chamber and he'd been drugged, he was not a simple man.

And he'd seen her when he was clearheaded. His mind and eyes were keen; certainly Elyn would look, smell, act, and, aye, taste different. Either Elyn or Kiera would have to admit the truth and then, God help them, the Furies of hell would surely be unleashed!

Hildy slipped into the room and closed the door softly behind her. "You cannot go, Kiera," she said in a rush. "You must tell your father and Lord Penbrooke the truth."

"Now?"

"Yes." She let out a long breath and fingered the stone dangling from her necklace. "I'm afraid that if you leave with Penbrooke tonight, you may never come back. That you will have to play the part of Kelan's wife for the rest of your life. That . . . you will be doomed to live a lie forever." She placed an old hand on Kiera's shoulder. "I . . . I think Elyn may not return."

Kiera nodded, absorbing the bitter reality. "I know."

Penelope shot off the bed. "You *know?* And you accept it? You're just going to leave . . . leave me alone?"

" 'Tis temporary. You have Father."

"Nay. I've never had Father," Penelope said, shaking her head in a fit of emotion. "Elyn and you, yes, you had Father, but he never had any interest in me."

"You were Mother's favorite."

"And I lost her. Now Elyn's missing and

you're leaving and . . ." Tears rolled down Penelope's cheeks and angrily she dashed them away. "Everyone's gone."

"I'll be here," Hildy said soothingly, but her eyes were dark with worry. "You have to understand, Kiera, that if you leave tonight, you may never return. You may have to live the rest of your life as Kelan's bride."

"Not if I find Elyn," Kiera argued, wondering how in the world she would ever accomplish that particular feat.

Hildy sighed and shook her head. "As I said, I fear it may be too late for that."

"I have to try! And you must help me. If we don't find her within a week, I will tell Kelan the truth. I had planned to this day, but then he received the news of his mother's condition and now I . . . I think it is not the right time."

"There will never be a *right* time," Penelope pointed out.

"Aye, but there will be a better one."

"After his mother dies?"

"I don't know. But if we leave now, I don't need to tell him now. No one at Penbrooke will recognize that I'm not Elyn." Kiera curled her fingers in Hildy's tunic. "I will not let this go on much longer, I swear, and I cannot risk drugging Kelan again, but I might need the potion to give to a guard or a stableboy if I am to leave his castle at will. Bring me more of the sleeping elixir, as many vials as you can hide in a small pouch."

"Oh, child, this is dangerous."

" 'Tis all dangerous! Please, worry not," Kiera begged desperately. "I must be able to escape Penbrooke in order to find Elyn." Kiera saw the doubts in the older woman's eyes, and felt them herself. Did she truly want to find her sister? Or would she be content to continue her role as Kelan's wife, to live and sleep with him for the rest of her days? Would that be possible, knowing in the back of her mind that she was living a lie? Nay. And though Elyn may have abandoned her, Kiera could never do the same to her sister.

"What if the baron finds you with the elixir?" Hildy asked, and Kiera shuddered at the thought of Kelan's fury. Oh, 'twould be terrible.

" 'Tis a risk I must take. Please, Hildy, you must help me. If not, all will truly be lost."

Penelope pouted. " 'Tis lost already."

"Not yet."

"Oh? Then what are we to say to Father, or anyone else who asks about you? How are we going to explain that *you're* missing?" she asked. "Father's not that blind! When you're not about, everyone in the castle will begin to wonder what happened to Kiera, not Elyn. How are we to explain that?"

Kiera had worried about the same thing, and the two choices she came up with were both sorry. "You must lie and tell him I went with Elyn. Just say that at the last moment Elyn begged me to come with her and I agreed," she said, her thoughts racing quickly ahead. "I will try to say good-bye to him before I leave, but if I don't, tell him I'll send word soon or return. That should allow us a few more days. Maybe then we'll find our sister."

"Unless we can't," Penelope pointed out, jabbing a finger at Kiera's chest. "And what then? What if we pretend that you're with Elyn at Penbrooke, and someone from Lawenydd visits Penbrooke and sees you, not Elyn, playing the part of the lord's wife. Then what?"

"It won't happen. Not before I return!"

Hildy sighed heavily and bit her lower lip. "We dig ourselves deeper with each lie."

"Please. Give me a week. If we do not find Elyn in that time, then, I swear, I will tell everyone the truth and take all the blame," Kiera said. "In the meantime, we must send a messenger to Oak Crest, to Brock." She looked from her sister to the old woman. "Mayhap he will know what has happened to Elyn."

"Then we will have to find a messenger we can trust," Hildy thought aloud. "Who?"

Kiera had already decided. "It must be Joseph."

"Joseph? The stableboy?" Disgusted,

Penelope tossed up one hand and rolled her eyes as if the mere suggestion was ridiculous. "How can he get away? Won't someone notice?"

Kiera was one step ahead of her. "He is someone we can trust, and he will have some time away from the castle with the excuse that he'll be looking for the mare that is missing."

"What mare?"

"The one Elyn took!"

"Oh, we are doomed. Doomed." Penelope dropped onto the bed and shook her head. "Now there are stolen horses."

"Borrowed horses," Kiera corrected, turning to Hildy. "You have sway with Father. Do whatever you have to do to convince him to let Joseph search for the missing horse, and then see that Joseph contacts Brock."

"What if he finds Elyn?"

"He must give her a message from me, that she must come at once to Penbrooke."

"And if she refuses?" Penelope asked.

Kiera's jaw hardened. "Then I will speak with her."

"From Penbrooke?"

"I will find a way, worry not!"

Footsteps shuffled outside the door and Kiera knew her time was limited. "I have to go soon," she said. "Joseph is clever, he will come up with a way. Now you, too, must do your part," Kiera warned.

"I know and I . . . I will try to keep your secret, but we can only do it for so long," Penelope vowed. "A few days, mayhap a week, but then, if you or Elyn have not returned, we will have to explain to Father."

"I will be back. As soon as I can. I promise. With or without Elyn." Kiera tightened the leather strings of her bag. Forcing a smile she didn't feel, she threw one arm around her younger sister's shoulder. She'd already begun to miss Penelope. "Have faith. Now, if only the fates will be kind."

Hildy's eyes darkened. " 'Tis not what I see," she admitted, shaking her head.

"You have been wrong before." Releasing her sister, Kiera opened the door. "Pray that you are this time as well."

As she said her good-byes to Hildy and Penelope, Kiera was suddenly seized by an icy chill. She hurried down the stairs of the keep, and all the while she felt as if she were drowning, drowning in her own cold lies.

Chapter Thirteen

Elyn felt queasy.

As she always did these days.

But tonight, after too brief a day spent making passionate love at the Gamekeeper's Inn, she and Brock rode to Oak Crest. Her discomfort was more than a bit of upset stomach. Since she'd met up with Brock the night before, on what should have been her wedding night to Kelan of Penbrooke, she'd sensed that there was something he was hiding, a secret yawning between them. He seemed quieter, tense, his demeanor shrouded in a darkness she couldn't understand, his lovemaking more desperate than ever before.

Aye, something was amiss and it worried her.

Holding tight to the reins of her headstrong little mare, Elyn wondered if she'd made a horrible, irreversible mistake. The road was deserted, light from a pale moon barely illuminating the muddy ruts. Brock was silent and brooding, his horse a few paces ahead of Elyn's temperamental jennet.

From deep within the surrounding forest

an owl hooted mournfully and Elyn swore she heard the whir of bats' wings, though it was improbable. Her guilt-sodden mind was playing tricks upon her. That was all.

She kneed her mare, and the animal, always fighting the bit, broke into a hasty trot to catch up with Brock's destrier. "Something's troubling you," she said, deciding that if Brock wasn't going to bring up whatever was wrong, she would. She'd mentioned his quietude twice before, but he'd suggested she was imagining things.

"I'm fine."

"I know you better."

He didn't answer, just slid a glance her way.

"What is it?"

"I already told you. Nothing."

Her stomach tightened and its meager contents roiled. "You're lying."

Astride his taller horse, he sent her a scathing look. "You risked your neck, your reputation, your very life, to be with me and now you call me a liar?"

"I think you're hiding something. Mayhap to protect me."

He snorted as if she were silly. "You are a romantic, Elyn," he said with more than a touch of sarcasm. "You always have been. You . . . you make more of any situation than there is."

"Brock." She reached across the small

space between the horses and grabbed his destrier's bridle.

"Hey! Watch out!"

Her own mount tried to shy away, but Elyn held on to the reins with a firm hand. "Tell me."

The stallion tossed his head, but she clung on desperately and both animals pulled up short. "Before we go another step, I want you to tell me what's on your mind, what's been bothering you."

In the dim moonglow she noticed his handsome face tense, his lips pinch. He avoided her eyes. A cold chill settled in her heart.

"Now!"

He was wrestling with a decision; she saw it in the moonlight. Before he made the damning admission, Elyn felt it, like a snake uncoiling in her gut. "It's Wynnifrydd," he admitted.

The snake struck. Bit hard. "What of her?" Elyn demanded, an image of Brock's scrawny, shrewish intended coming to mind. By the gods, she hated that wretched woman.

Again, Brock hesitated. Looked at the moon, then centered his eyes on her again, and in that instant she knew. Oh, God, she knew. She closed her eyes, wished she'd never asked the question, tried to block out the sound of his admission, but over the moan of the wind and the horses breathing, his voice rang clear as church bells. "She's pregnant, Elyn."

Her heart squeezed and she nearly passed out. In a voice she didn't recognize as her own, she asked, "The baby. Is it yours?"

Another damning silence.

"Nay," she whispered, shaking her head. He couldn't have betrayed her. Not again.

But he nodded curtly. " 'Tis mine."

"Why do you lie to me?" she gasped, refusing to believe him. This had to be some twisted, painful joke.

"I'm sorry, Elyn." Regret was heavy in his words.

"You're sorry? That's all you can say?" Her horse pranced nervously. Angrily, Elyn jerked on the reins. "No! You're lying! Or . . . or *she's* lying."

"Elyn —" His voice caught with reproach, and the icy wind wrapped around Elyn's heart.

"This can't be! It can't!" A dozen knives ripped through Elyn's soul. Thunderous denial roared through her brain. "You and me. 'Tis what we planned. 'Tis how it's supposed to be."

"I'm sorry," he said again and sounded miserable, but she didn't care. Pathetic, hideous cur! His betrayal burned through her. *Just like before!*

Elyn's jealousy, always easy to arouse, now threatened to overtake her. "That's not good enough," she hissed. "What were you thinking? Why . . . why were you with her?"

"It . . . 'twas a mistake. It just happened."

"Just happened? Breeches just happen to become unlaced — is that what you're trying to tell me? Tunics just happen to fall to the floor? You just *happen* to bed another woman?"

His silence condemned him.

"You're — you're certain that she's with child? That this is not some scheme of hers?" Elyn asked, sounding bitter even to her own ears. But her heart was breaking into a million pieces, shattered on the ominous stones of weakness and betrayal. Oh, Lord, the pain. Brock . . . how could he do this? How could he do it to her, the woman he'd vowed to love, when she'd given up so much for him?

"The baby will be here by summer."

"But —"

" 'Twas a mistake," he admitted, his throat working.

"You should have told me," she said, and the words seemed empty. Hollow. Spoken from someone else's mouth. The urge to vomit was overwhelming. Bile climbed up her throat.

"I only found out this week past," he said, but she barely heard it over the echo in her mind. She felt as if she were in a dark cavern, one with no escape. She couldn't breathe. Her stomach roiled. With all her might, she tamped down the urge to lose its contents. She had to get away. Now. She couldn't face him, couldn't let him see her tears, couldn't stand to hear any more.

Releasing the stallion's bridle, she dug her heels into her mare's sides. With a firm yank on the jennet's reins, she twisted the mare's head around. The high-strung horse responded, springing into a wild gallop.

Where to go? What to do? The mare stretched out, racing faster, night-dark trees rushing by in a blur.

"Elyn!" Brock called after her, but she couldn't face him. Wind stung her eyes, bringing fresh tears. The hood of her cloak fell off, her hair tumbling free as the jennet's strides lengthened further, flinging mud, iron-shod hooves pounding the wet ground.

Elyn's heart was leaden, her soul destroyed. She'd given up everything for him. *Everything*. Her life. Her home. Her heart. Her virginity. And he'd abused her trust so carelessly. With Wynnifrydd.

The road forked and she edged her mare toward the left, away from Lawenydd. She couldn't return and face her father, nor her sister . . . Poor Kiera had married the bastard from Penbrooke.

No, you did. He's your husband. Kiera just said the words in your stead. You, by right and intention, are the Lady of Penbrooke. . . . It had been only two days since she had left

Lawenydd and left Kiera to marry and deal with Penbrooke . . . could she return? Could her sorry excuse of a plan actually work?

But it mattered not. Not after Brock's betrayal. How could he have slept with Wynnifrydd? After all the times they had laughed at the skinny woman's expense.

Mayhap Brock and Wynnifrydd had laughed at your expense. What makes you think you were so special to him? Why would they not, after a night of passionate, heart-pounding love-making, have found humor in your pathetic love for a man betrothed to another?

The pain in her chest pounded. She rode blindly. Somewhere behind her she heard the sound of hoofbeats, loud and clamoring, faster and faster. So he was chasing her. That mattered little. She didn't want to face Brock now . . . couldn't look into his Judas eyes. Nor could she see anyone. Her stomach ached, her head thundered, and she knew firsthand how easily love and hate could be confused.

At the next bend in the road, she forced the mare to veer right toward the river that cut deep through this section of the woods. A few swift strides and they were crossing a narrow bridge, the jennet's hooves clattering noisily on the boards. Beneath the bridge, the river, black as night, roared and rushed as it flowed to the sea.

An escape, she thought wildly, though the

hoofbeats sounded closer.

On the far end of the bridge, she pulled her horse up and, while the mare breathed heavily, guided the animal down the steep bank toward the sound of the icy water tumbling over stones and boulders. Yes, the river. She could hide there, then follow the waterway along its banks.

But the sweating, nervous mare fought the bit. Rolled her eyes, tossed her head, and stumbled. Elyn pitched forward, scrabbling for the pommel as the mare caught her footing.

Heart racing, Elyn righted herself in the saddle, then reined the horse to a quick halt, hiding on the steep bank beneath the span of the bridge. Surely Brock would think she'd ridden onward. Certainly he wouldn't suspect that she'd stopped here.

Breathing hard, ears straining, she listened for her pursuer.

Hoofbeats reverberated through the forest. Elyn bit her lower lip. Tears rolled down her cheeks. She didn't bother brushing them away. Her mare stiffened as the stallion's racing hooves hit the bridge, iron-hardened hooves ringing frantically over the old boards. Elyn didn't dare breathe as Brock passed overhead. *Traitor*, she thought, *lying bastard! How could you?* Misery filled her soul.

His steed's hoofbeats faded as he rode deeper into the woods, farther into the distance. She listened hard until she could no longer hear any sound of his retreat over the rush of the river's current and the whistle of the winter wind.

'Twas over.

All her dreams turned to dust.

All her plans for naught.

She'd been a fool. A pathetic, love-sotted fool. Kiera had been right, she realized belatedly. There was no such thing as true love.

She climbed down from the horse, clambered over some rocks, and bent over. Her stomach contracted as she vomited. Over and over again until, weakened, she fell to her knees in the mud and stones.

She'd not even told him that she was carrying his babe, that though Wynnifrydd might indeed be pregnant with his child, so was she.

Brock and Wynnifrydd. Brock and Wynnifrydd. Brock and . . . oh, Mother of God, she couldn't believe it. How could he do this to *her?* Had she not stood beside him, loved him with all of her heart, forgiven him when once before he'd lied and betrayed her? Her fingers curled in the wet grass and mud. Pain blistered through her heart. *Fool, fool, fool. He and that* . . . *that skinny, smug worm of a woman.*

"Bastard!" she cried, scooping up dirt to shake in one fist. "Bastard, bastard, bastard!"

'Twas too much to take all in one night.

And the Judas hadn't told her on the first night at the Gamekeeper's Inn, oh, no. He'd waited. Bedding her at will for a full day. Waiting until she'd dragged the words from his cowardly lips.

He was worthless.

He always had been.

By the saints, she couldn't think of it, not now.

He deserved cold, hard Wynnifrydd with her icy eyes.

But he's the father of your child.

Fresh bile rose in her throat. Gritting her teeth and determined that no man would destroy her or her unborn babe, she pulled herself upright. Her mouth tasted foul. Her spirit was blackened, she was certain, beyond repair. The smell of the river filled her nostrils, the cool air of winter night pressing against her skin. Small sobs tore from her throat. Her life was ruined. She'd never been one to cry, but alone in this dark, cold night, she let loose all the pain and wailed, pounding her fist against her leg. *Ogre! Unfaithful, lying ogre!*

Images of her time with him burned through her mind. Their secret trysts where they seemed the only two people in the world, their passionate lovemaking, stolen hours wrapped up in each other, their plans of defying their parents and rebelling against tradition . . . all a lie. Because of Wynnifrydd.

Skinny, pallid, whiny Wynnifrydd, who could not hunt, nor ride, nor even smile. Barely seventeen, she seemed already a shriveled prune. To think that Brock had taken her to his bed . . . Elyn shuddered in the wintry forest, but vengeance burned bright in her heart.

Brock would rue the night he had seduced Wynnifrydd. They would both suffer. With the moon as her witness, Elyn vowed to make Wynnifrydd's life pure hell.

Holding on to the reins, she edged farther down the steep bank to the sandy loam by the river. There, between two rocks, she scratched a rune in the sand, a crude drawing she'd observed once while watching Hildy. It was the rune of separation, a sticklike image, an X with opposing straight lines.

In her mind she conjured up an image of Brock holding Wynnifrydd, kissing her, undressing her . . . no! Not after what Elyn had gone through, what she'd sacrificed for her one true love. Angrily, she spit upon the rune and swore. "May you both bloody rot in hell," she muttered, and turned her back on her handiwork. She scrambled up the bank and started to swing into the saddle again just as she heard the sound of a horse approaching. From the direction in which Brock had disappeared. Damn!

Her mare snorted and pricked her ears.

"Shh." Elyn touched the animal's velvet-soft nose, but the anxious mare sidestepped and minced.

The hoofbeats grew louder. Horse and rider were fast approaching.

Elyn would have to hide under the span again. She pulled on the reins just as an owl hooted and flapped its great wings overhead.

The mare started.

"Whoa —" Too late, the frightened animal reared.

Elyn's arm jerked upward. Hard. One sharp hoof hit her chin with a hard crack. "Ow!" Pain splintered in her jaw. The reins slipped from her fingers. Her boots slid on the muddy ground. Elyn fell backward, tumbling down the steep bank toward the inky black water. Desperately, scrabbling with her fingers, she tried to gain purchase.

"Elyn!" Brock's voice cut through the night.

The mare neighed shrilly.

She caught hold of a root. Held fast.

"Elyn!"

Oh, Brock, you miserable cur of a man. Her throat was thick, her arm aching as she tried hard to regain her footing. But her boots slipped in the slick mud. She tried to clutch harder, to hoist herself upward. But the root snapped and she tumbled backward, rolling upon the hard rocks, unable to stop herself, scraping and banging against stone and earth and roots. She scrabbled for a handhold, slid ever faster downward until she splashed into the icy, swift river.

Water as cold as demon's piss dragged her down, pulling at her clothes, carrying her into the swift current. Shivering and gasping, screaming, she fought and flailed, stared back at the bridge as she bobbed in the frigid torrent of a river. Through a swirling, raging blur, she saw him. The lone rider holding fast to the reins of his mount. Moonlight played upon his features and she recognized Brock, the traitor who had seduced her and turned against her.

I loved you. You pathetic bastard, I loved you! Then she was pulled under.

Chapter fourteen

Where the devil was Brock? Wynnifrydd tried to make conversation with Brock's father, but Nevyll of Oak Crest was half dead, a lord who should have long ago stepped down and let his son rule. She walked with the old man around the sorry excuse of a keep with its crumbling walls and overgrown gardens and pathetic workers. Oh, they were a miserable lot, and when she became Lady of Oak Crest, she intended to change things.

The first thing she planned was to find new servants who knew how to behave, who showed proper respect, who bowed and curt-sied and *hurried* to do the tasks she com-manded, instead of these lazy creatures who barely acknowledged her. Take that slovenly woman who tended to her while she was vis-iting. Daisy. A wretched beast with crooked teeth, ferretlike eyes, and a nose that twitched as if she could sense her own bad smell.

Wynnifrydd shuddered at the thought of the fat woman combing her hair or helping her into her dresses. She'd almost rather do the job herself.

As they made their way to the chapel

through a thick mist, she noticed a few of the workers leering at her. Hideous idiots with ogling eyes, they seemed to undress her as she passed. Two men pretended to be thatching the roof of one of the dingy huts; another peered at her as he honed an ax against his whetstone. From beneath an overhanging brow and an uneven fringe of reddish hair, his eyes followed her, his thick lips curving evilly. She hastened her step along the stone path that curved toward the chapel.

Even the House of God appeared worn and eroded, the stone walls rough and covered in years of dust and dirt, the door hanging at an angle from its jamb. Nearby, pigs were rooting and grunting and a boy with a stick chased after a snarling speckled bitch and four scrawny, yipping whelps.

Baron Nevyll didn't seem to notice that the dogs nearly ran her over. He too was a useless, tired man. It was no wonder his servants were unfit; they had a pathetic example in Nevyll of Oak Crest. She wondered how this man could possibly have sired a strong, strapping son such as Brock. 'Twas like night to day. She could only think that Brock's mother was a strong woman, one with fire, one with passion, for she couldn't imagine Lord Nevyll having ever been a warrior or a leader.

Unlike his son. A tall, well-muscled man with snapping green eyes and a fierce, uncompromising countenance. A man who once he had touched her had branded her as forever his.

"Come along," Baron Nevyll whispered in his creaky, irritating voice. "Let us speak to the priest about the upcoming wedding."

"Yes, let's," she said with a smooth, comforting smile as she sidestepped a puddle. The old goat. Nevyll of Oak Crest had agreed to the wedding only because of the dowry attached to her. And even Brock had been swayed by the wealth of Fenn, though Wynnifrydd preferred to think that her bridegroom was marrying her because he loved her.

But there was Elyn to consider. Brock had always had an eye for that one. 'Twas lucky that Elyn had been pledged to Kelan of Penbrooke.

As she entered the chapel Wynnifrydd glanced over her shoulder in the direction of the stable, where a young boy was whittling and another dozed beneath the overhang of the building. Lazy, lazy curs. Wynnifrydd pondered how she would take care of them and all the other disgusting, useless creatures as soon as she was married.

Surely Brock would return today, as it had been a couple days since Elyn's wedding, if that was where he had been. That particular thought lodged painfully in her mind. His "hunting excursion" seemed like a weak excuse for something darker. Something nefarious. Perhaps he had tried to stop Elyn from marrying Penbrooke . . . but if so, he'd failed, for already Wynnifrydd's spies had returned to Oak Crest, a mere day from Lawenydd, with the news that Elyn was married and on her way to Penbrooke.

Good.

The priest, a fat, shuffling man with a sickly smile stitched to his lips, was hurrying toward her, past the pews, the few candles flickering as he passed. He extended his fleshy hands, making her skin crawl.

"Welcome," he said, and she noticed the thin web of veins running from his bulbous nose to his cheeks. No doubt he drank more of the castle wine than he should have. Well, that would change, of course. He took her hand in both of his and she forced herself not to withdraw from him.

"Father Duncan," she whispered. "Please, tell us of the service for the wedding."

The priest glanced from her to the baron.

"Should we not wait for Sir Brock to return? Where is he?"

Good question, she thought, though she wouldn't voice her concerns. She couldn't help the suspicion that crept through her brain, the suspicion that he was, even at this moment, with another woman.

Kelan drove his men hard, and Kiera felt that she was going to die of exhaustion as she clung to the saddle pommel and guided her mount. The group bound for Penbrooke had not been able to leave Lawenydd until nigh midnight, though Kiera's father had pleaded with Kelan to await morning. But Kelan and Tadd would not hear of delaying their journey with their mother so perilously close to death's door.

They had not stopped until the following evening, when Kiera almost collapsed from fatigue.

Surviving on little food and with only a few hours' rest, Kiera's entire body ached. It had now been three days since she took her sister's place at the altar, and their journey was far from over.

The beasts were muddy and tired, the handful of men grumbling, especially the big, oafish Orvis, whom she sometimes caught staring at her — not leering, just looking at her as if she were some kind of puzzling creature. Throughout most of the journey the rain had been incessant, a steady cold drizzle that spat from a leaden sky.

Kiera was miserable. And weary. She'd had only one short night of sleep with Kelan. In their hastily pitched tent they had made love, sleeping only after they were both sated, and rising a scant three or four hours later to ride again. 'Twas but a few days since she'd donned Elyn's wedding dress and knelt at the altar to become

Kelan's wife, but in that time she'd slept little.

Nor had she told him the truth. Each time she'd tried to explain about the vials, she had been interrupted. Kelan, preoccupied with his mother's health and the ride, had not mentioned them again. He'd become distant. Whenever he looked upon her there was a dark mistrust in his eyes. Worse yet, she thought as she rode her once-spirited mare, lying had become second nature to her. She'd deceived her father, insisting that she had to go with Elyn to help her "settle into" her new role as the Lady of Penbrooke. And she'd taken advantage of him by slipping away and then, astride her horse at Kelan's side, waving as if she were Elyn, knowing that with his feeble eyesight, in the darkness and the confusion of horses and men, he would not realize what she was doing. If he had any questions, Hildy would have explained that she could see Kiera on one horse and Elyn on another.

There was no doubt that her soul would burn in hell for all her deceptions. Someday, she would have to right her wrongs.

Then find your sister and tell the truth.

Bone tired, her hood pulled high enough to hide her eyes from the soldiers riding to her left and right, Kiera clucked encouragement to her weary gray palfrey and watched the drops of frigid rain drip from her nose. She'd spent the past two hours contemplating telling Kelan the truth as soon as they reached Penbrooke. Or should she wait until she'd found Elyn and avoid the confession? Would it be better to blurt out what had happened and beg his forgiveness, or should she bide her time until she was certain she knew what had happened to the woman he'd supposedly married?

A wagon creaked behind her, and the opinionated priest who had married them insisted upon trying to make conversation.

"You'll love Penbrooke," Father Barton said for what seemed the dozenth time that afternoon. " 'Tis a lovely keep. Larger than Lawenydd by twice, nay, thrice, and busy . . . oh my, teeming with trade, it being on the main road and all. And the lord's chambers . . ." He clucked his tongue at the magnificence of the baron's quarters. " 'Tis five rooms, all connected on the highest floor of the great hall. Tapestries and rush mats specially woven, the like of which ye've never seen, I'll wager." He waited as if expecting a response, as the horses slogged on through the mud.

She sensed him staring at her, wondering about this odd woman who was Kelan's bride. She continued to look straight ahead, hoping that only her nose, red from the cold and dripping rainwater, was visible.

"And it's not just the great hall," he added

when she held her tongue. "The chapel, ah, 'tis a pleasure to hold mass there. A finely carved altar and gold vessels and . . . well, you'll see soon enough, as we're near now . . ."

He droned on and on about the grandeur of Penbrooke. The stables were larger than he'd ever seen, with a training ring attached; the kitchens were vast, requiring dozens of workers; the tailor was an artist of the highest order; the hounds were cunning and the best hunters in all of Wales; and the steeds were of some private, incredible lineage that ensured they were the swiftest and strongest in all the land.

Not to mention Kelan's family. His sisters were the most beautiful, well-mannered, and kindhearted in the surrounding baronies. Oh, and they knew their place. Kelan's brother, Tadd, though a bit of a ladies' man, was a fierce, clever warrior, an incredible strategist. Then there was Baron Kelan himself. The old priest practically genuflected at the mention of his name. Without a doubt Kelan was the shrewdest businessman, the fairest judge, the most caring, responsible baron in all of Wales and certainly England as well, considering how brutish the English were.

Kiera's head was spinning with all of the blessings attributed to Elyn's new family. She wanted to tell the old man to be silent, but didn't. He was, after all, a priest, so she didn't respond. The less anyone knew her, the more likely Elyn, wherever she was, could step into her place, though as each day passed Kiera knew that the chances of her sister's return were shrinking to almost nothing. And there would be little chance of a switch now — she had accepted that; she and Elyn would have to explain why she'd pretended to be Kelan's bride and suffer the consequences.

She let out a weary sigh.

"What is it, my child?" the priest asked from astride his mud-spattered mount, a once-white, even-tempered mare. "You seem troubled."

" 'Tis nothing."

"Ah, well, if you can't talk to me, then who? I know 'tis difficult to leave a family. Aye, I had a hard time of it myself when I joined the priesthood. Yes, and I know that marriage . . . well, can be a trying change. But the baron, he's a good man. Oh, he had his problems in the past, but that rebellion, 'tis long behind him now."

She wondered about Kelan's "problems" and "that rebellion" but didn't ask, and the priest, as if he realized he'd said too much, didn't elaborate. They rode onward but he wasn't one to keep his silence.

"Should you need any comfort, m'lady, please seek me out, and I will pray with you, or for you."

"Thank you," she said, hoping to end the conversation. It had carried on for longer than she thought, Kiera realized as she saw that daylight, through the wet gloom, was fast fading. Staring straight ahead, she watched Kelan ride. Astride a bloodred destrier, he sat arrow straight, his wide shoulders unbowed as he rocked with the steed's steady gait. She couldn't see his face from this angle but knew it was probably etched with the same worry it had been since Tadd had given him the grave news of their mother's impending death. From the moment of learning of Lady Lenore's plight, Kelan had driven man and beast mercilessly in an effort to return to Penbrooke before she passed on. Kiera only hoped that they would make it in time.

"Can we not but rest a while?" Orvis asked, pulling his fatigued destrier sidelong to Kelan. " 'Tis weary the men be and we've ridden so hard we are now but a day's ride from Penbrooke."

Kelan looked at the darkening sky, then at Orvis.

"And think of the lady. She's got grit, I'll give her that — she's not complained — but she needs to rest a bit."

Kelan frowned darkly. He was driven. Wanted to keep riding. But he felt the fatigue in his own mount and had cast more than

224

one glance over his shoulder to see Elyn riding silently on. Half the time she was listening to the old priest prattle on, the rest, as Orvis had mentioned, without complaint.

He knew he'd ignored his new bride, mayhap even punishing her for her deception. But then there were the cursed vials he'd found in the bedchamber and Elyn's own reticence about explaining them. Aye, he thought, his fingers twisting in the reins, let her suffer.

"We ride on," he growled, feeling like an ogre. What was he attempting to do? Kill his horse? Turn the men against him? All for what? Yes, he had to get to his ailing mother's bedside, but there was more to it. He was trying to prove to his wayward wife that he wouldn't put up with her lies. For all he knew she may have tried to poison him, murder him as he slept.

If so, it didn't work, now did it?

And if she hated you so much, would risk an attempt on your life, why then had she come so eagerly to your bed?

Images of their lovemaking burned through his mind. He remembered the taste of her, the feel of her skin, the thrill of her tongue running upon his shoulders and back. Had not her fingers lovingly explored him, had not she fired his blood as no other woman had? By all that was holy, what was he to do with her?

"Lord Kelan." The priest had ridden

closer. " 'Tis dark and time to rest. Even God set aside a day of rest."

"Aye," Kelan ground out. He was anxious to return to Penbrooke, but not at the expense of his men. "We'll camp at the river for the night."

"Praise God," Father Barton muttered, and Kelan felt a tiny jab of guilt when the riders pulled up at the river and he saw Elyn nearly collapse off her horse. No woman, even one who lied to her husband, deserved to be put through such a grueling ride. His soldiers had complained mightily in the last two days of riding at a breakneck pace, but his new wife had never so much as uttered one word against him.

The past two days Kelan had ridden so fast and hard as to cut half a day from their journey.

Still, he hoped they were not too late, that his mother was still alive, and though long ago he'd given up his faith in God, he sent up a prayer for Lenore of Penbrooke's life.

He ordered the men to their tasks. Within the hour a campfire was roaring beneath the carcasses of three unlucky hares and a small pig sizzling upon two spits. Fat drizzled and steamed in the moist night and a jug of wine was passed among the men. Elyn sat on a flat rock, still within the circle of firelight, a bit distant, apart from the soldiers, not yet accepted. Only Father Barton made an effort to speak to her, but even he, at last, gave up.

"Trouble in the marriage already?" Tadd asked, sipping from the jug and eyeing his new sister-in-law.

"No trouble." Kelan pried one of the hares off its spit with his knife.

"If she were my wife I would have already taken her to my tent and pallet and —"

"She's not your wife," Kelan reminded him gruffly and, despite his anger with his bride, carried part of the meat to her. "You must be hungry," he said. "And tired."

"We all are."

Her gaze met his in the firelight and his groin tightened. As weary as she was, there was still a spark in her eyes, a bit of rebellion that he found fascinating. "Mayhap you would rather eat in the tent."

"If that would suit you," she mocked, and lifted a precocious eyebrow. "For that is what this has all been about, has it not? The long hours in the saddle, the punishing gait. 'Tis to keep me in my place. And so, as you request . . ." She gathered herself and, head held regally, made her way to his tent.

A few men had heard the exchange and didn't bother to hide their smirks. Orvis cleared his throat. Tadd grinned. Kelan was left holding the damned meat — his peace offering — and grinding his teeth. As his men watched, he followed her into the tent.

She was seated on the pallet, her cloak

pulled tight around her.

"It would be wise," he said, trying to keep his voice steady, "for you to be respectful."

"Would it?"

"I will not accept any insubordination from you."

"Is that so?"

He crossed the short distance between them and loomed over her, still holding the damned piece of burned meat. "Aye. I'll suffer no disrespect from you, wife."

"As I have from you?" she shot back. "You have treated me more as a servant than a wife."

"Mayhap that is because I expect to trust a wife." He placed the meat upon the pallet and walked out of the tent before his temper was lost to him completely. The tent was too close, too intimate, with the firelight playing through the thin walls. 'Twould be better to leave her be for the night, for even now, angry as he was with her, he felt his member begin to rise. Just being close to her stirred far too many emotions, too many feelings at war with each other. The men were trying and failing not to look in his direction. He grabbed the jug of wine and took a long pull. Once the men had dispersed to their tents and were snoring off the long ride, then he would deal with his headstrong wife.

She shouldn't have baited him. Kiera knew

she'd pushed him too far, ridiculing him in front of his men, but she was tired, hungry, and furious at the way he'd treated her.

What do you care? He's not your husband.

That thought only made things worse. She finished eating alone in the tent, wiped her fingers as best she could, then wrapped her cloak around her and pulled the fur blanket tight to her neck. The pallet was lumpy, but at last she was warm, and though she intended to stay awake, to wait for Kelan's return, to at least try to find some grounds for a truce between them, her eyelids were heavy. Exhaustion had taken its toll and she soon fell asleep.

She didn't hear him return, didn't know that he'd slipped onto the small mattress with her, only became aware of him when she felt a cold hand upon her breast.

She sucked in her breath, but as soon as he kissed the back of her neck, his lips as warm as his hands were cold, her blood began to heat. She was too tired to resist, and though she knew things were far from settled between them, that she was weak where he was concerned, she turned in his arms and kissed him full upon the lips.

After all, what did one more night of love-making matter?

They'd ridden for hours, when the soldiers' horses' ears perked forward and their gaits seemed more lively.

Kiera, too, felt the excitement. She closed her mind to the night before, to the passion she'd been unable to allay. She couldn't dwell on the mistake, not now.

Kelan's band was no longer alone. Groups of travelers appeared on the road as they closed in on Penbrooke. Huntsmen and soldiers, peasants lugging huge baskets, older children running along the muddy ruts while younger ones clung to their mothers' skirts. Oxen, horses, and mules slogged onward, straining against their harnesses and yokes, pulling heavy carts laden with crops, goods, and trinkets.

The muddy road curved through thickets of oak and spilled into fields surrounding a keep the likes of which Kiera had never seen. The rain had stopped, and the sight before her seemed nearly enchanted as a pale winter sun cast rays against the castle and its surrounding grounds. Kiera had been certain the old priest had been exaggerating when he'd spoken of Kelan's home, but she'd been wrong. Penbrooke was a massive, sprawling castle sculpted from light gray stone. Eight square towers spired high into the sky, and a wide curtain wall extended far from the keep to encircle and protect the town.

"Did I not tell you?" Father Barton asked proudly. "As fine a keep as any in the land."

Kelan quickened the pace, urging his

mount faster, and the other horses followed at a swift gallop. The wind tore at Kiera's hair, slapping her face, tearing the breath from her lungs, and she felt exhilaration mixed with that awful, never ending sense of dread. Hoofbeats ringing, the horses raced across a drawbridge and into the town teeming with merchants, peasants, animals, and children. As impatient as Kelan was, he had to slow as the streets were cluttered. Artisans and craftsmen sold their wares off tables. Peddlers and farmers had positioned their carts and wagons on the sides of the narrow streets and were offering their goods while people milled about, clogging the road.

Over the hum of conversation and the creak of wheels, one man's gruff voice caught Kelan's attention.

"Bless you and your new wife, m'lord!" The skinny man was holding a cap in his hands, worrying the tattered wool. " 'Tis sorry I am about your mother."

Kelan drew up hard. "My mother." His face drained of color. "She's not already passed on!"

"Nay, oh, nay, Lord Kelan. I meant not to alarm you, but to express me concerns."

"Thank God." Kelan managed a tight smile at the rail-thin man. "Thank you, Tom."

"Surely the physician will be able to help her." This time it was a woman who spoke. She was carrying a baby while a toddler clung to her skirts and peeked up at Kelan with shy eyes.

"Lady Lenore, she's a strong one, she is. She'll be fine," said another woman wearing a heavy apron and a scarf wound around her head. She was nodding rapidly, as if agreeing with herself.

"Me and the missus, our prayers be with ye and yer family, m'lord." This from yet another man in a stocking cap and huntsman's garb.

The apple-cheeked woman at his side offered a bit of a smile. "Welcome home, Lord Kelan. 'Tis better I feel, knowin' yer here in the keep. And congratulations on yer wedding." Her gaze skated to Kiera before returning to Kelan. "May the Father bless you and the lady with many sons."

Astride her mare, Kiera closed her eyes, wished she could shut her ears. She felt the gazes of the curious turned in her direction and she dared not meet even one.

"Is that the baron's new wife? A tiny thing she is," one cackling voice observed.

Kiera's eyes flew open, but she didn't glance in the direction of the conversation.

"Shh, Esme. She's got ears, y'know."

"Is it true she didn't want to marry Lord Kelan? By the saints, what's wrong with her? Has she no eyes? I'd kick me husband out of the bed any day of the week for an hour or two with the baron. If he's half the man he looks, he'd know how to keep a woman satisfied." Esme cackled, amused at her own joke.

"Hush! Are ye daft? She can hear ye!"

"Oh, bother," Esme, the cackler, muttered, her voice fading only to erupt in another nasty laugh. Kiera wanted to shrink into the sodden ground. What was she doing here, riding past the shops of the village? She was an outsider, and not only that but she was a fraud. These people — freemen and serfs, knights and merchants, husbands and wives — all seemed to show respect for Kelan, even revered him a bit. And she was a traitor amid them all, a liar of the highest order, a pretender.

Kelan led them through another gate with its yawning portcullis to the grassy area of the outer bailey. He urged his tired horse to a lope, passing an eel pond where ducks swam through the reeds. Tadd spurred his horse forward so that he was on his brother's heels with Kiera's mount close behind.

Across the bent grass, beneath bare apple and plum trees, past sheds that housed the livestock, the horses galloped. Goats bleated while pigs rooted and grunted from their pens, and everywhere men and women who had been working stopped long enough to nod at their lord or wave at some of the soldiers. They all knew that he'd left Penbrooke to marry. Now he had returned with his bride, and Kiera didn't dare imagine how he would feel when the truth was known by all these people.

She swallowed against a dry throat and tried not to think of the days ahead, of what would happen to her. To Kelan. To Elyn. Oh, dear God, where was her sister? Why had Elyn abandoned her and why, oh, why, did Kiera now feel a tiny bit of hope that she would never have to give up her misgotten title of Kelan's wife? What had got into her?

For the moment she could only follow Kelan through another gate to the inner bailey, where huts lined the walls, and the whitewashed keep, a fortress within these wide curtain walls, rose four full stories. The kitchen was detached, with a covered walkway leading to the great hall. The chapel, too, was separate, and the huts lining the inner walls were crafted uniquely, each more of a shop unto itself.

Kiera had never seen anything so formidable, nor so grand, as Penbrooke Castle. The long-winded priest hadn't stretched the truth an inch.

Kelan's mount slid to a stop at the steps of the great hall, and he was off the horse before the page, a pockmarked boy with wild hair, had reached him.

"Take care of Fate, Will," Kelan ordered, his expression grim.

"Aye, m'lord."

"And the lady's horse as well."

He had turned to help her dismount from her tired mount as Tadd vaulted from his steed, tossed the boy his reins, and headed up the stairs to the keep.

As Kiera slid from the saddle, Kelan reached up, helping her land on the soft turf. "Come with me," he ordered, taking her hand and starting for the stairs.

Tadd had already disappeared within and before the door could swing shut, a tall, imposing woman dashed outside. "Thank God you're here," she said tightly. " 'Tis mother . . ." Her voice cracked. "I don't think she will last out the night." Tears glistened in eyes as blue as a midnight sky.

"Sweet Jesus." A muscle worked in Kelan's jaw, and his grip on Kiera's fingers tightened.

"You'd best see her now."

"Aye." He glanced at Kiera. "This is my sister, Morwenna. Morwenna, my wife, Elyn."

"Oh." For the first time the taller woman glanced at Kiera and when she did, something sparked in her eyes. "Elyn?" Tiny furrows drew her eyebrows together as wind tore at her hair and rain drizzled from the sky. "Nay." Impatienty she glanced at her brother again. "I have no time for jokes, brother," she said angrily. "This is not Elyn of Lawenydd."

Panic gripped Kiera. Her heart nose-dived. Oh, God, all was lost!

"What do you mean, not Elyn?" Kelan demanded furiously.

"Just what I said." Morwenna's eyes scoured every inch of Kiera's face. "I've met Elyn. Years ago. At Castle Fenn. And you," she said to Kiera, "are not the same woman!"

Chapter fifteen

Oh, by the saints, no! Morwenna had met Elyn?

Kiera's breath stopped still, but her mind was whirling. She could not have her web of lies undone yet. Sweat collected on her back though it was winter cold outside. "Of course we met," she said quickly, silently praying she wouldn't say the wrong thing and strengthen Kelan's sister's doubts. " 'Twas the time when my father sent me there to learn the ways of being a lady." She managed a coy smile. "I think he thought it was a waste of time."

Morwenna's frown deepened and her blue eyes clouded suspiciously as she stared at Kiera. "Mayhap I'm mistaken," she said, though she didn't sound convinced.

"You are," Kelan asserted, and Kiera shrank inside. She wanted him to believe her, but not to the point that he would embarrass himself later. Oh, how she hated this deceit. If she could get her hands on her sister . . .

"Well, there is no time to get reacquainted now. We'll talk of it later. Mother has been waiting for you. Please, we must hurry."

Kiera forced her wooden legs to move. As she walked into the great hall, her lungs were so constricted she could barely breathe. What if Morwenna could not be convinced that Kiera was Elyn? What then?

The keep was twice the size of Lawenydd's. A fire raged in a grate that was large enough to hold a horse, brilliant tapestries decorated whitewashed walls, and a musician's balcony was perched high on the far wall. Tables were pushed to the side, and a raised dais covered with rush mats supported an intricately carved table that ran the width of one end of the hall.

Rushlights flickered, servants scurried down hallways, and the castle hounds, shaggy, spotted beasts, barked and bounded toward Kelan, their tails whipping so frantically that their backsides wriggled.

How would she ever learn how to navigate through these intricate corridors? How would she ever be able to escape the castle to find Elyn? 'Twas impossible. Ridiculous. Immensely so.

Kiera hardly had time to contemplate her sorry fate, for Morwenna snapped her fingers at a servant woman gossiping near a thick velvet curtain.

"Rhynn!"

The woman's head jerked up. She sported hair that had once been fiery red but now had begun to gray. Her eyes were tiny and her chin had a deep cleft. "M'lady?" she asked, her skin coloring a bit as she realized she'd been caught being idle.

"This is the baron's new wife, Lady Elyn," Morwenna said, her lips pinching a little as she said the name. "Please, Rhynn, look after her needs. See that she's made comfortable in her quarters. Have a bath prepared, food and wine brought up. Make certain that she is able to get settled and rested."

"Aye, m'lady," the servant replied, though her eyes sparked rebelliously.

Morwenna didn't notice, nor pay any attention. She was already following Kelan up the wide staircase, leaving Kiera alone with this tiny, dour servant.

"Come along upstairs, m'lady," she said. She didn't so much as crack a smile as she caught sight of a slight girl with long arms and skinny legs who was diligently sweeping the staircase. Rhynn repeated Morwenna's instructions, sending the girl after bathwater, food, and drink. "I apologize for Nell in advance," she said as the girl scurried away. "Not right in the head is she. Your rooms are this way." Kiera immediately disliked the judgmental servant and hoped that the rest of the staff was more pleasant.

Rhynn led Kiera up three flights of stairs, the very steps that Kelan had dashed up only moments before. She'd watched him take the stairs two at a time and felt a stab of disappointment that he never so much as glanced over his shoulder at her.

Of course he had to see his mother; she understood that. But as she glimpsed only a portion of this immense keep, spying chambers and dark corridors that angled from the staircase on each floor, her despair grew. How would she ever sneak away from the labyrinth that was Penbrooke? How would she ever find Elyn? Was she destined forever to live this lie?

And would that be so bad?

Of course it was! Oh, she must be so tired she could no longer think straight. She had to tell the baron the truth. Soon. Before things got worse. Even if it meant she would have to suffer the consequences. But not tonight. Not just yet. Not until she had everything sorted out in her mind and had exhausted every opportunity of finding Elyn.

"In here," Rhynn directed, opening the door to a spacious chamber with a wide, canopied bed that faced a grate nearly as large as the one she'd glimpsed in the great hall. Curved windows overlooked the inner bailey. Tapestries, sconces, and weapons adorned the walls, and sweet-smelling rush mats covered the stone floor. Aside from the bed there were two chairs, a short bench, and a small table crowded together. Two alcoves veered from the main chamber, each opening to spacious rooms. "I'll check on Nell and see that a bath is being brought up, but that might take a while, so mayhap you would like to rest," Rhynn said as she turned down the bed. "There's water in the basin, and the latrine is just down the hallway, outside the door to the left. Now, is there anything else I can do for you?"

"Nay. I'll be fine. Thank you, Rhynn."

"I'll be back shortly to see that your bag has been brought up. I'll make sure that the cook realizes you need food and drink. A stubborn one, he is, and doesn't like his routine disturbed, but *I'll* see that you aren't forgotten." Her eyes glittered a bit. "You'll find that some of the servants here are a bit lazy, not that I'm gossiping, mind you, but they'll need to be watched carefully. The laundress, oh, she's a slothful one, always barking orders to the girls, the cook is stubborn, and the butler samples too much of the wine . . . oh, well, I've said too much. I'll see to them all, I will, and you'll not have to worry, for I won't let any of them take advantage of you."

"Thank you, Rhynn," Kiera said again, her dislike for the woman growing, "but I think I can deal with the servants myself."

Rhynn's smile tightened as she walked to the door. "As you wish, m'lady, but if you need any help, or . . . information about the keep, I'm at your service."

"I'll remember that." Kiera didn't trust this servant an inch and was grateful when she slipped into the hallway and the door closed with a soft thud behind her.

Thank God.

Kiera was left alone for the first time in days. She wanted nothing more than to collapse on the bed, close her eyes, and squeeze out the world, but she couldn't. Not before she figured a way out of this mess. Her mission was to talk to every person she met and find out about the workings of Penbrooke. As lord, Kelan would have a daily round to attend to, business to conduct, and surely he would be behind in his work. And the vastness and the intricacies of the castle would provide her excuses for hours alone. In that time, she'd either find Elyn or tell Kelan the truth.

"I want to meet your bride before I die," Lenore insisted as she lay in her immense bed with her children gathered around her. She looked so frail and birdlike, barely a skeleton. The physician was tending to her, but he was a useless man who scurried about appearing busy while Kelan's mother was wasting away.

"Elyn is weary from the journey, but she will visit you in the morn."

Lenore moved her head upon her pillows. "Promise me you will have sons. Many sons," she whispered, and Kelan caught the stiffening of his sister Morwenna's spine. All of her life she'd carried the weight of not being firstborn, and not being male. He'd heard often enough what she thought of that. "Some of us are not so lucky as to have been born with a royal scepter dangling between our legs," she'd said baldly when she'd been dispatched to learning embroidery and Kelan had been taken out hunting.

"Women have other attributes," their father had explained. " 'Tis a clever woman's wiles that cause men to go to war or create great alliances. Use what you've been given wisely, Morwenna, and you, Kelan and Tadd, be careful with your . . . what did you call them?" he'd asked his eldest girl. "Royal scepters? They can be the source of much pleasure or intense pain."

Morwenna had always harbored a bit of jealousy against her brothers. When Kelan had been forced to accept this arranged marriage, Morwenna at seventeen had swallowed a smile and told him it was his "duty" to marry the woman that their father had chosen for him. It was the curse of the first-born. Bryanna, his middle sister, had thought it incredibly romantic that he was to set out and claim his bride. But then at fourteen she was forever lost in romantic dreams. And Daylynn, the baby, not yet twelve, had giggled openly at the thought of her wayward older brother, who had at one time been banished from the castle by their father, now doing the old man's bidding. Even from the grave, Lord Alwyn's will had been imposed.

Now, however, all Kelan's siblings were stone-cold sober. Even Daylynn's usually laughing eyes were sad as Lenore of Penbrooke's children surrounded her bed.

"Take your lesson from Kelan," Lenore rasped, her voice rough and frail. "He married a woman he didn't know, a woman he didn't want, but he did it because it was best for Penbrooke. For the family. All of you must do the same. Form strong alliances, have children. . . . oh, I wish I would be here to see them all." She blinked rapidly and Kelan's heart tore.

Though he and his father had always been at odds, he had loved his mother. She had always been his champion, forever forgiven him his mistakes, even during those dark days when he seemed lost to her. Now, as she gripped his hand in her fingers, he felt a deep pang of regret. For his willfulness. For his rebellion. The subject of Kelan's marriage had always been a sore point between him and his father. Alwyn had forever been plotting about who would make the best alliance and on one particular night had been heavy into his cups. As always, Kelan had balked at his father's scheme. His father and he had exchanged words and the argument had escalated to the point that Alwyn had drawn a sword. Kelan had taken up the challenge, defying the old man and showing him up, stripping him of his weapon. His father had been mortified, and Kelan had only made matters worse by toying with the older man, for which he'd been banished. Alwyn had borne the scar his eldest had inflicted upon him, a neat little cut on his chin, and Kelan regretted that little flick of his wrist that had drawn his father's blood.

He'd left Penbrooke, run afoul of the law, and finally, realizing that his father was dying, returned. The old man had forgiven him but demanded that he marry Elyn of Lawenydd, and Kelan had agreed. Reluctantly, like the prodigal son, he had been restored to his place of honor as firstborn and to this day Kelan was tormented by his past. Oh, if he could change things so that he had never turned his back on his family and nearly broken his mother's heart. She, who had never lost faith in him, had prayed for him, welcomed him back into the family with open arms and tears in her eyes. And now she was dying and there was nothing he could do.

"You will see them, Mother; you will see all of your grandchildren," Daylynn said fiercely, her throat working. "You will get stronger. Do not . . . do not talk like this." Daylynn's red-rimmed eyes looked from her mother to each of her grim brothers and sisters, seeking some kind of agreement. She found none. The others knew that Lenore was slipping into the next life. Daylynn's little chin wobbled as she touched her mother's shoulder. "Rest, Mother, please, and drink the broth — you will be fine."

"Ah, Daylynn . . . 'tis weary I be."

"Then sleep. We will leave so that you can rest and gain back your strength."

"Shh, Lynnie. 'Tis my time. To join your father."

"Nay!" Daylynn flung herself over the bed and broke into heart-wrenching sobs as she buried her face in their mother's frail chest, and Bryanna choked back a cry. "Do not give up, Mother. Do not leave us. Not yet. We . . . I need you," Daylynn whispered.

Wearily Lenore stroked Daylynn's dark tresses. " 'Tis best, daughter."

Kelan saw the lines of strain on his mother's pale face, the pain registering in her eyes. He glanced at Morwenna and she nodded, for they had always been close enough to know what was on the other's mind. "Come, Lynnie," she said softly. "Father Barton has returned from Lawenydd; let us leave Mother so that he may be with her."

"But —" Daylynn tried to protest.

"Shh. Mother needs her rest." Carefully Morwenna peeled her youngest sister from the bed. With Bryanna's help, she shepherded Daylynn from the warm chamber.

From her bed, Lenore watched them leave,

then turned tired, glassy eyes toward her two sons. "It is your duty . . . both your duties . . . to see that they marry well. Now . . . please leave me be. I'm so weary. I hate to wait but I'll meet my new daughter-in-law come morning."

As the maid hovered nearby, Lenore sighed and closed her eyes.

The knot in Kelan's gut tightened. He knew his mother was dying and accepted it, yet it was hard to lose someone who had held him dear all of his life. As he strode out of the room, he sent up a silent prayer for her soul and nearly tripped on the steward as he approached.

"M'lord, I hate to bother you, but if you have a minute," he interjected, falling into step with Kelan. He was shorter by a head and had to half run to keep up with the baron. "There are some disputes you need to see to," he said breathlessly, as if the faster he talked, the more likely Kelan would stop and listen. "The farmers to the south are grumbling about the taxes, and there is a quarrel on hunting rights, and the wardrober found the cooper's son filching spices, and —"

"Must this be settled right now?" Kelan snapped.

"But you've been gone for days and —"

"It will wait. Everything will wait." Kelan didn't break stride. "I'll meet with everyone tomorrow, after the daily round. Today I have much to attend to."

"I know, but the spices are expensive and the wardrober's angry. He trusted the boy and feels played for a fool. He's been losing spices for months, been certain it was Girlie Flout and had a talk with her. She burst into tears, denying it all and running to Lady Morwenna; then he up and catches Robert Cooper with ginger or caraway seeds in his pockets. He wants the boy's head, let me tell you."

"One more day won't matter," Kelan insisted. "Let Cooper stew about what I'll do to him."

"And what will that be?"

He spun on his heel and glared down at the shorter man. "I'll decide tomorrow. Is that all?"

"Nay, there are still robbers and cutthroats in the forest. Two days ago a visiting priest was attacked. Unharmed, but his horse was stolen. And yesterday one of the merchants was robbed on the road to the north, by a bend in the river, on his way to Black Thorn."

"Now are you finished?" Kelan asked crossly. He had no time for this. Not now.

The steward opened his mouth as if to say more but seemed to think better of it as he saw the impatience evident in Kelan's features. "Aye, m'lord."

"Good. As I said, I'll see to all the complaints in the morning." Kelan stormed down the stairs and out the door. He'd deal with the petty bickering, thievery, and robbery and whatever other problems the steward planned to lay at his feet tomorrow. As it was already twilight, his visit with his mother having taken most of the afternoon, he intended to have a servant watch over his mother. Then he would take a long bath, eat a hot meal, drink wine by the fire, and spend the rest of the night making love to his new wife.

Chapter Sixteen

Kiera sank to her neck in the towel-lined tub. Hot, fragrant water washed away the grime of the journey and the aches from her neck and back. A fire blazed in the grate and candles burned on the tables and mantel.

Elyn's gowns, freshly pressed, had been brought up and were hanging in one of the alcoves. Thankfully, dour Rhynn hadn't returned and the girl attending her, Nell, was a chatty, pleasant little thing with a quick smile, keen eyes, and ringlets framing an elfin face.

Nell washed Kiera's hair, all the while talking and gossiping without hardly taking a breath. Kiera closed her eyes and let the soothing water run over her, asking a few questions and trying to learn as much about the keep as she could.

" 'Tis glad we all are that the lord has taken a wife," Nell confided without the least bit of concern that Kiera might repeat what she said. "He's a handsome one, he is, and oh, many of the ladies who have visited Penbrooke have fancied him. I've seen it meself, but he . . . well, he had his troubles, you know."

"Troubles," Kiera repeated as the girl's small fingers massaged her scalp.

"Oh, 'twas a few years back. Two . . . nay, more like three or four. He and his father, Baron Alwyn, they had themselves a row the likes of which hadn't been seen between these curtain walls." She leaned closer, her voice lowering, so that Kiera could barely hear her. " 'Twas about a woman. Well, now, isn't it always? Baron Kelan — well, he weren't the baron then — he didn't like his father makin' alliances and plannin' his life. When it was suggested that he marry the Lord of Hawarth's daughter, oh, there was hell to pay. Baron Kelan refused and they got themselves into a sword fight of sorts. 'Twas an awful thing, with blood bein' spilt. Baron Alwyn, he ended up with another nasty scar on his chin, he did, from his son's blade. Lady Lenore was fit to be tied, but the old baron he up and banished his son . . . and . . ."

"And what?"

Nell hesitated. As if she'd suddenly realized she'd said too much. "I don't know if I should be talkin' behind the lord's back."

"I'm his wife," Kiera said, running a cloth along her arm to rinse off the soap and trying to hide the fact that she was desperate to know anything and everything about the man to whom she was married.

"I know, but —"

"Whatever you say, Nell, I swear it will go no farther."

"Not back to the baron. He's been good to me and me mum, kept us on when she was ailin'. He's a good man, he is, Lord Kelan, and I shouldn't be tellin' tales. No one knows if they're true or not anyway. It's just gossip."

"Then why would anyone care?" Kiera asked with a smile.

Nell bit her lip and stared into the sudsy water, then shrugged. "Well, 'twas a few years back when Baron Alwyn was still alive and . . . and there were rumors that someone had recognized his son as an outlaw, part of a ring of horse thieves and the like. No one believed the rumor until one of the crooks was caught with a stolen horse and he claimed the son of a baron had sold it to him."

"And that son was Kelan?"

"So the thief insisted even as he was walkin' up the scaffolding to be hung by his neck."

"What happened?"

"Lord Kelan, he eventually returned. By this time his father was near to dyin', but they patched things up, forgave each other, they did. Though, if ye ask me, the lordship's other son, Tadd, he didn't like it much. Thought he was going to become the baron. But then that one . . . well, he's got his own problems, let me tell you. It wouldn't surprise me if the two brothers got in to it. The lord, he's got himself a temper!"

The door opened and Kiera jumped. Water sloshed and Nell, already flustered, gasped at the sight of the very man she was maligning as Kelan filled the doorway. "Oh, m'lord," she said, blushing. "I was just givin' the lady her bath."

One of Kelan's dark brows lifted. "Thank you, Nell, but I think the lady can finish herself."

"But — her hair is wet and . . . and . . ."

Kelan walked into the room and Nell, her blush intensifying, scurried away just as Kiera reached for a dry towel. "Close the door behind you, Nell," he commanded, his voice deep and sending a chill down Kiera's spine.

Kiera was wary. The room seemed suddenly close, and she far too unclothed. Kiera did not forget that on top of the issue of the vials, she now had to somehow explain Morwenna's insistence that she was not Elyn. "If you'll give me a minute to dress."

"There is no need." He was crossing the room and she sank under the water. He'd seen her naked before, but never here, in his keep, with candles flickering brightly, the fire giving off a warm, seductive glow. 'Twas unsettling. At Lawenydd, she knew everyone; here she was a stranger. Isolated. With a man who thought he was her husband and knew she had lied to him.

"Did you rest?" he asked as he reached the tub. His eyes moved from her face to the aromatic water and, she knew, the slightly distorted view of her body.

"Nay. I had not time."

"After dinner, then."

"Yes. Are . . . are we not expected to dine with the others?"

"Aye, and this time, wife, you will accompany me and sit by my side."

"Then I should dress and —"

"Not yet." She glanced up at him and watched as he slowly rolled up one sleeve. "I don't think you're quite done with your bath." Plucking the towel from her hand, he stared straight into her eyes and flicked the towel onto the bed. "Mayhap you need some help." Slowly, he lowered his hand into the tank.

"You're going to wash me?" she asked, stunned, when she realized what he had planned.

"To begin with." His fingers grazed her breast and a shock wave zinged through her. Her eyes widened and he brushed his lips across hers. "You know, wife," he whispered, his fingers sliding down her wet abdomen, "there are secrets you have kept from me, lies you have told, and I know not what they are or why. I have wondered what to do about them." He feathered his fingertips across her inner thighs, and the water swirled around them. "I've considered all sorts of punishments." She swallowed hard as his hands caressed her nest, teasing and stroking while the water lapped deliciously. "But what I want most is the truth." Again he swept his lips across hers, and this time his tongue traced the outline of her mouth. Kiera strained upward to taste more of him and one finger slipped inside her.

She gasped.

"Like this, do you?" He touched her intimately. When she didn't respond, he leaned forward and kissed her on the lips lightly before trailing his tongue down her neck.

Her blood was warm as the surrounding water, her legs parting, her mind swimming with the need of him, all of him. She writhed, arching upward, one nipple breaking the surface. He captured it with his lips and suckled hard. She closed her eyes, her head spinning as he stroked her, his hand plying sweet, sweet magic deep within her, his mouth and tongue laving her already wet breast.

"Kelan," she whispered, writhing. "Please . . ."

"What, little one? Please what?"

His fingers found that incredible spot and she cried out. "Ooooh . . . please . . . more."

"Precisely what I was thinking." He bent over and dragged her from the tub, then carried her, dripping, to the bed. Cold air caused her nipples to tighten. Drips from her hair rained on him. Together they tumbled upon the bedclothes and as he pulled off his shirt, she fumbled with the laces of his breeches. He was hard. Straining. She felt his length, hot and pulsing, withdrew it from its bonds, and kissed him, stroking him, sensing his muscles tense.

"Oh, love," he whispered, his hands in her hair, his breathing shallow with restraint. "You are a witch, you know that . . . you've . . . you've cast a spell over me . . ."

And then he was without words, rolling her onto her back and parting her knees with his. He kissed a drop of water still clinging to her breast. She arched, ready. With one hard thrust, he claimed her and the world began to tilt again. Hot and wanting, she met his pace with her own eager rhythm. Her hands traced the muscles of his shoulders and down his back, along his spine, past the scars, one deeper than the others in his hard flesh.

Faster and faster she spun. Candlelight swirled. Blurred. Kelan's face, his incredibly handsome face, swam in her vision, burned through her brain, and for a fleeting instant she thought she loved him. Would that be so wrong?

With a sharp jolt, she felt their souls fuse and become one. In that magical instant he cried out, every muscle in his body straining, every sinew tight. Kiera clung to him, her body convulsing as he spilled himself into her. With a rush of breath he collapsed, holding her tight, his shallow breath pulsing at her neck.

Her arms surrounded him.

His body slackened.

She thought for the briefest of seconds that she really was his wife and strangely, for no reason she understood, she felt a tear slide from the corner of her eye.

"Lord Kelan!" Thud. Thud. Thud. "Are you not coming down to dinner?"

Kelan opened one eye. The room was near dark, the fire having died, the woman beside him sleeping as if she would never waken. He brushed a curling lock of hair off her face and felt an emotion he didn't want to name. By the gods she was a beauty. She sighed and turned over, her lips moving. He wondered with a surprising bolt of jealousy if she was dreaming of making love and if so, who it was she was kissing.

"Lord Kelan?"

Again the pounding. Duty called. And his stomach growled. Playfully, he slapped his sleeping wife's smooth, white rump. "Time to waken."

She burrowed into the covers, and he leaned over and kissed her swollen lips. "Wake up, Elyn," he whispered, and her eyes flew open. He felt her tremble and the answering heat of his blood. As if it was second nature, she turned her face up to his, offering her lips.

"Lord Kelan?" the guard called through the door.

"I'll be down soon," Kelan yelled from the bed as his arms surrounded his wife, then added in a whisper only she could hear, "When I'm finished here."

In the end, they were late. For their first dinner. She'd plaited her hair hastily and donned one of the dresses she'd brought with her. The apple green silk rustled as she walked. The embroidered bodice was tight, the square neckline lower than she would have liked, but she felt radiant as Kelan's wife, no matter how false the title was.

"Hurry," he insisted, taking her hand as they hastened down the staircase. A loud buzz of conversation wafted throughout the corridors and seemed to carry with it the scents of roasted meat, baked bread, and all sorts of tantalizing spices. Kiera's stomach growled, for she was hungry. Yet the thought of meeting all of Kelan's servants, subjects, and family members was formidable.

As they reached the great hall, a trumpet sounded and a man with a deep voice announced, "Welcome back the Lord of Penbrooke and his new bride, Lady Elyn."

Kiera nearly tripped, yet Kelan smiled widely as, from the tables set up on the floor of the great hall, people rose and applauded, smiling as they took their place at the head table. Musicians played from the balcony, stopping only as Kelan greeted everyone within the hall and introduced her as "Lady Elyn of Penbrooke."

Kiera withered inside. She managed to smile and nod, but felt every bit the fraud she was. Hildy had been right; she should have told the truth before they left Lawenydd, for every day that passed made the truth more difficult to admit. The longer she played the part of Kelan's wife, the more likely his fury would rise, his shame and embarrassment double.

The feast was grand, course after course carried in by servants who wended through the peasants' tables to offer each succulent dish first to the baron and his new bride. Kiera died a thousand deaths knowing she was the reason for this incredible celebration. It was all she could do to force a smile and watch as stuffed heron and pike, salmon and roasted boar, custards, pies, and tarts, more food than Kiera could possibly eat, were brought before her. She sat wedged between Kelan and his brother, Tadd, the rogue who had ridden with them and now seemed amused that the Lord of Penbrooke had finally wed. Next to Tadd was Daylynn, a beautiful dark-haired girl who eyed Kiera as if she were an oddity, a person most rare. Another sister, Bryanna, was friendly and warm, though there was a sadness to her eyes, which Kiera assumed was because of their mother's ill health. But the person who worried her most was seated on the far side of Kelan. His sister Morwenna, who, while nibbling at her food, studied her new sister-in-law as they made conversation.

"So, you do remember Castle Fenn?" Morwenna asked, between bites of a fine fish pastry.

"Of course." Kiera nodded but felt the warning hairs on the back of her neck raise.

"And there was a squire there you fancied, wasn't there? Brock of Oak Crest?"

Kiera's heart dropped like a stone. Where was this conversation leading? "Aye, I remember him, I think."

"What happened to him?"

"I know not," she said quickly and plopped a jellied egg into her mouth in the hopes of ending the conversation.

Little lines of concentration formed between Morwenna's arched eyebrows. She fingered her knife. "Did I not hear that he was betrothed to Wynnifrydd, the Lord of Fenn's daughter?"

"Was he?" Kiera asked, lifting a shoulder and trying not to notice that any trace of merriment had left Kelan's face.

From the other side of her Tadd spoke up. "Aye. I'm sure of it." He motioned to a page to refill his mazer. "The wedding was planned for . . . what? This week, I think."

"This week?" Kiera repeated, her worries intensifying.

"Tomorrow, I believe." Tadd waited as the page filled his uplifted cup. "Thank you, John."

The floppy-haired page nodded, then, not once looking her in the eye, began refilling Kiera's mazer.

Tomorrow? Brock is slated to marry Wynnifrydd tomorrow?

Then what of Elyn? Had the wedding been called off? Or was Brock going through with the marriage? Kiera took a calming drink of wine. *Think, Kiera, think.* Where was her sister? Kiera had begun to worry that Elyn might not have returned to Lawenydd because she'd run off with the man she loved, that both she and Brock had spurned their intended spouses and ridden away to some unknown fate. At that private thought, Kiera became angry, then stupidly hopeful. Now, she had the quicksilver intuition of why her emotions had been at odds, for she could no longer deny the unthinkable idea that she was beginning to fall in love with Kelan.

Dear God in heaven. That ridiculous notion hit her hard and she nearly choked on her wine. *In love? With this stranger? A man I barely know? My sister's husband?* 'Twas folly. Worse than folly!

Now, with the fear that Brock was truly marrying Wynnifrydd, Kiera's worries redoubled. Had harm befallen Elyn? Or . . . even worse, had she somehow lost her life? An accident? A cutthroat in the forest? Her stomach squeezed painfully and it occurred to her that she might never know. Just as she'd never found out what had happened to Obsidian.

She was no longer hungry, her appetite having been chased away by worry. Yet support came from an unexpected corner.

"Morwenna, you and Elyn were at Fenn years ago; what were you, Elyn — around thirteen at the time?" Kelan's mouth was pinched, his jaw tight, yet he said, "What happened then, 'tis of no matter now."

"And we all know how things can change over the years, do we not?" Tadd asked, leaning back in his chair. With a careless smile, he looked at Kiera and winked slowly. "Your husband was not always the upstanding, honest man he is today, you know. There was a time when the baron was anything but law-abiding. 'Twas a good thing my father bribed the sheriff, or Kelan might well have ended up hanging from a noose rather than ruling a barony."

"He exaggerates," Kelan said, his eyes sparking as he scraped back his chair. "And as I said, what happened before matters not." His gaze moved from one upturned face to the next. "Lady Elyn and I are married." Kiera felt the color drain from her face. Oh, this was as bad as Hildy had predicted. Worse! Kelan lifted his mazer and the hall fell silent. "A toast," he proclaimed and glanced down at Kiera, then nodded in her direction. "To my wife, Lady Elyn of Penbrooke."

Chapter Seventeen

It was late in the day when Joseph slipped through the shadows of Oak Crest after hours of trying to locate Lady Elyn within the keep. Hildy had explained to him about Elyn's foolhardy and selfish plan. Before she'd asked, he'd volunteered to search for the stubborn lady. So far, he had failed. Three days had passed since the night Kiera, pretending to be her older sister, had left for Penbrooke. Joseph's gut tightened when he thought of what Lady Kiera must have had to endure with the Baron of Penbrooke, all for the sake of Lady Elyn. So what had happened to her? Where the devil was she? The answer, it seemed to Joseph, lay with Brock of Oak Crest. And so, hoping to find Elyn and drag her back to Lawenydd, he'd ridden as if Satan himself were chasing him. Unfortunately, Joseph had been unable to escape his duties for a full day, then it had taken another day to travel to Oak Crest, and today he had futilely spent his time spying, trying to hear word of Lady Elyn. As time passed he knew that he would be missed at Lawenydd.

Well, so be it.

Sometimes there was duty and other times duty had to be damned for a greater cause. And the search for Lady Elyn was the greatest cause of all.

He slid silently into the stables, exhausted, smelling the acrid odor of urine mixed with dust and the scent of horses — this, finally, was familiar territory. He'd grown up living with horses, and so he felt at home for the first time since leaving Lawenydd.

After riding hell-bent for a day and leaving his own mount in the forest tied in a copse of oak, he'd slipped through the castle gates with a group of peasants, then blended in with the farmers and merchants and peddlers setting up to sell their wares. He'd managed to search some of the buildings and the baileys, listening to craftsmen talk or the gossip of the women gathering eggs and hanging laundry. The castle was abuzz with the upcoming nuptials of the baron's son, Sir Brock, and Lady Wynnifrydd of Fenn.

"She's a bossy one, she is," one old crone had confided to another this morning as Joseph had found an ax and begun splitting firewood. Since it had been raining off and on for the past few days, he'd drawn his cowl over his head, and with his back to the women, no one had paid him any attention. "Sir Brock will have his hands full with that one."

"A pity," the other woman had sighed, "to

be married to a shrew." She'd laughed heartily while her friend had snorted. Joseph had hazarded a glance over his shoulder. The shorter, scrawny woman had filled her basket with eggs while the laundress had been hastily retrieving sheets before the rain began in earnest.

" 'Tis what he deserves, don't ye think? And then his father will be well rid of him. Sir Brock can become Lord of Fenn someday and it's good riddance, I say. He won't be botherin' us for a while, not until the Baron Nevyll, God preserve him, passes on." Sketching a sign of the cross over her chest, she'd stepped around a puddle and hastily tossed the half-dried clothes into a large basket. " 'Tis my guess that Lady Wynnifrydd will want him to stay on at Fenn as long as Lord Nevyll is alive. Have ye seen the way she looks down that long nose of hers, her nostrils flarin' an' all? It's as if Oak Crest isn't good enough for the likes of her." The laundress had snorted at this notion. "Nay, she'll not be wantin' to stay here a second after she's gotten that wedding band from Sir Brock."

Listening intently, Joseph had stepped beneath an overhang near the mason's hut and placed a chunk of oak upon the old stump that was marred by hundreds of scars from ax blades slicing into it.

"Then he can raise the skirts of the

wenches at Fenn and leave our girls alone. A randy one Brock is, and rough, I hear." The egg collector had raised her sparse eyebrows. "That's what Glyn told Beanie."

"Ach. The girls waggle their tongues too much. Especially Glyn."

"Nay, they waggle their hips too much and get themselves into trouble with the likes of Sir Brock."

"Well, he's Lady Wynnifrydd's pain now."

"And all the while I thought he'd marry Elyn of Lawenydd; she was sweet on him, I hear. My niece, she's a seamstress over at Lawenydd, and she swears Lady Elyn had her heart set on Sir Brock."

So that was it. Joseph gripped the ax, raised it over his head, and swung down hard.

Crack!

The dry oak had split. Two pieces had spun sharply off the stump, but the gossiping women had paid him little mind.

"If ye ask me, Lady Wynnifrydd and Sir Brock are made for each other. They'll make each other miserable, and that's just fine with me."

" 'Tis lucky for Lady Elyn that she didn't end up with him and married Kelan of Penbrooke instead. I know he was a black sheep and gave his father more than his share of gray hair, but compared to Brock, Kelan of Penbrooke's a prince."

The laundress had chuckled as she hoisted her basket onto one of her ample hips. "I'll have to be hangin' these in the shed," she'd muttered disgustedly under her breath. "I told Dellwynn that it would rain today, but would she listen? Oh, no. Not that one." Balancing the laundry, she'd marched off toward the great hall while chickens had squawked and scurried out of her path.

Joseph had heard other gossip as well, talk of the impending wedding, nasty remarks about the lordship's son, but never once had Elyn been mentioned again.

What to do? he'd wondered as he stacked the wood he'd chopped and cast a glance at the great hall. Joseph had considered confronting Brock, but decided the man would only lie or have him thrown into the dungeons or worse. Already he'd surreptiously scanned Oak Crest's herd of horses that he'd found in the outer bailey. There was no sign of Lady Elyn's mount, the missing mare. But he wasn't convinced that the feisty little horse wasn't hidden somewhere apart from the main herd.

While the stable master had been checking the hooves of a dappled stallion, Joseph had slipped into the open door of the stables. Now he moved quietly in the shadows. A few of the animals snorted, one nickered, and all the while there was the sound of hooves shuffling in the straw and the gentle snoring of a stableboy, his back propped against a post, his cap pulled down over his eyes.

With little trouble Joseph discovered the ladder leading to the upper loft and swung stealthily into the haymow, to settle into a spot in the corner. Noiselessly, he burrowed under the loose straw. Using his mantle as a blanket, he closed his eyes to rest and wait until dark, when he could move around more easily. If he found the mare, he'd take it as proof that Sir Brock had met Lady Elyn. If not, he'd continue looking for her.

And what if you find her? What are you going to do if she won't return to Lawenydd with you? Tie her with ropes? Shackle her? Force her back to her father?

"If needs be," he muttered under his breath. But first he intended to talk to the spoiled son of Oak Crest, regardless of the differences in their stations.

Standing at the fire in his chamber, Kelan fingered the vials he'd brought with him from Lawenydd. One of blood, the other empty. He was certain now that Elyn had used whatever was in the empty vial to make him drowsy, rather than poison him, to keep him in her bedchamber, though he didn't know why. The other . . . he knew not.

Did it matter?

Did she not pledge before God to be his wife?

Did she not come with him to Penbrooke and stand at his side?

Had she not met his mother this day, and was not Lenore pleased that she was his wife? Only Morwenna seemed not to trust her, and yes, there was something not right. The small vials in his hand were proof enough of that.

He glanced over his shoulder to his napping wife and his heart melted. Firelight played upon her white skin, turning it golden. Her dark hair was tangled on the pillows, framing a face he'd begun to love.

Love? That thought struck him hard. He wasn't a romantic, didn't believe in love. And yet this woman with her clever tongue, laughing eyes, and spirited lovemaking had found a way into his heart. He was lucky. Most marriages were for convenience only; the husband and wife only tolerated each other.

But . . . she'd deceived him. The vials were proof enough of her deception. His jaw grew so hard it ached. Why? Why had she lied to him? He could ask her again. Demand answers.

And what will that accomplish? A rift between the two of you? You are married. You agreed to this arrangement and you must make the best of it. Elyn is your wife and will be the mother of your children. Doubting her now is of no use.

'Twas time to start anew. To embrace this

marriage. To trust the woman who had vowed to be his wife. He tossed the vials into the fire. The full one broke, liquid oozing out and sizzling, smelling foul.

Kelan hoped it wasn't an omen of things yet to come.

"What do you mean you can't marry me?" Wynnifrydd demanded as she rolled off Brock's bed. He had arrived this morning, on their wedding day, and now this? She threw on her tunic and glowered down at him. "The wedding is in less than twelve hours. The guests have already begun arriving. My father has signed an agreement with yours, and we have a baby coming into this world! 'Tis far too late to change your mind." She was beautiful in her rage, standing above him, shivering with fury, pointing an uncompromising finger at his naked form. "If this is a joke, Brock of Oak Crest, 'tis a bad one. A very bad one."

He levered himself on an elbow and shook his head. " 'Tis no joke, but I can't marry you and keep the secret any longer."

"The secret? You mean that Elyn of Lawenydd was a ninny and ended up drowning?" she asked. "Is that the secret you're worried about? Because, Brock, I know you have many. Some more dark than even that one." Hitching her chin indignantly toward the ceiling, she folded her arms around her middle and her fingers drummed an agitated beat against her ribs. Oh, she was angry . . . but he could not appreciate the flare of her nostrils or the stormy clouds in her eyes. Not now.

"She died, Wynnifrydd," he said again. "Because of me."

"*You* didn't kill her. 'Twas an accident. So how does that affect the wedding?"

"She died running away from me when I told her I couldn't marry her."

"Then she was foolish!" Wynnifrydd said, exasperated. She walked to the fire and warmed her hands. "And what makes you so certain she died? I've heard through a traveling merchant that she married Penbrooke just as planned."

"Impossible. I was with her after the wedding," Brock admitted. Never in his life had he experienced the onus he felt now. Guilt was a new emotion, an unwanted burden.

"Then why does Penbrooke have a wife?"

"I think he married the wrong sister. 'Twas Elyn's plan that Kiera take the vows in her stead."

"Then *Kiera* is married to Penbrooke, but the baron thinks she is Elyn?"

"Yes, at least that's what Elyn's plan was," he said, rolling onto his back and staring at the crossbeams overhead. "Though legally Elyn would have been his wife. Oh, 'tis a mess and now . . . now she's dead." A heavy stone had settled in his heart for the first time in his life. 'Twas a weight that grew heavier with each passing day.

Wynnifrydd was unmoved, and he was beginning to think she had no soul. "Hear me out, Brock. Accidents are commonplace. They can happen to anyone. Anytime. And remember, we are in this together. Remember what I know of you. Things that your father would hardly dare believe and, should he find out, certainly banish you for. Do not ever try to cross me," Wynnifrydd warned. "If you do, I'll make sure you regret it for the rest of your life. We've planned this for a long time and now I'm carrying your child. I don't know why you're so concerned about Elyn. I should be angry with you for abandoning me to run off with that woman for a few days," she added bitterly.

"I had to explain to her that I was truly marrying you."

"Did you tell her that you loved me?"

"I told her the truth."

"Ah, ah, ah." Her voice rose an octave with each syllable. Wagging a finger back and forth, she walked closer to the bed. "Do you love me, Brock? Really love me?" she asked, leaning over him, her breasts visible above the neckline of her tunic and so near his face. Inviting him despite her wrath.

This was a trap; he knew it. Felt it in every one of his bones. And there was only one way out of it. Though he wasn't in the mood, he grabbed one of her wrists, pulled her atop him, and kissed her hard. "What do you think?" he asked.

"I — I think you would bed any woman to change the subject." Her voice was suddenly breathless, as he'd expected.

"Would I?" He smiled and cupped her rump. It did the trick. Feeling her tight ass, his manhood rose, stiffening in eager arousal.

"Y-yes. Oh, yes."

"But it is you I'm with," he said, and pulled her atop him, bunching her skirts and guiding her onto his ready shaft. She gasped and then, thankfully, didn't say another word. He shouldn't have told her that he wasn't going to marry her; nay, he should have just left her standing alone at the altar. It would have served her right.

As for the child, what proof did he have that it was his? Wynnifrydd hadn't come to him as a virgin and she could bloody well leave carrying her bastard. He cared not.

But he could not live having Elyn's death on his conscience, could not just forget her. Brock had committed more than his share of infidelities, told more lies than he could re-member, and even stolen when he needed to. But never had he let a woman die. Never had he felt this overwhelming burden, this horrendous sense of guilt.

As Wynnifrydd cried out in lust and Brock

spewed his seed deep within her, he held her tight, breathed hard, but could not dislodge thoughts of Elyn dying in that cold torrent of a river. Her death would forever be on his soul.

No matter what happened, he needed to tell the truth, to confess his part in Elyn's plan, to somehow balm his soul.

Chapter Eighteen

"Let me understand this," Kiera said to the tailor as they stood in the solar in the lord's tower. Two seamstresses were standing nearby, each with thimbles, scissors, and measuring sticks. Several pages were busy hauling rolls of fabric into the room. "My husband hired you to have a dozen dresses made for me?"

"That's right, m'lady. He asked me to bring you samples of my finest cloth. Oh! Not there, Gwayne!" the tailor called to a gangly page with bright red hair and a hooked nose. "Place the bolts here, on the table in the best light." Frowning, he jabbed a finger on the hard planks. He was a small, compact man with a finely cropped beard and a mouthful of ill-fitting teeth. In constant motion, he ordered the pages and seamstresses about while nervously rearranging the lace and pelts and ribbons by color on the table.

Never had Kiera seen such a display. Pale silks — some, the tailor assured her, brocaded in Italy — were set alongside bolts of rich velvet and damask, a heavy material brought from Damascus. Threads of silver and gold were woven into the plush fabric, and the tailor was already suggesting colors and trim for dresses that he envisioned.

"Sable is always in fashion," he confided as if it were a great secret, while placing a sleek dark pelt over a bolt of silvery gray damask. "And when summer comes, there is this lavender sandal — now, where is it? I had it just yesterday . . . Gwayne . . . oh . . . here it is!" He showed off the bolt in question, a shimmery lilac over which he draped a fine white lace and a plum-colored ribbon. "Is this not exquisite? This gown will be fitted at the waist, with a square neckline trimmed in lace and a train that you'll carry over your forearm. We could have the skirt in layers, some of the darker fabric!" He practically glowed as he described dress after dress. Kiera couldn't remember which style he put with the different fabrics, but told herself it mattered not.

"Now, let's measure you," the tailor suggested as he snapped a finger at the seamstresses.

While being measured, Kiera studied the vibrant colors of cloth and told herself she could not go through with this. The elaborate gowns would cost a king's ransom and were intended for Kelan's wife.

She decided she would have to speak with him, while the tailor rambled on and on

about sleeves, necklines, and hems as he envisioned not only dresses, but cloaks, man-
tles, headdresses, and shoes that Kiera would
never wear. While listening with half an ear,
Kiera imagined what her husband would say
when she told him the truth.

He would be livid. Mortified. And ready to
draw and quarter her. She would have to
throw herself upon his mercy and ask for his
help in finding his true bride.

Her stomach soured at the thought of the
extent of Kelan's humiliation and shame and
ensuing wrath. But she had to confess. She
had to. This morning, when Kelan had gently
awoken her with his caresses, she had wanted
to explain everything, but words had failed
her. After meeting his mother and earning
her approval, Kiera had made passionate love
to her husband again. But she could not continue to pretend to be Kelan's wife. No
matter what punishment Kelan meted out, no
matter what embarrassment they both would
suffer, she could no longer live this lie.

She put up with the fidgety little tailor
working around her only because Kelan was
now too busy to talk to her. She'd have to
wait until they were alone and in the meantime she could do nothing to alert the staff
that anything was wrong. Kelan deserved the
dignity of learning of her perfidy first.

"Ah . . . here's something special," the
tailor announced, showing off a roll of deep

blue velvet and accenting it with the long white fur of a rabbit. "Yes . . . with your eyes and hair, 'twould be elegant, nay, regal, m'lady. Pointed sleeves, I think, a high bodice, and a deep enough neckline to be daring. Yes?" He rubbed beringed fingers in his excitement.

"Thank you, but I'm not sure that I need so many clothes," she said as the energetic man kept up with his task, draping linens, silks, and velvets over her shoulders, only to step back and stroke his pointed beard as he imagined the fabric sewn into his creation.

"Your husband was very insistent. A dozen dresses. No less. With matching shoes, head-dresses, and cloaks." A twinkle lighted his dark eyes. "He must love you very much."

Kiera felt all the more miserable. Though she didn't believe Kelan was in love with her, she knew that he'd become fond of her and she . . . oh, blast, she was beginning to fall in love with him despite the fact that he was Elyn's husband.

"Come, lady, smile. 'Tis not every day that a lord orders an entire wardrobe for his wife."

She managed a thin pretense of a grin, for there was no explaining that the dresses would never be sewn, that by tonight Kelan would rescind his order for the clothes and probably strip Kiera of the ones she was wearing before casting her into the dungeon.

But there was nothing she could do about it.

She had to tell him the truth and somehow find Elyn, if her sister was alive. Then, assuming she could be found, Elyn could deal with her new husband.

Oh, what wretched, wretched torture. For as much as she wanted to locate her sister, she could not think of being separated forever from Kelan. To think of him with another woman, her sister — oh, nay. Her stomach threatened to lurch at the cursed image. So lost in thought was she, she didn't hear the door to the chamber open.

"Lady Elyn?"

Kiera turned.

Morwenna, the sister who knew Elyn and so obviously doubted Kiera, breezed into the room. With her raven-dark hair and intense blue eyes, she cast a quick smile at the tailor and said, "Lady Elyn, when you're finished here, my mother would like to speak to you."

Kiera's heart dropped. *Now what?* "But I already met with her."

"Aye. And now she wants a word with you alone."

"We are nearly done, m'lady," the tailor said as he snipped off a length of saffron burnet.

"Please, see to her as soon as you can." There was a deep sadness in Morwenna's eyes, underscored by distrust, and as quickly as she had entered the room, she left.

Why would Kelan's mother want to see her alone? Had she known by sight that something was amiss? Had she, like Morwenna, met Elyn years before? Yet Lenore had uttered not a word when Kiera and Kelan had visited with her. Though frail and ill, her body not recovering from her fall, Lady Lenore had smiled and her gaze had seemed friendly and warm. Kelan's mother had even grabbed Kiera's hand in surprisingly strong fingers and whispered a firm, seemingly heartfelt "Welcome to Penbrooke."

Kiera's throat had clogged and tears had burned behind her eyelids at the strength of the woman.

So why the urgent need to see Kiera again? Unless Morwenna had voiced her doubts about Kelan's wife to his mother.

When the tailor had finished, Kiera hurried out of the solar and up a half flight to Lady Lenore's chamber. She started to make one wrong turn, then corrected herself. Earlier, Nell had shown Kiera a trick of remembering passageways by pictures or furniture landmarks. She'd met two dozen servants, all of whom had tried to make her feel welcome. At home. Oh, God, she could not let this go on a second longer.

At Lady Lenore's door, Kiera paused, tucked a stray strand of hair behind her ear, wiped her sweaty palms on her skirt, then rapped on the panels.

Within seconds the door was answered by a nurse.

"I'm here to see Lady Lenore." Kiera peeked into the darkened interior where Kelan's mother lay, propped upon her bed.

"Yes, she's been expectin' ya. Askin' about ya she has been," the woman said. "Come in, come in."

"Is it Elyn?" Lenore called softly from the bed.

"Sure'n it is, m'lady."

"Good. Let her inside and please, give us a few minutes alone."

"But the baron, he instructed me ta stay with ya no matter what."

"Then wait on the other side of the door. If I need you, I'll call for you," Lenore commanded, displaying what Kiera supposed was her old fire.

"But Lord Kelan, if he catches me, will —"

"Let me deal with him. Now go, Rosalynn. I'll be but a minute." As the nurse grumbled her way out the door, Lenore lifted a tired hand and waved Kiera closer. "I'm glad you came."

"Of course I would come." Dear Lord. If possible, Lenore looked weaker than she had before. An embroidery hoop was at her side but remained untouched.

"Something is troubling you," the older woman stated. It was a pronouncement, not a question, and Kiera felt a moment's relief that Kelan's mother had not discerned the truth.

" 'Tis only that I'm new here."

"And?" Lenore prompted. "Something is on your mind. More than missing your home and family." She reached for Kiera's hand. "What is it? Does my son displease you?"

"Oh, no! 'Tis nothing of the sort."

"He treats you well?"

She thought of the fact that he hadn't brought up the vials for some time, his defense against Morwenna's attack the night before, the dresses he'd ordered made for her, the way he'd introduced her to the staff, and, most of all, the lovemaking, sometimes tender, other times so passionate she couldn't breathe. "Aye, he treats me well," she admitted, afraid a tremor in her voice would betray her.

" 'Tis because he loves you."

"Loves me?" Kiera repeated, torn between elation and despair. Oh, to think that Kelan cared for her, that he actually loved her, was heaven itself. Or was it hell? For he could never love a woman who had deceived him so. Never. Eventually the truth would come out.

Tonight.

She had to tell him tonight.

"Aye. I know my son. I thought him incapable of falling in love, and if I'd had even a glimmer that he would become besotted with his wife . . . oh, my. I only wish I could be here to see his child . . . your child."

Kiera's heart twisted. She realized that if she was not already pregnant, she would never have the opportunity to bear Kelan a child. Suddenly she felt empty inside. Bereft and hollow.

"I think there is something you should know," she said, hearing the beginning of her confession before she'd actually thought it through. Surely she should tell Kelan the truth rather than his mother.

Frail as she was, Lenore straightened in the bed, and Kiera caught a glimpse of the younger woman she had once been, the strong, vibrant woman whose aging body was set upon betraying her. "What is it that's worrying you? Do you not love Kelan?"

Love him? Love *him?* Nay, that was impossible and yet . . . hadn't she thought, nay, feared the very same? Desire was not the same as love. It could not be, but the feelings Kelan had evoked from her belonged not only to the body, but to the heart as well. " 'Tis not about love," she hedged, though she was certain Elyn's mother-in-law could see through her evasion. Though Lenore was ill, she was still clear in her mind. "The loving is not a problem."

"Then all is well. For he does love you, Elyn. A mother knows her own son and I see his love for you in his eyes. When the two of you visited my chamber, I caught him staring at you when you weren't aware that his gaze was following you. Oh, he tries to hide it, I can see that, but he's smitten." A tiny, satisfied smile curved her lips, and Kiera wished she were dead a thousand times over, knowing that this ill woman received a glimmer of hope and happiness in the knowledge that her son had married well. Oh, 'twas awful. She had to set things straight.

Lenore turned to her embroidery hoop. "This was to be part of a wedding present," she said with a sigh. "But, I fear, 'twill never be done." She picked up the hoop with its stretched fabric and intricate stitches, half-finished images of two doves holding a ribbon threaded through matching gold bands. "It was for you, and I will ask Daylynn to finish it after I pass."

"Please, don't talk like this. You don't know that your time is near."

Steady blue eyes held hers and the room seemed to suddenly hush, the sounds of the castle no longer seeping through the door, the fire's hiss softening, the echo of footsteps in the hallway nonexistent. "I know, daughter," she said, and Kiera cringed inwardly at the endearment. "When a woman's time is due, she knows. 'Tis not much different from sensing a husband's infidelity, or feeling that her unborn babe is about to enter the world. I've lived a full life. Grieve not for me. Just knowing that Kelan is married and happy, 'tis more than I could have wished for. I had only hoped that he would find some peace in the arrangement my husband made with your father, but this, seeing him smile and look at you the way he does, this is a true blessing."

Kiera's eyes began to fill and her soul was twisted in two. Should she hold her tongue and let Lady Lenore pass on to the next world without knowing, assuming that Kelan and Elyn were, indeed, happily wed, or did she owe the older woman the truth? She glanced at the embroidery hoop with its intricate stitches made by an ailing woman. "I — I think you ought to know that things are not as they seem," she said, her voice sounding far away to her ears as she steeled herself for the reaction that was to come.

Lenore's gaze focused hard on Kiera. "If not, then maybe they should be," she said. 'Twas almost as if she could sense the deceptions, feel the lies. "Whatever is on your mind, Elyn, please do not speak it. Ever. It's of no matter and sometimes a woman must turn her head away from the truth when it would be too painful for her family to withstand, or would serve no purpose other than to rend that which should be forever whole." She folded one thin hand over the other. "I have seen the pain of love gone awry . . .

Morwenna herself as a young girl . . . oh" — Lenore shook her head sadly — " 'twas a poor choice. Carrick of Wybren. How she fell in love with that rogue I'll never understand . . ." Her voice trailed off for a second as she remembered something that brought her eyebrows close together. " 'Tis of no matter now. What is important is that Kelan loves you and I think you love him, do you not?"

Kiera's heart twisted ever more painfully. How could she admit to loving her sister's husband?

Is it any worse than making love to the man? Worse than pretending to be someone else?

"I — I am not who you think I am," she admitted.

"Who I think you are is the only woman who has ever touched my son's soul." She grabbed Kiera's arm again, her fingers clasping as if in desperation. "Please, I implore you, whatever it is that's troubling you, whatever it is that haunts you, do nothing to thwart this marriage."

"But I am not —"

"Shh!" Lenore would hear none of it. "A true love is a rare, precious gift. Guard it with all your might. Promise me."

"I — can't."

"Promise me." Suddenly Lenore's eyes burned with a bright, fervid fire. "I ask nothing more of you. I need to go to my grave knowing that this, your marriage, the

children you will have with my son, will not be in jeopardy." Her voice was a harsh, demanding whisper. "For the love of God, Elyn, promise me this."

Kiera swallowed hard. Her throat was near swollen shut. 'Twas a vow with Elyn that had got her into this mess in the first place. With Kelan's desperate mother clutching her sleeve in a death grip, she was about to make another oath that she was certain would only lead to heartache.

"Do not deny me this. Let me go to my grave in peace."

"Aye, I promise that I will do the best I can to make the marriage work."

" 'Tis all I can ask." Lenore's tense features relaxed a bit. "Thank you, daughter." Her fingers loosened and she sighed as she sank onto her pillows.

Kiera could hardly breathe.

But I am not your daughter, she thought miserably. *Nor am I your daughter-in-law.*

"Now I grow weary. We'll talk another time." The fire in Lenore's eyes dimmed. Apparently satisfied that she'd got Kiera's word, she sagged, her strength suddenly dissipated. Slowly her eyelids lowered and she lifted one bony hand, her fingers fluttering slightly. "Please, call the nurse. Good day, Elyn."

Kiera didn't have to say a word. As if she'd been hovering on the other side of the door, Rosalynn bustled in. Casting Kiera a disparaging glance, she hurried to the bedside as Kiera said a quick good-bye.

"I'm here, m'lady," the nurse assured Lenore.

"Good . . . Please see that Daylynn finishes this bit of needlework," she said, her words following Kiera as she entered the hallway. " 'Tis a wedding present for my son and his new wife."

From his hiding spot in the hayloft, Joseph spied the missing mare. Nervous and fidgety, her crooked blaze standing out upon her dark coat, she was tethered in a stall away from the rest of the horses. Most of the animals that were not being used for pulling a cart or carrying a soldier were in the south meadow, grazing on the scrub grass that grew in an orchard. Joseph had sneaked outside and observed what seemed to be a daily routine. The idle horses were tended by a lazy, rawboned lad who wore a hat pulled down over his eyes to protect him from the rain. He leaned against the bole of a leafless apple tree, either whittling or dozing. Which was just fine. He seemed dull enough not to miss the mare.

Just as you didn't? his guilty mind nagged.

Joseph's jaw clenched as he considered his plan. He'd steal the mare that belonged to Baron Llwyd; 'twas the least he could do and might somehow make up for losing Obsidian a few years back.

But what of Lady Elyn?

His eyes narrowed thoughtfully as he climbed down from the hayloft and paused to pet the mare's soft nose. Tossing her head, she snorted. Silently Joseph slipped out of the stable. It was not yet dusk. He pulled his cowl over his head and kept to the shadows and away from the well-worn paths. The wind was brittle and cold, the rain once more spitting from the sky.

Despite the weather, workers were busy within the crumbling castle walls of Oak Crest. Women carrying jugs, platters, dead chickens, eggs, and vegetables followed after huntsmen with their kills and woodsmen with carts of firewood. Cows lowed, sheep bleated, and there was chatter everywhere, an air of excitement in the smoky air. High upon the north tower, the green-and-white standards of Oak Crest snapped in the breeze, and on a lower flagstaff, the crest of Fenn was flying as well.

Lady Wynnifrydd was soon to be Sir Brock's bride. So what of Lady Elyn? If her horse was here, did it not follow that Elyn, too, was within the keep? Yet he'd heard not one mention of her name, had seen nothing, aside from the skittish mare, to indicate she was nearby.

Or was she?

A dark trepidation had been growing in Joseph's heart. For over a day Joseph had moved within the population of the keep. He'd overheard dozens of conversations and filtered through enough gossip and rumors to surmise that Lady Elyn hadn't arrived at the castle. Unless she was secreted away, hidden from everyone but Brock. But why?

He frowned and wrapped his scarf tighter around his neck, hiding more of his chin. He didn't believe Lady Elyn would allow the man she loved to marry another woman. Not when she'd gone to such great lengths and taken such incredible risks to be with the bastard of Oak Crest. Joseph hated the man, not only for his brash manner, but because Lady Elyn loved him.

"Cur," he muttered sourly in the muffle of his wool scarf. The fear that something unspeakable had happened to her gnawed at his brain. He found it impossible to think that sharp-tongued, outspoken Lady Elyn of Lawenydd would cower and hide and be satisfied with living a lie to be . . . what? Brock of Oak Crest's mistress? Nay . . . that thought made no sense and brought a bitter taste to Joseph's mouth. If Elyn truly loved Brock, she would not settle for anything other than being his bride.

Yet Sir Brock's marriage to Wynnifrydd of Fenn was to take place this very afternoon.

Joseph didn't like the feeling that teased at his brain. Something was wrong. Very wrong.

Either Elyn was hurt, mayhap kidnapped and imprisoned, or she had escaped and was on her way back to Lawenydd without her horse, or — and this thought settled like lead in his gut — it could be that somehow she'd been killed.

By Brock?

Or Wynnifrydd?

Or someone else entirely?

It mattered not. If Elyn was dead at someone's hand, then that person would pay. Joseph would personally see to it.

Chapter Nineteen

"I promise that I will do the best I can to make the marriage work."

The vow to Kelan's mother haunted her, chasing after Kiera as she explored the castle, and reminding her that she had to find her sister and end this pretense as quickly as possible. Had Joseph gone to Oak Crest to find Elyn and Brock? Was her father, Baron Llwyd, even now waiting for Kiera's return? Was Penelope able to keep her secret?

As she made her way down a back staircase, smiling at a girl sweeping the stone steps and nearly tripping over a man carrying baskets of cold ashes from the great hall, Kiera felt like a cornered fox. There was nowhere to run, no one that her lies hadn't touched.

She could ignore her oath to Lady Lenore and tell Kelan the truth, thus breaking the old woman's heart, or she could wait until Kelan's mother had passed on and then admit all her sins. That thought was bitter. Kiera didn't want Lenore to die and hated the idea of basing her own freedom on her passing.

There had to be another way.

First thing she had to do was learn how Penbrooke was run. When the gates were open and when the portcullis was cranked down. She needed to know who the guards were, what their positions were, when they relieved each other . . . just in case she had to leave.

Outside, the day was cold as it neared sunset, the wind cutting as it blew against her face and toyed with the hem of her cloak. Kiera pulled her scarf tightly around her neck as she passed by the chapel, her gaze taking in every nook and cranny in the bailey. The priest was leaving the chapel, and Kiera looked quickly away and hurried down a well-trodden road. She'd prayed often for divine insight into her plight but heretofore had not been able to solve the dilemma. She'd considered visiting Father Barton but had not drawn up enough courage to confess her sins. Not yet.

Ducking around a corner near the kitchens, she came upon a fire pit where three girls were tittering and gossiping as they plucked feathers from half a dozen dead geese. At the approach of the lord's wife, the girls became suddenly silent as stones and went back to their tasks of removing feathers from the carcasses and singeing off the hairs before gutting out the innards.

Kiera slowed long enough to say hello to

the suddenly earnest feather pluckers, then met the stonecutter's wife and her brood as they bustled toward the chapel. "Good evening, m'lady," the woman said, and all of the girls and boys mimicked their mother with a chorus of greetings.

"And to you, Millie," Kiera replied before starting toward the outer bailey. How easily she'd come to know the people of Penbrooke — servants, freemen, and soldiers — all pleasant, all seeming to be pleased that their lord had wed.

If they only knew that the entire marriage was a lie. A horrid, ugly lie. On her way to the outer bailey she passed by the mews, where the falconer was training a young bird. The falcon was hooded and leashed, perched upon the trainer's gloved wrist. "M'lady," the falconer said, tilting his head as she swept by.

"Oh, Malcolm, good day."

"Same to ya." She was rewarded with his gap-toothed smile. He, along with so many others who lived within the keep, was trying his best to make her feel welcome, to make her feel secure and at home. She, in turn, had learned many of their names.

"Have you seen my husband?" she asked.

"Aye, hours ago, at the stable." He scratched his head and the falcon shifted upon his arm. "I think the baron went riding."

"Thank you," she said, and felt a jab of

disappointment that Kelan hadn't asked her to join him, though of course that was a silly notion, one she would have to shove aside. Just as she had to forget all her heated memories of making love to him. Absently she touched her abdomen and thought of the child that she could so easily have already conceived. And what then? She bit her lip and was surprised at how deeply she wanted a child, not just any babe, but Kelan's son or daughter.

"M'lady, are you all right?" Malcolm asked, bringing her out of her painful musings.

"Oh. Yes . . . thank you." She flashed him an embarrassed smile, and while the hooded bird let out a soft noise, Kiera walked briskly along the rutted path leading toward the stable. She met boys lugging buckets of water teeming with live eels and a fat woman hauling a basket of candles. Nodding to everyone she encountered, Kiera made her way to the stableyard, which, compared to the rest of the bustling activity of the keep, was surprisingly quiet.

The stable master was nowhere to be found, but the boy who assisted him was brushing the gleaming coat of a huge black destrier. "Excuse me, Francis, but have you seen my husband?" she asked.

"The lord? 'E was 'ere earlier," the lad said as he shook out the brush. Dust and horsehair fell from the soft bristles. "Rode off with

the constable to check on some poachin' in the woods."

"Then he'll be back soon?"

The boy lifted a shoulder. "I know not," he admitted as the horse swung his great head around.

Kiera's heart nearly stopped.

Obsidian!

Every hair on the back of her neck rose. This horse was the very steed she'd lost in the forest three years ago. She was certain of it. Her throat constricted as she stared, memorizing the steed's features. His coat gleamed blue-black in the frail sunlight slanting through the heavy clouds, and his eyes were wide-spaced and bright with interest. His ears pricked forward at the sight of her, and his forelock fell over one of his eyes. Just Obsidian's had. *How had Kelan ended up with this animal?*

"This is a beautiful horse," she said to the boy as she petted the stallion's velvet-soft nose. There, on one cheek, was a tiny scar, crescent-shaped nick from a sharp metal clasp of a bridle that had snapped when was just a foal. The stallion snorted, then lifted his head, shook it, and neighed softly. She knew without a second's doubt that was her father's horse. She clucked tongue and his ears flickered again. She whistled, softly, and he nickered.

"Yep, he's a good-lookin' one, 'e is,"

297

groomsman said with pride. "Strong a. ox, but fleet . . . and a good breeder. 'imself nine foals already, good colts a. fillies. Two more on the way."

"Was he raised here as well?" Kiera asked, but knew the answer before the floppy-haired boy spoke.

"Nay. We've only 'ad him a few years. The lord, well, he weren't the lord then, mind you, but 'e brought 'im back with 'im after the time 'e was banished. Lord Alwyn 'ad 'imself a change of 'eart about the banishment, though methinks 'twas more of Lady Lenore's doin'. Anyway, Lord Kelan returned and 'e brought this fella with 'im." The boy patted the horse's sleek shoulder.

Kiera's head was pounding, horror pumping through her veins. Could it be? Was it possible that Kelan was the thug who attacked her in the forest? It was true Obsidian had been long gone when Kiera had awoken in the woods, but didn't the mere presence of the horse indicate that Kelan could have been the attempted rapist? That thought was horrendous. Unbelievable. She had only to think of her coupling with Kelan to know that he was no attacker, no fierce outlaw who would force a woman . . . *but you didn't know him then, did you? When he was an outlaw, a highwayman, a horse thief banished from his home. What he was then may not be who he is today.* She had trouble keeping her

voice from trembling. "Did Lord Kelan say where he'd got the steed?"

"Nay. Not that I know. Some people think 'e stole 'im. Others claim 'e probably won 'im. Baron Kelan, 'e never explained it." Again the lift of a dismissive shoulder. "But Ares, 'ere, is a fine animal."

"Ares?" she repeated, chilled to her bones at the thought that the man with whom she was sleeping might be the very beast who nearly raped and killed her three years before.

No! No! No! 'Tis impossible! Kelan would never . . . But she thought of the battle scars upon his back, the deep gash in one shoulder, which could easily be explained by a wound from an arrow — Elyn's arrow.

Don't even think it!

But the thug was never found; whoever had attacked her that night had gone missing, his body having disappeared. Kiera had assumed that he was alive somewhere . . . hopefully somewhere far away, and now . . . Nay, she could not believe that Kelan was the man who had loomed over her that night. Though she hadn't seen his face, she'd smelled him, heard his gruff voice, felt his rough touch . . .

The Kelan she knew would never . . . no, 'twas unthinkable. A mistake. A stupid, idle notion. Just because no body was ever found in the woods, the horse lost . . . nay, it did not mean that Kelan was the thug.

Ignoring the doubts that continued to assail her, Kiera patted the horse and said, "Thank you, Francis." As she walked toward the great hall, her thoughts were tangled between the night that she'd lost the prized stallion, when she'd vowed to repay her sister for saving her life, and her new promise to Kelan's mother, that she would try to make the marriage — Elyn's marriage — work. Oh, she was forever getting herself into trouble. Would she never, never learn?

"I don't want to hear another word about it," Wynnifrydd growled. "We are to be wed this evening and that is that. If you bring up that miserable woman one more time, I swear, Brock, I'll cut out your tongue!" She was furious, her hands trembling as she tucked a stray strand of hair beneath her headdress.

Brock stood next to the fire, warming the back of his legs, appearing wan and miserable.

'Twas not the loving tryst one would have expected for a bride and groom upon the day they were to be married, Joseph thought with more than a little pleasure. He observed them from his hiding spot, a curtained alcove that he'd discovered when he'd taken over the job of carrying firewood to the upper floors. Everyone at Oak Crest — servants, peasants, guards, and even the lord himself — was busy with the dozens of tasks in preparation for the wedding. Already, a few guests and their servants had arrived, so no one noticed an unfamiliar man in his cowl and scarf as he carried bundles of oak to the fireplaces within the great hall.

Joseph had experienced little trouble finding Brock's roomy chamber with its private entrance and alcove, the tiny closet in which he now hid, peering through a crack in the worn curtain.

Wynnifrydd was in a rage, her disgust evident in the features of her face. "You are never to speak of the whore again."

"Elyn was not a whore."

Joseph's gut clenched. His fingers wrapped around the little dagger at his belt.

"It matters not. She's dead and you have . . . immortalized her like some angel, and I'll not have it, do you hear me?"

Dead? Elyn. Nay! Joseph's knees threatened to buckle and he couldn't draw a breath. Lady Elyn was not dead. She couldn't be. And yet his ears rang and the voices seemed to come from a great distance, echoing as if they were traveling through a long tunnel.

"You forget yourself. I will soon be the lord; you are but my bride."

"A wife who knows the truth about you, Brock, so be wary."

"I cannot live this lie."

"No? With as many as you've lived before?" she mocked, her eyebrows raising indignantly as firelight cast flickering golden shadows on the cracked walls. "Now I must return to my room lest anyone see us together before the wedding. 'Tis bad luck, they claim."

"This has all been bad luck."

She stiffened and advanced upon him. Though nearly a foot shorter than he, she glared up at him as if looking down her nose. " 'Tis about to turn. For the better. You will be not only Lord of Oak Crest one day, but also lord of a fine castle, much grander than this, when my father dies and you become Baron of Fenn. Trust me, love, your secret will never surface and I will be your wife. Whatever has transpired before matters not. Together we will restore Oak Crest and rule Fenn, making them the strongest baronies in all of Wales. So do not fail me now, Brock; do not cower and whine. Be the strong man I know and love, the ruthless man I admire. Be my husband." With that, she turned on her heel and stormed to the door. Once there, she was careful, slipping into the hallway and, Joseph assumed, skittering down to her own room to wait for the ceremony to begin.

There wasn't much time. He would have to work fast. Sir Brock was a tall, strong man, but this evening some of the starch had left him, and Joseph was certain he could overtake him. Oh, how he longed to slit the bastard's throat — the thought that Lady Elyn had died because of him was more than Joseph could stomach — but first, he had to find out the truth, and only the bastard knew what it was.

Joseph bided his time anxiously, careful to stay in his hiding spot. He had to remain cautious, could not make a mistake now, not when he'd learned the devastating news of Lady Elyn's death. Revenge would have to be served, and who better to deliver it than he? He let go of the knife and withdrew a leather strap from his pocket, a fitting weapon as it was the tether that had been used to restrain Lady Elyn's mare. Now it would choke the cur who had seduced and possibly killed her. A slow, determined smile curved his lips as he wrapped each end of the leather around his fists.

Muscles tense, a tic of anticipation starting near his eye, Joseph waited until Brock had tossed down a mazer of wine and was staring listlessly at the fire, his back to the alcove. The fire hissed, muted voices drifted through the thick panels of the door, and somewhere a mouse or rat scurried, its nails scratching on the stone floor beneath the rushes. Silently Joseph made a sign of the cross and sent up a small prayer, then slowly pushed back the curtain and crossed the room.

Brock didn't hear him. Didn't turn. Was too caught up in his morbid thoughts and self-pity.

Joseph struck like a lone, hungry wolf. In one easy motion, he flipped the leather around Brock's neck. The big man gasped and twisted, nearly bucking out of his chair as he frantically scrabbled at the noose with one panicked hand and reached for his knife with the other. Brock was strong and desperate, his weight turning and writhing, but Joseph only pulled tighter. "This is for Lady Elyn, you dirty bastard," he growled, not so much as flinching when he felt Brock's blade slam into his thigh.

Brock made gurgling sounds and fought like hell, pulling out his knife from Joseph's leg, then hacking frantically, trying to wound his attacker again. 'Twas pathetic. The big man was losing strength now, flailing wildly, and Joseph easily sidestepped his blade as he twisted the tether more tightly. Brock's knife clattered to the floor. He reached upward, trying to grip the leather strap with both hands, his fingers digging into the skin of his throat to no avail. Joseph, straining, his muscles bulging, only pulled the noose tighter, refusing to let up until he felt the miserable bastard shudder and collapse, his hands falling to his sides as he lost consciousness. Only then did Joseph release the tension.

For the moment, he had to keep the

bastard alive. Much as he would like nothing better than to take his miserable, greedy life, he would let him live.

But only for the moment.

Chapter Twenty

"Kelan, something is amiss. I feel it in my bones," Morwenna insisted as she met him at the stable door. He was tired, having ridden most of the day through the forest looking for poachers' traps, listening as the constable droned on and on about the increase in crime, the thievery within the castle as well as without. A band of cutthroats had been hiding out in the forest and terrorizing travelers, getting bolder by the minute. Then there were the peasants who were cheating on their taxes and fees for the right to use the lord's land. He'd heard enough for one day and yet here was Morwenna, her pretty face a stone mask, trouble knitting her usually smooth brow.

"What is it?" he asked. Had something happened to Lenore? No, Morwenna seemed more vexed than sad.

"Lady Elyn."

"Don't tell me," he said, sighing. His thoughts were already up the tower stairs to his wife and their marriage bed. At the image, he felt the corner of his mouth twitch upward. "I know. You don't trust her. You think she's . . . what? Not herself." He scoffed at the idea but, seeing that his sister was sincerely worried, placed an arm around her shoulders and shepherded her toward the great hall. "She's my wife, you know."

"You're in love with her." Morwenna's voice dripped ice.

"Would that be so bad?" They walked through the evening mist past huts where fires glowed through open windows. The night was closing in. A hint of moon shone above the clouds, muffled barks sounded from the kennel, the sails of the windmill moved slowly overhead, and somewhere far off a sheep bleated.

"Does she love you?" Morwenna asked, and some of the serenity of the evening cracked.

"We don't speak of it." He inclined his head toward his sister. "And what would it matter to you?"

"I just . . . I just don't trust her."

"Because you remember her as a girl."

"Yes. I don't believe that people change, not like that, not in their hearts. Elyn of Lawenydd was a stubborn woman only interested in herself. Well, and Brock of Oak Crest."

"And what of you? Did you not once lose your heart?"

Morwenna stiffened. "That was a long time ago."

"Aye, and now you feel differently about Carrick of Wybren."

She didn't answer, but he saw her blanch as they climbed the steps to the great hall. Inside, workers were already setting up the tables for the evening meal.

"Lady Elyn and I are wed. That will not change, sister," he said, finally releasing her. "You must accept it."

"I've tried."

"Try harder."

Kelan dropped into his chair by the fire and began working off his gloves. He heard footsteps hurrying down the steps. He looked up to see Elyn dashing into the chamber, her hair flying, her beautiful face as white as weak milk.

"Thank God you're here," she said. "The physician is searching for you." He shot to his feet. " 'Tis your mother, Kelan," she said, her face ashen and drawn. Compassion filled her eyes and Kelan felt his entire body tense. "She's asking for you and . . . and there is not much time."

Morwenna gasped. She bolted out of the chamber and Kelan overtook her on the stairs. He heard Elyn behind them, but he didn't look back, thought only of what he would find in his mother's room. No matter how much time one had to prepare, there was never enough. He nearly ran into the nurse as she flew from Lenore's chamber.

"Oh, Lord Kelan, I'm so sorry —" she cried, her voice trembling.

"No!" He wouldn't believe the worst. He burst through the doorway and found Daylynn sitting near the bedside, tears streaming down her pale face, the physician wringing his hands and the priest mumbling a prayer over the bed.

"Mother . . ." He charged to the bedside but his mother was unmoving, her chest beneath the bedclothes not rising or falling. "Nay," he whispered, pain welling up from the very depths of his soul.

"I did what I could," the physician insisted. "I gave her comfrey for her bones and used leeches and —"

"Enough!" Morwenna ordered. "You are not to blame."

Kelan's heart crumpled. He knew this day would come, of course, had told himself he was preparing for it. But now his throat clogged and his eyes burned and deep harrowing sorrow burned through his soul. His mother had been forever on his side, forever his champion, and now . . . and now she was gone. 'Twas unthinkable and yet he'd known it would come to this, had convinced himself he'd expected it. But he hadn't. Not deep down. "Leave us," he said to all the servants, and his voice sounded strange. Strangled. "Leave us alone with our mother."

Boots rang up the stairs and Tadd, disheveled, his clothes askew, flew through the open door. He stared at the bed in horror. "Why did someone not call me? Why was I not told that . . . that the end was at hand?" he demanded, his face twisting in pain.

"The end came on quickly," the physician said, puffing up his chest a bit. "I had been with her earlier, and though she was very weak, her passing did not seem imminent. She had been the same for days."

"She was ill," Kelan snapped, tired of the bickering. His mother had passed on; there was no need for blame or recriminations.

"Elyn was the last to see her," Morwenna said, her voice harsh. "Did you not notice that she was failing?"

His wife nodded. "She was tired."

"You spoke with her alone?" Kelan asked.

"Aye. She asked to see me."

"Alone? But we'd seen her just . . ." Was this not odd? For a second he thought of the vials he'd found in the bedchamber at Lawenydd. Had she not drugged him then? Did she not have some knowledge of potions that made a person sleepy and sluggish or never want to wake? Would this woman that he married dare give his mother something that might slip her into death? Oh, nay. That made no sense whatsoever. Why would Elyn wish to harm his mother?

"She sent for me."

"So the nurse was with her?"

"For a while." Elyn swallowed hard and took in a deep breath. "But she sent Rosalynn out of the room."

"Why?"

"She wanted to speak to me alone."

"What about?" Morwenna demanded, moving closer to her.

Kiera felt every grieving eye upon her, every face turned to her, as if in her last conversation with their mother she could provide them some kind of insight or comfort. She looked from one to the other, but there was no solace in her words; she had no answers, and she felt a strong need to unburden herself, to admit the truth about her duplicity, but not now when the family was in shock and grief. She could not. *Coward*, the hideous nagging voice in her mind taunted, but she refused to listen. Refused to tell of her deception. She had to talk to Kelan alone. "Lady Lenore wanted to talk of my marriage to Kelan." Kiera glanced at him, noticed his lips tighten with distrust. "And what would be expected of me as the Lady of Penbrooke." Not really a lie.

"Please, I implore you, whatever it is that's troubling you, whatever it is that haunts you, do nothing to thwart this marriage." Lenore's dying request echoed through Kiera's mind.

"Why would she call you up here just to tell you of your duties?" Morwenna demanded, her thunderous blue gaze focusing

311

suspiciously on her new sister-in-law.

"Why wouldn't she?" Kelan said, and stepped closer to his wife.

"Yes, why wouldn't she?" Daylynn nodded and sniffed back her tears. "Mother was concerned with what would happen to Penbrooke. We all know that. Did she not ask us all to marry and have children and . . ." Daylynn's voice broke and she buried her face in her hands.

Gently, Morwenna touched her sister's shoulder. "Shh, Daylynn. 'Twill be all right." Bryanna folded Daylynn into her arms.

"Will it?" Tadd asked, and his lips compressed into a tight, angry line. He glared at his brother. "I guess we'll see now that you, brother, and you alone will be running this keep. Without Mother's counsel, without her support, without her damned insistence that you were destined to be master of Penbrooke."

" 'Tis the natural order of things," Kelan insisted.

"Is it?" Tadd asked. He stepped to the bed and, after touching his mother's fingers, turned on his heel, cast a disparaging look at Kiera, and left.

Morwenna's gaze softened a bit. "There is much to do," she said, as if to herself.

"I am so sorry for your loss." Kiera glanced down at the bed where Lenore, serene in death, lay.

"Thank you." The tears that had been once stemmed now ran down Daylynn's cheeks while Bryanna stiffened her shoulders and attempted to appear brave. Kiera said, "If there is anything I can do —"

"There is," Morwenna cut in swiftly, her gaze fastened on her sister-in-law. "All we want, Elyn, is that you, as a member of this family, as the baron's wife, never lie to any of us. That your loyalty is to Penbrooke. I hope that is not too much to ask."

"Enough," Kelan snapped, his face drawn in grief. "We're all upset, but we must do as Mother wished. And that, sister, was not to fight and bicker among ourselves."

"As you wish, m'lord," Morwenna muttered sarcastically before leaving the room with Daylynn at her heels.

"Please give me some time alone with my mother," he said to the priest. As Father Barton retreated, Kiera started to follow. "No, Elyn, you stay with me," Kelan asked, and laced his fingers through hers. She felt awkward but held his hand. His fingers were tense, his eyes dark with sorrow, as he silently said good-bye to the woman who had borne him. With his free hand, he brushed a strand of hair from Lenore's pallid cheek, and he blinked hard against tears.

Kiera was surprised that he would share this moment with her, that he would allow her to see him so raw and aching. Her earlier suspicions concerning Obsidian, the questions she had designed to discern the truth about that night three years ago, were lost. How could she have thought such unkind thoughts, have such dark suspicions? Oh, if she could do anything to ease his pain, to balm the grief that was so evident in his features. Then she remembered Lenore's faint voice and her plea.

"I think you are the only woman who has ever touched my son's soul . . . Please, do nothing to thwart this marriage."

Dear God, Kiera thought, *how in all of heaven and earth will I ever be able to tell him the truth?*

Chapter Twenty-one

"He's gone," the idiot of a soldier said with such maddening authority that it was all Wynnifrydd could do not to take her hands and claw the man's piglike eyes from his head.

"You're mistaken," she insisted as she stood in her wedding dress, her veil affixed to her head, in the decrepit solar of Lord Nevyll, Brock's father.

Not only were the soldier and the baron in the chamber, but her own father was as well. Two guards stood near the door, one belonging to Oak Crest, the other from Fenn. All observing her disgrace. And the guests . . . lords and ladies who had come to this horrid keep to witness her wedding and now would be able to be shocked by and eventually gloat over and gossip about how she'd been left standing alone, waiting for a bridegroom who had left her. She would be a laughingstock. No. She couldn't allow it.

"Find him," she ordered, panicking inside. "Brock is somewhere in the keep; I'm sure of it. You just have to locate him. He was half in his cups earlier; mayhap he's dozed off somewhere."

But even to her this excuse sounded feeble. Worse, it seemed to come from a desperate woman. Fury singed her brain. Embarrassment clouded her vision. How dare Brock not appear in the chapel for her wedding? How *dare* he? Who did he think he was, this lowly son of an aging baron with a keep that was about to fall to pieces? He had no right to treat her this way. Oh, when she got her hands on him, she would show him what it meant to leave a lady waiting for her own wedding! "But be discreet. It would not do for the guests to think that he'd nearly missed his own wedding!" Just the thought of it brought a dreadful heat up the back of her neck and to her cheeks.

"Aye," Nevyll agreed hurriedly. He swallowed hard and worked his hands as nervously as a virgin about to bed a rogue. "My son is in the keep. As Lady Wynnifrydd suggested, mayhap he began celebrating his nuptials too soon and took a nap somewhere and lost track of time . . ." He sounded hopeful, not that he believed his pathetic excuse but at least he wanted everyone else to accept his explanation. "Check the battlements, the towers, the dungeons, and every square inch of the castle. You'll find him . . ."

Nevyll was grasping at weak straws. And he must have known it for his smile was twitchy and unsure. 'Twas preposterous to think Brock had lost sense of time or forgotten his own wedding! And yet what other reason but the one that Wynnifrydd feared most, that he'd abandoned her at the altar? Her teeth gnashed so hard her jaw began to ache, and a headache began at the back of her skull, reminding her that Brock had never been faithful. Never. Not even when she'd told him of the baby . . . which, of course, did not yet exist. She had hoped to feign a miscarriage after the wedding and then quickly get pregnant.

Where the devil was he? She smoothed the folds of her wedding dress, a gorgeous creation of white velvet and lace. Now a useless garment, a mockery of her situation.

An ugly black thought snaked its way through her throbbing brain.

What if Elyn of Lawenydd is not dead? What if she did marry Kelan of Penbrooke and even now Brock was hastening away to steal her away and claim her? What if he mortified Wynnifrydd on purpose? What if he knew there was no babe as she'd claimed, that she'd only wanted to force him into marrying her?

"My men and I have looked everywhere, m'lord," the soldier said. He was a big bear of a man with a huge girth and a ruddy complexion. He spread his hands in a gesture of perplexity. "We have gone from the highest tower to the lowest dungeon and every spot in between. His bed is undisturbed; his wedding clothes are lying upon his wooden chest. 'Tis as if he up and vanished."

That much seemed right. Wynnifrydd had seen Brock's handsomely tooled mantle, his finely woven tunic and breeches, pressed and waiting upon the chest. She'd ordered them from the tailor herself and they'd been there when she'd sneaked into his room earlier. Was it possible this half-wit of a soldier was telling the truth? Had her worst fear come to pass? And all because she'd made the mistake of loving a heartless rogue who had used her and left her without a second thought?

Tears of mortification burned the back of her eyelids.

Her heart and pride ripped as painfully as if they'd been fused together. What a stupid, love-duped fool she'd been! "Look again," she ordered the beefy constable, feeling her cheeks flame with her shame and outrage. "Talk to everyone. Find out if anything is amiss. *Anything!*"

"Yes, yes, check again," Lord Nevyll commanded, rubbing his fat hands together.

Her own father stepped in. A small man, he nonetheless had the voice of a bellowing bull. "And when you find him," Lord Seth said, "tell him I want to speak to him *before* he marries my daughter."

Wynnifrydd panicked. "Nay, Father, the moment Brock returns, the wedding is to go on as planned."

"What? And have the guests sit idle?"

Better than to let them go at this point when there was still a chance she could reclaim some of her rapidly disappearing dignity. "They can roam the castle and be entertained by the jesters and musicians or watch the bearbaiting or cockfights," she said, thinking fast. "Certainly the cook can serve some of the food that has been prepared for the wedding feast. Then, as soon as Brock is located, the marriage will commence as planned." She glanced to Lord Nevyll for support. "Well, unless you and the servants of Oak Crest are unable to keep the guests satisfied."

"Oh, nay!" Nevyll shook his head quickly. " 'Tis a grand idea, Lady Wynnifrydd. I'll alert the cook —"

"Stop. Do not." Her father shook his head, and she noticed his face was so flushed with rage that she could see his red scalp through his thinning white hair and beard. " 'Tis too late. We had an arrangement," Lord Seth insisted, pointing a beringed finger at Brock's father. "And if your son has shirked his duties and embarrassed all of us in the process, there will be no marriage, no alliance, nothing. My daughter has had her choice of suitors, from Wybren to Rhydd, and neither she nor I will suffer this kind of humiliation. If Brock doesn't appear with an apology within the next three hours, consider the wedding never to take place."

"Father! Nay!" Desperation clutched Wynnifrydd's throat, nearly strangled her.

"You will not be compromised, daughter, nor mortified." His head snapped toward the soldier who was in charge of the search party. "Find him," Seth ordered, "and find him fast. I'll have a word with him."

Wynnifrydd wanted to collapse into a pile of tears. She wanted to kick and scream and gnash her teeth. Oh, Brock would pay. Whenever she looked upon his handsome face again, she would make sure he would never forget the raw disgrace she'd suffered at his hand.

Someone rapped upon the closed door.

Wynnifrydd's heart soared. Brock had been found! Surely this was all a horrid mistake.

"Who is it?" the guard demanded.

"Willis. I've got John, the stableboy, with me."

The guard opened the door. Two men, one yet another soldier, the other a lame little man with one droopy eye, bustled into the room. No Brock.

Wynnifrydd wilted inside.

"You've found my son," Lord Nevyll said hopefully.

The soldier shook his head. "Nay, m'lord, but John, 'ere, 'e knows something that might help. Go on, tell 'im," he said to the crippled little man.

"There be a horse missin'," the man said, seeming about to jump out of his own skin. "I work with the stable master, and Dafydd, he's worried sick about it."

"What horse? Brock's steed?" Lord Nevyll asked angrily.

"Nay, the big sorrel, he's where he should be, with the others. But Sir Brock, he had another horse, a high-strung little mare he swore he won in a game of dice a few nights back and . . . she's missin'." The man was sweating profusely and Wynnifrydd suspected he was lying or was somehow responsible for losing the horse, but he continued rambling on. "Now, it could be that she ran off. God knows, Dafydd, he sometimes sleeps on the job, but Dafydd, he claims the mare was locked up in a stall, and just today when he awoke, the mare was gone. He figured Sir Brock had taken her out for a ride, but now everyone says Sir Brock's missin', too, and I thought ye should know about the mare."

"So what are you saying?" Wynnifrydd demanded of the little worm of a worker. "That Sir Brock left me to wait for him at the altar, just to embarrass me?"

"Oh, nay, nay, m'lady," John was quick to answer. "Mayhap he took a ride or hunt and an accident befell him. That's what I'm sayin'."

Now this made more sense. A second's relief washed over her. Of course Brock wouldn't leave her alone on the wedding day intentionally. Why, she'd seen him earlier today . . .

Lord Nevyll took the man's word as that of the Bible. "Assemble the troops," he ordered the soldier. "I want every man available to start looking in the surrounding forest." Lines of worry etched his face. "But be careful. Brock is an excellent horseman, so it could be that he's not been involved in an accident, but that someone has attacked him."

"Who?" Wynnifrydd's father scoffed.

"Mayhap an outlaw who recognized him as my son and would hold him for ransom."

Lord Seth raised a dubious eyebrow as he glanced around the sparsely furnished room with its threadbare tapestries and cracked walls.

Baron Nevyll was undeterred. "Or . . . or perhaps someone did not want the marriage to happen."

"And who would that be?" her father again snorted.

"I know not, but mayhap someone who had his own reasons for not wanting an alliance between Oak Crest and Fenn."

Wynnifrydd stopped short. This was a new wrinkle. And one that was even more plausible than the excuse that Brock had been out riding and had an accident. The skin on her scalp prickled, for she felt a new fear.

"You are covering up for your lazy son's

impudence, rudeness, and disrespect. But whatever the reasons for his absence, I suggest you find him and soon," Seth countered.

Elyn, Wynnifrydd thought in a moment of sickening clarity. Somehow Elyn was behind Brock's disappearance. Either she'd come back to haunt him from the grave, or she was very much alive, and the two lovers had played Wynnifrydd for the worst kind of fool.

She felt suddenly sick. Disgusted. Mortified beyond belief. This was far too great a dishonor to allow to happen. By the gods, she wouldn't allow it, wouldn't suffer the injustice and humiliation. Wynnifrydd's fists bunched in the skirt of her fine white dress. Whatever the reason, be she dead or alive, Elyn of Lawenydd wouldn't get away with it.

Feeling the winter cold seep through her cloak, Kiera listened to the priest as he intoned a final prayer over the coffin of Lady Lenore. Just the day before, she had spent time with the woman and made a vow she couldn't possibly keep. Now Kelan's mother rested in a grave next to that of her husband. The funeral had been rushed at Kelan's insistence. He couldn't bear the thought of his mother's lifeless body lying within the keep's walls.

Lady Lenore of Penbrooke's band of mourners was large, everyone in the keep standing around the freshly turned earth.

Peasants, knights, tradesmen, servants, friends, and family had gathered on the slight rise outside the bailey as dark, ominous clouds scudded over the sky. They whispered their own soft prayers and held the hands of their loved ones as the chapel bells pealed plaintively.

Kiera made the sign of the cross and, with her head still bowed, stole a glance at the Lord of Penbrooke. Dressed in black, his tunic decorated with stripes of leather and silver, he stared into the grave. His face was set in stone as he quietly grieved, his gray eyes darker than ususal, his hair as black as his boots as it ruffled in the brisk breeze. A timid sun dared peek from behind the roiling of clouds, and frost covered the bent, trodden grass of the cemetery.

Kelan had been distant from her since his mother's death, caught up in his private thoughts as, through his grief, he saw that the castle ran smoothly. His siblings, too, were quiet and had kept their distance from Kiera. Which was expected, but it gave Kiera too much time alone with her own morbid thoughts, her own guilt. She'd passed more hours than she cared to think of in prayer, hoping for divine intervention from her dilemma and, beyond that, the courage to face the man who thought he was her husband. She'd tried to broach the topic of their marriage since Lenore's passing, but late last night in bed, it seemed all Kelan wanted to do was lose himself in desperate, passionate lovemaking.

As the crowd dispersed and two workers began to shovel dirt over the casket, Kelan let out a long, shuddering sigh. "Find peace, Mother," he whispered so low that Kiera barely heard the words. And then it was done. Lenore of Penbrooke was finally at rest.

The mourners filed through the gates of the castle into the outer bailey, where most of the horses were penned. Standing taller than the rest, his head turned toward the mourners, Obsidian let out a quiet neigh.

Kelan glanced in the stallion's direction. "Shh, Ares," he said, though he sounded distracted, his thoughts far away.

"He's a fine steed," Kiera said, hitching her chin toward the destrier.

Kelan nodded as if jarred from his dark thoughts. "Aye. One of the best I own."

"How long have you had him?"

"Only a few years." He managed a thin smile. "I won him in a game of dice."

Desperately Kiera wanted to believe him. "From whom?"

His eyes slitted with an evil glint. "From one of your old suitors, wife. Did he not tell you?"

"Who? Tell me what?"

"Brock of Oak Crest."

"Brock?" she repeated, stunned. Brock had owned Obsidian? How? Had he bought him? Found him in the woods that night . . . ? And suddenly she understood.

" 'Twas a few years back when I . . . when I was out of favor with my father." Kelan shoved a wayward lock of black hair from his forehead as the first drizzle of sleet hit the ground. "I was drinking at an inn not far from Castle Fenn and Brock arrived upon Ares. He'd been in some kind of battle and was healing from a nasty wound, but he began drinking and clamoring to wager, so I agreed."

"And what did you wager?"

"My horse, of course. At the end of the evening, I had two and Brock had none."

Kiera's mind was spinning. Had Elyn ridden into the woods that night not, as she'd said, for fear of Kiera's safety, but because she was going to meet Brock? Was the man who attacked her, who had nearly raped or killed her, Brock of Oak Crest? Had Elyn shot her own lover, then left him in the forest to die? Why? Oh, God, why? Jagged memories, bits and pieces, cut through her brain. It had been so dark that night, too dark to see the face of her attacker clearly, but somehow Elyn had been near enough to wound the man with her arrow. Kiera's stomach clenched painfully. Was Brock not trying to rape a woman he'd come upon in

the forest? Or did he think she was Elyn and
. . . and what? Was he angry with his lover?
Planning to make her pay for some slight
against him? Her knees began to quiver. Why
had Elyn shot the man she loved?

*Because she saw him attacking you, and either
out of jealousy or fear for your safety, she saved
your life, or at the very least your virginity.*
"Did Brock tell you where he'd got the
horse?" she asked, forcing her voice not to
quaver and hoping to hide her warring emotions.

"I didn't ask."

Brock hadn't been trying to rape her as
much as teach his lover a lesson, and Elyn
had been jealous and angry and decided to
shoot him and save Kiera . . . that's how it
was. How it had to have been. Walking
quickly as the storm began in earnest, they
passed through the smaller gate to the inner
bailey. Kiera, lost in her own revelations,
barely noticed all the activity though the
peasants and servants were already back at
work, hammers banging, bellows blowing,
wheels creaking from carts that were moving
through the keep again.

Kelan's voice lowered. "Mayhap I didn't
want to know where the horse came from. It
mattered not and I knew the stallion to be a
prize. Those were dark days, Elyn. Days
when I was banished from Penbrooke and
cared for no one but myself. If the horse had

been stolen, it was not of my concern," he admitted, with a self-deprecating twist of his lips. That he rued those murky days was evident in the shadows in his eyes. "In truth, I thought Brock had probably taken Ares from his own father." He glanced her way and managed a thin, humorless smile. "There is much we don't know of each other. Now come." He glanced at the darkening sky. "The storm worsens."

She withered inside but kept up with his faster pace as icy pellets rained from the sky. She thought of the night she was attacked and the horse was lost, how Elyn had lied and deceived her, and how she, in turn, was deceiving Kelan. Her legs were leaden and her heart was heavy as they hurried up the steps to the great hall. Finally, to start untangling the intricate and painful web of lies, she said, "The steed is my father's horse."

Kelan stopped at the door and his countenance tightened as if he didn't believe her. "Ares is from Lawenydd?"

"Aye." She nodded as a servant opened the door and they stepped inside to the warmth of the keep. "But his name is Obsidian. I recognized him from the scars upon him when I saw him in the stable yesterday. I called to him and whistled and he responded, just as had my horse. You see," she said, unwrapping the scarf that had been tied around her neck and forcing the damning words past her lips, "three years past, I went against my father's wishes. I took Obsidian from the stable behind my father's back and went riding in the woods. He shied and threw me and then he was gone."

"Gone?" They walked into the great hall, where servants were already setting up tables for the next meal.

"Disappeared. My . . . my sister helped me back to the keep."

"She rode with you?" he asked, and she thought about the answer, deciding to hedge.

"Yes, she was in the forest with me."

"Kiera?" he asked, and she nearly jumped at the sound of her name. It had been days since she'd heard it. Rarely from Kelan's lips. "Did she steal a horse as well?"

"Yes, Kiera was there," she said carefully, her heart pounding with dread as she began to reveal parts of the truth. "I didn't think of it as stealing the horse, more like borrowing him. We . . . my sister and I . . . were together. But losing the horse was my fault." She didn't tell him about the rest, about the attack. Perhaps she would later, but not now, not until she'd finally revealed her own secret, that she was not his wife.

"The next day we found no sign of Obsidian. 'Twas as if he'd disappeared into the night. I feared that something wretched had happened to him, that he'd had a horrible, tragic accident, mayhap that he'd somehow run upon the ridge only to stumble and fall over the cliffs by the sea." Shuddering at the mental image that had haunted her, she added, "But his carcass was never found. I never knew what had happened to him. Until I saw him in the stable yard."

"And you're certain this is the same horse?" he asked, obviously skeptical.

"Aye." She nodded and explained in detail about the scars and Obsidian's traits, but again she didn't mention the fact that someone had attacked her, nor did she admit to her identity. That would all come in time. As soon as she knew what had become of Elyn.

And what if you never know? What if she is like the horse, and has disappeared without a trace? What will you do then? Sooner or later you will have to tell him the truth.

And she would. When the time was right. She could not live this lie forever.

Chapter Twenty-two

Had she misread them?

Or had the stones lied?

Hildy cupped the cold pebbles in her hands and tossed them across the worn planks of her table. They tumbled and bounced, stopping before sliding onto the dirt floor, shining in the fading firelight. Outside, thunder cracked and storm clouds roiled, but here within her hut, she studied the rocks, and for the first time in her life, she doubted what fortunes she read. She'd seen in the pebbles' placement that one of the baron's daughters was to die, though she didn't know which, and now . . . now the stones said that there might be another as well . . . two children killed or maimed from Castle Lawenydd.

Her old heart was dark with fear, her blood cold as the sleet falling outside.

Could she tell the baron?

Could she not?

From habit, she deftly sketched the sign of the cross over her chest.

If only Joseph would return, or she would hear from Kiera or Elyn. "Please be with them," she whispered in a quick prayer as she scooped up the stones and placed them into her tattered bag. 'Twas her walk in life, to balance her beliefs of the old, pagan rituals with that of the Church. Sometimes it seemed as if she was destined to fall from favor with both the Mother Goddess and the Holy Father. Mayhap her own torn faith was the cause of this hellish curse that the stones foretold.

There was trouble brewing, worse than ever, she feared. A plaintive wail came from beneath the table and Hildy bent down to find her cat cowering in the shadows.

"Come along, Sir James," Hildy said, coaxing the frightened beast from his hiding spot. " 'Tis naught but a storm." But a shutter banged loudly as if to disagree. The cat slunk farther from her, his eyes wide, his pupils dilated with fear and the darkness. Hildy managed to grab him by the scruff of his neck and pull him close enough to pick him up. He let out another terrified cry, his claws sinking through the rough wool of her tunic. "Ach . . . calm down, will ya, now? 'Tis not as if you've been seeing the future and how dire it is. Why don't you kill me a fat rat or a mouse, eh, instead of hiding beneath the table?" The cat crawled up her arm to settle onto her shoulders. "Hey, now, look what I've got for ya. See here, I took it out of Cook's scraps and she was going to use it for fish-head stew." From her pocket she retrieved the head of a small eel and dangled it in front of the cat. He batted at it and pulled it close. "Spoil you, I do," she groused under her breath. She was still disturbed by the images she'd seen in the stones. "Come along, now."

As she placed the cat and morsel by the fire, an alarm bell clanged, pealing loudly throughout the castle walls. Hildy's old spine turned to ice as she hurried to the door. What now? She thought of the omen in the stones and prayed it was not bad news of the baron's daughters, for she loved Elyn, Kiera, and Penelope as if they were her own.

"Halt! Who goes there?" the sentry's voice boomed over the storm.

" 'Tis I, Joseph," another voice answered.

Orson's son! Mayhap with news of Lady Elyn! Hildy's worried heart nearly leaped from her rib cage. Hurriedly wiping her hands on her skirt, Hildy half ran outside, her footsteps carrying her to the main gate, where the portcullis clanked upward. Soldiers with knives, swords, and maces at ready ran from the barracks. Through the frigid drizzle two horses with riders appeared.

Hildy squinted hard and pulled her scarf over her head. Aye, it was Joseph on a small, skittish mare who pranced with mincing steps and tossed her dark head, fighting the bit. Despite the icy rain pelting from the sky, the bay was covered in lather. Hildy hurried along a muddy path, caring not that her skirt was trailing in the mud and puddles, hungry for news of Elyn. But it wasn't the lady who was with Joseph. Nay. She narrowed her eyes at the second horse, a larger, sand-colored animal with darker mane and tail. The rider atop this steed sat awkwardly, listing badly to one side. Only when she got closer did Hildy see the reason. The man appeared to be a prisoner with his hands tied in front of him and a gag cinched over his mouth. He had to balance upon the horse using only his leg muscles while his fingers clutched the saddle pommel. The reins to this mount were held in Joseph's free hand. The captive seemed about to topple over, and though it was dark, Hildy recognized him. All her fears gelled in that instant.

Sir Brock of Oak Crest was Joseph's prisoner.

No good could come of this. None whatsoever. This was sure to bode ill. A lowly stableboy capturing the only son of a baron. "What happened?" she asked, eyeing the bound man.

Wincing, Joseph climbed off his mud-spattered mount. His face was dark, his expression harder than she'd ever seen it. "Lady Elyn is dead," he said through clenched teeth. "I heard the bastard say as much, so I dragged him here. We've been riding for

334

hours; we rode straight through the night."

"Nay!" she whispered, taking a step back as her legs began to fail her. She thought of the stones, the damning, cursed stones of fate and what they'd forewarned. "Nay, oh, nay."

" 'Tis true." Joseph spat on the hard ground. His jaw trembled a second and he wouldn't meet her eyes.

Hildy felt her insides turn to stone, and images of Elyn as a child flitted through her mind. Bold, reckless, with a keen sense of humor, she was oftentimes more son than daughter to Lord Llwyd. It had been Elyn whom he'd taken hunting, Elyn whom he'd taught to handle a falcon, Elyn who had been allowed to ride even the most spirited of destriers, Elyn who had been as good with a bow and arrow as any of the soldiers within the keep.

Hildy's throat grew thick and tears welled in her old eyes. She loved each of Llwyd's daughters. She'd helped raise them, and had promised Lady Twyla that she would see to their safety and now . . . now the firstborn was dead? Though she'd feared as much, though the stones had foretold of a death, Hildy found it hard to believe. Impossible to accept. Nay . . . not Elyn. Not headstrong Elyn. Nor vibrant Kiera. Nor sweet Penelope. But had not the cursed stones bespoken of not one, but two of the baron's children dying? Oh, Great Mother, it couldn't be. Hildy's throat was choked and she had to force out the painful words. "If Elyn be dead, then where — where is she? Where is her body?"

Joseph's jaw clenched. "I know not. Washed away in the river, he says." Disgustedly the stableboy hitched his jaw in Brock's direction.

Hildy gazed up at the son of Oak Crest, his shoulders still stiff with false pride, his chin lifted angrily as the soldiers gathered around and the guard, carrying a sword in one hand and a torch in the other, hurried down from his tower in the gatehouse. He took one look at the prisoner and stopped dead in his tracks.

"Go back to your post, Peter!" Hildy ordered, forcing out the words as she was dying inside. *Elyn. Not Elyn.* She couldn't think that Elyn had drowned, had been pulled under an icy curtain of death. Nay, she wouldn't believe it, not even though the stones had warned of disaster, of heartache. Suddenly, she felt older than her years.

The guard was undeterred. "But Joseph's brought a prisoner."

" 'Tis personal," Hildy snapped, then swept a hand at the soldiers. "All of you, go back to your posts!" Guilt burned bright in her breast. With the warning the stones had given her, could she not have somehow prevented it, or was this . . . this terrible death Elyn's destiny?

"Should not the baron be awakened?" Peter insisted.

"I'll speak with Lord Llwyd. You've done your duty. Now return to the tower and lower the gate!" Hildy ordered imperiously despite her grief. She had to take control, to save the baron from waking to this horrid news delivered by a thoughtless guard. Nay. The castle could not be awakened now. Not until she had time to think, to sort things through. Everyone at Lawenydd understood that she had the baron's ear, that he turned to her for advice and sometimes comfort. Few dared argue with her. Peter, the guard, however, appeared to be one of the stubborn.

"Should I not call the sheriff, or the captain of the guard?" he asked, though he sheathed his sword.

"Nay! Why wake them? I will handle this, Peter. I told you to go back to your post. I will speak to the baron myself in the morn. If there is any trouble, I'll take responsibility. Joseph here is my witness. You will not be blamed." Motioning with one hand, she said, "Joseph, take the prisoner to the dungeon."

"Who is he?" Using his hand to protect his eyes from the sleet, the curious guard held his torch aloft to get a better view.

"A common horse thief, is that not right, Joseph?" Hildy asked, her mind spinning with quick excuses. Silently she hoped the stableboy wouldn't blurt out the truth. Not yet. "Did this man not steal Baron Llwyd's mare?"

"Aye. This very horse," Joseph assured the guard, who scratched his beard and looked from Joseph to Hildy and back again while Brock shook his head vigorously and made mewling noises behind his gag.

"Worry not, Peter. We will deal with this thug. And the rest of you, too. Disperse!" she ordered, and the men talking among themselves drifted away. No doubt there would be speculation. Many of them had known Brock, but the broken man on the horse with his bloodied face could have been anyone. The mud on his clothes and face, the curtain of sleet, and the darkness helped disguise him.

Finally the wary guard rubbed his beard but slowly nodded. "Just see that he's locked up proper. I don't want no trouble on me watch."

"There will be none," Hildy said despite the muffled protests of the prisoner and the wild gestures of his bound hands. Reluctantly Peter walked into the gatehouse, his boots scraping the stairs as he ascended the tower. Soon, with a creak of old gears, the portcullis began to lower.

Once they were alone, Hildy and Joseph led the horses and prisoner to the stable. "What's the matter with you?" she demanded of the stableboy. "Have you suddenly gone mad? Why did you bring him into the castle?"

"What was I to do with him?" Joseph was angry. Furious. And limping slightly.

"Why bring him back at all?"

"He has to pay," Joseph ground out, pain reflecting in his night-darkened eyes. "Because of this bloody cur" — he hooked his thumb at the prisoner — "Lady Elyn is dead. Drowned in that river. I'd love to slit his gut myself and watch his innards spill on the ground! Drawn and quartered would be too good for the likes of him."

"Nay! Vengeance is all well and good, Joseph, but we have others to consider. What of Lady Kiera?"

Joseph glowered into the night as they walked past a roost, and several chickens, wakened from their slumber, let out disgruntled clucks. "Mayhap 'tis time for the truth to come out," Joseph muttered as they reached the stable yard.

Much as she wanted to, Hildy couldn't disagree. "Aye, but we need time . . . Kiera needs to be told what happened so that she can deal with Kelan of Penbrooke."

"Christ Jesus, what a mess."

Hildy nodded, though her thoughts were already whirling ahead. "Does anyone other than our soldiers know that Elyn is dead? Did he tell anyone?"

Casting a hateful glance up at Brock, ignoring the cold sting of sleet, Joseph muttered, "Lady Wynnifrydd is aware that the lady lost her life. I overheard the bastard telling her. There could be others who have heard the news as well, but I know not who."

This was worse than Hildy first thought.

Not only was Elyn dead, but Kiera's identity was about to be exposed.

"We'll need to send a messenger to Penbrooke, to warn Kiera. Someone we can trust," she thought aloud as Brock struggled with the rope binding his wrists. "Stop it," she warned, "or I will throw you in the dungeon and tell the baron how you were responsible for his daughter's shame as well as her death."

He quit moving.

"I'll ride to Penbrooke," Joseph offered.

"But you've only arrived. And you're wounded. You walk with a limp."

" 'Tis only a scratch."

"Mayhap I should tend to it."

"As long as it's done so I can leave again." Joseph was adamant. "The less people who know of this, the better. I'd like to kill Brock this very night and I can't."

At least he was beginning to understand the need for secrecy. " 'Tis true. You will have to ride day and night to reach Penbrooke so that Kiera can tell Lord Kelan the truth before the news reaches him. At the same time, I will confide in her father." Hildy shuddered to think what Lord Llwyd would do when he realized one daughter was dead, another living a lie, and the third, along with the one woman he thought he could trust, keeping secrets from him. And Kiera . . . when she confided in Kelan, what would happen to her? Pray that the Lord in heaven was with them all. Hastily she made the sign of the cross over her chest.

But the wind howling through the bailey cut straight to her soul.

"I need but a few hours' rest and a meal. I can leave in the morn." Joseph cast a glance up at his prisoner. "If I stay here, there's no telling what I would do to him." His lip curled in disgust and his big hands balled into fists.

"Leave him to me. I will take care of him."

"Throw him in the dungeon and let him rot or kill him outright. I care not. He's a murderer and any death, no matter how long he suffers, is too good for him," Joseph said, his eyes glowing with the need for revenge.

"Sir Brock is the son of a lord," Hildy reminded him.

Joseph spat on the ground. "He's a bloody cur."

"But someone will come looking for him."

"Aye, and soon, I'd wager," Joseph admitted as he tied the mare to a post. "He was to have been married later the day that I

. . . persuaded him to come with me."

"Will they think he left on his own, or that he was taken prisoner?"

"I know not," Joseph said, then thought for a moment. "There was no evidence of a struggle except for a little of my own blood. And only one horse would be missing, the mare that Brock stole from the lady."

Brock growled behind his gag.

"Shh!" Joseph hissed. "Or I'll kill you now, I swear it."

"Come along. Leave the horses here and we'll take him to my hut," Hildy instructed.

"Gladly." Joseph yanked Brock from his saddle and prodded him forward along the starlit path. Shards of ice glittered in the few puddles, and the frozen earth crunched beneath their boots.

So Lord Nevyll as well as the Baron of Fenn would soon arrive and demand answers, for certainly one of them or Wynnifrydd would eventually surmise that Brock might have gone looking for Elyn. "In the morning, before dawn, once I've cleaned your wound you can leave. I'll let you have a few hours' head start; then I'll speak with him," she said as they reached her hut. The sleet was letting up, but the wind was bone-rattling cold and the clouds overhead were dark with night, ominous and close. In the next few hours, Hildy knew, she wouldn't sleep a wink. And in the morn, after Joseph was well on his way to Penbrooke, she would strip the gag from the bastard of Oak Crest and hear what he had to say.

Did it matter?

Nay.

For no matter what Brock of Oak Crest said, what lies or truths passed his thin lips, only one thing was certain. There had been too many half-truths and lies. Soon, the devil would demand his due.

The night wrapped around them, its darkness broken only by the dying fire. Kiera curled up against Kelan, resting her head on his shoulder, sensing that he, too, was awake. And restless. Despite the hours of fervent, nearly desperate lovemaking they'd shared. "Can you not sleep? Is something wrong?" she asked, running her fingers through the whorls of hair upon his chest.

"Shh. 'Tis nothing."

"I wish I could help," she whispered, assuming that his thoughts were upon his loss, his memories of Lady Lenore. "I, too, lost a mother," Kiera said softly. " 'Tis difficult."

He didn't answer, but she saw him staring at the ceiling. His brow was creased, his jaw tight.

"Is there . . . is there something else?" she asked.

"Do not worry about it."

"But if I can make things easier . . ."

" 'Tis not about my mother," he said, and she felt a sliver of dread slide down her spine. In a heartbeat she knew the time had come for the truth.

"Then?" she prodded, every muscle in her body rigid, her brain clamoring for her to keep up her ruse, her heart knowing she could not.

He paused, then said softly, "You never answered me about the vials I found in your room."

The temperature of Kiera's blood dropped. She gathered herself. "You did not ask again," she said, knowing that she was doomed. She had to tell him the truth. Her promise to his mother could not be kept any longer. While it had only been a short time since she had made her promise to Lenore, she could not continue lying, even if it had been a dying woman's wish.

"I told myself not to think of it, that it was over, and yet . . . it bothers me that you put something in my wine, a potion to make me weak and tired. For a reason I don't understand, you wanted to keep me prisoner in your chamber."

"Did we not already speak of this?" She tried to roll away, to break free of his embrace, but he held her fast against him, his long, sinewy body pressed against hers.

Levering upon one elbow, he gazed down upon her, waiting. "You never explained why."

Kiera closed her eyes, drew in a deep breath. 'Twas finally the time; there was no escaping the truth. "I did not want to marry you," she admitted, her heart thundering, her stomach knotting in dread.

"Because you loved someone else? Because of Brock of Oak Crest." His voice was low. Barely a whisper. As though if he made the distasteful charge softly, it would not be true.

"I loved no one else," she said from her heart. "I have never felt the way I feel with you, Kelan, and I did not expect to care for you. I thought it impossible." She fought tears as she stared up at him.

"As did I."

Her heart nearly cracked. This was so hard. Did she dare touch him? Would it be the last time? When he found out the truth, he would never speak to her again, would recoil from her touch, would no doubt banish her from his sight forever. Agony echoed through her soul. "I love you, Kelan. Only you."

He smiled. Touched her hair. "And I love you, Elyn. With all of my heart."

Her insides shriveled at the sound of her sister's name. *Oh, Lord, help me,* she thought as the fire hissed and glowed a dying red. "I — I've done much that I'm ashamed of," Kiera admitted.

"It matters not. 'Tis done. But the vial of blood? Why would you need blood unless you were not a virgin?"

"But I was."

"I know." His breath stirred against her neck, and she gazed into his eyes knowing that never again would she be able to look at him thus. Never again would she feel the strength of his muscles against hers. Never again would he trust her.

"I can't explain it," she said, unable to force the truth over her lips just yet. " 'Twas a foolish idea."

"You thought if I was drugged, I would think we'd made love before I had slept and then I would leave you alone?"

"If not forever, for a while," she said, grasping at this frail explanation.

"But you knew it would happen?"

"Aye, eventually."

"And still you were willing to trick me? To give me a potion and lie to me?"

"Yes, Kelan," she said dully, her heart aching painfully. *And knowing what I do now, how I feel about you, I would do it again. Just so that I could lie here in your arms, so I could feel your breath on my face, so I could know what it was like to make love to you.*

"You vex me, wife."

" 'Tis not my intent."

"No?"

She heard the disbelief in his voice, felt his hand run up the inside of her leg. Her pulse jumped wildly.

"I think you lie, Elyn. I think 'tis surely your purpose to puzzle me."

"Nay, I . . ."

"You what?"

Oh, God. It was now or never. She closed her eyes, took in a deep breath, and, ignoring the fingers brushing the sensitive skin on her leg, said in a rush, "I am not who you think I am, Kelan. I'm not Elyn. I think . . . I fear that Elyn is dead."

"What?"

"I'm her sister. Kiera."

He laughed and amusement rang throughout the room. "Not Elyn? You must have been talking to my sister."

"Your sister?"

Morwenna. Of course. She knows I am not Elyn.

"So now you are playing tricks on me," he said, his arms surrounding her, his lips tickling her bare shoulder.

"Nay . . . yes . . . 'twas Elyn's idea that we change places." Now that she'd made the admission, she was desperate for him to believe her, to understand how much she loved him, how hopelessly she'd hated her lies.

"Was it, now?" He rolled her onto her back and stared deep into her eyes. "And now I am with my wife's sister, with her blessing."

"Yes," she whispered, her heart beating wildly over her shallow breath.

"And you are here, willing to take her

place? To do whatever I want?"

"Nay, yes . . . I mean . . ."

His smile was deliciously wicked as it slashed white in the night. "Many men would envy me this."

"I think not —"

But it was as if he could not hear her denials. "Well, then, sister-in-law, it is my desire that you make love to me until dawn."

"You don't believe me," she said, realizing that he thought she was somehow trying to enhance their lovemaking by pretending to be another woman.

"I believe anything you say to me," he whispered, kissing her in the hollow of her shoulder as her heart beat crazily and the fire in the grate softly hissed. "Anything."

Chapter Twenty-three

Elyn's head ached, and her body felt as if someone had taken a mallet to every one of her muscles. Drawing in the shallowest of breaths burned her lungs. Slowly she opened a bleary eye and saw a pale woman leaning over her. Her skin was so white as to be nearly translucent, her hair a silvery blond, her eyes a watery blue. An angel, surely.

I've died and gone to heaven, Elyn thought wildly as the room, a small chamber with a tiny fire, came into focus.

"Ahh. You awaken. 'Tis time." The angel offered a kind, ethereal smile.

"Who are you?" Elyn asked, her head clearing. This wasn't heaven. She hadn't died. No, the aches in her body made her realize that she was very much alive and lying upon a narrow pallet in this chamber decorated with beads and smelling of herbs from the candles that were placed around the room.

"My name is Geneva. And you are?"

"Elyn of Lawenydd," she blurted before remembering that she had given her identity to Kiera, that she now had no name, that she was lost. But the woman was not surprised at her admission. 'Twas almost as if she'd divined who Elyn was before she'd even asked the question. Lifting her head, Elyn asked, "Where am I?"

"This is my room at Castle Serennog."

"Serennog?" Elyn repeated, her throat scratchy. She'd heard of the keep, of course, but had never visited. "How did I get here?"

"I found you. Tossed up on the bank of the river. Near dead."

"The river," Elyn repeated as piece by sharp-edged piece, her memory returned and she recalled riding away from Brock, hiding beneath the bridge only to fall into the icy depths and be swept under.

"You were lucky," Geneva said, though Elyn didn't believe it for a minute. She'd been anything but lucky these last few weeks. There had been her impending marriage to Kelan of Penbrooke, then the realization that she was pregnant, and then . . . oh . . . *the baby.*

As if she'd read Elyn's mind, Geneva's smile faded. " 'Tis sorry I be," she said, "but the child . . ." She shook her head, her ashen hair shimmering in the fire glow.

"What of my child?" Elyn asked, though she understood, saw the sadness and pain in the thin woman's gaze.

" 'Twas lost. I found you on the edge of the river nearly three days ago and I thought you were dead."

"You're saying that the child is gone," Elyn said, aching inside, but she wouldn't believe it. Couldn't. Surely the woman was mistaken. She had to be pregnant. *Had* to.

"Aye. The babe did not survive."

"No!" She closed her eyes and her ears to such blasphemy. She was pregnant. The child was Brock's and . . . and she would marry Brock and they . . . they would be a family and . . . But Brock was marrying Wynnifrydd. He told her so himself, the lying, cheating bastard. Her heart wrenched so painfully she nearly cried out. She couldn't have lost the baby. But why would this strange woman lie to her? "I — I don't believe you."

" 'Tis not easy."

" 'Tis not true!" Elyn insisted, rising to a sitting position, but she felt it then, the ooze that had not stopped between her legs, the hollowness in her body and soul.

"There will be others," the woman assured her. As if she believed her words.

Elyn didn't.

Now that Brock was lost to her, she couldn't imagine having a child fathered by another man. Nay. She closed her eyes and willed the blackness that had swallowed her to come again, but she felt Geneva's cool fingers upon her own hand.

" 'Tis not your time," she said with a steadying calm that, had Elyn's heart not been splitting into a million pieces, she might have found comforting. Instead she drew back her hand. She didn't want to be touched. She was beyond consolation.

"I, too, lost a babe," the woman admitted sadly as the fire crackled. She seemed distant for a minute, swept up in memories that robbed her of her serenity. Her pale eyes grew cold as the winter sea, her expression hard and angry, and her hands curled into fists. "It happened not long ago. 'Twas a boy child and the father . . . he is dead now. He lived here at Serennog."

"But he wasn't your husband."

"No . . . nor was he destined to be." She sighed and stared at the flames. "Payton was not a good man and he was killed by a band of men he led, cutthroats."

"And how did you lose the baby?"

Her icy eyes slitted. "He was taken from me," she whispered bitterly, then stood. "I will get you clean, warm clothes and something to eat."

"I am not hungry."

"But you can eat, and you need your strength."

"For what?" Before she could draw away, Geneva placed a smooth hand over her patient's heart.

"To fulfill your destiny, Lady Elyn. What else?"

Yes, what? Elyn thought, and moved enough

to realize that she could use her legs and arms, that if she put her mind to it, she could leave the keep this very night and, as the pale-eyed sorceress had claimed, fulfill her destiny.

He was gone. Kiera reached over to Kelan's side of the bed and found the sheets cold, the bed empty. In the hours before dawn he hadn't believed her when she'd tried to explain that she wasn't Elyn. He'd been amused that she'd pretended to be her sister, but no matter how insistent she'd been, he hadn't believed a word of it. He'd held her close, wrapping his arms around her body and burying his face in her hair, only to fall asleep.

Recriminations had plagued her for most of the night, tearing at her as Kelan's warm breath ruffled the back of her neck. How could she make him understand the truth? Now that the hateful words were said, how could she ever face him again? Around and around the tormenting thoughts had spun until she'd finally fallen asleep only to awaken hours later and discover him gone. Had she made a mistake confiding in him? But what else could she do? She couldn't lie to him forever.

Forcing herself out of bed, she threw water over her face and dressed without the aid of the maid that was always fussing about. The girl, Nell, was sweet enough, but she was a gossip. Kiera was certain that whatever Nell heard went in her ears and out her mouth within seconds.

She started out of the chamber and glanced at the bed. Memories of making love to Kelan teased at her mind and she realized with a horrible sense of doom that it wasn't just Kelan's touch she craved, but so much more. Aye, he was an exhilarating lover, but there was more to him that she would miss were she to leave.

Or be forced to leave.

Hurrying out of the room, Kiera bustled down the stairs to the great hall, where Rhynn was haphazardly strewing fresh rushes over the cleanly swept floor. The dour-faced maid glanced up, then turned back to her work with only a mumbled "Good mornin', m'lady" as a greeting.

"And to you, Rhynn." The aroma of fresh-baked breads and tarts filtered through the rooms, and her stomach rumbled. Everywhere servants worked. One girl hummed as she replaced burned-down candles with new ones; boys brought in stacks of firewood; young children toted water or, leaving their vessels, chased after each other, running up and down the stairs or disappearing around corners until their mothers' sharp voices drew them back to their tasks. Kiera smiled to herself, for she was beginning to feel as if

Penbrooke was truly her home and that Kelan was . . . was her husband.

Don't think like that, she warned herself as she tucked her cloak around her and stepped outside to feel a bit of warmth from a rapidly rising sun. *This is* not *your home and never will be. And if you're foolish enough to fall in love with Kelan, then you are asking for heartache, sure as anything.*

"M'lady," a male voice rasped, and she turned to find Timothy, the gardener, following after her. "A word, if you have a minute."

"Certainly." She stopped at the corner of the wine maker's hut, where a cooper's assistant was rolling empty barrels inside.

The gardener scraped his hat from his head. "I wanted to ask ye about the herbs ye'll be wantin'. We'll plant the usual — some have wintered over — but is there anythin' special ye'd like? We've got thyme and rosemary and comfrey and yarrow, o'course, but I was thinkin' ye might want me to try and grow some of the more exotic ones. I haven't had much luck in the past, but . . . I thought if there was anything you'd like, I'd find me some seeds or starts."

He seemed so eager to please her, and though Kiera was late for mass, she said, "That's a fine idea, Timothy. Let's try anything that we can grow ourselves. I'm sure the lord will purchase whatever else that the cook would like."

He offered her a gap-toothed, shy smile. "Thank you, m'lady."

"Thank you, Timothy," she said, then took the time to inquire about his pregnant wife and three children before hurrying to the chapel. The door creaked as she entered. As her eyes adjusted to the darkened interior, she searched for Kelan and was disappointed.

"Is not my husband here?" she asked Father Barton.

"Nay," the old priest muttered, obviously irritated. " 'Tis my guess that Baron Kelan thinks his own business is more important than that of the Lord."

"Do you know where he is?"

"On the far side of the barony." Father Barton tried and failed to hide his disapproval in the tightening of the corners of his mouth.

Morwenna, from the single pew, had overheard the conversation. "There was a dispute last night, near the border of Serennog. A daft woman was found trying to steal a horse, and a farmer was badly injured. She kept insisting upon seeing the baron, so Kelan and the sheriff rode there. He should be back late tomorrow unless there are problems."

"He should have told me," Kiera said, feeling an odd sense of doom. Mayhap it was because of her own admission and Kelan's disbelief. Now that he was away from the castle, she was worried, would like to have had time this morning to explain herself. That he was gone didn't bode well; why, she didn't know, but the sense of foreboding settled deep in her bones.

"He didn't know until this morning that there was trouble," Morwenna explained, "and he didn't want to wake you."

The door to the chapel opened and a gust of wind banged it against the wall. Daylynn, horrified, cringed as she entered. "Sorry." On her heels, Bryanna followed.

Father Barton cast an extremely unholy glare in the girls' direction, then sighed and lifted his hands. "Now, ladies," he finally said, motioning to the wooden bench, "if you will kneel, we will begin."

Everyone bowed their heads. But as Kiera closed her eyes in an effort at piety and Father Barton began to intone the prayer, her mind was far from this tiny chapel in the middle of Penbrooke. She couldn't stop thinking of Kelan, of the man she loved, of her sister's husband.

She was disturbed that he'd left her, and her premonition of doom was as strong as if Satan himself was watching and waiting for just the right moment to strike.

"You lied to me?" Baron Llwyd bellowed, glaring at Hildy and Penelope with his faded eyes. "*Both* of you?"

Penelope wanted to die a thousand deaths. Never before had she deceived her father. Now, standing in the solar of Lawenydd with Hildy, facing his rage, his disappointment, she felt as small as a runt in a litter of piglets.

Her own gaze downcast, Hildy fingered her necklace. "Aye."

"And Kiera and Elyn lied as well." He clucked his tongue, and as if the shame of it all was too weighty, he dropped into his chair by the fire and absently rubbed his favorite hound behind the ears.

" 'Twas Elyn's plan," Penelope tried to explain. "She forced Kiera to go along with it."

"No one forces Kiera to do anything."

"But Elyn left and promised to be back, and Kiera, she owed Elyn a favor and —"

"Enough." Her father held up a hand, cutting off the rest of her rambling explanation. "So you all decided to lie to me, to shame me, to humiliate me . . . Christ Jesus." He mopped his thinning pate with one age-spotted hand, and to Penelope he looked older than his years. "Does Penbrooke know?"

"Nay."

"And Kiera . . . she . . . oh, Mother of God, did she sleep with him? Oh, why even ask . . ." the baron bemoaned.

Innocently, Penelope responded, "Yes, but she had a potion to keep him from rousing, so all she had to do was lay beside him and not . . . not . . ." Her father looked up at her as if she were a simpleton. Penelope actually shrank away from him.

"So he was duped, too. And still he thinks the wrong sister is his bride? Oh, by the gods, why couldn't I have had sons? They be so much easier than daughters." Sighing, he said, "Surely this ruse has ended." A muscle worked in her father's jaw. "We must ride to Penbrooke today. We must tell him the truth, that he is wed to an imposter, as the woman to whom he was betrothed fled the castle before she was married." Llwyd paused, his hand reaching up to his throbbing head. "Oh, Lord," he moaned as he realized that Kiera had given herself to her sister's husband, as Elyn's name was on the marriage contract, and the name was binding. "By the gods, when I get my hands on Elyn, I'll shake the very life out of her. I swear I will."

" 'Tis too late," Hildy whispered and tears slid down her weathered cheeks.

Penelope knew what her nursemaid was going to say before the words passed her lips. *Nay! Nay! Nay! Not Elyn! Not any of my sisters!*

"Hildy, oh, no . . ." she whispered, but her father hadn't understood.

"Lady Elyn met with Brock of Oak Crest," Hildy explained.

"What?" Llwyd shot out of his chair, and

the dog was on his feet in an instant, barking angrily. "She left to meet another man?" Penelope's father's face flushed to dark crimson. "Like a common whore? My daughter? You're saying that Elyn gave herself to another man while she was betrothed to Penbrooke?"

"They were lovers," Hildy said tonelessly.

"I believe it not!" A vein stuck out in his neck, pulsing with hot anger.

Hildy didn't respond.

"You knew it, didn't you?" he charged, pointing a crooked finger at Hildy's narrow chest. "You knew this and said nothing? Did nothing? Even when I asked you to toss the stones for me, when I wanted the truth, you lied and kept secrets from me while my first-born shamed me and shamed Lawenydd?" Slowly he advanced upon her. "What kind of a sorceress are you?"

"I did not want to hurt you, and I had made an oath with Lady Elyn and Lady Kiera."

"Hurt me? You were concerned for my feelings?" Llwyd's rage was palpable. "I think not. And you'd best remember that you made oaths with my daughters. *Mine.* Not yours. You miserable, lying Jezebel. You are to be banished from this castle at once!" So enraged he was shaking, he glowered down at her. She didn't bother to dash away her tears, nor did she bow her head.

" 'Tis not her fault," Penelope said quickly. "Hildy tried to talk Elyn out of her plan. And when Kiera decided to go to Penbrooke, Hildy tried to stop her as well. But Kiera insisted she had to because of some oath she'd made to Elyn. But now . . . now . . ." Penelope began to sob.

"Now what?" Llwyd demanded, though the edge to his voice indicated that he was beginning to understand. "What is it, Hildy?"

"Brock of Oak Crest is in my hut, a prisoner."

"What? God's teeth, what do you mean, a prisoner?"

" 'Tis true," she said, explaining Joseph's mission and how he'd kidnapped Brock on his wedding day.

"So now Fenn, Oak Crest, and Penbrooke have all been insulted. Compromised! By all that is holy, Elyn, what have you done?" he said, rolling his eyes toward the rafters as if his missing daughter could hear him.

"There is more," Hildy said quietly, her expression as grim as it had ever been, and Penelope steeled herself for what was to come.

"More trouble?" he flung out with a shake of his head. "What more could there be?"

" 'Tis as I feared," Hildy admitted, her tears again tracking down her hollow cheeks. "Lady Elyn was killed. She and Sir Brock had a fight; she ran off and was thrown from her horse into the river."

"What?" Llwyd grabbed hold of Hildy's arms. His anger quickly gave way to disbelief. "Nay . . . I heard you not. Elyn, she's alive somewhere. Hiding mayhap."

"I fear not, m'lord. I am sorry. So sorry."

Penelope could stand the pain no longer. Sobs erupted from her throat and she crumpled into a chair. How had this happened? And why?

"I don't believe you," Llwyd said, but despair was evident in his face. "No. 'Tis not the truth you speak but some lie, some witchcraft. Have you not wounded me enough tonight, woman?"

"Brock is here. In my hut. I spoke with him earlier and he agreed to tell you himself." Hildy's voice trembled. Penelope thought she might be sick. Penelope's hands curled into fists and she remembered all the times Elyn had tried fruitlessly to teach her to shoot an arrow, or to ride a galloping steed, or to bet while rolling dice, none of which Penelope had ever learned. She couldn't be dead. She couldn't!

"Have him brought to me," the Baron of Lawenydd ordered as he dropped heavily into his chair and his dog settled at his feet again. " 'Tis far past time that I knew the truth."

"As you wish." Hildy half ran from the room, leaving Penelope to face the disgraced man who had sired her.

"Father," she said, grief-stricken, "I am so sorry. If there is anything I can do . . ."

"You can do naught," he said bitterly, hopelessness and shame evident in the grooves surrounding his mouth and eyes. His shoulders bowed as if under some invisible weight, and he shook his head in great, overbearing sadness. "You can do nothing to bring your sister back to the living, can you?"

Her heart broke into a thousand pieces. "Nay, but —"

"Nor can you restore my reputation or that of your sister Kiera, isn't that true?"

"Nay," she said miserably.

"I have lost a daughter and you a sister. If that heartache be not enough, there is more. And it will last forever. No baron who is not daft will ever sign an alliance with me again when they learn how my own children and servants have made a mockery of my agreement with the Lord Kelan of Penbrooke. Aside from the original deception, now I will be accused of plotting to kidnap Sir Brock, Lord Nevyll's son, and ruin his marriage to Lady Wynnifrydd of Fenn, whose father will surely blame me and will never again trade or barter or align with Lawenydd. Nay, Penelope, there is naught you can do," he said fiercely. "You have all done far more than you should have."

"But, Father, please," she whispered, broken, her nose running, tears blinding her as she threw herself at his feet and the dog grunted in irritation. "Let me make this up to you."

"Ahh, Penny-girl," he sighed, absently patting the top of the crown of her head. " 'Tis too late. Far too late. Too much damage has been done."

She swallowed back her tears and, taking in a deep breath, forced herself to her feet. "I will make things right . . . well, righter than they are," she swore, and her father's opaque, saddened eyes looked up at her in weary disgust.

"The best thing you can do right now is leave. Go to your chamber or . . . or anywhere. I care not. You and your sisters have disappointed and embarrassed me to the marrow of my bones. I want not to look at you any longer."

Stung, she held back a gasp. 'Twas as if she'd been slapped. Surely he didn't mean it . . . but when she opened her mouth to argue, he waved her away as if sick to death of the sight of her.

Fresh tears filled her eyes and she ran to the door, only to have it flung open. Hildy burst into the room. "M'lord," she said, her eyes wide with worry. "Sir Brock has escaped."

"What?" Llwyd jumped to his feet, the dog barking and growling.

" 'Tis true. His bonds were left in my hut

but he's nowhere to be seen!"

"Oh, for the love of God, call the captain of the guard. He must be found at once!"

But Hildy didn't move. She stood rooted to the spot, and the terror in her eyes warned of something far more dire than Brock's breaking free of his bounds and slipping away. "There is more," she admitted. "Lady Wynnifrydd has arrived. With her are the barons of Fenn and Oak Crest."

Chapter Twenty-four

"He's not here?" Wynnifrydd demanded, her lips tight, her spine as stiff as a flagpole. "Brock's not here?"

She couldn't believe it. Of course Brock had fled to Lawenydd. Where else would he ride to but the home of his beloved? Standing in the great hall, she glared at the broken old man Baron Llwyd, the Lord of Lawenydd no less, and wondered if the old goat was lying to her. Or perhaps, because of his blindness, he just hadn't noticed Brock. The baron seemed defeated and weary, as if he had no strength in his aging bones.

And what of the others milling about him, a gaunt woman servant who seemed rife with secrets, and the younger daughter, a pretty thing whose face was cast in sorrow? The whole place was gloomy and dark, though not as tired and decrepit as Oak Crest.

"Sir Brock was here; one of my men brought him to the castle," the old man explained as servants scurried with trenchers of meat, cheese, and tarts that they laid upon the lord's table. Already both her father and Baron Nevyll had mazers of wine. As if there was time to tarry over a cup! "But he left."

"To go where?" Wynnifrydd cried, despite a quick sign from her father indicating that she should be still.

"I know not," the Baron of Lawenydd said.

He was lying. There was a secret between him and his daughter and the old crone of a woman, who, though obviously of peasant birth, was allowed to hover close to the lord, more as a wife would than a servant. Aye, there was something between them.

"Please, come and eat, 'tis a day of mourning here, for I've been told that my daughter was killed. 'Twas your son," he said, hitching his chin toward Nevyll, "who told Hildy what happened to her and . . . well . . ." He lifted a tired hand. "There is more involved than just that. Much more. Come, sit. We'll talk." Using a cane, he led them to the high table.

"Your daughter, meaning Elyn?" Wynnifrydd clarified, and the old man nodded. Though it seemed impossible, his shoulders stooped further. Something was very wrong here. It chilled Wynnifrydd to the bottom of her soul. She pretended not to understand. "Did she not marry Kelan of Penbrooke?"

"Aye, I thought so, but I was mistaken," he said, throwing a hard glare at the ashen-faced serving woman. " 'Tis a long story, one that I do not fully understand myself. The marriage

. . . it occurred, but there may have been some deception to it." He explained it all quickly, including the stableboy's mission to Oak Crest and his capture of Sir Brock. With a weary sigh, he added, "It appears that I may have been duped and I was not alone."

Nor was she, Wynnifrydd thought, but she had no patience for the stupid old man. Nor did she care about Kelan of Penbrooke's marriage to Elyn, except as it had to do with Brock. Reluctantly, only to appease her own father, she accepted a bit of the food that was offered. But she was going out of her mind. Where the devil was Brock? Who cared about anything else? "What of Brock?" she asked. "He was here, as your prisoner, but he's escaped?"

She suspected that he'd ridden to Penbrooke, even knowing that his beloved Elyn was dead. He would probably have to see for himself that she hadn't somehow survived and even now slipped into her rightful place as Penbrooke's wife. When all else failed, Wynnifrydd supposed, he would scour the towns and castles along the river, searching for Elyn's body, hoping to convince himself that she was alive.

Unfortunately Wynnifrydd understood the man she intended to marry far better than he understood her. With the knife she'd been given, she picked at a bit of pheasant and started plotting. She'd ride much more quickly alone and she wouldn't have to put up with her father's orders or Baron Nevyll's groans about his aches and pains. She could go where she wanted and as fast as she had to. Nothing could stop her. Not her father. Not the threat of outlaws. Nothing.

Her fingers clutched the knife a little harder. Brock of Oak Crest would rue the day he'd left her for another woman, the day that should have been her wedding day. It mattered not that he was probably forced from the keep. He was a strong man, a great warrior, so the fact that some mere stableboy had been able to overpower him and drive him away from Oak Crest seemed ludicrous. Unless he wanted to leave, to have a ready excuse to avoid his own marriage. Stupid, stupid man.

Did he really think she would let him go? That she wouldn't chase him down and mete out his punishment for her humiliation? She cut off another morsel of the bird's carcass and ate slowly, savoring the few bites she'd taken as she considered her revenge.

If by some miracle Elyn had survived the river, or if the story that she'd died was only a part of an intricate plot to deceive them all, then Brock would pay. As would Elyn. And Kiera and anyone else who dared to think that he or she would get the best of Wynnifrydd of Fenn. Nay, she wouldn't let it happen. She'd had plenty of suitors. Plenty.

Rich men, handsome men, men whose prowess at lovemaking was legendary, but she'd spurned them all to be with Brock.

Because she loved him. With all of her foolish heart. And he'd betrayed her . . . Anger burned up the back of her neck and she set her jaw.

He would pay.

And soon.

At her hand.

Until he came crawling back to her. It would happen. As she pushed her trencher aside, Wynnifrydd sent up a silent, determined prayer for vengeance. It need not be swift, nay, but it would be sweet. She would set out tonight for Penbrooke.

"That's it, I tell ye, Lord Kelan," the farmer insisted nearly two days after being robbed, his expression hard beneath his beard. The sun was high in the sky but the day was winter cold as Kelan, the constable, and this farmer stood in front of a weathered shed where five half-grown pigs rooted, oinked, squealed, and grunted in a small pen. Frost covered the dry grass and muddy dirt clods. Ice glittered from small puddles.

"Just at dawn, it was," the man said, nodding to himself. Dressed in a patched tunic and baggy breeches, he kept the pigs at bay with a pitchfork that he held in his good hand. His other was wrapped in cloth that

370

was crusted in blood. "I was out to check on me pigs here, and I found this wild-eyed woman tryin' to steal me best horse. Just comin' out of the shed she was, and startled, near as much as I. She ran as if possessed and I yelled, runnin' to catch up with her.

"That's when she turned on me, came at me with a knife, she did. Slashed and cut me arm. She acted as if she was hurt, y'see. Seemed about to swoon as she tried to climb onto old Sadie's back. But when I yelled at her to get off me horse, she ignored me. She dragged herself into the saddle. Still holdin' her middle, she took off at a gallop, and by the gods, that witch could ride." Giving out a breathy whistle, the farmer held his bandaged hand and stared across his fields and into the woods, his gaze presumably following the path of the crazed horsewoman.

"Did she take anything else?" the constable asked.

"Nay. Nothin' else is missin'. But I'm thinkin' she's the outlaw who's been givin' us all so much trouble."

"Who was she?" Kelan asked, disturbed at the image. "Did you recognize her?"

"Me, nay." He shook his head and rubbed the back of his neck. With his head bowed, he rolled his eyes up so that he could focus on Kelan. "That's the oddity, y'see. Even though she rode like a man, she had an air about her, acted like she was better'n me, as if she was a noble lady or such."

"What did she look like?" the constable asked.

"As I said, it was dawn, just gettin' light, and she was close enough to cut me with a knife, so I got a good look. She was regal-like, with white skin. Long hair, kinda curly, dark brown with some red in it." He motioned toward the tip of his jaw. "She had a pointed chin, but it was her eyes that I noticed. Wild, like I told ye already, but a deep green color. Dark."

Hair, skin, and eyes like Elyn's, Kelan thought with a smile that faded quickly when he remembered his wife's strange admission the night before, that she wasn't Elyn, but Kiera, her younger sister. Nonsense of course, and yet . . . he felt the first little tingle that things were not as they seemed.

"What was she wearing?" the constable asked, and Kelan tried to dismiss his concerns. What was he thinking? He left his wife sleeping in bed . . .

Or the woman you think is your wife.

"A white dress covered with a dark mantle. The dress, it looked like a peasant's. Me own wife has some from the same rough fabric. But the mantle was from a noblewoman or from the wife of a rich merchant, a thick, deep blue that was near to black and lined in fur."

A noblewoman.

"The mantle could have been stolen," Kelan said aloud, to convince himself, for Elyn's confession along with this strange tale was beginning to pull at the underpinnings of his trust.

"I suppose," the farmer said.

"Was there anything else distinctive about her?" the constable inquired.

The farmer snorted, then glanced sideways at Kelan. "Aye, that there was." Jabbing the toe of his worn boot into the dirt, he said, "As she left, she yelled that I could get me horse back. All I had to do was to ride to Penbrooke."

"Why?" Kelan asked as an ill wind kicked up, but the underpinnings of trust began to fall away and the premonition of ill he felt was stronger. Something in the farmer's eyes warned him of bad tidings. His fingers clutched the reins in a death grip.

" 'Cuz she said, 'I'm just borrowin' your horse, farmer,' " the man said, rubbing his wounded arm. " 'The horse, he'll be at Penbrooke tomorrow, and I'll see that my husband returns him to ye.' I asked her who her damned husband was and she laughed and said, 'Don't you know, farmer? Surely you recognize me.' I told her I didn't and she laughed that crazy laugh again, and tossin' her hair over her shoulder, she dug her heels into old Sadie's sides and said, 'I'm the lady of the keep. Elyn of Penbrooke, Lord Kelan's wife.' "

The skin over Kelan's scalp crinkled. His heart dropped to the cold stones of the earth. Christ Jesus, what kind of fool had he been? He had dismissed as a joke what his wife had told him the night before he'd left. How could she not be Elyn? He tried not to consider it, but there had been so many questions since he met her, and as he thought about it, images swirled in his mind, images of the short time he'd known his wife, the few days since he'd met her. There had been the wedding when she'd only hazarded a few glances at him from beneath her heavy veil, then her unexplained illness directly after taking the vows, a sickness that kept her from joining in the celebration of her marriage, their marriage. Not only was Elyn missing from the great hall, but her sister, Kiera, had not shown her face the entire time Kelan had been at Lawenydd.

Kelan felt a slow dawning, and it was a dark dawn as he realized there were other hints as well, signs that indicated all was not as it should be, foreshadowings that he'd ignored. The vials he'd found hidden in the rushes, blood and some potion that surely kept him from thinking clearly, and Elyn's unexplained absences as she'd nearly kept him prisoner in their bedchamber while she'd gone off riding in the forest . . . her reticence about returning to Penbrooke, the hushed voices of the women of Lawenydd, as

if there were secrets within the castle walls
. . . and then when he and his new bride
had finally arrived at Penbrooke, Morwenna's
assertion that his wife wasn't Elyn of
Lawenydd after all. He'd pushed aside all of
these little inconsistencies, didn't want to
think that he'd been duped, but now . . .
now with the black dawn, he was beginning
to wonder if he had not been a greater fool
after all.

At the constable's insistence he had ridden
across the barony to talk to several peasants
who were suffering at the hands of thieves,
those whose livestock and goods had been
stolen, no doubt by a band of rogues and
outlaws, but this farmer's story was different.

*"I'm the lady of the keep. Elyn of Penbrooke,
Lord Kelan's wife."*

The thief's own words. They cut deep into
Kelan's heart, and though he wanted to deny
the suspicions that swirled darkly through his
mind, he could not. He'd seen the torture in
his wife's eyes — nay, not his wife's, but the
traitor's eyes. He'd thought it was due to separation from her family, from her loss of
home, from her unhappiness at the marriage,
but now he knew different; he knew that
she'd lied, the impish sprite who had teased
him, flirted with him, eagerly loved him in
her bed, the virgin who had been frightened
and curious . . . His jaw tightened.

Deep in the pit of his stomach he felt the

cold stones of betrayal gather and rub, causing pain, creating doubts, reminding him that his beautiful, intriguing wife was a stranger to him. And a liar.

Rage burned through his soul. Dangerous fury blasted through his bloodstream. He thought of his wife, his lying, beautiful Judas of a wife. By the gods, how could she do this to him? To her own family? What kind of calculating, heartless bitch was she? His teeth clenched so hard they ached, his hands around the reins were stiff, and he imagined grabbing her by the shoulders and shaking her and . . . An image of her smile, teasing and naughty, seared through his mind. He re-membered the lift of her eyebrow, coy and seductive in one gesture, and the way her hands played magic along his spine.

Bile rose in his throat. He'd thought he'd loved her, and she'd used him. Played him for a fool. *Oh, cunning, heartless woman, just wait until I see you again.*

'Twas time to return home.

Time for the woman claiming to be Lady Elyn to bare her soul and face his wrath.

Chapter Twenty-five

"There's someone here to see you," Morwenna announced, breezing into the great hall, where for most of the time since Kelan's unannounced departure, Kiera, sitting in a chair near the fire, had been besieged by the servants, one after another.

She'd spent hours listening to their questions, making decisions, and telling herself that she did not miss Kelan. She'd talked with the cook about the next week's meals, with the steward about the need for more cutlery and linens, with the priest about distributing alms, with the carpenter about building more tables and chairs. Her head was spinning with all the choices she'd made, choices that weren't hers to make.

"Who is it?" Kiera asked from her spot at the table.

"A messenger from Lawenydd."

Kiera's head snapped up and Morwenna lifted an eyebrow. "He says his name is Joseph."

"Joseph?" Kiera's pulse leaped and she jumped up so quickly she banged her knee on the table. "Ouch!" He must have news of

Elyn! Finally she would know the truth, discover why her sister had not returned to take her place as Kelan's bride.

Perhaps Elyn had returned! Yes, that was it! Why else would he have ridden here?

Then what will you do? You don't want to leave Penbrooke. You love Kelan. Oh, God, but you want word of your sister, to know that she's well.

Kiera felt ripped in two, but she was grateful for word of Elyn, any word. From the corner of her eye she spied one of the servants loitering near the washbasin. "Rhynn. Please, see that my guest is sent in, then get him something to drink and something to eat. And . . . and have someone prepare a room for him, as he will be weary."

"Aye, m'lady," the surly maid agreed.

"Who is Joseph?" Morwenna asked as Rhynn slipped out of the chamber.

"The son of the stable master."

"He's visiting you?" Kelan's sister couldn't hide her surprise. "A peasant. And you're preparing a room for him?"

"Yes!" she nearly snapped. "He . . . he must have news of my family," Kiera said. She started for the door as Joseph, his clothes caked in mud, his hair lank, his face weary, barreled his way into the great hall.

Escorted by Rhynn and a burly guard and limping slightly, Joseph grinned as he saw her. "M'lady." He swiped his cap from his head.

"Joseph!" She ran to him, and despite the curious stares of the servants and Morwenna, she threw her arms around the stableboy, nearly sending them both sprawling. The hell with social stations. She didn't know until that moment how much she had missed Lawenydd and everyone within her father's keep. Her heart lurched and tears burned behind her eyelids as Joseph, stunned at her demonstration, awkwardly embraced her. "By the saints, it's good to see you," she said, her voice catching as she finally pushed off his shoulders to stare at him. "Please, come in, come in. Warm yourself. Rhynn!" She turned to the woman, who stood rag in hand, mouth agape at the lady's display. "Get food and wine for our guest." When the woman remained as if rooted to the floor, Kiera said more harshly, "Now."

"Oh, er, yes, m'lady."

Kiera motioned Joseph toward the fire when she finally noticed his expression. It was more than weariness that tugged at the corners of his mouth and eyes. His countenance was hard. Angry. His jaw worked as he tried and failed to repress emotions that burned through his soul.

Oh, God . . . something was wrong. Terribly wrong. Her lungs constricted as horrid image after horrid image burned through her mind. "You must be tired and cold. Here, sit by the fire." Shepherding him toward the chair she'd just vacated, she motioned for one of the boys carrying firewood to add the logs to the flames. "Oh . . . forgive me, this is my . . . Kelan's sister, Morwenna."

"M'lady. A pleasure," Joseph said, but his expression remained grave and there was a flatness in his eyes that frightened her.

"Sit," she said, dropping into one chair by the fire and motioning him into another. "You have news? Something is wrong, I can tell."

Morwenna dallied.

"Aye." His throat worked and Kiera knew the darkest dread of all.

" 'Tis your sister, lady."

"My sister?" she repeated, and a roaring started in her ears.

"We think she's dead."

"Nay!" Kiera shot to her feet. *Elyn dead?* Nay, oh, nay! She felt the color wash from her skin. Her voice, when she spoke, was raw. "There must be some mistake." She wouldn't believe it. Much as she loved Kelan and wanted to stay as his wife, Kiera couldn't believe that Elyn was dead. Even though it was odd that she hadn't returned when she'd promised, Elyn had to be alive. She was young. Vibrant. Strong. "No, it cannot be."

But even as she uttered the words, a dozen questions rattled like bones through her mind. *Have you not wondered if she'd been harmed? Haven't you in your darkest hour sus-*

pected that she might have died . . . and yet you kept your secret, remained here with Kelan in happy oblivion, denying your fears, living a lie, rather than finding a way to help Elyn.

"She was out riding, and disappeared," Joseph explained wearily.

"But surely she'll be found." Was that her voice? It sounded so weak. So far away, though she was certain the words had fallen from her own tongue.

"Nay, I think not." He rubbed his jaw and shook his head.

No, no, no! Elyn was just hiding somewhere. Aye, that was it. She would be found. Alive. Mayhap she was injured, but not dead. Never dead. "This is a mistake, Joseph . . . she's missing, I know, but . . . you said 'We *think* she's dead.' So no one is certain. You have not seen her body."

Joseph stared at the fire. "She was to meet someone and he saw her horse later. Without her. She . . ." He cleared his throat and looked down at the fists he'd clenched over his knees. "She fell into the river and was pulled under. Swept down. No trace of her found."

"No." Kiera was shaking from the inside out. Her hands were trembling, her legs threatening not to hold her. Despite the fire, she felt cold as death, shivering outwardly at the thought of Elyn drowning, being pulled under swift, winter waters, her lungs filling . . . no, oh, no. Her bones seemed to crumble beneath her. She could barely stand as she thought of Elyn, panicked and flailing, battling a deadly current. "This is wrong. Who saw her?" she demanded.

"Sir Brock of Oak Crest."

Every muscle in her body became rigid. "That cur saw her drown and was unable to save her? No, I don't believe it. Nor do I believe him. He's a liar . . . and a horse thief and a rogue."

"Why would he lie?" Morwenna asked, and Kiera tensed even more. So intent was she on Joseph's information, she'd forgotten that Kelan's sister was in the room, hearing the entire conversation, trying to piece it together. "You and I both know Sir Brock," Morwenna reminded her gently, though her eyes were suspicious as they trained on Kiera. Frantic, Kiera replayed her conversation with Joseph in her mind. Had she mentioned Elyn's name . . . oh, what did it matter? Now Elyn might be dead. *Dead!* Tears filled her eyes as Morwenna said, "You . . . you once fancied yourself in love with him, did you not?"

"Not I," Kiera said tightly.

Morwenna's cold expression charged her with the lie. "But why would your sister go to meet him? You are speaking of Kiera, is that not so?" she asked Joseph, whose guilty gaze concentrated on the crackling flames in the grate.

He hesitated, his gaze flicking to Kiera. "Aye, I am speaking of the lady's sister," he said.

Balancing a heavy tray, Rhynn bustled into the chamber — though not so much out of duty as to hear the gossip, Kiera thought angrily as Rhynn, with a smile for Joseph, laid the tray on a small table. There was a mazer of ale, a brick of cheese, and a bowl of eggs set near a trencher of wastel bread.

"Thank you," Kiera whispered to the serving maid, who lingered, casting a smile in the stableboy's direction. Kiera sighed as she battled tears. "I — I cannot believe this." Kiera's throat burned painfully and distant memories of her older sister and their childhood flashed through her mind. Elyn with her adventures, crossing a stream on exposed rocks in summer, riding bareback through the autumn leaves, hunting with their father or aiming her deadly arrow at Kiera's attacker, and, most recently, pressing Kiera into this insane plan and then abandoning her to Kelan . . . *Dear God, please, please, bless her soul. Redeem her.* "How . . . how is Father? Penelope?" she asked, then shook her head and buried her face in her hands. Tears of grief and remorse spilled from her eyes. "Oh, this is so wrong."

"I'm sorry," Morwenna said, and Kiera felt a gentle hand upon her shoulders. Through a sheen of tears, Kiera looked up at Kelan's sister. Morwenna's face, so often suspicious, had softened with concern. "If there's anything I can do . . ."

Kiera sniffed. "There is nothing," she said, anger, regret, and grief tearing at her soul. "Nothing anyone can do."

Breathless, her body aching from the punishing ride, Wynnifrydd saw the castle looming in the moonlight.

Penbrooke.

Home of Baron Kelan and . . . no doubt, Elyn of Lawenydd.

The bane of Wynnifrydd's existence.

Surely Brock was within the tall stone battlements, even now searching for his beloved. Wynnifrydd's betrayed heart twisted so hard she shook. Brock wouldn't have rested thinking that Elyn might have survived, that his eyes had played tricks upon him the night on the bridge, that she may have returned to her rightful place, that she might even now be married to the baron.

Lying, miserable bastard.

Digging her heels into the mare's sides, Wynnifrydd urged her horse along the rutted dark road leading to Penbrooke. The moon and stars offered small illumination and the night air was raw and chill. Wynnifrydd hardly noticed. Though she was tired, she felt a Stygian tingle of anticipation.

Tonight belonged to her. Wynnifrydd would

exact her revenge from Brock and Elyn and anyone else who had been a part of the mortification she'd suffered when her groom had left her standing alone at the altar. Even now, she felt the humiliation of it all, the ghastly embarrassment to her, her father, and all of Fenn. She set her jaw and lowered her head, riding even faster, feeling the wind rush by, whispering in her ears, telling her that finally she would be able to even the score and exact her revenge.

Soon Brock and Elyn and whoever else had been a part of the scheme to demean her would pay. No matter what it cost.

Kiera pushed open the door of the chamber and stepped inside. Another day was drawing to an end, and Kelan had yet to return.

In the bed, Joseph opened an eye and struggled to a sitting position.

"Nay, don't," she said, walking into the darkened room. "I was just checking to see if you're being cared for."

One side of his mouth lifted, though there was no spark in his eyes. "Bothered more like. Nell, she's brought me mead and food," he said, motioning to a table bearing a jug and empty trencher. "Some other girl carried up hot, wet rags for me to clean myself, the priest was here wanting to pray with me, and the physician cleaned and bound my leg."

Kiera smiled. "Welcome to Penbrooke."

He managed a humorless laugh.

"Rest now. I won't bother you."

"You don't, m'lady," he said, and sighed. "I think I've had enough sleep. 'Tis all I've done since I arrived."

"You need it."

Joseph didn't seem convinced and glanced at his clothes, still tattered but clean as they warmed atop a stool by the fire. Near his boots were his knives, the larger one that he'd had strapped to his waist, a smaller one that had lain hidden in the scruffy boots that now rested on the hearth. "I only wish that I could have saved the lady," he said, his voice husky.

"As do I," Kiera said. Her heart felt as if it were made of stone. Her eyes burned from the tears that she'd shed, and her head pounded with guilt. 'Twas time to bare her soul again and make Kelan believe the truth this time, even if it meant losing him. She'd waited all day for Kelan, but he hadn't returned.

Darkness had fallen hours before and she'd spent the evening in anxious anticipation with her ears straining as she hoped to hear his voice rising up from the lower floors or the sound of his boots on the stairs. She'd been disappointed and she understood forlornly how much she'd come to love him. Her heartbeat always kicked up a bit at the sight of him, her pulse leaped when he looked at her, and she grew warm inside at his touch. She looked forward to spending days with him, learning the routine of the castle, and she anticipated each night of making love.

Foolish, foolish woman.

And now you must unburden your heart and confide in him. For there may be a child. You are already a day late; your ever regular cycle has been disturbed. The thought that she could very well be with child was comforting, but only a little. Until she told Kelan the truth, she could find no solace.

"Lord Brock is to blame," Joseph muttered.

" 'Twas Elyn's choice to meet him."

"But he should have saved her." Joseph's lip curled in disgust. "I'll cut out his black heart," he vowed, then closed his eyes and sighed. "I should have stopped her; I should never have let her take the horse."

"You couldn't." Kiera placed a hand upon the stableboy's shoulder. "No one could talk her out of meeting Brock, nor could you have denied her requests."

"Because she is a lady and I am a servant," he sneered, and for the first time Kiera witnessed Joseph's loathing of his position in life. His eyes held hers and she noticed the flare of defiance in their depths, recognized the rebellious thrust of his jaw. "And so she is dead."

"You must not blame yourself."

"Nor should you, m'lady. But Sir Brock, he is guilty as Satan himself, and he'll pay."

"Shh. We'll talk of this another day; now you must rest," she said. She saw him glance to his clothes as if he intended to get out of bed the instant she left the room. Not that she blamed him. Wasn't she, too, restless, in need of distraction?

With thoughts of her sister and Kelan heavy on her mind, Kiera hurried to her room and gazed out the window. The moon rose high over the battlements of Penbrooke, silvering the ground and stone walls of the keep. Sadly she accepted the fact that Kelan wouldn't return until the morning. Or later. She would have to live her lie through one more night. Yes, she had told Kelan the truth, but she hadn't fought hard enough to make him believe her words, that she was Kiera, not Elyn. Tomorrow, she swore to herself, she would be forceful, making Kelan believe that his true wife had died, that she, the impostress, had lied over and over to him. Then she would suffer the consequences.

Her punishment when Kelan accepted the truth would be severe, she knew, but whatever penalty Kelan meted out, it would be less painful than seeing the hatred and loathing that were certain to be evident in his gaze. No sentence could be worse than having him detest the sight of her.

"God help me," she whispered, making the sign of the cross over her bosom. "Help us all."

She could stand the waiting in this room no longer. Slipping her mantle over her head, she hurried downstairs to the great hall, where only a few servants moved through the darkened corridors. The dogs slept near the dying fire. The lazy hounds raised their heads as she passed to the main door, where a guard was posted, but seeing nothing seriously amiss, they let out soft grunts, yawned, and settled back to sleep. "Are you going out, m'lady?" the guard inquired.

"Aye, Jeffrey, for a while."

"But 'tis dark."

"I know. I won't be long." She pushed past the guard and threw him a quick smile.

Outside, the night was cold and crisp, a bit of a breeze tossing dry leaves along the path. Through the slatted windows of some of the huts, a few strips of firelight seeped into the night and she heard whispers of hushed conversation and the cackle of muted laughter. Overhead the sails of the windmill creaked in the brittle night, and in the distance she heard the lonely cry of a wolf.

She didn't know where she was going, just that she needed to walk, to think, to grieve for her sister, and to plan what she would say to the man who still thought she was his wife. Her boots crunched on the frozen ground, and her breath fogged in the night air. Her cheeks were chilled and she thought of Elyn, fun-loving, daring Elyn, being dragged beneath the surface of the icy river. "God be with you, sister," she whispered as she made her way to the eel pond, where moonlight rippled across the water. She wondered if when Kelan arrived home she should reemphasize the truth as soon as he returned, or delay and spend a few more moments in sexual surrender, making love to him.

She thought she heard a footstep behind her and turned, squinting into the night, but no one appeared. The keep was nearly deserted and yet she felt a presence, as if someone was watching her. Goose bumps pebbled her arms. 'Twas foolish. No one was about. And yet . . .

Was it her imagination or did she hear her name whispered over the breeze?

"Kiera."

Kiera's blood turned to ice. No one knew her by her given name.

"Over here." The voice was weak, as if in pain.

Kiera whirled, her eyes searching the darkness.

"Kiera!" Louder this time. More distinct. And clearly from someone who knew who she really was.

Elyn's voice.

But that was impossible. Elyn was dead.

Lost in the icy current of the river . . .

Heart thudding, she scanned the night-shadowed bailey. Past a hayrick and the well, beyond the garden, she scoured the shadows.

Had she imagined it? Was her mind playing cruel jokes upon her, conjuring up the haunted, frail voice of her sister?

Squinting, she saw a figure hiding behind the ferret kennels. Kiera's heart beat crazily as the woman stumbled forward. Wearing a fur-lined cloak that didn't disguise the tattered, bloodied tunic beneath, the ethereal figure slipped out of the shadows. She made a faltering step forward.

Elyn! The woman was Elyn! Oh, God, she was alive and here or . . . or . . . Kiera stopped short. Was this really her sister, or was it Elyn's ghost?

Chapter Twenty-six

Her heart wedged in her throat, Kiera flung herself toward her sister or the damned apparition, whatever it was.

Tears of relief filled her eyes and she wrapped her arms around the stiff form of her sister. Not a ghost. Not an apparition. Not a cruel image of her mind, but her real, flesh-and-blood sister. "I thought . . . oh, thank God you're alive! I thought you'd drowned! Where have you been? I've been waiting so long . . . oh, God, look at you. What happened?"

Kiera held her sister at arm's length and saw the dark accusations in Elyn's eyes, the haunted expression that aged her face a dozen years.

"You knew not what had happened to me and yet you stepped willingly into my shoes," Elyn said, her voice condemning, her face pale as death in the moonlight. "I'm certain you never thought you'd have to give them back to me."

"But you wanted me to do this! You left." What was Elyn thinking? Why was she making such bizarre accusations? Did she now want to claim Kelan as her husband? How? 'Twas too late.

From one of the towers there was a cough — one of the sentries. Kiera dragged her sister down a path toward the stables. "I never considered myself Kelan's wife."

Elyn snorted and held her middle as if it ached. "Do not lie."

"I'm not. You didn't return to Lawenydd as you promised, nor were you here when we arrived. I didn't want to do this deed, Elyn. It was your idea. Your plan. You left me without a word, to face — what did you call him? — the Beast of Penbrooke and marry him." Anger tore through Kiera's soul. How could her sister blame her? "You abandoned me. To be with Brock, remember?"

Elyn's features twisted, making her appear grotesque in the moonlight. "Brock," she said as if the man were dead.

"Oh, please . . ." Kiera lowered her voice when she witnessed her sister's bald pain. "Let's not fight. I am so glad that you're alive. Joseph came with the news that you'd lost your life in a river and I . . . I thought I'd never see you again."

"I've heard the rumors, sister," Elyn whispered, undeterred by Kiera's plea. "I hid in a closet by the kitchen where the wenches gossip. They are half in love with the lord themselves and made jokes about bedding him, but they seem to think it impossible

393

now because the baron appears quite taken with his wife, meaning you. And they say that the two of you are in love and that he's never been happier in his life."

Elyn's voice raised an octave with each new charge, and Kiera was torn between elation that her sister was alive and dismal regret at her sister's hostility.

With difficulty, Elyn pushed a wayward strand of hair from her eyes. "So is it true? Do you love him?"

Kiera's heart wrenched. She swallowed hard and felt the weight of the barony upon her shoulders. Yet she could not lie. There had been enough lies as it was. A harsh wind cut across the bailey and scraped her face. She loved Kelan of Penbrooke with all of her heart. The truth was impossible to hide. "Aye," she admitted, nodding. " 'Twas not expected, but oh, none of this was." She reached out to touch her sister's arm, but Elyn recoiled swiftly, as if the thought of her sister's touch was repulsive.

"And he loves you?"

"So he has said."

"Then you've slept with him? Made love to him?"

"Aye," she whispered.

"I knew it!"

"How could I not?" Kiera demanded, suddenly angry. She was vaguely aware of a noise in the bailey, but she was so incensed at Elyn's ridiculous accusations and recriminations that she ignored it. "You didn't return when you said you would. When you first told me of this plan of yours, you were to return that night, and when I didn't want to go through with it, you left me anyway. I thought you would be as good as your word, but nay, I waited and waited. Me, Penelope, and Hildy, and you sent no word. Not one," she reminded her sister. Her fists were clenched, pride stiffening her spine. "Even if you had returned, Elyn, it was too late. Your plan was flawed, so horridly flawed. Kelan's no fool and he'd already seen me far too often to be deceived by my switching places with you."

"I was detained."

"It matters not," Kiera declared. "I drugged him, but he caught me the next day. I skulked about the keep trying to find you, I lied to Father, and I worried . . . never knowing what had happened to you. I did everything you asked, it didn't work, and 'tis not my fault. The only blame I will accept is that aye, I fell in love with him. Despite everything, and my promises to myself, I love him."

Elyn's jaw tightened. "So now you want to remain his wife?"

"Nay . . . I want not to be his wife if he is to think I am you," she admitted, though the admission hurt. "And there is no other way.

You cannot return now and pretend that you have been his wife all along. Too much time has passed. Everyone here recognizes me as his wife. *Kelan* considers me his wife. And that is what you wanted, isn't it? You had no intention of returning," Kiera said, speaking the suspicion that had gnawed at her soul.

Elyn's lips compressed. She didn't answer. Probably couldn't face the truth. "Tell me of Lawenydd."

" 'Tis no different. Hildy and Penelope kept the secret and I pretended that I left Lawenydd to spend some time with you. I lied and said that you wanted me to accompany you to Penbrooke, so that Father wouldn't miss me. But now the truth is known, and no doubt Father is furious with all of us. I know all this because Joseph came here to Penbrooke." Stung by Elyn's unfair accusations, she turned away from her sister.

The sound of a horse whinnying within its stall echoed through the night. Not able to face Elyn, she asked, "Why did you not return as you'd said you would? What detained you?"

There was silence and when Kiera looked over her shoulder, she found Elyn bracing herself against the wall of the stable, both her arms wrapped around her torso. " 'Twas foolish," she admitted, a tear tracking down her cheek. "I thought Brock . . ." Her voice broke and she shuddered, then cleared her throat. " 'Tis true. I wasn't coming back, Kiera. Brock and I had planned to run off." Her eyes seemed to flatten with a dark rage. "Then he changed his mind. Claimed that he had to marry Wynnifrydd, as she was with child." Elyn's lips twisted at the irony. "Fortunately he never knew of ours. And now 'tis gone."

"Of yours? Gone? What are you saying?" Her heart nearly stopped, and though she was barely listening, she heard the sound of the portcullis opening, of hoofbeats thudding against the cold ground.

"Aye, Kiera. I was carrying Brock's babe; that's why I could not return, why I couldn't marry Penbrooke. I wanted to spend the rest of my life with . . ." She choked and sobbed, then, as if mentally slapping herself, took in a deep breath. "But when he told me of Wynnifrydd and her babe, I rode off angrily. I just . . . I just had to get away from him. From the thought of another woman . . . from everything. The horse shied. I ended up in the river. I nearly drowned, only I was saved and survived. The child did not."

Kiera's heart wrenched painfully. What if it were her? What if she'd lost her child before it was born? Would anything be worse? More tragic? "I'm so sorry . . . Elyn . . . dear God." She turned to embrace her sister, but Elyn held up a hand, stopping her again. Clearing her throat, Elyn looked away, and her sadness seemed even greater than before.

Whispering, she said, "So I have returned. To relieve you and tell my husband the truth." She leaned heavily against the wall as if she could no longer stand. "Except that you are now in love with my husband, and mayhap with a child of your own." Her hand shook as she brushed her hair from her eyes. " 'Tis a dismal mess I've made."

"One we shall straighten out," Kiera insisted as she placed a firm grip upon her sister's arm. "Come. You're weary. Let's go inside. You can rest and I'll have Cook bring up some soup and wine and we shall talk."

"What good will talking do?" Elyn wondered aloud. Then she glanced past Kiera's shoulder and in the weak moonglow seemed to pale even further.

"I know not, but somehow we must find a way to tell Kelan the truth. I tried but he did not believe me," Kiera was saying as she heard the hoofbeats behind her and knew in that one heartbeat that someone had overheard them. She froze for a second, then gathered in her breath and turned slowly.

"The truth," Kelan said from atop his destrier as he looked down his nose from one sister to the next. His expression was harsh. Dark. Uncompromising. His eyes reflected the icy moonlight; his lips were blade thin. "And what, I wonder, is that?"

Kiera died a thousand deaths in the span of that one heart-stopping second.

Kelan dismounted and another horse came into view, a dappled animal ridden by the constable. If possible, Kiera's heart felt heavier. Slowly, each step seeming to take forever, Kelan approached. His jaw was set, and the cords in his neck stood erect. Fury radiated from him in hot, hostile waves.

"Explain yourself," he growled.

She reached a hand to touch Kelan's chest, but he caught her wrist and glowered down at her with icy gray eyes. "What is it, *wife?*" he demanded, his fingers clamping over the bones in her forearm like a vise. "What have you got to say for yourself? Who is this woman who looks so much like you?" He hitched his chin toward Elyn cowering in the shadows; then his eyebrows rose as he focused hard upon her. "Is she your sister?"

"Aye," Kiera said, sick inside.

"Kiera?" he asked, his voice taunting.

Kiera's head snapped up and she glanced at Elyn. Then she shook her head.

"Well, 'tis not your younger sister, Penelope. I met her at the wedding." His eyes narrowed and Kiera sensed the wheels turning in his mind, his thoughts a tangle of doubts, suspicions, and lies. "Or is it the other way around?" he bit out, his face set in white-hot fury.

From atop his stallion the constable cleared

his throat. "M'lord?"

"See to the horses," Kelan ordered, then, to Kiera, sneered, "Come, *wife!* Into the great hall. You, too!" He motioned toward Elyn. "We have much to discuss."

"She's ill," Kiera protested.

"We'll tend to her, but I'll not have this conversation in the middle of the bailey where any servant or freeman might hear!" Jerking on her arm, he led her along the path to the keep while Elyn, trying to hold on to the rags of her dignity, hoisted her chin and slowly followed after.

So it had come to this: the great reckoning. Kiera's insides were knotted as she, looking over her shoulder at her sister, was half dragged into the great hall. Some of the guards looked their way but said nothing, while Kiera's heart was knocking wildly in her rib cage. How could she explain herself? How could Elyn? And what did Kelan already know? 'Twas as if he was already taunting her, scorching her with his gaze. The fingers surrounding her arm were punishing, his grip a manacle.

Once they were inside the great hall, Kelan pointed with his free hand to a wooden chair on the hearth. "You, whoever you are, sit," he ordered Elyn. She hesitated, seemed about to argue, then seeing the flare of determination in his gray gaze, dropped like lead onto the seat near the fire. "Now, who are you?"

Elyn looked miserable as she searched for words. "I'm . . ."

"She's your wife," Kiera said quickly. The truth had to come from her lips.

"My *wife?*"

Kiera nodded and saw the twist to his lips, the flare of anger in his eyes. He'd known. From the moment he'd found the sisters in the bailey, or even before. What she told him was not the surprise she'd expected. "Elyn of Lawenydd."

"So you were telling the truth the other night when I thought that you were joking?" Kelan said with a quiet, burning rage. "Why did you not correct my assumption . . . Kiera — isn't this your given name?"

Oh, God. Help me. He glared at her so intensely she wanted to shrink through the floor, but she couldn't. "Yes, Kelan," she whispered, her heart in her throat. "I am Kiera, Elyn's sister."

"But you have been here, with me, these past . . ." His voice drifted off and Kiera knew he was thinking of her erratic behavior during the wedding ceremony and directly after, of her refusal to join the guests and pleas of illness, of the hidden vials, of his drugged state, of her aversion to being with people who might recognize her, of her desire not to come to Penbrooke. Every muscle in his face tightened and the skin over his cheeks stretched taut. His lips barely moved as he whispered, "You've deceived me all along; you lied to me, to my family . . . when I thought you were telling the truth, you were lying. When you were telling the truth, I thought you were jesting. How can I ever trust such a woman?" Kelan asked, his heart hardening against the woman he had thought was his wife. "How can I trust any woman? It turns out the woman I thought was my wife is an impostress, and the woman who is my wife is a liar and a horse thief. You both plotted and planned to ruin me, my family, and my name."

Kiera felt her face drain of color. "Nay." But her denial sounded weak, so she forced herself to toss her head and meet the anger snapping in his eyes. "Never."

"You dare to deny that you willingly plotted to make me a fool?" His glance sliced from Kiera to Elyn and back again.

"Forgive me," Kiera whispered. " 'Twas not my . . . er, our intent."

His was a quiet rage, one that transformed his features from disbelief to a florid, ruddy fury. "Why else?"

Kiera swallowed hard, forced herself to stand her ground. She finally had the chance to explain the totality of the foolish plot that Kelan had not allowed her to mention before he had left. " 'Twas only supposed to be for a night," she said in a rush. "I would say the vows, hide in the chamber, and see that you didn't leave . . . The vials, they were to trick you, aye, into sleeping as if you were dead and, when you awoke, to see that the sheets were stained so that . . . so that . . ." She gulped and her courage faltered.

"So that I would mistakenly think we had made love," he said through lips that barely moved.

"Yes . . . I know it sounds foolish, daft even, and — and 'twas wrong, but we thought there would be no harm done and after that first night, Elyn would return and . . . and then we would switch back."

"Switch back," he repeated, spitting out the words. His lips were bloodless. His face tightened with a seething, growing wrath, and a tic above his eye pulsed against the restraint that was evident in the cords of his neck. "I don't believe you," he charged, his voice low. Deadly.

"Why would I lie?"

"That is the question, is it not?" Kelan sneered while still he held her wrist with his deadly, crushing fingers.

"Kiera speaks the truth," Elyn said boldly as she stared at the fire. "I didn't want to marry you or anyone my father chose. I thought I should be able to pick the man I was to marry. Father, of course, disagreed. He thought of me as a prize he could barter and trade at his will." Her nostrils flared as if she'd just smelled cattle dung in the castle.

The fingers around Kiera's wrist clenched so tight she thought her bones would snap. "So if you truly are Elyn of Lawenydd, and you're the shy Kiera, why did you agree?"

Kiera said, "I owed her my life. I told you of Obsidian, the horse you call Ares. The night I took him out I came upon an outlaw who attacked me. Elyn followed me and wounded the man before . . . before he hurt me. I felt I owed her my life and so . . ." Her heart wrenched and she could barely breathe as she admitted the rest. "And so I swore I would do anything she asked in return."

"And that favor was to stand in for her during the wedding ceremony, to bed me while she was . . . where?" Kelan's gaze moved to Elyn in her tattered, dirty blue mantle and stringy hair. Despite her bedraggled appearance, she lifted her chin, tossed her hair over her shoulder, and glared back at him, all the while remaining stonily silent.

Kiera didn't say a word, couldn't betray her sister. And so the room grew cold. Unspoken accusations and alibis hid within the dark corners. Only the quiet hiss of the fire broke the silence.

Kelan turned his harsh gaze back to Kiera. "Tell me."

"I wasn't supposed to bed you. You . . . you were supposed not to awaken 'till morn," Kiera quickly said, skirting the issue of Elyn's relationship to Brock. It worked; Kelan became even more furious.

"From the potion you slipped into my wine," he snarled, his temper snapping and all restraint lost. "You lied to me. Both of you and probably others as well. You pretended to be my wife, acted the part while making me a fool for you."

Kiera's arm ached; her heart tore. Kelan must've guessed her pain. In disgust he dropped her wrist and strode to the fire to glare down at Elyn. "Speak, Elyn of Lawenydd."

"All right. Kiera speaks the truth!" Elyn finally admitted, blinking against tears and rubbing her arms with her hands as if she was cold to her bones. "All of it, 'tis true." She managed to climb to her feet, and though her legs wobbled, she met Kelan's — her husband's — incensed gaze with her own. "This plan was all my idea. I forced Kiera to be a part of my plan because of the debt she owed me."

Kiera touched the chain around her neck, and the jeweled cross felt as heavy as an anvil.

"She was *forced?*" he mocked, shaking his head.

"She owed me a debt. By standing in for me at the altar and pretending to be me, she paid it. She did everything because of honor, no matter what you may think. And the bald truth of the matter, Kelan of Penbrooke, is that I am your legal wife, if only in name, but I am here to take my place . . . Kiera took the vows for me, in my stead, with my blessing."

The words echoed through the room, reverberating painfully in Kiera's heart.

"You are not my wife, nor will you ever be," Kelan spat in disgust. He glanced over his shoulder to Kiera. For a heartbeat she caught a glimpse of pain, of raw agony, but it disappeared quickly.

Kiera wanted to die.

"You will both be locked into separate rooms until I find out what the devil is going on," he said.

An alarm bell sounded, clanging loudly, pealing through the keep. Outside the door, men shouted wildly and footsteps thundered.

"What the devil?" Kelan muttered, reaching for his sword as Tadd and Morwenna raced from the upper hallways only to stop stock-still at the great hall.

"Elyn!" Morwenna said, her gaze landing on Kiera's sister.

"What's the trouble?" Tadd demanded.

"It seems as if I married the wrong sister," Kelan said as the door burst open and a guard, dragging a screaming, wild-haired woman behind him, entered. She was kicking and fighting, looking half mad.

"Unhand me!" she snarled, drawing herself

up to her full height, her eyes scanning each face in the room only to halt at Elyn's. "I knew it," she muttered, pulling free of the burly sentry.

Kelan's gaze landed upon her. "Who are you?"

"Wynnifrydd of Fenn," Elyn answered boldly, some of her old fire returning.

"Where is he? Where's Brock? I followed him here." Wynnifrydd advanced upon Elyn as if she intended to rip her eyes from their sockets.

"Are you mad, woman?" Tadd demanded.

Wynnifrydd's gaze darted quickly from the corridors to the great hall, searching every corner, every shadow. "He's here," she insisted, "but you've hidden the coward. That disgusting stableboy dragged him to Lawenydd, but he escaped and he came here to see for himself if she" — Wynnifrydd's gaze landed on Elyn — "was dead or alive. You've hidden him," she charged, advancing upon Elyn again. "Where is he, you filthy bitch — where in God's creation have you hidden him?"

"Stop!" Kiera ordered. "Brock isn't here."

"Then where?" Wynnifrydd demanded as Elyn pushed herself upright. Though weak and shorter than Wynnifrydd, Elyn held her stare.

"I thought he was to marry you. That you were carrying his child," Elyn stated.

Something flickered in the taller woman's

gaze, a lie that couldn't quite be hidden.

"There was no child," Elyn said, understanding Wynnifrydd's lie, and whatever color was in her face drained. Pain, unlike any other, surfaced in her gaze. "You lied to him. So that he would marry you. There never was a babe."

"I just need to find him."

"You pathetic witch." With all her strength, Elyn flung her body at Wynnifrydd, knocking over her chair as she pushed the other woman onto the floor. Together they fought, arms flailing, nails clawing, teeth bared as they screamed at each other.

"Wait! Stop!" Kiera cried, and threw herself upon the rolling women as she vainly tried to drag her sister off Wynnifrydd. But the fight was in full heat, the women struggling, hands at throats, fingers pulling hair. Tadd and Kelan each grabbed one of the women, but still they lunged at each other.

From the corner of her eye, Kiera saw the glint of a blade, a long, curved blade that Wynnifrydd had pulled from her cloak.

"Watch out!" Kiera cried as the wicked knife arced upward above Elyn's chest. "Nay!" She flung her body over her sister's.

Wynnifrydd's blade slashed downward.

Kiera twisted, scrabbled blindly, trying to wrest the weapon.

Morwenna screamed in warning, but it was too late.

Pain burned through Kiera's chest. Roaring, Kelan picked up Wynnifrydd and flung her across the room. "Nay! Oh, nay . . . not here . . . not this one . . ."

Wynnifrydd landed hard, but even in her pained state, Kiera saw the tall woman struggle to her feet. She wasn't finished. Tadd vaulted a broken chair and tried to restrain the madwoman, but Wynnifrydd, in full fury, slashed and chopped, her deadly blade slicing anything that came into its path.

"Stop!" Tadd held Wynnifrydd around the waist, picking her off the floor and hauling her kicking, screaming, and clawing toward the far wall. Her sharp knife hacked at him and he sucked in breath through his teeth as it found his arm. "Christ Jesus, stop it!" he growled, grabbing her wrist and banging her hand against the wall until her fingers opened and the long blade clattered to the floor.

"Call the physician!" Kelan barked, holding Kiera close as she felt blood oozing from her wound. The world was growing darker, but the strength of Kelan's arms was comforting. Elyn was alive . . . alive. Kiera glanced at her sister, feeling the lifeblood draining from her, knowing that a dark stain was spreading over her clothes. There was a horrid, plaintive cry from the hallway, and Joseph, half dressed, rounded the corner. He took one look at the bloody great hall and ran to Elyn's side.

"Oh, lady," he whispered. "Oh, lady, lady . . ."

Kelan's arms tightened around Kiera. "Elyn, please . . . do not leave me. Do not."

"I'm not Elyn," she said, fighting the blackness threatening to close in on her. The room was dimmer, the fire far away, and as she stared into Kelan's tortured eyes she felt incredible remorse. "I'm sorry," she forced out, and blinked hard as she lifted a hand to touch his cheek. "I love you."

He swallowed, and the words she'd hoped to hear, the admission that he cared for her, did not come. As she struggled with consciousness, she knew he would never forgive her. Never. How could he? What she'd done was unforgivable, a sin she would take with her to her grave.

Chapter Twenty-seven

"Are you going to punish her forever?" Morwenna demanded as she sighted on a stag, drew back her arrow, and let the deadly missile fly. It zinged over the deer's shoulder. The animal sprang lithely over a fallen log and disappeared into the forest. "Damn!"

The hounds, baying woefully, took up the chase but it was too late. She slid a glance at her brother, who, astride his horse, was watching the fleeing stag escape.

"You can't keep her locked away like a common thief. Tadd, Bryanna, Daylynn and I all agree. 'Tis madness and has to end." It had been nearly two months since Kiera had been injured by the crazed Wynnifrydd of Fenn in what seemed like a bad nightmare.

"Why not?" He dropped to the ground next to her. "Bad luck, that," he said, nodding toward the disappearing deer.

"There is no reason for Kiera to pay any longer. 'Tis cruel. You, brother, have made your point."

"I'm having the marriage to Elyn annulled."

"And what then?"

He shrugged. "I know not," he said, and wished the ache in his heart would subside. He knew that he'd loved the woman who had pretended to be his wife, had trusted her when he felt it was obvious to everyone that she had been lying to him. Made him a laughingstock.

He had given Elyn a choice. She could stand trial or join a nunnery. To no one's surprise, she'd become suddenly devout. He was lucky to be rid of her. "Why do you care? You never trusted Kiera."

"I felt something wasn't right about her." Morwenna shouldered her bow. "But I don't doubt that she loves you, Kelan. I see the misery etched upon her face. 'Tis a pity, for you will never find a woman more devoted to you than she is."

"The liar."

"Aye. The liar." She climbed astride her little mare and cast Kelan a glance that was far older than her years. "A piece of advice, brother. Do not lose this one, for I believe what Kiera feels for you is true love. And believe it or not, you aren't the most lovable creature in all of Wales."

"Nay?" he asked, lifting an eyebrow, trying to tease and failing.

"Especially now. You are so damned miserable that it's a wonder any woman, especially one with any mind whatsoever, would find you bearable." With her final remarks,

Morwenna spurred her mount toward the castle, and Kelan listened to her horse's hoofbeats fade. She was right, he thought, and hated the inner admission. He was torn and miserable and, oh, God's teeth. He kicked at a pebble and set it flying into the bole of a mossy oak.

Once before, he'd left Penbrooke, intending never to return. But the draw of his home and family was too strong, and he'd found a way to have his father lift the banishment that he'd suffered. And now . . . how he wanted Kiera. By the gods, he lay awake each night thinking of her, of the way she smelled, of her laughter, of the feel of her warm flesh pressed to his.

But his pride would not allow him to go to her. He'd only agreed that she could stay at Penbrooke until she had her child; then she would leave. But not with the babe. The child, his heir, was to stay here.

But it will be a bastard, for you have never been married to Kiera.

Unless you claim it as your own.

Kelan gritted his teeth. Silently he rued the day he'd first seen her, the shy bride behind her thick veil. From the first moment he'd laid eyes upon her, he'd been smitten. And she had proved herself, had she not, throwing her body between Wynnifrydd's knife and Elyn's heart? She'd nearly died herself for her act of bravery, but could he

413

trust her? After all the lies?

Climbing upon his steed, Kelan scanned the horizon, watching the winter-white clouds skim over the hills and forests. For the first time in his life he didn't know what to do. His heart ached each day at the thought of Kiera's lies, of her betrayal . . . and yet the thought of living without her, of being unable to see her smile, or not feeling the gentle bite of her sharp tongue when they argued, or . . .

He kicked his horse and felt powerful muscles unleash beneath him. The wind screamed against his head, but no matter how fast the beast raced across the grassy fields, he couldn't outrun his own mind and the sorry fact that he was still in love with a woman who had betrayed him to his very bones.

"I'm leaving." Joseph's voice reached her through the fog and Kiera opened a blurry eye. Her chest ached from the wound, her head thundered, and she felt the weight of doom upon her heart. She was locked in this chamber, allowed to wander the floor, but not allowed to join the rest of the keep in the great hall. Twice daily, she was allowed to walk outside on the curtain wall with a guard. Absently she rubbed her abdomen, which was not yet showing, but Kiera knew her child lay within. The child Kelan had demanded. The babe she was to abandon. The thought gave her new misery, a pain so deep she couldn't bear to contemplate it. Though the babe was not yet born, she loved it with every breath she took, every beat of her heart. Could she ever leave it here to its father's charge, never to lay eyes on its sweet, innocent face? Oh, God. She saw that Joseph was staring at her with sad eyes, as if he, too, felt her pain. "Where will you go?" she asked.

"I know not. I'm banished from Lawenydd and Elyn is gone." He offered her a sad smile. "Mayhap I'll join a band of outlaws." He was sitting at her bedside, and now he rubbed his hands upon the knees of his breeches. His eyes darkened a shade. "I still have something that is unfinished."

"Brock of Oak Crest," she said miserably, for Joseph was determined to run the bastard to the ground. "Could you not go to Serennog? Join Hildy? I think she is lonely after being banished by Father." Another tragic result of their deception.

"I think not." He straightened. " 'Tis time. Farewell, m'lady," he said as he stood. Kiera watched him leave and she felt a deep loneliness. Penbrooke was not her home; she was only staying until the babe was born.

And then what? Will you return to Lawenydd without your child? To live in a castle where your father will never let you forget your be-

415

trayal? That thought stung. She couldn't be separated from her baby. No matter what. And she couldn't go home. Llwyd of Lawenydd had been more than angry when he had heard of his daughters' plan. Not only had he banished Hildy, but he had supported Kelan's decision and forced Elyn to the nunnery. He had made it very apparent that Kiera was not welcome at Lawenydd. She was an embarrassment, a soiled woman, a liar, and little better than a whore.

Before she'd left, Elyn had suggested that Kiera go to Serennog to meet Geneva, the sorceress.

But she couldn't leave her child.

Nor could she take her baby. Kelan would hunt her down to the ends of the earth. Above all else he wanted his child — her child.

She couldn't stand it another second. This idleness when she was left with only her tortured thoughts for comfort. Her wound was nearly healed and she'd spent too many days locked up. Painfully she dressed herself and let herself out of the room. The guard was at her door. "I want to see the baron," she insisted.

The sentry shook his head. "You know he won't see you, m'lady. 'Tis his rule."

"Then it must be bent. Please, Paul, take me to the solar."

"He gave instructions that you were to be locked up here."

"And I need to talk to him."

"I can't go against his wishes," the sentry said as Tadd rounded the corner by the stairs.

"I can," he said as if he'd heard the entire conversation. He took Kiera's hand. "I'll take responsibility, Paul."

"But —"

"I said, I'll take responsibility. Come, m'lady."

"You'll infuriate the lord," Kiera said.

"Maybe he needs infuriating."

"You need not do this for me."

"Mayhap I'm doing it for him," Tadd said, one edge of his mouth curving up. "Asides, he's not growled at me in two days. 'Tis time to give him a reason to be angry." Gently he tugged on her arm, his jaw set in determination as he guided her down the stairs to the great hall. "My brother is miserable without you," he explained as they entered the hall, and he motioned to a serving maid for wine. The girl hurried out of the room. "And I'm sick of his short temper."

"So what are you going to do about it?" Kiera asked as Nell appeared with two mazers and a jug of wine.

"The only thing I can." Tadd took one cup, handed it to Kiera, and held his own aloft. "Lady Kiera of Lawenydd, would you do me the honor of becoming my wife?"

"Wha-what?" she sputtered, nearly dropping the mazer as the door swung open and Morwenna and Kelan appeared in the doorway.

"You heard me," Tadd insisted, a little more loudly. "I just proposed to you."

"What the devil's going on here?" Kelan demanded, striding into the great hall. His countenance was grim; his eyes were blazing, his lips thin and flat.

"I was just asking the lady to marry me," Tadd explained with a crooked smile. "Here, let me pour you a cup, brother, and you and Morwenna can toast us."

"What?" Kelan roared. "Marry her? What nonsense is this?"

" 'Tis not nonsense." Tadd seemed pleased with himself. "I just asked her to be my bride."

"And what did you answer?" Kelan's eyes burned into hers.

"I hadn't just yet."

Morwenna grinned. "What an inspired idea. Then Kiera can be close to her first-born, married into the family, and any other children she and Tadd have will be related and —"

"Stop!" Kelan looked at everyone in the room. "Do I appear such a fool that you would think I can't see through your plan? This is a shallow attempt to dupe me again, to force my hand."

"Nay, brother," Tadd said, his smile falling

to the side. "It is a simple answer to a hard problem. My offer is sincere."

Kiera closed her eyes. Could she do it? Marry a man she didn't love? The brother of the only man she knew she would ever want? " 'Tis true, Kelan. You have left us all with few choices. I would do anything to stay with my child. To think that you would take my babe from me rips my heart out. I've thought of leaving, of trying to escape, because I find it impossible to live here in this keep, knowing you are nearby, wanting you, hoping that you will find it in your heart to forgive me. 'Tis foolish, I know, but I love you and I always have loved you, from the moment you lifted my veil in the chapel. I would do anything for your forgiveness, but you cut out my heart by demanding my child." Tears rose in her eyes. "Would that it were not so," she said, seeing the impassive set of his jaw, "but if Sir Tadd means it, aye, I will marry him, just so that I can be a part of my child's life. Of your life." Her knees threatened to give way as she saw Kelan swallow hard. He blinked and looked away.

"How can I trust you?" he asked, his voice husky.

" 'Twill take time. But we have it, Kelan. Let me prove myself." She fought the urge to break down altogether. "I promise you I will be forever faithful. Either to you because I love you, or to Sir Tadd because he has made a noble gesture."

She waited, her heart barely beating, her breath stopped in her lungs. Kelan stared deep into her eyes. "God forgive me for being a fool," he ground out, then reached for her. "Aye, Kiera, I will keep you, marry you, and give my child his rightful name," Kelan said, breaking into a smile. "And this time I will make sure that the correct name is on the marriage contract, and that there are no veils so I can be certain I get the right bride!" he joked.

From the corner of her eye she saw Tadd grin and let out a breath of relief.

"And I vow, Kelan," she said, staring into his eyes once more, "to never lie to you again. I will love you forever."

Epilogue

The bells chimed loudly through the winter air, echoing against the wide curtain walls, ringing to the nearby hills. Kiera stood at the archway to the chapel at Lawenydd. Kiera's sisters stood beside her: Elyn, dressed in a nun's habit, and Penelope, happy that her father's anger was slowly lifting.

Her father had grudgingly forgiven Kiera as the alliance with Penbrooke was sealed, and Tadd, Morwenna, Bryanna, and Daylynn were in attendance to witness their brother marry Kiera of Lawenydd, the woman he loved. Even Hildy had been allowed to return for the ceremony.

Kelan, dressed in black, took her arm and they walked inside, where the priest was waiting. Candles burned and flickered, and the few guests stood until they reached the altar, where Kiera and Kelan repeated their vows.

But this time Kiera of Lawenydd was wearing her own wedding dress and a sheer veil that allowed her to see all of the angles and planes of her husband's face. This time, as she knelt at the altar, she spoke each word loudly and with conviction. This time she meant them.

And when it was time to stand and have Kelan lift her veil, she smiled into the dove gray eyes of her husband and kissed him soundly, with all the love in her heart.

For this time, she knew, her marriage to Kelan of Penbrooke was forever.

About the Author

Lisa Jackson has been writing romantic fiction for more than fifteen years. Over sixty of her books have been published and reprinted in more than a dozen languages. A single mother, she is a native of Oregon, where she still resides with her two teenage sons.

Lisa is often asked what the key to her success is, and her unfailing answer is a keen imagination, incredible friends, a loving family, and always loads of laughter. As Oscar Wilde is purported to have said: "Life is too important to be taken seriously."

If you would like to write to Lisa, her Web address is www.lisajackson.com.